THE BRASS WYVERN

BRONTE-MARIE WESSON

Bronte-Marie Wesson of Brass Wyvern Books is the owner and publisher of this work.
978-1-7636821-2-2
978-1-7636821-1-5
978-1-7636821-0-8
Year of first publication: 2025

Published with the assistance of Authors Own Publishing Services Pty Limited
Edited by Danikka Taylor & Henry Sinclair
Cover design by Casey Grills
Cover illustration by Eleonor Piteira
Map Cartography by Lark Sloan

For more information, visit:
www.thebrontemarie.com
www.authorsownpublishing.com

To my mother, who brought me into this world and then gave me the gall to believe I could do anything I set my mind to.

THE HEART OF THE IMPERIUM
ROYAL ENCLAVE
THURLOWE TOWER
LA PIETA
IMPERIAL LIBRARY
BRASS WYVERN
ROASTED APPLE
golden quarter
pilgrim's rest
red light district
the emperor's castle
nord hollow
traveller's corner

MOROUQDI
THE FIRST TEMPLE
TRAINING HALLS
ENTRANCE HALL
KITCHEN
WEAVING HALL
STORAGE
DRAGON NURSERY
DINING HALL
MASHJOR GALLERY
BRONNUQ'S ROOM
BIRTHING ROOM
HOLY MOTHER'S QUARTERS
BABIES' ROOMS
IDUNN'S CLOISTER
STORAGE
RENASCI LIVING QUARTERS
CHILDREN'S QUARTERS

'Svarna is the jewel of the south. We have advanced magicks beyond what the Imperium could manage in its many millennia on this planet, we walk as dragonfolk through the ephemeral plane, and we have seen the ocean of sky that exists above the clouds. We were the greatest of countries. That is why the Imperium will not leave us alone.'

~ A letter penned by Samir the Dragon Rider, sixty years before the fall of Muqdah.

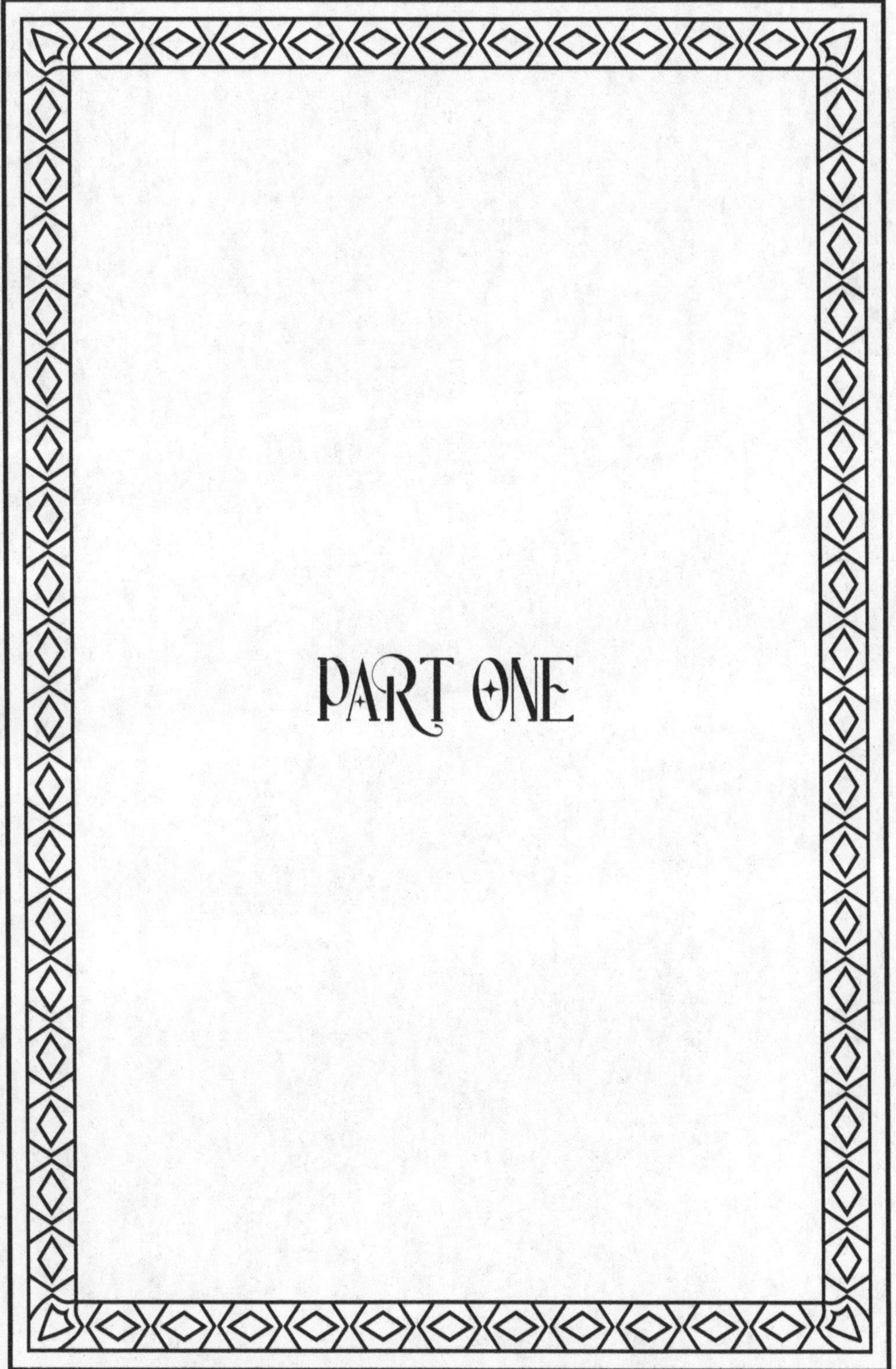

PART ONE

Chapter One

THE IMPERIUM

If the Imperium had been a city built for the rain, it may not have hidden Zuri so well, her laboured breathing drowned out by the strained rage of flooded gutters and rattling pipes. The rain washed away her crimson footprints before they could set into the cobblestone and betray her path to those that followed. The broad road was devoid of its usual thoroughfare, the lateness of the hour and the apocalyptic deluge driving its regulars out of the open. Elegant, pale-barked trees adorned the streets – perfect cover from straying eyes as she slipped down the alleyway.

Ducking beneath a lit window, she studied the boulevard that lay before her, her horns rimmed by the inklings of light that could reach her. The brothels were stacked tightly – long, boxy buildings that leaned upon each other as friendly drunks would. There was not a singular establishment in this strip that dared snuff out its lights and miss an evening of trade. They often left a narrow alleyway at their base to slip through; the buildings bore no concept of personal space or privacy.

One particular brothel was otherwise nondescript, its burgundy walls turned purplish in the lowlight. Settled amongst its garish neighbours – one establishment entirely covered in titanic peacock feathers, the other a visual cacophony of silver pillars – it would be easy to miss.

She paused only briefly in the alleyway, eyes flicking along the promenade before she sprinted across the way and dove in beside a tall flowering bush, crouching amongst great blue blossoms and huge, pointed leaves. She listened intently to the storm. Zuri knew that although the rain hid her well, it would also hide her enemies in turn.

Somewhere, a dog let out a single bark. Her dark eyes snapped back to the alley she had come from, gaze burning into the grey haze to try and distinguish a figure in the mist.

'She went this way!' The elvish voice was closer than she had expected.

Panic rippled through her, and she broke cover, tearing her fingers on thick thorns as she launched herself from the bushes and across the path. Her feet battered the cobblestones as she passed the feathered storefront. She shot up the stairs of the plain establishment nestled beside it and through its lit entryway. The house greeted her with a symphony of music and voices.

Zuri stopped herself from rushing forward, standing for a moment in the entryway. It was a long room with cherrywood doors on either side, and a huge sitting room ahead. People milled about in the haze of golden warmth within, a refuge from the storm. They did not notice her arrival amidst the downpour and their revelry.

She needed to hide. Swivelling on her heels, Zuri pulled open one of the doors. The long hallway beyond was mercifully empty. Clinging to the shadows, Zuri skirted along the hallway, pausing every few metres to listen to the night. She did not know this place well, but that did not matter, for anywhere would have been better than out on the streets. She slowed her walk as the sound of the rain quieted and was swallowed by the creaking of the house. Someone within the establishment was putting on quite a show with their distant moaning. A wry smile teased at the corner of her lips.

There had been rumours – whispers of a place in the red-light district where people like her were protected, safer than anywhere else in the Imperium. The servants had whispered amongst themselves when they'd felt safe enough to do so. Never to Zuri – they were never permitted to speak to her – but she had keen ears. She had heard enough. Zuri had thought it was a fantasy, but when making a break for her freedom, she was not about to discard the fantastical.

She came to a quiet corner that hid a door behind a velvet curtain, given away only by the door frame that peeked out beneath the curtain's hem. She inched the door open and let her shoulders drop when she found the room behind it packed with supplies, blowing out a long sigh of relief. Soft linens and boxes were stacked amongst the shelves, a cluttered collection of cleaning tools propped in the corner.

She closed the door carefully behind her and retreated into the furthest corner of the cupboard, collapsing upon the hardwood floor.

You're free, a quiet voice breathed in the back of her mind.

Sitting in a stranger's linen closet was the first moment of solace in which she allowed herself to grasp at the alien concept of freedom. She closed her eyes and allowed herself to drift off.

A huge, glassy eye watched her beneath a jagged brow, its thin black pupil burning into her mind. She jerked out of her daze, head throbbing.

Footsteps approached down the hallway. She started, pulling herself upwards against one of the shelves. They'd found her. She had no clue how long she had drifted. At a glance, the only weapon at her disposal was the broom. She grabbed it with trembling hands, hoisting it over one shoulder. If they came at her again, she could maim them. Ruin a perfect nose, or an eye, make it so that no one else could look upon them without seeing her mark. It was not an elf that opened the door. It was a stranger, and better yet, a Svarnish stranger.

'Hey,' the stranger said, first in Common. When he spoke next, it was in their mother tongue, a remnant of the old country. 'Are you alright? Did you come in from the rain?'

He seemed to be no older than her. He was also absurdly beautiful – emerald-green eyes set above fine cheekbones and a full mouth. Horns turned in elaborate spirals above his head, covered in brass jewellery that glinted in the dim light. She knew then she was safe – for mounted on her own skull were ram horns as black as onyx, rounding out on either side of her face in one great turn. They marked them both as kindred, Svarnishmen in an unfriendly land.

'You have to help me,' she gasped, discarding the broom and throwing her hands over his. Her knees gave out and she stumbled. 'They'll kill me if they find me again. They've set their dogs on me.'

The man planted his stance to balance their weight, gently helping her upright and onto her feet. A lightning shot of pain rocketed up the side of her calf to her knee, and she gasped, nails digging into his hands. Her moment of reprieve was proving swiftly to be her undoing, as the adrenaline faded from her body and her wounds began to make themselves known. She sucked in a huge, shaking breath and released the stranger's hands.

He glanced down at her bloodied feet, eyes narrowing as he stepped back.

'The elves running around outside like headless chickens?' The man reached to his waist, fingers slipping beneath his open shirt to withdraw a knife. It shimmered beneath the light, iridescence skimming along the edge of the blade. 'My name is Takuma. As long as you're within these walls, I will take care of you.'

'Zuri,' the girl said, her name slipping from between her lips before she could decide if there was wisdom in sharing it. 'My name is Zuri.'

'Nice to meet you, Zuri. You've been bleeding on my floors.'

She looked down and saw the blood on the hardwood, the uneven trail she had dragged in from the doorway. It was only then that she took notice of her broken feet. She didn't remember when she'd strode through glass, but the shards had sunk deep within the rough skin. Zuri let out a sigh of relief. Her wounds glowed, the golden mark that wrapped around both of her feet emitting a gentle shine.

Her Blessing was still intact.

'I will be back. Stay out of sight and away from the windows,' Takuma said.

He turned away briskly, asking no more questions of her. She waited until he was a few feet down the hallway, studying the brusque pace of his walk before following him, treading lightly on the balls of her feet. She stopped only when he crossed back into the entryway. Instead of following him through the cherrywood door, she pulled it carefully closed, leaving a narrow gap that she could spy through.

'Virnoi!' Takuma called sharply into the sitting room, the music within quieting at the sound of his voice. 'Elves outside. They're to stay outside.'

The elf who emerged from the room was draped in shadowy layers of sepia fabric, hollows beneath his eyes. He ducked under the doorway as he approached, a towering frame too large for this world. Zuri found herself staring at his boots, practical and creased with age. They were caked with dirt, as if they'd been buried in the ground for a few hundred years and only recently been unearthed.

'The rats scurrying around?' Virnoi asked softly, his voice a whisper of rustling leaves. Takuma nodded, a sharp bob of the head.

The mismatched pair stood in the entryway, sharing a muttered conversation. Takuma stood tense, flicking a knife over his knuckles and back between his fingers. Virnoi was still, seemingly unfazed by it all. He spoke to Takuma with his shoulders dropped and his head twisted to one side, as if he might close the distance between their great heights with a slouch.

'The Imperium greets you, good fellows!' A call came from out of the storm. At the sound of the voice, Zuri froze behind the doorway. 'Mind if I step within? If you'd lend me your eyes, I'd be so grateful.'

There Llewelyn was, standing beneath the evening downpour. His silver hair was slicked to his head, framing his handsome features, and the remnants of magic that had burned in his eyes had faded to a glittering amber. The beast at his side could have been a dog in a dim light, if one squinted, paid no mind to the details, and perhaps had never seen a dog before. Its heavy, rounded form strained against its leash, thick with muscle, as though crafted from the gnarled roots of a great tree. A thick, greenish tongue lolled out of its mouth as it snuffled intently at the porch.

'What's your business here, stranger?' Takuma asked. He held one hand aloft, the knife flipping idly between his fingers. 'It's a late hour for a stroll, even in this neck of the woods.'

The handsome man's smile was unnerving in the gloom. His brother emerged from the shadowy side of the brothel – milky skin with similarly pale hair, Maldwyn's icy stare lacked any of the charisma of Llewelyn's façade.

'We're looking for a thief,' the first man said. 'A Svarnish girl going by the name of Zuri. She robbed my brother here and fled up this way, according to my hound's nose. Got away with his coin purse and a family necklace that we're fond of. It was an heirloom from our mother.'

'A Svarnish girl?' Takuma asked, vaguely flourishing at the house behind him.

Laughter burbled up from within the brothel, and Zuri realised there was a crowd of rosy-cheeked girls in sheer linen dresses who'd come to watch the stand-off.

'If you hadn't noticed,' one of them said in a sing-song tone, 'there are quite a few Svarnish girls here. It's sort of our speciality. You're going to have to be specific – what did she look like?'

The man considered his words, peering past Takuma and Virnoi to the gaggle of girls behind them. The hound pulled forward, itching to investigate. Virnoi put a foot down in his path, a quiet motion that stopped the hound immediately. Though the man's smile remained warm, there was a chill in his stare that cut. 'Dark-skinned, round horns, long hair, no taller than your shoulders. Not ... wearing much.'

This provoked another wave of giggling from the doorway. The girl who'd spoken before waved a bare leg at the man, gasping in mock scandal.

'Why wasn't she wearing much?' she called. There was a knowingness to her question, and the brother's mouth set in a hard line. 'How'd she get your brother into such a position that she could steal a necklace from him?'

'She's not here,' Takuma interrupted. 'Never met a Zuri in my life, and we've had the same girls here all day. None that fit that description. All these girls are ones I've hired who've been here for some time. Maybe if you came to proper establishments, people wouldn't be taking advantage of you.'

'A proper establishment,' the brother muttered, turning away. 'That's a joke.'

The handsome man nudged his brother with a hard elbow, and the two shared a baleful, burning look that could have easily killed the other. Zuri's lip curled. She could sense the silent argument they were having. In the years she'd spent with them, the brothers had never needed to speak aloud to have conversations. The silence that stretched on was filled only with the endless drum of rain.

There was also the moaning – that one distant woman set on her grandiose performance.

The pair of waterlogged High Elves made some silent decision between themselves. Lips pursed, one brother nodded, and the handsome one turned back to the brothel. He was almost always insincere – his deceit came as natural as breathing.

'Do you mind if we take a look inside?' he pressed, his smile waning as he glanced down at Virnoi's firmly planted boot on the edge of the porch. 'Surely it wouldn't be much of an imposition. We'd just do a quick scout of the property to be sure you don't have a thief hiding in some shadowy corner of this house. You wouldn't want that. Then we'll be out of your hair, and you won't have to see us again.'

Takuma chuckled darkly, settling his knife from its idle turns in his hand, gripping the blade in such a way that would do plentiful damage if swung with any force. The brother's eyes narrowed; it seemed each participant in this conversation understood the nature of nonverbal communication. Takuma's voice carried through the boulevard. 'I do mind, actually. As the owner of this establishment, I don't want my clients disturbed because you couldn't keep your pockets sealed. That's not my problem.'

'You own the place?' the less-handsome elf shot back, taking a threatening step forward. Takuma did not flinch. The two stood glowering darkly at one another. 'How'd a goat like you come to own land in the Imperium?'

Takuma, unbothered by the insult, let out a harsh laugh. 'Your mother paid for it, knife ears. We're quite close.'

Zuri could have laughed if the look in the handsome man's eyes had not turned her blood to ice. His hand loosened on the leash, an inch of leather slipping between his fingers as another wave of laughter swept the gallery of onlookers. There was a man or two amongst them now, drawn by the spectacle evolving on their doorstep.

'What exactly did you just say about our mother?' the elf asked, his tone polite and even. The arcane glow returned to his eyes, a ghostly blue flame flickering to life. He stood, silently threatening to set his hound on this stranger who denied him. Virnoi took a long stride forward, leaning out of the entryway that had so far kept him dry.

From her narrow vantage, Zuri thought the elf looked like a phantom – an impression of a yawning shadow, stretched long by some distant light.

'This is private property – you and your scent-hound aren't welcome.' Virnoi's voice cut through the rain as a venomous hiss, softly spoken but with a hefty threat coiled within. 'If you want to come back, bring the city guard and hope we're not better friends with them than you are.' He did not raise a finger, his hands still hooked into his many layers of clothing. Yet, his eyes took up the same arcane glow, both men's features illuminated by an otherworldly light.

Two magi, weighing up their power against one another.

For half a breath, Zuri swore it would turn to a brawl. The handsome elf's fading friendliness shifted to cool indifference, and his brother swore quietly, sharing an uncertain look with him. The beast made one final strain against its leash, curiously pricking the leaves that constituted its ears. It was only then that it saw Zuri. Its eyes, a pair of gleaming lights peering out from within the vines of its brow, met her own. She saw the tic of recognition in its face as it lunged forward, tail lifting, winding up to let out a decisive bark.

'Get your dog off our porch,' Virnoi warned, stepping in the thing's way and blocking the beast from Zuri's view. He ground his heel into the wood. 'Or I'll bury it down the road.'

'Fine,' the handsome elf muttered, heaving the beast back with the leash. 'We'll be back come sunrise, with the morning behind us.'

Paralysed by fear, Zuri could not bear to move, convinced that a single sound would give her away. She sat, ice in her veins, legs burning as she watched her pursuers vanish into the storm. The tension drained from her, leaving her body racked by silent, convulsive sobs. Her shoulders shook as she pressed a trembling hand to her mouth.

The hound had certainly seen her, but had not been able to betray her to its master. Though the girl had once loved the beast for its company, it was loyal only to those who held the leash upon which its existence hinged. Any friendship the two had shared in their cage was that of two pets.

'Like hell they will,' Virnoi muttered, once convinced that they'd truly left. He withdrew back beneath the shelter of the porch, black hair dripping rainwater onto his cloak, angular features written with utter disgust. 'They wouldn't risk us calling them for what they are.'

Together, Virnoi and Takuma closed the house's double doors and locked them, the Svarnishman's blade vanishing into the folds of his clothing as he turned back to his audience. 'Girls, when the clients leave, you escort them yourself through the doors. Tell them we closed up due to the storm. We don't have the money to risk a leak in this place.'

A wave of affirmative noises came from the retreating women as they filtered back to their work, the brief entertainment of the evening gone with the prospect of a fight.

'Nuru—' Takuma called, and the girl who'd been taunting the elves turned back, arms folded at her chest. 'When the rain lightens up, it would be good if you'd fetch Taliesin. Wear one of my coats when you go, dress like a boy; we don't want anyone else picking you up because those bastards have money out for the arrest of any scantily clad Svarnish girl. We're going to need a healer.'

'Oh, so she *is* here.' Nuru tossed her head back and laughed, eyes sparkling in the lamplight.

Zuri, finally safe in her hallway, dropped slowly out of her crawl, collapsing forward onto her arms. She would have to apologise for bleeding more on his floors. She was growing more aware of torn fingernails and her shredded palms, the graze that wrapped up the side of her leg. The mortal shell that carried her so far began to collapse beneath the pain.

'Of course, she's here,' she heard the Svarnishman respond, his voice growing distant. 'Where else would she have gone?'

CHAPTER TWO

SVARNA

It all began with a great bolt of lightning.

It was a clear, hot day in Muqdah. The crystalline sky sprawled above the city in its endless splendour, sandstone buildings shimmering in the quiet summer heat. The lightning, bright and glaring against the perfect afternoon, bloomed from the earth itself – a colossal bolt, taller than the greatest of Muqdah's temples, arcing upwards and skittering across the shields that sheltered the holy city within. A thousand eyes turned upwards to stare into the sky as the protective cocoon woven around the city *shuddered*. It was a strange thing to hear the air shudder. The shields should not have made a noise at all. Yet, a groan rumbled from above, growing louder as it reverberated through the city.

Morouqdi, Svarna's First Temple, had an unobstructed view from the peak of Muqdah. The First Temple was an institution of Svarnish power, built of ancient alabaster that climbed towards the sky. That fateful afternoon, a dragon curled around the greatest of its towers, wrapped protectively around the tower's hatchery. The hatchlings crowded around on a stone platform, large enough to fly but still shy of taking to the sky and leaving the temple.

Far below, upon the forecourt of that Blessed place, a temple child sat with her brethren, dark eyes peering up at the magic bolt. Unease brewed in her belly.

A priest stood upon the stairs, having gone still the very instant that the light rent the sky. He was crowned with thin, curling horns and a great length of deep, auburn hair. The Child had always wanted hair of that colour, finding it far more vibrant and interesting than her own black curls.

'Children,' the priest called. 'Come here.'

The Child, no older than thirteen, picked herself up, glancing between the game at hand and the priest who had summoned them. Her brother, barely two summers old, had little understanding of the game that she had been trying to play anyway.

'Ohba, what is that light?' the Child asked. Ohba was the adult of whom she asked almost all things. 'Where did it come from?'

Ohba did not tear his eyes away from the sky, instead reaching out a hand to wave them over. She wrinkled her nose but obeyed without any question, tugging her brother over until they were within arm's reach. The Child reached out and put her little hand in his, watching his face intently. She squeezed it, hoping to draw some sort of attention from the priest, but found his fixation unerring. 'It is danger. A dangerous thing – but we're safe within the temple, little one. Just stay close.'

The Morouqdi forecourt had been relatively empty mere minutes before, but its occupants had been drawn out by the resonate groaning from above – what an almighty sound it was, like the straining of sundering wood on a divine scale. Yet, the Child did not think her little brother could hear it. He seemed more distressed by the confusion than the clamour of the heavens.

Holy men clustered outside together, and as the Child looked upon them, she saw unfamiliar knots of fear on their faces. Some cocked their ears to the side, listening to the air, just as she was. The holy mothers were emerging alongside them, women of many ages with round bellies and babes tucked in their arms. The Child looked for her guardian and saw Eulalia weaving through the growing crowd, one hand resting atop her protruding belly.

Eulalia was as tall as an oak tree – or so the Child thought – strong-limbed and certain. Thick of brow and chin, a tangled, curling mane fell to her waist, and atop her skull were curved horns adorned with copper jewellery. Her eyes filled with a passion like dragonflame, Eulalia's gaze was not turned upwards – she was searching the crowded court for her wards.

'Mamina!' the Child called. She had not immediately forgotten Ohba's warning, but she would argue that they were still close, simply not within reach of the priest. 'There's a light in the sky! Something's struck the shield!'

'I can see that,' Eulalia mused. 'Stay close now, little ones, don't go wandering off.'

And because it was Eulalia who said it, The Child nodded dutifully and kept only mere steps away from her. Her baby brother, Rasyl, was quieted by Eulalia's presence and toddled between them, one hand clutching at the woman's long skirt. The Child pondered the image of them both before she bowed down and picked up her little brother, clutching him to her side.

A second bolt tore from the earth. It shot up into the shield that surrounded Muqdah and, after a breath, pierced through the transparent wall, dissipating above the city proper. It did not shatter the shield entirely, but it created a narrow keyhole in the warded sphere, a dozen streaking lights branching upward to the highest reaches of the shield – excess magic let loose with no control. The Child shrank back towards Eulalia, who patted her.

One would expect a catastrophe to be loud, but Morouqdi was silent for several long moments. The wards that were meant to protect the city were failing – had failed. For centuries the wards had stood stalwart, all the city's battles occurring beyond its walls. Muqdah had survived countless sieges, with enough land and produce to feed its people. The Child knew that was how they had managed many a conflict, having sat obediently through her histories. The holy walls were meant to be eternal.

New voices joined the discontent. The Child twisted and saw the active renasci lingering around the temple's pillars, their staffs held firm at their sides. Their ringed tattoos shifted and hummed with quiet magic as they stared upwards. The renasci would protect them – that was why they had been made. That was why they had been given to the temple.

'Ohba,' Eulalia muttered. 'What's happened? That is not Svarnish magick.'

The sweet priest, who had often played pretend with the Child, could not feign lightheartedness now. 'They have come, Eula.'

He was maintaining a measured calm. The Child knew the feeling. She felt the same when she stood upon one of the perches on the high tower and watched a storm approach from across the distant realms of Svarna. The stillness that preceded a hurricane hanging by a slim thread above her head.

Eulalia made a strangled, odd noise of pure disbelief. She had never heard such a sound from Eulalia before. 'We are a city of temples – to bring an army here would be criminal. They would sully themselves before the whole world.'

The look Ohba gave was a dark one, which told the Child all that she needed to know. She did not know exactly who *they* were, but they were going to commit some great atrocity. She had always been precocious, but had recently begun to learn of adult things, the wicked ways of the world. Which meant that she was suddenly aware of how soft her brother was. How small and clueless he was. How he was upset only because the adults were crowding around in a way he had never seen before – not because of the lightning in the sky or that groaning magic he did not yet have a sense of. The renasci had aspects of their magic refined as they grew, but Rasyl was so little that his bands were still iridescent and shifting, glimmering upon his unblemished skin.

When the adult world worsened, it came for the littlest children first. The smallest and the most vulnerable felt the repercussions of change like the hammers of war upon their backs. She reached out and he grasped her hand with his chubby fingers, the magic of Morouqdi tingling between them.

'The riders are all in the field,' the Child heard Eulalia whisper. Ohba looked down and noticed the Child watching them. But the Child held her ground – there was adult business unfolding, and all the temple children eavesdropped upon adult business. 'How is Muqdah to defend itself?'

'We have renasci, and the dragons are dragons – they will fly with or without someone on their backs. All of Muqdah will rise to protect us. But we—we must go.' Ohba reached out and cupped Eulalia's cheek for a moment before his eyes flicked down towards the Child and Rasyl, letting the hand fall. He swallowed. 'The council will convene. We can put out a call for the war dragons.'

She nodded, and within moments, they were wading through the crowd back into the heart of Morouqdi. Eulalia strode ahead before she looked back, waving the Child forward. 'Come along, little one. There's no more time for games.'

Chapter Three

THE IMPERIUM

Mornings in the red-lantern district were a soft affair, with the bedworkers and courtesans recovering from their raucous evenings. It was bitingly cold that morning, the aftermath of the evening storm leaving the smell of damp, fragrant earth in the air. Takuma sat atop a dresser on the far side of the room, still mulling over the events of the evening before.

Zuri lay where Takuma had delicately placed her, swathed in patterned blankets and woven creations crafted by Virnoi's hand. The elf's bed was the largest and the cleanest of the lot, and she had not shifted since she was lain upon it. Takuma found himself reluctant to leave her side, eyes pinned upon her chest to ensure that it continued to rise. She was entirely too still.

It had been a long time since he had seen anyone treated so poorly by the world. Those bastards had mangled her horns in an attempt to train the shape of them, leaving them misshapen and asymmetrical in a way that made his headache to contemplate.

'You're telling me that she just showed up in the middle of the storm like ... this.'

'With a pair of knife-eared pricks on her tail, no less.' Takuma kissed his teeth. 'She'd wrapped her ankles with fabric to try and quiet the bells ringing as she fled. They put those anklets on slaves to stop them sneaking up on their masters, you know?'

'Slave trade is illegal in the Imperium,' Taliesin said. The priest was bent over the slave girl, brow furrowed with focus, his pointed ears twitching as he worked. He was the only Imperial High Elf who was tolerated within The Brass Wyvern without being a paying patron, having delivered more than one child within their walls. It had been good of him to come so early in the morning, but Takuma could only take so much of his naïveté. His pale blue eyes glanced towards Takuma, alight with the arcane glow of spellcasting. 'It has been in all of my life. It's a horrible, archaic practice.'

Takuma rolled his head backwards, tapping his horns against the wall at his back. His adornments chimed idly.

'Sure. I'll let the guards know that some rich elvish bastards are abusing Svarnishmen. I'm sure they'll be right on that.' One raised within the trappings of authority struggled to see the flaws that were only apparent from outside of it. It was like living within a gem – everything appeared dazzling when the finely cut edges of your existence are designed to camouflage the flaws in its formation. Takuma shook his head at the priest. 'Laws aren't real, Taliesin. Not for nobility.'

'I believe our friend is awake,' Taliesin remarked, neatly sidestepping what could be another hard conversation. He circled slowly around the bed, his periwinkle robes blocking her from Takuma's view. 'Zuri – my name is Taliesin. I can help you get that sedative out of your system. I'd just ask that you try to take it easy. I'm still in the process of healing your feet, but they're not quite done. You'll do more harm to them if you get up too swiftly.'

The woman's hand twitched. Taliesin's eyes homed in on it, after hours without any movement from her.

'Good,' Taliesin remarked. He leaned over Zuri as Takuma eased himself off the dresser. 'Now, let's take care of that sedative keeping you sluggish. It was your survival instinct that kept you on your feet, burning it out of your system, but it took right back over once you got a chance to relax.'

The priest did, truly, have a saintly visage. Ivory-skinned with a halo of golden curls, he was the picture of Elvish nobility.

As Zuri's eyes shot open, Takuma realised his personal miscalculation. Zuri coughed up dark fluid, and it flew from her into the priest's magical grip, her body sputtering back to life. Tension rippled through her as she fought through the sensation, shifting each limb and clenching each hand. Once the spell was done, an inky black liquid swirled in the air beside Taliesin.

'I'll just take that,' the priest remarked airily, removing a vial from beneath his robe. He unstoppered it and the liquid flew within, trapping itself. The priest blew out a puff of air and straightened the gleaming medallion that hung around his shoulders. 'Nasty piece of work when used outside of hospice – patients can often take weeks to come down if a mage isn't handy.'

Before Takuma could warn Taliesin, Zuri had rolled onto her back and lunged for a scalpel resting among the elf's other tools.

At least Taliesin was hard to take by surprise, as profoundly Blessed as he was. He tapped his heel against the hardwood flooring beneath him, and magic ballooned around Zuri in a sparkling cushion, catching her as she tipped forward. All it took was a sharp breath and Zuri was left suspended in the air, floating lazily in the direction she'd thrown herself.

'You owe me a sovereign, priest.' Takuma plucked the scalpel from the tray and made a show of inspecting it, turning it between his index finger and thumb. 'I told you she'd swing for you.'

'I never took that bet,' the priest responded mildly. 'I promise I've no intention of hurting you, Zuri. That would be counterproductive after spending the better part of my morning healing you. Are you going to go for the blade again if I put you down?'

She absolutely would go for the blade, which is why it was now in Takuma's hands. If there was one thing that he was good at, it was keeping a hold of his weapons. He saw Zuri's dark eyes flick over to the gleaming tool and then to his face, utterly transparent in her motivation. Mollified by force, she conceded with a single nod. The spell that held her aloft collapsed carefully, deflating until she rested back upon the mattress.

'I can hear you lurking, Nuru,' Takuma called. The woman was quite talented at navigating the brothel without making any noise at all, so the creaking floorboards in the hallway were no mistake.

'Feeling lively, are we?' Nuru asked, pottering in with her daughter tucked on her hip. She was a petite woman with an abundance of rounded curves, though her horns hadn't sprouted in the way that Takuma's had. Instead, they sat as short, rounded cones at the top of her forehead surrounded by wispy curls that she couldn't tame into her elaborate braids. She was the picture of Svarnish beauty. A lifetime ago, Takuma had caught a glimpse of a goddess of fertility in one of Imamu's locked caravans. Nuru was an echo of that deity, down to the rosy flush in her cheeks.

They were as beautiful as one another. It was why Takuma tolerated her.

The sheer, gauzy fabrics of the evening had been shed, and Nuru donned an ensemble of many-layered skirts belted at the waist, paired with a sea foam linen blouse. 'You gave Takuma quite the scare last night.'

Takuma huffed in Nuru's direction, wondering why he was being made out to be the distressed one when neither he nor Taliesin had slept particularly well.

'You don't have to worry about Taliesin,' Nuru continued. 'He's only an elf by blood. Abandoned all the noble pomp for the clergy, though we're still trying to get him to abandon the pomp of the clergy for us.'

'Still an elf,' Zuri muttered.

'An elf who's about to close your wounds,' Taliesin sung, his eyes aglow, the very picture of serenity. 'Your feet, please.'

Takuma snorted at the disgruntled look on Zuri's face as she thrust both her feet in the priest's direction. The priest was not going to let Zuri leave, and Takuma wasn't going to let her knife his best cleric, so she didn't have much of a choice. With a breath from Taliesin and a flourish of his hands, the open wounds on Zuri's feet knitted closed. The priest probed at her anklets. 'I didn't want to do this while you were asleep and risk harm to you – that would be a terrible breach of trust. My magic has a delicate touch, but it isn't perfect.'

'They're solid Imperial gold,' Zuri murmured, staring down at herself. There was a distant look in her dark eyes. 'I want them off me. I'll melt them down and sell them. I need them off.'

They could have been pretty things in any other context, thin chains that wrapped her ankles, adorned with bells the size of grapes. The warm gold sung to her complexion. Takuma despised them and all they stood for; he had only ever seen them on the dead. One needed a mage of significant prowess to break them, and most enclaves were predisposed to turning in slaves to the Imperium rather than handling the trouble that came with freeing them.

'I like your spirit,' Takuma remarked. He smiled weakly, stomach turned by a lingering memory of slave bells in the dark.

'*Allante,*' the High Elf breathed, pinching one chain between his pale fingers. The air crackled with latent energy, and the chain collapsed beneath Taliesin's touch, melting away like ice beneath the heat of a sun. He repeated the method on the other anklet, and they fell onto the mattress. Zuri scrambled back on the bed, out of Taliesin's reach, and frantically checked her ankles.

Nuru took one look of appraisal around the room as an unfortunate silence descended, and she thrust her babe towards Taliesin.

'Would you mind putting Nema down in the crib, Taliesin?' the Svarnishwoman asked, pulling a face at the fussing child. 'Andraste can watch her once she's down, but she's not settling, and you know how she gets if she doesn't nap.'

'Oh! Of course!' Taliesin responded, entirely accustomed to this. He scooped up the child, bouncing on his feet as Nema burbled happily, clutching at his collar. 'You little troublemaker, you're going to make me late for the midday mass, aren't you?'

Whatever Takuma thought of elf-kind in general, there was a tenderness to the way that Taliesin handled Nema, from the moment he delivered her into the world, that revealed his true nature. Cruel men could not be trusted with the helpless – they would not offer their fingers to children or tolerate them drooling on their gilded robes.

Taliesin swept out of the room, Nuru humming idly as she slid the door closed behind him, as quiet as a mouse about it. Takuma listened to the creaking floorboards until he was certain that the priest was well out of earshot before turning to Zuri.

'I need to ask you what happened.' Takuma broached the topic, finally placing the scalpel back amidst the medical equipment. 'Purely so that I can be prepared for whatever those men might bring to my door if they figure out that you're here, which they might. I think myself a realist.'

It was a fair question, even if Takuma felt like a bit of a beast for asking it. He would bet good money on the fact that those elves knew Zuri was within The Brass Wyvern, and he needed a better idea of what he was dealing with.

'The brothers you spoke with are Llewelyn and Maldwyn. The third or fourth sons of an absurdly rich Elvish family, the both of them mages and the both of them bastards. They'll never have a lick of any real responsibility, but they still have access to the family vault. They picked me up off the street when the head of my caravan was imprisoned by the guard. There was a scrabble. We scattered, and in the confusion I lost track of my parents. I should have known better than to trust those bastards, but what in the winds was I supposed to do?'

Growing restless, Zuri slid to the side of the bed. She stood, shifting her weight and staring down at her newly healed feet. Nuru had discarded the scraps she'd arrived in and instead dressed her in clean, loose trousers and an oversized tunic that tied at the front, covering her from collarbone to her calf.

'They kept me locked in what I think was the guest wing of their family estate, where only the servants would see me.' Zuri paced the room as she spoke. 'Last night, they came in acting odd – put me to sleep with a spell, and when I woke, I was in this dark room facing a wall of glass. I thought I was still asleep because they pushed me forward and I just ... I went straight through it. I shouldn't have been able to go through it.

'It was a habitat. They threw me into a habitat with a hunk of meat, this huge chamber with an island at the centre of it. They'd never taken me there. I'd never seen it or heard anything about them keeping an animal so large. Llewelyn kept his hounds, but I thought they were the only living things he minded.' She stopped and took a long breath, taking an uncertain glance at Takuma. 'It was a dragon.'

'That's not possible,' Nuru mumbled. Takuma saw the warmth of her complexion turn sallow, his old friend smoothing her skirts with her hands. Her tone was gentle but distant, stuck somewhere in a memory. 'The dragons didn't survive the war, Zuri. The elves made sure of that.'

There were some that had survived the war, but they had not snuck this deep into the Imperium. They had not made it to the capitol.

'I know what I saw,' Zuri insisted, shaking her head. 'It wasn't an illusion, some magical thing with no substance. I may not have seen a dragon up close when I was in Svarna, but I remember them from afar. I remember the way my father used to describe them. It radiated heat, and the whole chamber stank – a peculiar stench I'd never smelt before. For a second, it just sat there, staring at me. Then something came over the beast, and it did laps around the enclosure, bellowing so loudly that I thought I'd go deaf. I am not a madwoman. I have never seen or heard things that weren't there.'

The world had gone quiet to Takuma. Blood had begun to pound in his ears, but all he could hear beyond it was Zuri's breathing and the creaking wood of The Brass Wyvern. He raked his hands through his hair as he tried to calm himself.

'The dragon charged into what I thought was a door at first. The door did not survive – it fell straight off its frame. In a rage, the beast turned on the glass wall they'd thrown me through and bought me enough time to get out. I knew I wouldn't get another chance if they'd thrown me in here like this, so I ran for the door. Turned out it was actually a cover to a vent that went up a few dozen feet and fed out into the garden. After that, I only had to find one of the servant's passages, and I was in the Imperium.'

Takuma whistled. 'You climbed up a vent?'

'Blessed feet,' Zuri pointed out, waving at her feet. He had studied the golden banding of her feet for hours as Taliesin worked, terrified that the wound would steal her magic away from her. She lifted a sole, and it cast a warm halo on the hardwood flooring. 'I have perfect balance. I would have gone into entertainment if I'd stayed with the caravan. I can find my way on little ledges or, you know, a tightrope. The magic runs in the family.'

'Useful,' Takuma muttered. He turned his eyes on Nuru, trying to gauge her reaction, but she had turned away from him. He would need to speak with her later.

'Those bastards from last night have a dragon?' a familiar voice chirped, surprising them. A feminine face poked over the windowsill, pointed features pinched in disbelief.

Takuma swore under his breath as she emerged from where she'd been eavesdropping, swinging her heels through the window and settling on the sill. Hotaru's horns were once both thin and tall, gently curved, but one was now broken near the base. It had left her silhouette utterly lopsided, rakish.

'No way some half-pint High Elves are keeping a whole dragon. They couldn't even decide on which route to take home, you could hear them three blocks over.'

Takuma strolled towards her, leaning onto the windowsill, caging her body with his so that they could not escape. .

'Hotaru,' he said lowly, 'how would you know what they squabbled over?'

'I followed them,' she admitted reluctantly, glancing behind her, no doubt weighing up her chance for escape.

He quirked an eyebrow at her.

Takuma's favourite pickpocket had shockingly blue eyes, hidden amidst a mane of untidy dark curls and a nest of linens wrapped around her narrow shoulders. She watched him with those eyes now, a glint in them reserved just for him.

The silent exchange ended as quickly as it had begun, Hotaru letting her eyes slide from his once more as he stepped back and allowed her to drop to the floor.

'They were loud,' she said as she shifted past him into the room, hands behind her back. 'They were kicking up such a fuss, I was curious what had their breeches in a twist.'

All her clothes were threadbare, holes torn in the knees and repaired by hand, the only clothing of value being the burgundy boots that Takuma had bought for her when she'd formally joined them in The Brass Wyvern. She glanced over her shoulder at him, clearly uneasy at his continued silence, and he weighed up how he'd most enjoy punishing her later for putting herself in danger.

'We'll have to deal with you breaking house rules later,' he concluded. 'How far did you follow them, exactly?'

Hotaru perked up the instant the topic shifted, vibrant eyes sparkling as she realised she had a chance to make herself useful. 'All the way back home! Some big building in the Golden Quarter – they're loaded. I could have caught six sovereigns from the jeweller down by Daine's just by lifting one of their timepieces.'

'They have wards on everything,' Zuri warned. 'Absolutely everything. Not worth stealing from, it would cost you more than just a finger.'

'Too risky to steal from, but perhaps worth following,' Takuma mused, head bobbing thoughtfully. Caution was good, it would keep them alive, but it would stop them from making any real progress. 'Do you think you could retrace their steps?'

'Of course I could,' Hotaru said with a toss of her curls. 'Nuru, will you go get Feliks? We might want a Nordic-looking face if we're wandering into the upper echelons. He has a way of making the rich folk feel at ease.'

Nuru nodded and vanished through the door. Takuma watched her go, studying the way she held her shoulders and her silence. That was going to be a much larger problem.

When he'd settled on the semblance of a plan, he turned back to Zuri. 'Do you want to come with us, Zuri? You can stay here if you want, but I need to see what we're dealing with.'

Given what Zuri had gone through in a single night, he expected her to stay within the confines of the brothel. Instead, her jaw ticked and she set her shoulders. 'I'll come with you.'

What spirit she had.

Feliks appeared, filling the doorway, fair-skinned with a head of reddish curls, his horns far more akin to antlers than those of a dragon. Though Feliks' smile was friendly, Takuma watched Zuri withdraw from the intensity of his stare.

'Finally awake, are we?' he asked. 'Where are we all hopping off to?

Chapter Four

SVARNA

Death had come, an ominous wind that was too hot and stung at Eulalia's eyes. The Imperium had worked their way through all of Svarna and brought their violence to its holiest abode.

Ohba helped her back within the temple, one hand clutching hers and the other resting gently upon her back – trying so intently to impart an aura of calm. It was for the sake of the children, but it was at least somewhat to quiet her, which was sweet if misplaced. She was not prone to hysteria.

The children trailed behind them. She did not want to let either babe out of arm's reach. Eulalia knew very well the ways in which people became sheep when panic overwhelmed them, how they might trample one another to escape danger. She could not leave the children with the masses and trust that someone else would care for them while she worked.

They passed the renasci as they went, who had congregated swiftly to discuss the predicament amongst themselves. Priests of Morouqdi would most certainly be strategizing deep within the temple, making sense of the threat at their doorstep, and the renasci would move to enact their will.

Morouqdi had a deceptively deep entryway, complementing the complex, multi-layered labyrinth that lay within. Dozens of chambers broke off from the first chamber, winding tunnels all in that geometric stone. Those who resided within the temple called it the Dragon's Den for how elaborate it was. It harkened back to the lairs that dragons burrowed into the sides of mountains when left to their own devices. They could hide the population of Muqdah in these channels, protect them if the temple sealed the doors, but they would need magi at the ready to reopen the doors after the conflict had passed. There were not many magi left to do that work.

'You are thinking,' Ohba said, breaking the quiet they'd sunken into. 'Of what, Eulalia?'

'Hidey holes.' She looked back at the children to ensure that they were following. 'Places we can tuck the hatchlings to keep them out of danger.'

Her children were both so little. She could not think of either of them as growing people when she had birthed them, when she had nurtured them – Eulalia had felt them grow and kick within her, and that was how they remained in her mind. The world continued on, but her babies would always remain cuddly newborns to her. The Child was approaching the bridge of womanhood, but she was still young and soft-faced, clueless to the grimness of the world. Rasyl was still so little that all he could do was follow the nearest familiar face, concerned for little else than when his next meal would arrive and that the people around him were at ease.

'Nothing will happen to them.' Ohba was attempting to reassure her, but she glanced at him, lips pressed, and a shadow passed between them. Now was not the time to be making promises that they could not keep.

'Not as long as I stand,' she said simply. That was the truth. Eulalia could swear to herself that no harm would come to these two temple children, but it meant nothing if she did not move into action. There were more practised mothers than her who'd once tried to coach her out of this mentality – tried to persuade her that she could not control the world in such a way that she could protect her children forever. They soon gave up.

The hallway through the centre of the Morouqdi stretched on for an eternity. The lamps set into the wall burned quietly with dragonflame. It was how the keepers taught the hatchlings to breathe fire on command and allowed them to expend any excess heat growing within themselves. Every now and again, the lamps would need to be reset, but dragonflame was long-lasting. It was how most of Muqdah kept its light.

At last, they came to a broad chamber, a half-sphere that was home to the council of the First Temple. The room's centre was filled with a hearthfire of human design, the fiery core to the spiralling glass structure that defined the room. The legend went that when the first council of priests had convened, it had been under the stewardship of a dragon who had settled in Muqdah long before any Svarnishmen had gone to ground in the city. The dragon – whose name differed depending on the tale – had blown this glass with pure fire and made it impossibly strong as it did. It was how they'd decided how many priests should make up the council. As the crystalline material had spiralled out, it had split the chamber and looped in on itself, leaving clear the space for twenty-four to stand comfortably within its circles.

It was usually a place of immense beauty. When the hearthfire was lit, the glass refracted its warm light and set the world ablaze in its glorious warmth. Now, it stood grey and still in the quiet, devoid of the bustle of council. Cuinu was already there, his fine silks and embroidery rumpled, face pinched with worry. He crouched in the centre of the room, feeding a log to the fire. When the council had been full, they had taken their formal positions around the hearth – in the twenty-four seats scattered about the room, loosely forming two concentric circles. They were evenly dispersed so that even in the furthest corners of the room, one could still feel the comfort of the fire on a cold night.

However, they had dispensed with formalities years ago, settling into having their discussions at the very centre of the spun glass. A central opening meant for debate, now designated to petty squabbles and collective grief.

'Why are the temple children here?' Cuinu asked, casting a confused look over Eulalia's shoulder.

Eulalia cast a glance back at the Child, knowing that the girl would be listening, as she always was. Being a mother meant that one grew quickly, acutely aware of how they now had a resident eavesdropper at their side. She did not usually keep the girl within arm's reach, so she was quite accustomed to losing her for hours at a time and trusting that she would be cared for by whomever she was on an adventure with. But Eulalia could not have the girl vanishing off when they did not know how much time they had with the shields left standing. 'Because,' Eulalia replied, 'if I don't bring them along, our little hatchling will run off to the nursery, and we may lose her before the Imperium arrives at our temple. We wouldn't want that.'

Cuinu grumbled discontentedly but did not dare contend with Eulalia.

Rasyl was far too young and valuable to be left on his own. A child of the temple, he'd been spelled in the womb, destined to become a warrior. The renasci were birthed by holy mothers, who brought themselves to temple ground when pregnant with a child that they could not fathom keeping on their own. But Eulalia had chosen this life for him, the reason for his conception. Rasyl would join their ranks one day. Until then, Eulalia was not about to take her chances with her babe.

The Child was precious in an entirely different way. Bright-eyed and quick-footed, she was the herald named in a prophecy that Eulalia had never really believed in. She could not fathom that anything prophetic had come from her womb and refused to believe that their fate was shaped by strange prophets, dead for centuries.

Yet, everyone else believed that the Child was a beacon of a bright future. When she'd been born, the once glorious stewards of Morouqdi had declared her the herald of a new age in Svarna. Eulalia did not need her daughter discovering the harsh reality of her destiny amidst this war, and if she was not careful, Eulalia believed she would. The girl was trouble, and trouble did not mix with warfare.

The council who now resided within Morouqdi had dwindled to four priests in total. When Eulalia had first come here to birth the Child, there had been upwards of twelve who cared for all of Muqdah. As the war crept across Svarna, devastating all in its path, some council members had left, desperate to save what relics they could. When the council had shrunk to four, the remaining holy men formally admitted Eulalia and Fidela to Muqdah's stewardship. Eulalia and Fidela were only considered for membership of the council as the pre-eminent leaders amongst the holy mothers. To be a mother was important in its own right, but they had none of the training that the holy men did. Eulalia herself didn't even have a Blessing, incapable of even the smallest of magics.

Cuinu returned to stoking the fire. From the entryway, Eulalia also spied Adil wearing a path into the stone as he paced around the hearth. Staring at the holy men's features, lined by age and the gravity of their situation, she grieved her lack of Blessing. A mage of distinction or someone with even a minor Blessing, somebody with a trick up her sleeve. Had she been a powerhouse of magical energy, she might have been able to make a real difference.

Fidela came, far less pregnant than Eulalia. She had taken to pregnancy like a duck to water, thriving despite the growing life in her belly. Eulalia had never shared Fidela's splendour for childbearing; she did not think of them as wondrous miracles, they were simply a fact of life. Yet for Fidela, pregnancy had turned an already exquisite woman into a queen, flush with wealth and warmth.

She was accompanied by the eldest of the holy men, Bronnuq. He had just passed his ninetieth summer – half the reason he was still on the council was because it had been entirely unfeasible to send him off into greater Svarna to join the war efforts. He leaned heavily on the staff of Muqdah, a profoundly magical artefact that was bound to the holy workings of the city. It held the purest distillation of the city's power, stored in a clear gem secured in a golden lantern at its top.

'This has to be Thurlowe or the Emperor. There's no other caster in The Imperium who would be able to break through our defences,' Bronnuq said, his staff planted firmly into the stone floor as Fidela eased him into his seat.

Neither of those were excellent options. Thurlow Thurlowe had been carving his way through Svarna, having slain the queen and her children – an unhinged force whose violence had sent whispers spinning all the way to the coast. He would not hesitate to tear through a city populated by the nonviolent and the holy. Yet, if it were the emperor of the Eschalion Empire amassing at Muqdah's border, that meant the elves were so assured in their conquest that they'd risk their monarch in this final confrontation. Eulalia looked at Ohba out of the corner of her eye

'How is he breaking through them at all?' Fidela pressed, heated. 'We're supposed to be protected here. How did they break through the wards?'

Adil swallowed, approaching Fidela. He reached out with one broad hand and squeezed her shoulder. 'We don't know. I began researching after the first strike, but this could just be brute strength. If a rune had been worn down, it would have only been one of hundreds. Those runes work like an interlocked net, so if one fails, the rest should protect Muqdah long enough for one of our magi to find it and reinforce it.'

Fidela pressed a hand to her mouth and patted her belly with the other, dark eyes full of watery dread. Eulalia narrowed her eyes at her fellow holy mother and failed, for a breath, in her attempt to avoid judgement. She loved Fidela, loved her in ways that only a woman could. She loved the way that she twisted her hair into spirals when she was anxious, the way her fine fingers thumbed at her jewellery, the set of her mouth. Now, they were pregnant together. Yet, Fidela was not exempt from Eulalia's bouts of frustration. Fidela needed to find her spine.

Ohba drew closer to the burgeoning fire, closing his eyes for a moment. When they reopened, they were ghostly, glowing a pale gold. He blinked and they returned to normal. 'The wards that shield Muqdah are damaged, but not destroyed. However, if they continue to strike with such force, they will break through. I've never seen our protections strained in such a way.' Her holy man wiped his hands on his robes, and Eulalia found herself chilled, goose flesh prickling on her arms despite the warmth of the fire.

She took a long breath and tried to restrain her confusion. There was no time to worry about how the army were forcing their way through their defences, only that they could do so. 'They've figured out something that nobody else has in all the centuries Muqdah has held its peace. They've found one worn point in our protections and exploited it.'

'They took the royal city. It is very likely that they learnt something there that might have helped them break through our defences,' Bronnuq said quietly. 'They would have had the royal library at their disposal.'

Eulalia felt as if she were floating above her body, watching herself talk to the priests from above. She should have been panicked, desperate to protect her and her children's lives. Yet, the turmoil within her was dangerously quiet.

'We should call for dragon riders,' Eulalia found herself saying. 'If they can make it back to Muqdah before the shield falls entirely, they'll decimate the army. We're only at a loss because they know we're unprotected, but we don't have to be.'

'If we call them back, we may also cost Svarna the last of its riders. Did you see the bolt that broke the shield?' Cuinu barely let her finish her last word before he cut in, tone clipped and his words tight. A hot flush began to crawl up the back of her neck as he tore himself away from the fire and levelled a look at her that once would have inspired violence in Eulalia. Long ago, the temples had been the sanctuaries of women. The holy mothers had ruled and been respected. But hungry wolves had crept in when their numbers had faltered and clawed their way into place.

'Do not condescend to me – we all saw the bolt. We'll see how long they can maintain that level of power. They'll need several more bolts to shatter the shield entirely.' She was posturing somewhat as she spoke, making guesswork out of what she knew. Eulalia's stare flicked briefly from Cuinu to Ohba.

He gave her the smallest of nods before he took up her argument – it was an unfortunate truth that Ohba's opinion held more weight than hers with these men. 'The dragon riders are our greatest defence. Idunn is a powerhouse, but she won't leave the eggs in the nursery. The most practised warriors have left Muqdah to fight. Maybe calling the dragon riders back might be necessary.'

'Of course it's necessary. They've done this on purpose,' Eulalia snarled, her frustration rising. 'They know all the dragons were sent out to defend the countryside, and they've come here because we've left ourselves defenceless. I fucking told you—'

'We've told each other many things in these last months. Let's not argue in front of the children,' Ohba reasoned quietly. 'None of us could have foreseen this. The Imperium should have been stopped along the Golden Reach, but instead they've come west to us. A hundred small and large skirmishes have gone awry, none of which we could have predicted from here. We are not veterans of war.'

'Muqdah needs help,' Bronnuq stated, his voice creaking like ancient wood. 'We are a holy city with no military of our own. We must do whatever we can. It's the duty of the dragon riders to assist those who are in need in our vast nation – we should put out the call. Those who swear their service to Svarna know the risks of war.'

Ohba made an uncertain noise. Eulalia pinned him with a long, even stare that was undermined by the quiet burbling of Rasyl at their backs. She did not want to think of what the Child was drawing from their conversation, how much their doomsaying was sinking beneath her skin.

You and I can argue about this later, she thought. When we've rid the army from our door.

'I agree that we cannot afford to be conservative.' Ohba finally spoke after a great deal of consideration, watching her all the while as he spoke. 'I don't think it matters if it's Thurlow Thurlowe or one of the Eschalion. If the shield falls, the army will show no mercy. Only... if there's something that we can do in our power to stop them, it is our responsibility as Muqdah's guardians to do so. We might need to rely on our dragon riders.'

Eulalia was pressuring him into this, she knew, but with two children at her back, she did not feel bad about it. She thought of every temple child, each strapping warrior who'd left their city and peace behind to serve in the war.

They were vulnerable. They would need every weapon in their arsenal if they were going to defend themselves. The renasci were their eternal guardians, but they were not dragons; they could not raze a battlefield.

Within the womb, the renasci were made magick; it was a sacred art that made them more than they were, bound them to the land and allowed them to commune with the world in a way mere mortals could not. It took twenty summers for the entirety of the work to be done, to pour molten magic within them, but what was twenty summers when traded for an eternity? Their magic granted them abnormally long life. One renasci could stand watch over a dozen generations, care for hundreds of people. They could marry within their ranks and produce Blessed children. But they could not breathe dragonflame and incinerate their enemies in a single pass.

'I will not make that call,' Cuinu cut in. 'I will not condemn any dragon rider to death. The invaders are stuck outside that shield, and they cannot come any further. The shields have never fallen, in all the years this city has stood, and they will not now. If we simply leave them out there, they could starve to death at our door. That crack is a show of force, but they do not have the capability to bring the shield down. They are attempting to bully us into preemptive submission.'

Eulalia's face warmed at the implication that she could be bullied into any form of submission. To allow her anger loose would be disastrous upon any breath of diplomacy. Her rage had a way of strangling politeness in its crib and drawing out the honest, blunt meaning of a person.

'Should we all cross our fingers and pray that crack does not grow?' she goaded, leering at him. 'Perhaps they'll be here in time to attend the autumn festival if we're really lucky.'

'The First Temple needs a consensus amongst its council. And there are children here. It is our duty to protect them.' Ohba's gentle, plying ways turned onto Cuinu and Adil while Eulalia simply glared. 'We should be doing something. At least Eulalia is presenting a path of action.'

Most holy mothers who had walked Morouqdi's walls were soft, loving figures. They cared for all equally and never snarled or snapped, so coddled by the holy men that they could not find anything to rage about. Eulalia was pregnant. She was a mother. She was, however, not particularly kind or gracious in her own mind and did not consider herself a good person.

She considered herself even less of a good person when she knew she was correct and someone was being stubbornly, adamantly wrong. Cuinu had decided at some point in their lengthy acquaintance that she was a foolish woman who was prone to diving into action without a second thought.

'We have so few dragons left,' she heard Fidela say. The beautiful woman's voice was far smaller, less settled. Eulalia's gaze turned on Fidela, disbelief etched on her face as she felt the tide of the conversation shift.

'And we will have no dragons or temple children left if we let them march on us!' Eulalia threw a hand into the air. 'Do you not understand that? This is the last frontier for them. If we fall, so do the nurseries and the temples. That's the last of us.' The way of Muqdah and the First Temple was that the council must come to a consensus on any decisions they made; the magic embedded in the stones of the Morouqdi would then do all it could to enact that decision. A distress call, if enacted properly, would ring through every city in Svarna that had a temple. It would ring out over the prayer towers they'd built deep in the draconic territory that surrounded Muqdah. They need only raise the alarm and the riders would come.

'You're doomsaying,' Adil accused. 'Just because they are at our door does not mean that the city is lost. Our shields will hold.'

Eulalia wanted to smack him sideways. 'Doomsaying is not an unreasonable thing to do when doom sits on the horizon,' she snapped. 'I am trying to circumvent our eradication, and you are standing in my way.'

'Ohba—' Cuinu began.

Eulalia, sensing where this was leading, turned on him too. 'Think twice before you ask Ohba to manage me, unless you'd like the two children in this room to witness a murder.' She did not have a weapon, but she had two perfectly good hands, and Cuinu's neck didn't look terribly thick. 'Most of the dragons here have never fought in a battle. Our most powerful dragon hasn't flown in thirty years and will not leave her eggs. Yes, we can send up renasci on the few that do fly, but there are dragons out in Svarna whose sole purpose is to protect us. It is astounding idiocy to not raise the call for help. And the renasci – to rely on them as if they are soldiers ... have you forgotten why they were given to the temples? Mothers give their babes to you because they do not think themselves capable of giving their children the lives that they deserve. Not for us to treat them as disposable warriors.'

'Eula ...' Fidela started.

'Don't.' The two women were fierce friends, but even fiercer foes when they found themselves at opposite ends of these arguments. Having given the church two children, though, and sitting on her third, Eulalia outranked Fidela. She was not opposed to pulling rank. 'We cannot rely on the renasci to defend us. Not unless you're going to put a weapon in the hand of every man, woman, and child. They are the sentinels of Svarna. We make babes magic so that they can do what we cannot – speak with the land and care for the dragons without being eaten. Not fight for us.'

That tension, strung tight like a drawn bow, hung in the air between the council of priests and the two holy mothers. Her eyes went from one face to the next, waiting for one of them to break that hellish silence and speak. Fold. They had to fold. They had to call the dragon riders in. It was an absurd thought that they had weapons of mass destruction at their fingertips, and yet, they'd remain out of reach until they'd come to some half-formed consensus.

It was unlikely that six adults would even agree on small matters, like the colour of the banners they hung at the change of the season. Yet even their imminent destruction could not move the bar for these stubborn bastards.

'I understand you have a personal investment in this, Eulalia.' Adil's eyes darted towards the Child, who was crouching with her back turned away from them. 'Everyone in this room knows that your girl must be defended at all costs. She will one day be the beating heart of all of Svarna. And Ohba—'

Having learnt his lesson from dragging Ohba into a discussion he was not a part of, Adil paused. He glanced nervously between them, as if expecting immediate interjection, but Eulalia waved him along.

'Ohba is the anchor of our city. He cannot leave, and you two have always been quite close, so I don't think anyone in this room doubts that you would stay with him through any fiery end.' It was a respectful way of quietly accusing them of being in love, in some great or small way. 'But we cannot be irrational in how we handle things. We have avoided destruction thus far. We are going to stay in our city and remain safe while they hammer away at shields that have stood for an eternity.'

'Not once in eternity have we faced destruction like this,' Eulalia said. 'We have been hiding away, hoping that the north squashes the invasion in their tracks. They did not. We need to use our dragons.'

The pair glowered at one another. Had looks been deadly, they would have both dropped on the spot.

'A deadlock will get us nowhere.' Those words sounded far too close to an admonishment coming from the ancient Bronnuq, so Eulalia quietly wound in her own aggression lest she lose him too. The fact that the magic that bound Muqdah required a consensus from its caretakers was something only a man could think was clever. It should have been a majority rule, but the first Svarnishmen who'd bonded had wanted to ensure that there was no margin of error in which the temple power could be abused.

'We can start with the tapestries,' Bronnuq continued, his tone gentle. 'We need to cut free the tapestries currently in progress and wrap them up. There are two caravans down in the dock that we can man with those of able body to get as many citizens out of here as we possibly can. Any fineries and focuses should go with them – there will be little space for much else, but the mashjor cannot fall into elvish hands. Eulalia, I sense this will be a nonstarter, but should we move your little one out with them?'

The group murmured sounds of mild agreement, though Adil and Eulalia had yet to break eye contact. Their contest only ceased when Cuinu's hand brushed against Adil's elbow, quiet words passing between the stubborn pair. Eulalia snapped her attention away from him and only then recognised what Bronnuq was suggesting.

'I could not be parted from her,' she said, slowly. 'She – she should be here. With us. Do we want to lose the herald of Svarna to a war-torn country?'

'You could go with her,' Fidela pushed tentatively, only sympathy in her gaze. Yet, it was not an option that Eulalia could envision. They had lived all these years in relative quiet in Morouqdi; she did not know how to be away from this place. She suspected that the world had not grown any kinder to women in her absence.

Eulalia pressed her lips together, shook her head, entirely untrusting of her tongue.

Cuinu nodded. 'We can revisit this discussion once that work has been done.'

She could have screamed. Demanded that they change their mind, cursed their bloodlines off into the furthest wastelands. She could have raged against their obstinance, but that would fix nothing. For a woman who was intimately familiar with her own fury, she'd grown quite accustomed to knowing when it would get her nowhere. Some people grew skittish and folded like long grass in the wind when faced with the hot tide of Eulalia's anger. Some grew stiffer and sealed over with stone. Those who turned to stone could not be moved by more fire. She'd have to find another way to turn them quickly or circumvent the need for them entirely.

'We should go talk to the dragons,' Eulalia said. It was an excuse – the look she shared with Ohba told him so. They would need to talk to the dragons, but they also needed to talk with one another. 'I don't know what they will do, but they deserve to know what is coming to our door.'

Chapter Five

THE IMPERIUM

The Imperium was a churning monolith, under which everyone was welcome – if they were capable of assimilation.

Svarnishmen were incapable of being anything but what they were – garish, gauche, gaudy – but they were also adaptable. When thrust into a crowd, they were great at disappearing into the throng. It made it easy for the High Elves who populated the Imperium to disregard Svarnishmen in their midst. No one wanted to spend any length of time considering the existence of the disenfranchised – not in an empire that believed itself benevolent to those it crushed within its grasp.

Nuru kept her shawl tucked tight around herself, conscious of the bare stretches of skin that would draw the eye to them if they were not careful. The culture of modesty throughout the respectable corners of the Imperium was a shield of anonymity; the most scandalous thing one could be was a woman who dared to flash her décolletage. She could play at this game, as long as they weren't rushing headfirst into scrutiny.

'They were swearing the whole way back.' Hotaru recounted Llewelyn and Maldwyn's retreat as she trotted beneath a narrow cobblestone bridge, Nuru and the Wyverns in tow. 'Fighting like they'd lost their last meal and bitching to high heaven. They knew she was in The Brass Wyvern, they just didn't know what to do about it. Didn't want to risk Virnoi knocking them upside the head, I guess.'

'You followed a pair of angry High Elves all this way?' Nuru asked, sensing Takuma's roiling anxiety about Hotaru's nightly escapades as he kept pace beside her.

'They were sniffing around the brothel,' Hotaru shrugged. 'I wanted to know what they were looking for.' She had been dubbed Takuma's 'little crow' because she was constantly perched on their roofs and had a penchant for picking up shiny things.

'It's not a brothel,' Takuma muttered. The Wyverns chuckled, a cascade of laughter falling from them in response to the familiar protestation. 'It's a … community home. For the promiscuous.'

'Sure,' Feliks said with a chuckle. 'Because nothing says community like paying people to have sex.'

'Shut your mouth.' Takuma swiped at Feliks. 'It's a different licence if we're functioning as a business. You think we could afford to pay that much to the city? You think I want to deal with Imperium diplomats?'

If Nuru had pressed Taliesin, she could have had the paperwork taken care of for them. There were more reasons to remain questionably licensed than simply the monetary cost.

'Nobody wants to deal with Imperium diplomats,' Hotaru responded tonelessly. Nobody believed her, considering her wandering Blessed fingers and the small treasure trove of stolen goods that she'd pilfered for them throughout the years.

'Anyone who needs to know about The Brass Wyvern and what we do there already knows,' Nuru said. 'If the guards have an issue with us not being licensed to the city, they should let us know. We see them often enough.'

Nuru attended to half of them alone. She sent them stumbling into the evening lamplight, heady with liquor and laughter, and knew their wives by name.

'Bless you, holy mother, and your infinite wisdom,' Hotaru sang. Nuru swiped at her, pulling a face. She had been the first one to bear a child, but that did not make her feel any more mature than the rest of them – just another wyvern lost on the wind.

The Brass Wyvern, at its essence, was an establishment that could not exist. Imperium property law was meant to be airtight, and the Svarnish hadn't been factored into it. Out in the broader Nordlund, the laws were more lenient from town to town, but within the capitol, one had to be of a certain sort to own their home. Nuru and Takuma had got around this by having one of their old clients sign on as the benefactor of the brothel that had stood in The Brass Wyvern's place prior to their establishment, The Stuck Pig. The Nordic name got them a foot in the door, then they'd finagled the rest.

The Brass Wyvern didn't have to be on any formal listing or registry. People found the Wyvern regardless. They came from all over the city, following whispers and traded drinks, and they left happy. There wasn't a bedworker in The Brass Wyvern who was bad at their trade, and Nuru and Takuma together – they were legendary.

Nuru had been Takuma's bedmate for longer than most people were married. It was a purely platonic arrangement, though it came with … complications.

Zuri stayed quiet through the entirety of their transit. She was as slim as a whip, dark-skinned and darker-eyed, but her horns cut a concerningly crooked silhouette. Nuru kept checking on her wordlessly, her eyes seeking Zuri to ensure that they had not lost her entirely.

The crew stuck close to the buildings as they approached the Imperium's Golden Quarter, its windows hung with colourful banners embroidered with the insignia of the Eschalier, the familial symbol of the emperor. The Golden Quarter surrounded the palace, the closest one could come in this city without treading on the hallowed grounds of the living royalty. This was the holy land for the nobility and all those who hoped to one day join their refined ranks. With the influx of immigrants, the quarter was split between those who'd sell to the royals – wineries, academies, and bauble peddlers – and those descended from age-old dynasties.

Hotaru made a show of shoving her hands deep within her coat pockets as perfumed women swanned past with long, slashed pockets. The High Elves floated in perfumed clouds, wearing their high-necked gowns and their mithril chains.

'Focus,' Takuma spoke quietly, ruffling Hotaru's curls. He pressed a kiss to the top of her head. 'You can go plucking the fruit later – you just need to show us the orchard first.'

'Together?' Hotaru asked.

'Deal,' the proprietor responded. Nuru remembered when they'd met. Takuma had been utterly incensed by Hotaru nearly making it off into the city with his coin purse. He may not have Blessed fingers like Hotaru did, but he'd been a pickpocket for long enough to spot them a mile away.

Hotaru led the way along the side of the road, occasionally guiding the group into the narrow alleyways between buildings when someone was paying them too much mind. Nuru did not avert her gaze so thoroughly from their stares, instead ducking her head and allowing the red ribbon she'd woven into her hair to do the speaking for her. It was the universal colour of service for bedworkers in the Imperium and beyond.

Amidst the crystalline spires and the colossal reaches of the High Elf estates, a dome emerged slowly upon approach, as though it were a trick of the eye. Seemingly shaped from the firmament itself, the azure reaches of the sky cracked apart to reveal the glimmering sphere against the furthest corner of the heavens. The structure was nestled beside a castle split in half, an imposing slate grey beast that contrasted against the pastel gardens that lay at its feet and the trees that flowered in vibrant lilac tones along the estate's perimeter.

'That's not just some nameless noble's estate,' Takuma said, eyes turned upwards towards the dome's peak. It was an obnoxiously large thing, and from the ground, they could see magic swirling within it as thick as smoke. 'That's the Thurlowe estate. The Emperor's Justice.'

A feeling crept into Nuru's stomach, a thread of ice that had her drawing her shawl tighter around her.

'The dread mage. Taliesin's father.' She massaged a spot just above her jaw, her own eyes turning to the spiny buttresses that supported the dome's immense weight.

She did not know all the Thurlowe clan. She had been introduced to a select few and had heard even fewer names from Taliesin, but she pushed the thought of them aside, unwilling to approach the reality of Thurlow Thurlowe fathering her sweet priest. There were always rumours of Thurlowe bastards – the dread mage took women as he wanted, when he wanted. Taliesin's own sister, Nahia, was half Nord. She had only been accepted into the fold because the church had wanted her.

'The ones that tried to register all the Svarnish caravans?' Feliks asked, cocking his head to the side. He had never lived in a caravan; he wasn't familiar with the revolving swarm of politics that surrounded their mere presence within the Imperium. It was the easiest way for the Svarnish people knew to move en masse. It was how they had escaped the war.

'The very same,' Nuru affirmed. She remembered the headache of when they'd tried to regulate the caravans, and how Imamu had sworn up and down that he'd never let it happen. 'Our old caravan kicked up a stink about it because they didn't think it was a smart idea to have every man, woman, and child listed under the Imperium. It would have let them quantify the threat of the Svarnish to their precious order.'

'You can get closer,' Hotaru chirped, unperturbed. The little pickpocket had never been in close enough proximity to Thurlow Thurlowe to fear him – the mouse had little to fear from the elephant – if the mouse could see the elephant's approach. 'I can show you where they went inside.'

'You went closer?' Zuri hissed, horrified.

'It's fine! People pass through the Golden Quarter plenty to get to other parts of the city. It's just smart not to linger.' To illustrate her point, Hotaru went trotting out across the Golden Quarter. Nuru blew out a sharp, frustrated breath and made chase, though Feliks was just as quick. It was his job to care for them, and he had a talent for looming over his wards.

'Little crow,' Takuma called. 'You better know what you're doing.'

'You taught her this,' Nuru shot back. Hotaru could have benefited from some level of fear of the Imperium.

Takuma's only response was to chuckle, but he could not deny her claim. He had taught Hotaru how to handle a blade and to spot trouble with a keen eye, but he would not teach her fear, despite how nervous it made Nuru. Takuma had done nothing but make Hotaru braver, allowing her the confidence of being a part of a group rather than a crow without a murder.

A collection of glass bridges surrounded the Thurlowe estate, lining the greenery for those who wished to peruse the public gardens. Nuru and Hotaru trotted over one together with the Wyverns at their back, passing the occasional disinterested guard on the way. The Imperium's ruling class allowed the peasantry to use the bridges and bask in their splendour, without realising the area could be used to scope out the estate for those who had the eye.

Nuru was familiar with the Golden Quarter, but she far preferred to frequent it under the cover of night. She had been squirrelled into guest wings and estates, into secret rooms and servants' cottages. Places where young lords could feel fine throwing her onto a soft-pillowed bed without the eyes of an empire bearing down upon them.

They came to a short stop on the third bridge, which was the emptiest corner of the overlook. The nobility were not so unwise that they'd allow visitors close enough to the estate to sneak within, of course, but all the Wyverns needed was a good look at the place. With most of the Imperium hard at work as the sun ticked into the high point of the sky, the glass overlook was largely devoid of people except for a few besotted High Elves. It was hard to make oneself inconspicuous in the Golden Quarter, especially when standing on a glass pedestal. Nuru was conscious of wandering stares, but the guards were underpaid and lazy in the sunlight.

Hotaru peered over the railing, her huge eyes seeking something in the surrounds. Nuru's eyes followed hers, lips pressed together.

'They went in there.' Hotaru had swapped tongues to Svarnish, pointing to the estate. 'Came all the way around here instead of going through the front. Maybe they didn't want to wake everyone up?'

'That's a service passage,' Nuru responded. She kept her distance from the Thurlowe estate, but she'd been snuck into a neighbouring estate several seasons prior. She had made friends with the kitchen staff who'd been lingering outside the passage. 'If they were actual Thurlowes, I doubt they'd be getting in the same way the servantry does. High Elves are too proud for that, especially Taliesin's family.'

'Being Thurlowe-adjacent doesn't particularly improve matters,' Takuma chimed in. He had propped himself up on the balustrade, resting his chin on his hands as he surveyed the estate. People often believed that Takuma was far more lackadaisical than he was, but Nuru had known him long enough to know he was painfully intelligent. The gears in his mind were churning, clicking as he regarded the sumptuous corner of the world that lay before them. 'It could be far worse if they were in the Eschalier household. Do you think this is where you were kept, Zuri?'

As he spoke, Hotaru had grown distracted by something in the gardens. She attempted to hook herself over the railing, only to be tugged firmly back to the floor by Takuma's protective hand on her waistband.

Attention turned to Zuri, almost forgotten in her quietness. She had pulled a scarf up around her face at some point, though it did little to hide her horns from view. It was the unfortunate reality of being Svarnish – they all cut distinctive figures. Hotaru did a better job than most of obscuring her silhouette, braiding her hair into elaborate buns that could hide her horns.

'I came out the side of the dome chamber, not the gardens,' Zuri said. Her eyes, framed by dark lashes, peered out at the estate. She joined Takuma and pointed, subtly, down the side of the gardens and along the castle. 'Back where those guards are. This is the place.'

Nuru followed her gaze to the end of the public gardens, where there was a narrow gap in the wall that led back into the further reaches of the estate. There were two guards stationed out front, but Nuru spotted more guards at their backs. There was something going on behind that wall, but they weren't going to be able to get back there to investigate – not without Virnoi. The gravedigger was a spellcaster with a talent for unsavoury magics, but he worked odd hours and had been utterly comatose when they left.

There was a flash of movement out of the corner of Nuru's eye, and when she turned back, Hotaru was tucking a colourful blossom behind one ear.

'So, she came from inside Thurlowe's estate,' Hotaru shrugged. 'Thurlow Thurlowe, the Emperor's Justice, has a dragon. It's not like he can do anything with it. Right?'

Chapter Six

THE IMPERIUM

Hotaru's revelation went down about as well as could be expected.

Personally, she thought that the panic was a tad dramatic. It was an unfortunate thought, that Thurlow Thurlowe had a dragon, but it was not the end of days. She had never even crossed paths with a nobleman of Thurlowe's station, and if she did, she suspected he'd think nothing of her. It was no more offensive to her than the treatment of other poor Svarnishmen in the city.

Being a beggar made one nearly invisible in big cities. That meant that, in the great, monolithic beast of the Imperium, Hotaru made a practice of disappearing. Beneath the layers of a stolen coat and linen scarf, the world presumed her to be one of the wayward women lost in the mire of the capitol. That suited her just fine. It opened the world to her slender fingers. She was a child of misfortune and sorrow, like so many others dragged in by the Eschalion's far-reaching claws.

Her compatriots at The Brass Wyvern did not understand what it was to beg and scrape for their meal – other than Takuma. There had been a time in his life where he'd been just as feral as Hotaru. When he'd felt his stomach twist with hunger and not known when his next meal was. And in that common struggle, their bond had been forged.

It was why Hotaru was surprised by the debate that broke out as they returned to the brothel. She barely listened to it on the way back, her fingers itching to do something. Community would not be enough to save them from the brutality of the Imperium. Thurlow Thurlowe had a dragon, and that changed nothing, really. Not in Hotaru's world. She would merely need to seek out some potions of fireproofing, some insurance should she tread anywhere near the Golden Quarter in the future. She would ask Virnoi if he knew how to brew them.

She felt better once they were back within the red-light district. There was no honour amongst thieves, but there was solidarity between bedworkers. Within The Brass Wyvern, there wasn't a soul who worked there who would throw them to the wolves.

The stray that had come in with the rain was tucked up in a chair beside Takuma, her pretty face utterly indecipherable to Hotaru. She had spent the walk back trying to concoct something to say to the stranger and failing, intimidated so thoroughly by the look of her that she kept blanking. Zuri had little to say about their predicament and had resorted to the same strategy Hotaru had, returning to her quiet and watching the argument unfold like an entertaining scrap.

'If Thurlow Thurlowe really has a dragon, it's probably smarter for us to leave. We can pack everyone up, get a caravan together and make our way south. I'd rather risk it on the road than be here when he lets whatever's in that dome loose.' Feliks had seemingly decided that they should all flee, that none of this was worth the trouble they were likely to find from interfering.

'Smarter for whom?' Takuma shot back. 'Do you know how expensive it is to actually buy the number of caravans you're talking about? It's not as if I can exactly sell this place, we don't technically own it.'

Hotaru sighed and pushed herself off the wall she'd been watching from. This was a non-argument as far as Hotaru was concerned. She had never been on the road, and she didn't find the idea of rejoining the wandering masses particularly appealing. Her own blood family, caravan dwellers and traders, had abandoned her to the capitol in the first place. She left the boys to their bickering and went to trail after her nocturnal companion, having tracked Virnoi's emergence from his slumber. Distinctly removed from the argument occurring within, Nuru had taken to standing out on the porch. Virnoi moved first to join her outside, and Hotaru followed, comfortable in remaining within his shadow.

The argument continued, well within earshot. There was little privacy within The Brass Wyvern.

'Does he really have a dragon?' Virnoi asked.

The shadowy High Elf had taken up in the corner of The Brass Wyvern several winters prior, when taverns without a proper hearth could no longer hold off the biting chill. He usually made himself scarce throughout the daylight hours, yet here he was, out in the warmth of the afternoon.

Nuru sighed, turning to face him. Hotaru watched from around his robe, curious.

'Zuri certainly believes that she saw one beneath the dome that Thurlowe's been building. And she described a stench, which makes sense if the dragon produces gas from its flight bladder while remaining grounded. But we have no way of being certain, otherwise.

'Thurlowe's estate has been shrouded in wards so that no one can see inside while they finish construction on the new addition. So there's a chance that this is all nothing more than overblown whispers. There's a chance that Zuri's never actually seen a dragon, and that it was a manticore or a drake or a wyrm, that maybe the shock confused her after all she had been through. There's a chance that the wards are just the product of Thurlowe's paranoia, given half the country wants his head on a pike.'

'But it's a hell of a lot of smoke for there not to be fire,' Virnoi murmured. He was wrapped in a great knitted shawl, enchanted to hold the shifting hues of dying leaves. The gravedigger let out a long breath, and it fogged, clouding upwards in the chill. Fall had descended upon the Imperium, and the weather would soon turn. The streets would gloss over with frost and sleet, and sparkling icicles would sprout from the rooftops, turning the city to crystal.

'Thurlow Thurlowe, right hand of the arch mage of the Eschalion, has a dragon.' Nuru and Virnoi stood together in horrified silence, while Hotaru stuffed her hands in her pockets and tried not to disturb their moment.

Virnoi resorted to the basics. 'Fuuuuuuck.'

Hotaru snorted.

'I don't know if there's really anything we can do about a dragon,' Takuma was saying. They had migrated to the very back of the brothel for this discussion, wary of any listening ears amongst their clientele. There were too many knife-ears floating around the Wyvern today, watching for any sign of insubordination. Hotaru's eyes flicked between the balcony and the discussion table, wondering how long it would take for Takuma to transition out of his minor panic. He could certainly handle himself when arguments came about, but he tended to fall into a certain frenetic energy when racing through prospective options.

Virnoi was a quiet creature, so alien to the Svarnishmen. For the whole of the first season that Virnoi had spent in The Brass Wyvern, Hotaru had known him to be entirely nonverbal. He still lapsed into bouts of silence at times, but Hotaru did not mind. One got to know the world more intimately in silence.

'Thurlow has a dragon. We already knew that after the war he'd have the choice of whatever he wanted from the ruins of Svarna, but I think the presumption was that he'd slain them all.' Nuru spoke once more, and as she turned, Hotaru saw that her Blessing was casting a distant radiance. Hotaru had never been told the nature of Nuru's magic, though she had certainly heard the jokes of the whore with a Blessed throat. But in all the time they had known one another, she had not seen Nuru's Blessing in action.

Between her clipped tone and the pensive way she kept smoothing her skirts, there was something dangerous unfolding within their holy mother. 'Elves have no grounds to even commune with dragons, let alone keep them like playthings.'

Hotaru stared at an interesting spot in the garden, uncertain of what to make of this traditional talk. She had been born in a caravan and never met a dragon, had never stepped foot within a temple. She knew that the Svarnishmen had built draconic temples and helped protect eggs from the frost, had constructed great pyres in their honour – had died for their dragons. Most of the High Elves Hotaru knew wouldn't have the commitment to sacrifice themselves for anything within the Imperium's bounds.

'He can't be permitted to keep the dragon,' Virnoi concluded. There was an edge to his voice that very few people were familiar with. Hotaru sensed violence within it.

Nuru nodded. 'He can't.'

To them, that was really all there was to it. Thurlow had a dragon, and that could not be permitted. If he found a way to control it, to breed it, to foster the growth of those eggs for the Eschalion, he would ravage the remaining Svarnish population. All there would be left then would be for him to start dressing Svarnish – and that would be offensive not only to their sensibilities, but also to their eyes.

Hotaru followed her elvish companion as he dropped himself into an empty chair at the round discussion table, climbing into his lap and tucking herself beneath his shawl until her back was pressed up against his chest. Virnoi let out a small, half-huff of repressed laughter, and she elbowed him in the ribs.

'Thurlow Thurlowe has a dragon. We may be the only people in the empire who know that he has a dragon, and we're certainly the only people who care. Dragons are thinking, feeling, intelligent beings. The fall of Svarna cut them just as deep as it cut us. We either free the thing ourselves, or we go to the merchant kings and tell them what we've seen. They'll want it freed, too.'

The merchant kings were the makeshift rulers of the Svarnish people, who had been crowned when the caravans had become a primary mode of transport for their people. There were kinfolk who had not left the homeland, who could not be moved from their homes, but so many had found safe harbour within the caravans that the caravan heads suddenly found themselves guardians of thousands. The title of merchant king had started as a whisper.

Now, with Queen Taena dead, the Svarnish had five kings in her stead – and they did not quite measure up. Hotaru didn't think they were much more than upstart patriarchs, but they did make a great deal of money.

Takuma sneered. 'Fuck the merchant kings,' he said, his green eyes glinting. 'If I can steal from them and get away with it, they've got no hope of stealing from Thurlow. They're only good at thieving through trade. If this is really happening, we'll be the ones to do it.'

'We could ask Taliesin to get us in,' Hotaru proposed. It seemed unwise to ignore their one direct connection to the manor, but Nuru shook her head.

'Taliesin hasn't lived with his father for some time. They don't get on. He lives in the enclave.' Nuru sat slowly down at the table, her jaw set as she cast her eyes across the chaotic spread of papers before them. Her soft hands began to rifle through them, brows furrowed in thought. 'And I won't ask him for help in this. He's too good to be dragged into our business. And he's too noticeable, too prominent. His older brother Truls, however, is far less morally upright.'

'I don't want Taliesin to hear a whisper of this,' Takuma said, eyes boring a hole into Nuru's skull. She did not glance up.

'You think he'd help us?' Zuri finally spoke up.

'Not in the way that you're thinking. Truls is a family man – he's got a good relationship with his father, but he prioritises his brawn over his books, if you get my meaning. We'd have to work him indirectly,' Nuru explained. Hotaru had seen Truls regularly throughout the seasons she'd spent within the Wyvern. A rare exception to the usually willowy High Elves, that was a man who had some muscle to him. As an afterthought, Nuru added, 'He's mostly harmless.'

Hotaru doubted it. She had watched him and the way that when trouble rose, he turned to his blade.

'Then that's a start.' Takuma bounced with a sense of rising excitement. A nervous twitch set his boots tapping on the stone floor as he sorted the scattered sheaths of paper on the table. He cast them aside to reveal their own map of the capitol. It was neatly labelled 'The Heart of the Imperium' and had been bought from a questionable group of traders who boasted a great collection of wayward goods. Hotaru had nicked one just to see if she could. It sat on the western wall of this room, in Takuma's cabinet of curiosities.

She had been waiting for this shift in the wind. This was where Takuma came alight, when the beginning of a plan came blustering into him.

He was good at many things, but he had a talent for thievery, which was why Takuma had taken to tomb robbing as a hobby. Hotaru had gone along with him to see what the thrill of it was. The dead cared little for keeping what they were buried with and when they did, they objected as liches and the undead. She had not seen him rob the living on such a grand scale. It seemed to Hotaru that the very thought of thieving from the elvish nobility he despised so thoroughly delighted Takuma.

'First thing's first – if there's a flaw in that dome, we need to find it. Which means that we need to talk to the people who built it. It would be an expensive waste of magic to use elvish mages to build the thing, so they likely hired the least offensive labourers they could find and still underpaid the lot.'

'Nords,' Feliks said with a nod, tapping a cluster of taverns on the lower part of the map. Before the Imperium had been the Eschalion's, it had been the Nordlund's, and the Nords remained. They were joyous, rowdy and an infinitely strong lot. Most were still adjusting to the presence of the Svarnish amongst them, the oldest of the Eschalion's colonies trying to make sense of the newest. Feliks was fantastic with them, in a horrifically dissonant kind of way that contrasted with his usual looming temperament. 'There's a pub down there that's owned by an old clan that was here before the elves settled. We can go sniff around, there's always someone drinking who wants to vent about their old boss. I know these people.'

They continued, Hotaru watching from beneath Virnoi's shawl. She interjected occasionally, but largely spent the time watching Nuru, who sat quietly in her seat. The golden radiance of her Blessing cast a light upon the map of the city. She seemed distracted and distant. Andraste wandered in at one point with a bleary-eyed Nema on her hip, and between them, they shuffled the baby into Nuru's lap to feed. Nema was a healthy and sizeable child. Nuru sat stroking her babe's feather-soft curls while they talked, and Hotaru watched from her peripherals.

She was Nuru. She was the steadfast guardian of The Brass Wyvern. It was strange to see her off balance.

'This is all well and good,' Hotaru spoke, interrupting something Feliks had been saying about the oncoming festival. 'But how exactly does one go about stealing a dragon? That's not exactly a lift and run. This isn't some mark on the streets where you can just swap out his coin purse with a rock and call it a day. What are we even going to do with a dragon?'

'You don't just do anything with a dragon,' Nuru remarked. 'They're usually quite opinionated about what they'd prefer. I imagine they'll tell us where they're going, once we've freed them.'

Takuma loved a grand plan. It was the aftermath that grew problematic.

'I mean, they got the dragon beneath the dome somehow,' Virnoi reasoned. 'If it's of the size that Zuri says, it's not freshly hatched. It was large when it was brought into the city.' Hotaru was surprised to hear his voice rumbling behind her, but there was no uncertainty in his tone. 'If you can figure out how to do that, shouldn't we simply be able to reverse engineer its escape? If it went in through the tunnel, we should be able to get it back through that same tunnel. If they used a spell to transport it inside, you use the same spell. Easy.'

The stream of chatter lapsed, several pairs of eyes turning on the elf.

Virnoi grew still beneath Hotaru and made a contemplative noise. He did not like this much attention being directed at him.

'If you're dragging Hotaru into this mess, I'll lend a hand,' Virnoi ceded quietly. Beneath the shelter of the shawl, one of his hands snuck onto her leg. Takuma's face lit up with unadulterated joy. 'And anyway – if you're trying to rob the dread mage, I imagine having a mage alongside the crew will be a requirement.'

'I think Takuma would like to kiss you,' Nuru remarked, lips pressed together.

Their courtship was a peculiar thing; the elf had spent several weeks silently sitting at the end of the bar buying Takuma drinks, which Takuma had presumed to be from any of his dozen clients. Hotaru had known Virnoi from the alleyways before the Wyvern and had been entirely bemused by their connection. His whispery voice never changed.

'Later,' Takuma said with a dismissive wave. 'Once you all piss off. I don't need you lot staring at us.'

Chapter Seven

SVARNA

'They're *idiots*,' Eulalia groaned.

Ohba hummed as he helped her down, easing her onto one of the nursery benches. 'They're frightened.'

She snorted. 'They're frightened idiots, then.'

Her feet were swelling like balloons, and despite the fact she could not see them beneath her round belly, she could feel an ache in her ankles that needed quieting. She did not mind being pregnant until she reached the final stretches of it and found her body protesting at every small movement.

'Little one, go check on your friends,' Eulalia prompted the Child. She needed to vent without her eavesdropping, and the nursery was a thorough distraction. The two shared an uncertain look, lingering, before Eula waved her off. Taking it as permission, the Child deposited her younger brother with Eulalia and fled from the decidedly adult discussion. Eulalia would tell the dragons who needed to know what was happening, and then they could elaborate when they knew more.

The nursery was the heart of the First Temple, a chamber that swirled several hundred feet upwards towards the clouds. At its heart was a stone tower covered in hollows and round balconies. Not all of them were inhabited, but many were filled with dragons of small to moderate size, gleaming like bright gems in an elaborate sceptre. Clutches of eggs were half-buried in soft bedding and sand, anything they could gather in great masses that would insulate the warmth they needed to thrive. It was the renasci's job to ensure that the nests were well-protected. Clutching an egg when it was close to hatching could burn human skin until it bubbled and boiled; they needed their magical helpers for that.

A she-dragon emerged from within the network of dens, scales such a rich green that she shone ebony in the sun. Zoraida, Hellfire's Dawn, was friend to few, so nobody had been surprised when Eulalia had taken a liking to her. A century old, Zoraida had never tolerated a dragon rider upon her back or incompetency from those around her.

She was investigating their presence, and it was not long before both Eula and Ohba were kissed by her hot breath. Ohba watched her carefully as she approached. Eula bounced Rasyl on her hip, unbothered by the dragon's approach.

'The priests are being stupid.' Eulalia explained with a hiss. 'There is an army waiting at the city gates, and they are refusing to call back the war dragons. They will not think of how few saddles we have or how so many of our dragons are too young to know battle.'

A single dragon would destroy a dozen soldiers, but they were not hatched with the instincts necessary to fight in a human war. They hunted in the mountains, dominating broad empty skies – they were not born knowing how large a bolt would be before it pierced their rib cage or of the weird magics the elves wielded. The nursery was filled with younglings who had not ventured into the further stretches of Svarna, who would be unruly to ride and harder to drive, who had not even learnt how to hate their enemies. The matriarchs, like Zoraida and Kine, could be ridden and knew enough to be dangerous, but they resisted leaving their children.

Eulalia did not blame them. Zoraida reared in her distaste and let steam loose upon them, hissing as she did. A flush began to grow on Eulalia's olive skin, turned by the sheer heat that radiated from Zoraida.

The dragon's vocalisations sounded like they were speaking through great, clashing stones in their throat.

'They are frightened, Zoraida,' Ohba insisted, though he was gentler when he was trying to convince a dragon of the matter.

Had the she-dragon been able to roll her eyes, she likely would have, as Eulalia and Zoraida shared a heated look between them. Instead, Zoraida shook herself from her crested head to the tip of her tail and then settled down beside them. Her tail swayed from side to side at her back. Eulalia huffed and there was another soft rush of warmth. 'Being frightened is not an excuse for refusing to do everything in their power to protect this city.'

Idunn, the mammoth dragon that they called the matriarch of this nursery, had been grounded for several decades and now regarded the entirety of this place as her den. If and when the temple was breached, she would be their final defence.

The matriarch was unfazed by their passage. Her great shadow sat on the far side of the nursery, half-tucked away in a huge spherical chamber that she filled entirely. She was older than any of them, a resident of Muqdah for several centuries, and she was intensely fond of the Child. When the girl had been only a few days old, the holy men had presented her to Idunn – and that had been all the two had needed to grow as thick as thieves.

It had been the only part of the Child's prophecy that Eulalia had not been able to ignore. The herald of Svarna, the bringer of the new age, reportedly could speak with the dragons in a way that mere mortals could not. Even the temple children and the renasci did not have conversations at length like Eulalia's girl. They did not find themselves resistant to all flame and heat, unfazed by the dragon's warmth.

Nobody had ever articulated to Eulalia what a new age meant for Svarna, or how her child was meant to bring it. Bronnuq had told her that prophecies never had particulars – that he could have explained to her all the conjecture about Svarna's saviour, and it still would have little meaning. Destiny was a complex force that did not always work within the rules. That aside, Svarnish history was steeped in oral tradition, a tale so old Eulalia would have no way of knowing what the original prophet's wording had been.

That was the weakness with prophets. They could pop up anywhere in the world, speak their magic words, and remake fate without a single historian at their side. She was not the first to think that they should have simply kept their mouths shut.

Eulalia did not know how to articulate what was occurring at the city's edge to a being of such age as Zoraida. It was beyond her.

'They think of our dragons as sacred guardians,' Ohba continued, only speaking once he'd turned to check that the Child was not nearby. The Child was calling greetings to the youngest hatchlings, sitting down at the edge of the nursery pit to greet the scaled babes. Dragon cries filled the air, some pleasant and some unsettled – it covered their voices well. Ohba crossed the stone slowly to stand closer to Eulalia and Zoraida, reaching out to allow Rasyl to grasp at one of his fingers. 'Not everyone on this earth can be as pragmatic as you, Eula. They do not want to sacrifice the holy for the mortal.'

'Dragons are sacred, yes, but they're also intelligent. They would not have flown off with those riders on their backs had they not agreed in some way to defend us. Let us at least call for them, rather than sit here and resign ourselves to death.' The idea that any human could climb upon a dragon without the beast's consent was an absurd thought. Hundreds of idiots lost their lives presuming that a dragon would not mind their company and ended up devoured.

If she could, she would have also devoured those who presumed upon her personal space. It would have made the world a better place.

'Nobody is resigning themselves,' Ohba said. His hands worked at her ankles, trying to massage out her frustration in some small way. 'I think they just hope that the wards hold. One crack is dangerous but does not mean the fall of Muqdah – the shield is a powerful thing.'

Ohba was wrong in that, Eulalia thought. Once the access to Muqdah was allowed in some small or large way, they would find their way in. Whether it was one of the Eschalion or, gods forbid, Thurlow Thurlowe – they would not rest until the temples were theirs. She could feel it in the very bottom of her gut.

After a protracted and tense silence, Ohba spoke again. 'We should call them, Eulalia. I agree with you. We should make the call to the dragon riders. We should bring in anyone who can help save Muqdah. I simply cannot make them change their minds.'

She harrumphed. The holy men of Svarna were ideologically diverse, but one of their standing principles was the sanctity of free will. She respected free will, she truly did, but people were also profoundly stupid and could not be trusted to act without guidance.

Fidela slunk in, as quiet as a house cat. Eulalia watched her, yet to forgive her for the meeting's course of events. People called Eulalia beautiful when she was pregnant, but Fidela could make a man weep with a look. She had the patience to set her hair in elaborate braids and artful curls, as though forged by dragon-fire in her perfection. Even as their world teetered on the edge of destruction, she remained a vision. People listened to Eulalia because she'd borne the nebulously sacred babe – but they adored Fidela. If only she'd kept her usual spine and backed Eulalia when she needed her.

'Adil won't budge,' Fidela admitted after yet another uncomfortably long silence in which the two women stared at each other. 'I tried, Eula. Bronnuq and I both did. He swears that the wards will hold, that the dragons we have will be enough. I'm not sure he's wrong.'

'Thank you for your faith.' Eulalia rolled her eyes before she met her gaze again. 'Are you willing to bet our city on uncertainty?'

She knew Fidela. She knew what Fidela's answer should have been. In her mind, she silently willed her friend to join the fray. As holy mothers, they were the fighters. While the holy men of Svarna weaved at their looms, working at their tapestries, the holy mothers birthed the renasci. They defended the temples and fought tooth and nail to shape the world as it should be. To shape the world for those who would come afterwards.

'No,' Fidela concluded with a decisive nod. 'No, I am not.'

'Ohba, are you willing to bet all of Muqdah on uncertainty? On passivity?' Her sweet priest paused at her feet and their gaze met, dark stare on honey brown.

He swallowed. 'No. We should be doing everything we can to protect our own.'

'Then we need to persuade Adil and Cuinu into changing their minds.' Persuade was a kind term for the things she would do to Adil and Cuinu if words failed them. 'There is work to be done. Work that would only need to be done if our city was going to fall. Bronnuq wouldn't be having us cut the looms if he believed that the shields would continue to stand – and he's a veteran of conflicts coming to Muqdah. He knows what is coming to us. Those of us who give a damn are going to need to handle those who can't put two and two together. We'll oversee the work and then, Fidela, you'll need to work on Adil. You're the only one who'd have a chance of changing his mind.'

'I can do that. I think with a few hours of thought, Adil will loosen. His adrenaline will settle.' An argument with Eulalia, evidently, was enough to send the man spinning. She would have usually appreciated it, had it not stopped the council from coming to a consensus.

She looked at Ohba and then turned to Zoraida, whose tail still swung in great swoops. Her hissing and vocalising had quieted, but her icy, greenish eyes were fixed on Eulalia. Waiting. 'We will deal with Cuinu.'

The she-dragon opened her jaw – there was the threat of flame in her steaming breath.

The Child, who had decided that this discussion was not meant for her, flocked to the dragons as a family that embraced her. She swanned through the hatchling pit, skimming her hands over their young backs and chittering back at them as best she could. To the others, the nursery was a beloved but alien place, the dragon's many voices indecipherable. To her, it was calamitously loud; a chorus of a hundred cousins who all wanted to greet her.

'Hello, hello, hello,' she called. She knew most of them by the names the denizens of the First Temple had given them, but the younglings often didn't respond to them, unaccustomed to the idea that another being could name them at all. The mothers and younglings had grown old enough to understand the human tongue, and they called to her, pleased to be acknowledged when the Child named them in her own tongue.

The temple rumbled and shifted beneath her feet, cutting her a clean path along the nursery. Temple stones shuffled and corrected themselves in the way that they could for all temple children, sensing her intent and catching her feet. Once the greetings were done, she knew where she was going. She had to tell Idunn about the calamity approaching them.

Eulalia was one of the many temple mothers, but Idunn had always been the Child's mother. Her earliest memories were of clambering around the nursery, barely managing to stay out of trouble with the great dragon's eyes upon her. She thought that it was a great disservice that Idunn was often the last of the First Temple to be informed of new developments. As the Child had grown, she'd chattered to Idunn about everything. Every new birth, every new arrival, every time one of the temple children passed a trial that allowed them to continue in their training.

She could not climb the tower on her own, so she called up, shouting and whooping, and the dragons cried back. Bejewelled heads emerged from sheltered nooks. The Child searched for her companion amongst them but caught only a glimpse of the she-dragon slumbering at the back of an alcove she would have had to climb to reach. She would find Kine later, when she got a moment away from her mother.

The Child! It is the Child! Hello, Child!

She did not quite understand why she had been adopted by the nursery as the Child of note, other than the frequency of her visits and the nights she'd spent by their sides. The holy men had shuffled her into the draconic thoroughfare whenever she'd had a spare minute.

Idunn was not bejewelled like the smaller dragons, but the Child found her twice as magnificent. Her scales were the colour of river water from afar, not a vibrant shade but a gossamer grey that glistened in the light. Heat rolled off her in long waves, but the Child, who had long ago grown unbothered by it, felt her own magic unfold within her like a cool wind. The great dragon rose slowly from where she had been resting, bowing her head until the Child could reach up and press her hands to her burning scales. She gave the big dragon a quick greeting kiss.

'How are your babies?' the Child asked, fluttering across each egg. Idunn's eggs were always large, reaching up to the Child's shoulder; she pressed her face against each one and listened intently. Dragon eggshells were dense and strong, so she could hear little except for an occasional rumbling. They were beautiful, marbled spheres, no two eggs alike in their pattern or colour. Some people waited until the hatchlings had fled the nest and then harvested the shells for armour and equipment, as tough as dragon hide without any of the slaughter.

Yet to move, Idunn responded. *They will come when they are ready.*

The Child pressed her lips together. She was impatient to meet her new siblings, to have new hatchlings to fuss over. There was almost always a clutch in the nursery that was about to hatch, but even after their many centuries of care, they had no way of telling how long an egg would gestate for. The holy men thought it was something to do with the nature of magical creatures, that their power manifested within the egg, growing in its unpredictability.

It was all magical theory. The shift from the ephemeral to the physical, it was of little real consequence to her beyond the fact that it delayed her meeting Idunn's newest children.

'Something has come for Muqdah,' she began. She spoke the words softly, sensitive of how the stone of the First Temple carried words. 'They're saying it's an army. Whatever's been happening in the north has come down to us.'

They'd been trying to keep the war quiet, speaking of it only in hushed tones and shooing away the children when they tried to listen to what was going on. The adults had kept any talk of conflict to the evenings reserved for long, boring dinners and discussions meant to be driven only by maturity.

War, Idunn spoke in her rumbling tones. *Destruction.*

The Child shook her head, brows knitting together. Perhaps that was what Idunn saw in their panic, but it could not be the truth.

'War means nothing to Muqdah,' she huffed. 'The temple will protect us. They will call for the war dragons once they've realised Eulalia is right. They're refusing to right now, but they will. The shields will hold long enough for the riders to return.'

I will protect you.

She had always wanted to ride Idunn, but the holy men had been adamant that they would not saddle the matriarch until the Child was grown. That to mount her without enough experience would be certain death. Idunn was so large that the temple would need to rearrange itself entirely to allow her to take flight again, as she'd been happily grounded for several decades. The Child did not quite understand. She knew that a dragon and their rider were supposed to be uniquely bonded, and there was not a world in which Idunn would have harmed her. If she'd cared for the Child as a toddling infant, she would carry her to the sky just as well as Kine would.

It was more likely that the holy men and the renasci were frightened of Idunn and what would happen when she finally set flight once more. She reached for as much of Idunn as her arms would allow her to hold and pressed her face against her mother's scales.

'You will not need to,' the Child said. 'There's a whole city between us and them – and Eulalia would never let anything happen to this temple.'

Chapter Eight

THE IMPERIUM

Working at a brothel wasn't exactly easy work, but Feliks preferred bedwork to murder – which once had been the family trade.

The Brass Wyvern was a fine place. Unlike most of their neighbouring establishments, it was not a place that was built for High Elves to frequent. It might have been a little squatter in comparison to those that surrounded it, and the peeling paint on the second floor was largely left to deteriorate, but Takuma claimed that it gave the place character.

It was better than the Deep Forest, where Takuma had found him. Having heard whispers of a beautiful man luring elves into the dark tangle of trees, Takuma purposefully wandered off the main forest trail, unafraid of the axe or the shadows that stretched after him. It had seemed unhinged to Feliks that someone would risk their life on the off-chance that the forest folk might have made the city their hunting ground, but Feliks appreciated unhinged. Takuma thought Feliks the perfect addition to The Brass Wyvern, and the pretty Svarnishman had offered him the work, citing a need for pretty men and muscle in an entirely Svarnish brothel. Entirely charmed, Feliks had agreed to come along for two hot meals a day and a lesson on hand-jobs.

A deal was a deal, so Feliks took to watching The Brass Wyvern. He was taller than anyone working there, barrel-chested and stronger than any of the men that Takuma employed in the Wyvern – and most Imperium guards. He made friends of the brawny Svarnishmen that were hired after him and guarded his burrow jealously.

He did not sleep when the evening's work was done. The working hours at the Wyvern stretched into the early mornings as the clients shuffled out into the Imperium. They scuttled away from the Wyvern before dawn, disappearing into any crack in the city that they could find. It tickled Feliks to watch them scatter, as if each house did not have its own eyes that studied the passing customers from the dimly lit windows.

Takuma slept sparingly, in fleeting naps between clients, eventually wandering out when noon had broken over the city and most of The Brass Wyvern were asleep. He dressed down for his usual tastes, in flat colours that veered on refined rather than his usual flashiness. Though he liked to pretend that his broken rest did not affect him, he had hollows beneath his eyes. On Takuma, it was balanced – a flash of imperfection on his otherwise perfectly rumpled self.

'Time to go?' Feliks asked.

'There's no better time,' Takuma sighed. 'Nema is down, Nuru's finally asleep. If we wait any longer, they might insist upon coming along.'

'We go out the front then,' Feliks said. 'Hotaru's hanging around the back, waiting for Virnoi to get up.'

With a nod, they were off, two Svarnishmen winding their way into the monolith of a city. In a pair, it was easy to vanish into the city, despite their horns. It was rare that Takuma allowed another to take the lead, but for Feliks, navigating the city was no different from the forest. He could sense predators and knew how to avoid notice, slipping out of the way of guards. On his off evenings, he spent the darkest hours trawling through the Imperium, conversing with the strangers who only emerged in the dark.

He led Takuma down to the main road, a broad thoroughfare that brought almost everyone into the city. It was where the Imperium truly went to work, a host of gilded arches and a veritable army of guards welcoming visitors to the city. As they slipped down the road, the pair found themselves approaching the immense walls that surrounded the city. To the elves, they demonstrated the foresight and care of the emperor. To the Svarnish, it was a show of power. No one had ever broken through those walls.

The emperor of the Imperium, Eschalier, had his face all over the city. On banners and signs, his aquiline nose and features wreathed in laurels. There was nobody the Imperium loved more than its glorious, benevolent leader and his endless dynasty.

Feliks had wandered along this stretch of the Imperium when he first took to the streets to explore his new hunting ground and stumbled upon The Roasted Apple Inn. A building set only a short walk away from the Imperium's great entry, it overflowed with pale-faced Nords at any time of the day. The two-storey establishment could have swayed with the drunkenness let loose within its walls. Feliks suspected that this building was older than the Imperium itself, and the High Elves had simply built around it rather than uproot it.

An age ago, someone had told the tale that the ancient Nords were made from the first drops of snow as they melted upon the great peaks of the Nordlund. Flowers bloomed from the water and out came warriors, with translucent skin and snowy eyelashes. Feliks did not quite fit the look, but he was apparently close enough – the first time he'd wandered past, they'd hollered at him to come join their drinking song. He was fair and strong looking, so they'd presumed him a distant nephew or cousin of a friend and assimilated him within the throng.

Back when he'd lived in the forest, that was how they lured the Nords out, his looks familiar to the pale-faced travellers who wandered down their roads. They'd never had to contend with Svarnishmen until the war drove people north, but they were often too frightened of the forest to disrespect those within. That was how his father met his mother.

'What's the story?' Feliks asked idly as they regarded the pub from afar, hands hooked into their pockets.

'That we had one of Thurlowe's boys in, talking about how his father was raging about a mishandled job at his estate and blaming the local Nords for it,' Takuma explained in Svarnish, drawling through his words. It was a good story. 'We wanted to give them some advance warning that the Imperium might come down on them, lest the goodwill between deer thwart the lions and all that.'

Feliks cocked his head at the smaller man, making a thoughtful noise. Though Takuma didn't speak perfect Common, occasionally he spouted wisdom that took them all by surprise.

'Makes sense, I guess.' It didn't make sense to Feliks, but it wasn't his job to be the thoughtful one. He didn't come up with these plans. He did, however, try to mitigate any potential risk of chaos. 'Let me do most of the talking.'

'This is the only time you get to tell me that,' Takuma said with a laugh.

Feliks stepped forward and began to shoulder his way through the crowd of warriors lingering at the front of the inn clutching tankards, in an intense debate about the logistics of shield warfare. He reached behind him and grasped Takuma's forearm, pulling him along before a curious stranger could strike up conversation with him.

The roof of The Roasted Apple Inn sagged significantly. Feliks had to duck slightly to fit himself through the doorway, only straightening when he emerged onto the other side. It was just as crowded inside as it appeared to be from the street, the room filled with raucous revelry. They could only stand momentarily in the doorway before they were pushed past by a heavily scarred man who took a seat at a bar that looked entirely too small for him. People were willing to perch precariously on tiny, ancient stools for the sake of a good drink amongst their own.

'Feliks!' The bellow came from behind the bar, erupting from a robust man with half a head of silvery blond hair. He had a heavily scarred face and was missing one eye entirely—he'd allegedly gotten on the wrong side of a bear's temper.

Feliks chuckled and hauled Takuma down the bar, using the breadth of this body to make way for them. Feliks hopped up onto a stool and reached over, grinning from ear to ear.

'Ebbe! How is business treating you?' He clapped shoulders with the strong bartender and the current owner of The Roasted Apple Inn. Ebbe had owned the inn for as long as Feliks had been within the Imperium. Anyone who spent more than a few hours at The Roasted Apple Inn knew that Ebbe liked to serve the drinks because he didn't trust just anyone with his liquor. Considering that a portion of the front room had been burnt down some years ago when a regular got into it with a fire mage, Feliks didn't blame him.

'Winding up lately, plenty of travellers in!' Ebbe nodded thoughtfully. 'How is the Wyvern treating you?'

'Always fun having our own little home away from the elves,' Feliks said, provoking a round of chuckling from the patrons at the bar. 'Is Grenh in?'

'Aye, she is, down the back.' He filled a tankard with foaming ale and thrust it into Feliks' hand. Feliks knew that a small part of Ebbe saw him as unhuman. Yet, he treated Feliks like one of his bevy of friends all the same. Feliks would pay him back in time, in the way that he had been taught to. 'Take a pint with you if you're talking to her.'

'Thank you, Ebbe. Don't let the demons keep you late tonight.' With a wink, Feliks swooped up the tankard and hopped off the stool. He trusted that Takuma would follow him and went bouncing down out of the main tavern room, down a short hall, and making a sharp turn at the first open doorway. He tapped once, firmly on the frame.

'Horns,' Grenh said as the pair of Svarnishmen shuffled into her corner of the pub. Grenh was someone Feliks spoke with sparingly, if at all. She was a bulldog of a woman, squat and broad-shouldered, with a pile of snowy hair atop her head. She managed plenty of Nords who were looking for labour – those who weren't talented or rich enough to have their own workshops. She claimed that she'd been working out of this corner of the Imperium since she was a girl, but Feliks suspected she'd always been just this old. He could not picture her as a child.

Feliks slid the tankard he had just purchased towards her, nodding.

'Granny,' he chuckled. She stared at him, weighing whether the conversation was going to be worth the tankard he'd proffered. She swished a mouthful of ale around before swallowing, slamming the cup back on the table. With a sharp nod, Grenh gave them permission to speak. 'Any crews out putting their muscle to building our glorious Imperium at the moment?'

'A few, as always. You want to put your muscle to good use, Freckles?'

With a relieved sigh, Feliks dropped into a waiting chair, knowing that her speaking at all was an invitation for them to sit. 'Unfortunately, I'm fully booked – The Brass Wyvern keeps me busy.' It was a half-truth. Feliks had seen the way other brothels had their bouncers working, and arguably he had quite the relaxed employer in Takuma. It helped that half of his job was to look pretty for anyone passing through the red-light district who may have glimpsed him. Takuma had explained it to him once; brothels with super mean looking muscle often scared away soft-hearted clientele. One had to strike a balance. 'I was actually wondering if any of your lot were out working in the Golden Quarter recently.'

Grenh snorted. 'In Thurlow Thurlowe's estate?'

'Mm,' Feliks affirmed. He glanced at Takuma out of the corner of his eye.

'Yes, we did a job there. Why are you asking? That was done a while ago now, nightmare that it was. Three of the workers are still being cared for by the church healers.' The pinched woman let out a long sigh before she turned her attention back on the ale, somewhat mollified by the drink.

'We had one of Thurlow's boys over at mine ranting about how a bunch of Nords fucked up construction on the estate,' Takuma interjected, explaining the story away. 'Seems like Thurlow really threw a tantrum about it, and we didn't want y'all to be taken by surprise. I like this place too much.'

Grenh fixed Takuma with a shrewd stare. Feliks gave his employer a fleeting look that bordered on irritation. The elderly woman asked with a huff, 'Do I know you?'

'I run The Brass Wyvern,' he said, his voice dripping with a saccharine sense of charm that would not go down well with any Nord. Feliks pressed a foot on Takuma's boot under the table, fixing his stare on Grenh. Takuma continued unperturbed. 'It's a pleasure to meet you.'

'Sometimes I forget you're half Svarnish,' Grenh muttered at Feliks as she took a significant swig from her drink. With a breath like a death rattle, she began to talk, unleashing a torrent of frustration upon them. 'That Thurlowe job was a catastrophe. He hired three crews of men to work on that addition to the estate – that's more than half of the labourers we have. Everything was mismanaged. They didn't mention that they wanted Prismarium glass for the dome until all the work contracts were signed. Do you know how hard it is to find that much Prismarium glass on such short notice? It's impossible.'

'I've never seen that much Prismarium glass. Ever,' Feliks said with an affirmative bob of his head. He tried to sound empathetic, but was not sure he succeeded.

'It can be found if you know where to look, but there's no gaffer this side of the Imperium who can work at small notice. So, the heads of the crews go and do the groundwork. They convince their mates and the workshops they know to work for Thurlow Thurlowe – which isn't an easy fucking task, mind you – and then things start going wrong on site. The wards on the estate meant that those on the ground couldn't see anyone working at the top of the dome, which botches more than you think. Then workers started dropping.'

She only paused to take a drink of ale, leaving a long moment in which the two Svarnishmen exchanged a long look.

'Dropping?' Feliks prompted. Grenh had evidently been wanting to vent about this – she was positively irate. Her crinkled cheeks flushed a hot red as she talked.

'Thurlow wouldn't admit that anything was wrong, but the workers started complaining of a stench coming from the estate. They complained of nausea, dizziness. You know that us Nords can stand a strong stench better than most, but this was unreal. When the first one passed out at the top of the estate and fell to his death within that tower, I tried to pull the workers out. He had me trudge all the way up to his fancy house just to yell at me about my workers. I screamed right back at him. Told him that with half a dozen men injured, with a man dead, there was no point going on. Told him that we didn't owe him shit, that he voided the labour contracts when the site wasn't up to code. Bastard didn't give us much of a choice in the end.'

The idea of Thurlow Thurlowe yelling at an elderly woman painted him in an unflattering light, even when that woman was Grenh.

'We got the job done, but he has some gall complaining about the work that was done. We did everything within our power to get that inane dome made, and lost a man for it. So, if he wants to come shout about it? He can come shout at me. I've got an axe for his kneecaps.'

'I think you'd win that fight, Granny,' Feliks said, uncertain of how to settle her anger. This was also not something he excelled at. 'We just wanted to warn you.'

'You're a good boy for that.' Grenh nodded. 'But I know he might be coming, especially if whatever's living in that dome goes astray, and he blames us for it. Though, unlike you Svarnishmen, those of the Nordlund have more protection under the Imperium. I'd be safer than you if he came after me.'

'We'll leave you be,' Takuma said, giving them an out from the conversation. Feliks could have bought him a drink for that alone. 'I'm sure you've got better things to do – we only wanted to drop in.'

'Course.' Grenh watched as they rose from their chairs, ready to flee from whence they came. They were halfway out the door when her voice called after them. 'Don't go near the Thurlowe place, Freckles. Even you might find something to fear from them.'

All he could think to do was laugh and toss his hands up in the air. Feliks knew that if he spoke, she'd likely catch him in a lie. Secrets were a funny thing amongst humans – a truth possessed and often given away. Yet, the moment the words were spoken to one person, they would inevitably spread like a plague through a burrow.

Feliks and Takuma slipped out a back door of the tavern, avoiding the questions that Ebbe would undoubtedly lob at them.

'It's made from Prismarium glass,' Takuma remarked quietly. 'That's something.'

The High Elves used it all over the Imperium – a shimmering, magic-resistant glass that was supposedly indestructible. Feliks had never seen someone shatter it, though he'd certainly seen people try. But it was the fact that it was almost completely impervious to most magical attacks – the primary threat the Imperium concerned themselves with – that had led to its almost ubiquitous use. The elves built crystalline towers and vast arenas for mages and their shows, containing the powers that may otherwise decimate the city.

'We can't go through the dome, then,' Feliks mused. 'We go around it.'

'Exactly. Easier said than done, though. We'll need to know how they got the dragon in the estate to begin with. Virnoi might have been right for once.'

'Occasionally, other people are right, Takuma.' He rolled his eyes. 'Markets?' Feliks asked with a cocked eyebrow, altering course when Takuma made an affirmative noise. The alleyways that surrounded The Roasted Apple were bustling, forcing Feliks to mutter pardons as they jostled through to avoid ending up on the wrong end of a Nordic war hammer. Once they were free of the inn's surrounds, they swivelled, Feliks drawn to the markets like an iron to a lodestone.

They took to the backstreets, the easiest way to cross between districts and keep out of the guards' view. The pair had only gotten two buildings over into an alleyway before Feliks sensed a shift in his companion, a thoughtfulness. He slowed his pace and turned lazily.

'Boss?' That was all Feliks said as he saw another Svarnishman appear at the end of the alleyway. A wolfish man covered in tattoos.

'Do me a favour, Feliks, and piss off,' Takuma warned with a bright, charming grin.

Feliks took one look at the tension in his face and nodded, knowing that he was not paid enough to concern himself with all of Takuma's drama. He disappeared into the brickwork and alleys of the Imperium, leaving his friend to face his demons on his own.

He'd find him later. Takuma always came out of these things intact.

Chapter Nine

THE IMPERIUM

As Takuma was thrust against the wall, he found himself wishing that he had not grown accustomed to manhandling.

It was the nature of most of his professions. Prostitution, tomb-raiding, running a brothel for a handful of beloved ingrates who drove him insane; whenever things went awry, it turned to a fight. When he was younger, he'd fought everything, believed that every slight deserved a knife between the ribs. Now, Takuma knew there were other ways to inflict his sense of justice upon people. Someone had once told him that was the plight of the impoverished – to take the beatings for the world and still stay on their feet.

That man now stood, blotting out the light at the end of the alleyway, horns gilded in gold, a pair of fat garnets sitting pretty on his fingers while his offsider held Takuma against the wall.

'Imamu,' Takuma greeted him over his attacker's shoulders, trying to keep his chin lifted in a lofty way. He took a sparing glance at the man who held him. 'Mosi.'

There were certainties in the world that Takuma had come to appreciate. He wouldn't pay for anything he could get for free; he didn't take appointments from anyone who'd been in the Imperial Military; and where Imamu came, Mosi was sure to follow. A dog and the hand that fed it. The pair were about as different as two Svarnishmen could be – Imamu a robust bull of a man, and Mosi a jackal. Where Imamu adorned himself with gold, Mosi wore the plain green linens of their holy men. It was a curious choice, considering that he had laid the foundation for Svarnish bedwork within the constraints of the Imperium.

Mosi was lithe with muscle, body tattooed with rings that were prone to change but currently overlapped at the neck. It was the regretful look in Mosi's eyes that gave away the nature of this fight – no inkling of violence, only an arcane glow that Takuma had come to learn was not his own. Imamu's magic was the warmest copper, even when present in someone else.

He gave Mosi a wry look. 'I won't hold this against you, Mosi.'

Mosi scoffed as he readjusted his grip, holding Takuma's collar firmly. There was no point attempting to break his grasp; they'd spent many of Takuma's teenage years in an elaborate song and dance of submission and deviance. One only made an escape from Mosi if he'd yet to lay an ironclad hand on you.

There was an exhaustion in Mosi's glowing eyes as he sighed, rolling his head to one side. 'I wish you would, actually, I might feel better about this.'

He would have laughed if he hadn't wanted to avoid this beating.

'Far be it from me to weigh on your conscience,' Takuma muttered, eyeing off Imamu as the merchant approached them.

'You scrub up well for a blood traitor, Takuma,' Imamu said, strolling down the alleyway.

'We're not family,' Takuma bit back. 'One can't be a blood traitor to someone who isn't blood.'

'No, but we're both Svarnish, and I once clothed you, fed you, gave you a place to rest your head. That makes us blood.' That was one way to phrase spoiling someone until they could be tricked into indentured servitude. Takuma sneered at the thought, his distaste plain on his face. He need not appeal to this brute of a merchant – there was no way this would come to an amicable end. Imamu slowed to a halt at Mosi's back, staring down his nose. 'What are you doing in the Imperium, Takuma?'

Takuma studied the merchant's face, silently recalculating this encounter. Imamu was either feigning ignorance or he truly knew nothing of The Brass Wyvern, which meant that Takuma's plan had worked. The brothel was not supposed to be easy to find. It wasn't listed as a licensed establishment in the red-light district. The man whose name was on the deed had purchased it in coin – an upstanding paladin who happened to live several leagues out of town on a sprawling farm. He was not the city type. If one were to go looking for the floor plans in the royal archives, they'd find those of The Stuck Pig.

'I figured I'd find a wealthy High Elf looking for a Svarnish boy toy, make myself a mint,' he responded flippantly. 'There are plenty of brothels in the Imperium looking for workers.'

'Where's the babe, Takuma?' The amusement in Imamu's face fell away like a cloud across the sun, the pleasantries dropped.

Takuma feigned ignorance. 'Who knows? I left Nuru in some nowhere town in the middle of the southern reaches. Your baby's living it up out there with the Nords and the Wood Elves.' Takuma was lying out his ass and everyone in that alleyway knew it. 'You could have maybe asked about your ex-wife, at least make a show of pretending that you care about her.'

It was slight – a small shake of Mosi's head. If Takuma weren't so familiar with Mosi's face, he might have missed it entirely. They knew Nuru was in the Imperium, which meant that finding him in this alleyway would be enough to set the dogs on their tracks.

'Like hell you left her, you and Nuru were attached at the hip. Always pining after her like a hopeless puppy, praying that maybe she'd turn around and marry you. How'd that work out for you?'

Takuma should have acted cowed. He could have bowed his head and convinced Imamu that he was just too pitiful to bother with. Yet, he couldn't find the restraint. Takuma reached inside himself and found only a burning venom, tilting his head to the side and laughing. 'Worked out pretty well, actually. I fucked the wife of a merchant king and got paid for it. Can't say it's the worst deal I've ever made.'

Imamu's gaze filled with that copper glow, a blaze that swelled until it overflowed and swam around his brow. Takuma was wise enough to struggle at the show of magic, lashing out against the bruiser in the hopes that his grip had slackened. The huge man leaned back as he readjusted his grip on his staff, nodding once. 'Mosi.'

His voice was quiet and even, an unspoken command in the words that he did not say. When Takuma had been a boy in Imamu's caravan, that tone had never heralded anything good. It was the sound of a silent decision being made

He tried to brace, though the most he could do was curl up to protect himself. Mosi lifted him off the ground, slamming him against the cobblestones. Pain jolted through his ribs as Mosi kicked them, heavy like a battering ram. He swung again and again, black stars bursting into Takuma's vision.

The reprieve came with a sharp whistle from between Imamu's teeth. Mosi stopped, foot pressed lightly against Takuma's chest. It took a great deal of effort for Imamu to lower himself, falling into a crouch with one broad hand propped on his knee.

'You'll pay back every copper piece you stole from me,' Imamu said. He reached out with a hand and cupped Takuma's chin. 'And you tell my wife that I'd like to see my babe. And I want my tapestries returned.'

'What tapestries?' Takuma managed to sputter, spitting a glob of bright blood across the street. He and Nuru had stolen plenty from Imamu – a snowy mare that had been a bridal gift, a beautiful caravan, the contents of said caravan, and a small trunk of goods they'd sold during their escape. None of Imamu's magical tapestries had been among them – great woven paintings that he spent days on and rarely sold. They were a remnant of the old country, and Takuma hadn't stolen them. Any merchant worth his salt would have recognised them as Imamu's work, and they would have been branded as thieves in a second.

Imamu nudged him with his staff, digging it painfully into his chest. 'Don't play dumb, Takuma. It doesn't suit you.'

'We didn't steal any tapestries,' Takuma said through gritted teeth.

The merchant king rose, leaning on his staff. Seemingly satisfied with the beating, he strolled away, pausing at the end of the alley beside the two men who'd blocked it. Mosi lingered above Takuma as the magic faded from his gaze.

'Stay down,' Mosi hissed, which single-handedly motivated Takuma to get to his feet. He forced himself upwards despite the pain.

'What are you doing in the Imperium, Imamu?' he asked, not expecting an answer. 'You don't come to mingle with the knife-ears of your own free will.'

Taking on an entrepreneurial air, Imamu turned back. He dusted his hands as if wiping them clean of this mess, motioning for Mosi to join him with an easy smile on his face. His eyes were alight, burning with a cold sense of murder.

'Some big-shot elf is throwing a bash, and the city is going to be flooded with people here to soak up the revelries. More people lead to more trade, and if there's money to be made ...'

'You're there to make it,' Takuma echoed dully. He didn't bother to move from his place against the wall until Imamu and Mosi had long vanished into the thoroughfare.

When the pain had settled enough for him to walk without flinching, he turned on his tail and limped back through the alley. He was stopped abruptly when a pale arm reached out from amidst the crowd outside the tavern and dragged him back within the wash, pressing him into an alcove. Feliks had an obnoxious talent for vanishing into crowds despite his significant stature.

'Woah, boss.' Feliks remarked in his oddly accented Svarnish, keeping a strong arm crushed around his shoulders. 'You've got a pair of shadows. Best hold out before we go back to the brothel, unless you want them trekking all the way back to the Wyvern.'

'Good spotting,' Takuma muttered.

'What do they look like?' Takuma asked, pondering whether he had a broken rib.

'One's skinny, few inches taller than you, with straight horns. Silver jewellery, hair cropped short like he did it himself. The other could be a man or a woman with braided hair, short, thick horns, and a mean mug on 'em like they're smelling a barrel of rot. Sound familiar?'

Takuma wracked his rattled brain briefly and found nothing. Imamu's caravan was a vast collection of Svarnish folk – the money that flowed through it drew in anyone who could ply their trade. Many stayed only a mere season before they were promptly deposited at the nearest city of repute. He shook his head. It was hard to tell upon description alone. 'Must be new hires. Either that or I'm concussed.'

Feliks chuckled, gently pushing Takuma further into a tavern. Knowing that the throng would protect him from keen eyes, he slipped back into the waves of Nordic flesh. They wound their way back through The Red Deer to the stretch of bar where a brawny warrior sat. Feliks swung up onto one of the barstools, elbows propped on the wood as he turned to the builder.

'Oi, Darrin! You hear about the two Svarnish guys out the front?' Feliks asked, clapping the man on his shoulder. The redhead whistled to the bartender as Darrin roused himself, Feliks holding up two fingers. 'They were out front asking Runa if she was a bedworker for the place, rude little bastards.'

Takuma could have gaped at the audacity of the lie; instead, he frowned with a sense of mock concern, nodding thoughtfully as though aghast that anyone would behave so poorly in this place. There was nothing that those of the Nordlund took more personally than affronts against their women. They handled the finances, their men, and anyone who crossed into their homestead.

If you wanted to lose a handful of teeth, you insulted a Nord's wife or his eldest daughter. If you wanted to lose your liver, you insulted his youngest – and she'd cut it out of you herself.

Two clay mugs slid down the bar full of a frothing beer, one of which Feliks passed along to Takuma. He stared into it for a moment with narrowed eyes before taking a tentative sip. The Nordic drink was strong and chunky in a way that was deeply concerning to someone who'd spent several months curating his own bar.

'They said what about Runa?' Darrin asked, face going blotchy and reddish as his brow furrowed. He downed the last of his mug and stood, clapping his hands together before he turned towards the crowded tables. He bellowed something in a language Takuma did not know and drew just about every head in the tavern, pointing to the door. 'Outside!'

Fucking Nords, always down for a brawl. A roar went up, and the drunken lot piled out into the Imperium, some with weapons in hand. Takuma would have felt sorry for the poor men, had he not been wondering if one of his ribs was broken. Feliks tossed his head back and laughed in a feral howl as he dragged Takuma to the back of the bar, through a river of people pushing in the opposite direction. He kept one hand on Takuma's shirt, the other wrapped around the mug of ale he hadn't paid a coin for.

'Darrin is Runa's uncle! Those shadows will run, or they'll die, but they'll learn their mistake all the same. Come on!'

Takuma choked at that, staring at the back of Feliks head. 'If you told a Svarnishman his niece was being propositioned by people calling her a whore, they'd be stabbed!' Takuma crowed. As if he had a choice, he allowed himself to be dragged along, depositing his mug unceremoniously on a nearby table. The pair trundled up to the second floor of the tavern to the balcony. It was a crush atop that narrow walkway, Takuma squeezed between a swarthy woman with a war-axe strapped to her back and an elderly man with a tattooed skull.

The street below was developing into a full-blown brawl, other Svarnishmen having joined the fray. Ebbe had a thin Svarnishman by the neck and was tossing him around like a rag-doll, bellowing into the air. Takuma leaned over the balcony railing and spotted the shadows then, attempting to make off down the road, only to be blocked off by a small handful of red-faced Nords. Laughter broke over him, a wave of petty satisfaction – there was euphoria in watching someone who might have threatened you getting their teeth kicked in.

Upon return to The Brass Wyvern, Takuma sent Felix around the front of the brothel while he took the side path. It wasn't difficult for him to shimmy down through the flowery alleyway and unlatch the gate to allow him into the brothel's garden, a sly manoeuvre he'd been using since they bought the place to avoid unwanted attention. Better his workers didn't see him battered like this.

'Ouch,' a small voice chirped from above. A pair of great, blue eyes peered over the ledge on the second floor.

'Hello, little crow.' Takuma called, standing on his tiptoes to get a better look at the slight woman in her many layers of cloth. 'Want to come give me a hand?'

Hotaru was always back there, tucked up on Virnoi's windowsill. She preferred the view to the chaotically maintained garden over the gutter, for which he couldn't blame her. He wouldn't want to watch the brothel's clientele come and go without monetary compensation.

Hotaru climbed down from her perch, slipping along the patio and skilfully dropping onto the grass beside him. She plucked at his shirt and peered down at his bruised torso, his skin a watercolour canvas of crimson and deepening purples. She wrinkled her nose. 'You're walking pretty straight for someone who looks like they got their spine bent.'

'Merchant kings make shitty plumbers.' Takuma laughed. 'Let's not let the others know about this if we can, no?'

'That can be done. Can I get a second breakfast for my trouble?' An eternal haggler, Hotaru was raised with the tried-and-true Svarnish edict that one should never do anything for free. Takuma would have given her an extra meal if she'd only asked for it. When they'd first met, she'd been nothing but a slip of a girl, lurking in the puddled darkness of the Imperium. It had taken time to get her to trust the food at all, let alone ask for more.

'Sure, sure.' He waved his hand in the air. 'I'll tell the cooks. What do you want – two weeks of second breakfast? Three?'

Beaming at his concession, Hotaru trotted back the way she came. 'Three!' she called.

She was as quick as the wind, slipping up the side of the brothel and onto the latticework covered in dense greenery. Within moments, Hotaru was back on Virnoi's windowsill, sliding the window open and vanishing within. Takuma lowered himself delicately onto the grass, the spot where he and Hotaru often sat and debriefed.

When she returned, it was with an armful of healing supplies and a replacement shirt from his collection. They sat together, nestled in the vines, as Hotaru meticulously washed off the blood and pressed pastes to each vibrant bruise, chiding him all the while. Takuma had taught her that all blows were avoidable – had slapped her hard over the ass for mere close calls more than once – so it was his own fault that he copped an earful for it now. Hotaru was not the most practised healer, but she would get the job done until he could get Taliesin to skim over the damage.

Dealing with the priest was akin to dealing with a double-edged sword. Having a healer was a fantastic asset for the brothel, but the fact that he'd wander off and snitch to Nuru if he was concerned could prove problematic.

Only once he was presentable did he go in search of his business companion, patting Hotaru on her nest of dark curls and leaving her in the garden. He found Nuru dressing for an evening of work in front of the vanity that he had salvaged. She was framed by the baubles that she'd collected throughout her years in the Imperium – peacock feathers and patterned scarves, small trinkets and jewelries – a veritable queen of Svarna.

'Nuru,' Takuma began, his train of thought lapsing as his gaze traced the curve of her behind. She was bent over, slipping her shoes on. Of course, she was working, he made the roster. He should remember this. 'You're seeing Truls tomorrow?'

'At the library, yes. He's indulging me and my request to have a romp there.' Nuru's head bobbed as she straightened up. 'I know what must be done. I should be fine with Truls. He lets me get away with a lot.'

This was true. Takuma didn't know much about Truls in practice – he'd largely left Nuru to deal with the nobleman's machismo. She was better at managing that particular type of man, batting her great long eyelashes at them until they melted. He hadn't been born with that talent or the anatomy to back it up. When Takuma batted his eyelashes at men, they were often possessed to hit him.

'The package to drop is on your bed,' he remarked mildly. He'd tucked it neatly wrapped beneath her pillow as he came through, as they did often to exchange notes and packages. Nuru looked up at him in the reflection of her mirror, eyes widening as she regarded his battered face. She jumped to her feet, turning towards him with her brows furrowed.

'Whose tree did you piss on?' she asked as she studied his bruised face, unsurprised by the state of him but unamused. It would put him out of work for a handful of days at the very least, which meant that she would be on her own. Takuma knew it threw off Nuru's whole routine when she did not have him to fall back upon. But, once he had broached the topic that he was gathering the bravery for, there was nothing he could do to mitigate it. Nuru crossed the room to brush a finger against his throbbing cheekbone. He hissed beneath her touch. 'Must have been a pretty important tree.'

'Imamu's, but that's nothing new.' The woman stilled. It was only for a breath, which Takuma would have missed were he not intimately familiar with the planes of her face. She did not draw away from him, instead trailing her hands down to the graze he'd sustained on his jaw.

'You ran into Imamu?' she asked softly, head tilted to the side. Takuma nodded once, watching her through his lowered lashes.

He took a deep breath and asked the question that he knew would start a fight between them. 'Why, exactly, does he think that we stole one of his tapestries?'

'Why would I know?' She stepped away from him. Nuru was good at this – pretending that someone had insulted her to distract from the truth of it. She clearly did not want to have this conversation. 'I stopped being privy to what goes on in that man's head when I got pregnant with Nema. We both know what we stole.'

'Yes, we do, and a tapestry wasn't amidst that list of treasures. We had the trunk, the horses, the caravan, and the cutlery. The linens in the cupboards, the fixtures, the rugs. We had the gold necklace that we stole from his first wife and a handful of half-made jewellery.' Nuru waved a hand at him dismissively. She certainly wanted to ignore the conversation, pretend as if it had no merit, but he knew her too well for that. They had stolen away into the night together;

they'd both agreed on what they took. 'What we did not have was a magical tapestry. A mashjor – we did not have that.'

'And we still don't,' Nuru said, finally crossing her arms across her chest. There came that familiar wall of frustration, yet after having the shit kicked out of him, Takuma was ready for this argument. He was ready to brave the vast, unwavering desert of her temper if it meant he got the truth from her.

'Why would he lie about that, Nuru? Why would he make that up?' Imamu was many things. A despot, for one, someone that Takuma wanted to bury six feet deep and abandon, but he did not lie about his debts. He had enough on Nuru and Takuma without having to concoct an imaginary tapestry for the final nail in their proverbial coffin.

'I don't know! I don't know, Takuma.' She rounded back towards her vanity, plucking a soft iridescent feather from her baubles to tuck into her braid. She did this all as she spoke, making quite the show of her storytelling. 'Maybe someone took advantage of the chaos and stole a tapestry while they were still figuring out where we went. I've got no clue what happened after we left that caravan, other than the fact that they started following us.'

It was plausible enough. Some of Imamu's crew were career thieves, peddling pickpockets who lived to funnel money and profit back to their bull-headed boss. Had Takuma not been so pretty, that may have been his lot in life. It was plausible that one of them would be underhanded enough to steal a tapestry from beneath Imamu's nose, but there was a story that made more sense. One that he'd arranged in his mind as he'd limped home to his brothel.

Takuma leaned over to stare at her properly, eye to eye, knowing in his marrow that she was lying. 'If you have a tapestry, Nuru, it better be so buried that even Virnoi can't find it.'

Nuru rolled her eyes as she pushed past him, finished with the conversation. Her cold shoulder could have set the room in frost.

'Go lick your wounds, Takuma, and stop picking at the old ones. We've got far more important things to worry about.'

Chapter Ten

SVARNA

The great looms of Muqdah wove the magic of the world and made tapestries of renowned splendour. The gravity of their situation weighed heavy on the souls that cut them, each thread drawn taut and sliced free, the mashjor carefully removed from where they had once sat. The weave spun upwards, spiralling into a web of a thousand threads that joined to form a god's eye at the apex of the chamber.

'Please, move carefully!' Ohba called, his usual gentle tenor taking on an authoritative ring. 'I understand we're all shaken, but the magic in a half-finished mashjor is temperamental. I would not want any of you harmed because we rushed this.'

The Child darted from loom to loom, trying to make herself useful wherever a spare pair of hands could be used. Rasyl slept restlessly on Ohba's hip; Eulalia had been unable to carry him in her current state. She had tried to crouch briefly to lift him, but found her knees protesting and decided that if she'd lowered herself, there was a good chance she'd never rise again.

'Ohba!' a voice called. 'We're having trouble over here!' Her holy man sighed, raked a hand through his hair, and walked.

Eulalia turned, brows knitting as she saw a cluster of the temple residents crowding around one of their greatest mashjor mounts. It was a place to hang the tapestries when the temple was not in active worship, a golden frame with brass tributes piled at the bottom. There was more money lain in honour of this tapestry than there was in any other place in the First Temple – the resident there demanded it.

The being sat cross-legged in front of the tapestry was a slim, sparkly-eyed woman with tightly cropped hair. Her warm-brown skin glistened, golden bands that glowed like Blessings wrapped around her legs and arms. She was not totally solid before Eulalia's eyes. Her form shimmered like a mirage in the heat, thrumming with latent magic.

Eula had only heard her speak from afar. It was the domain of the holy men to handle the denizens of their mashjor, and considering she did not take her chances with gods, she kept well out of their way. She was a holy mother because she performed a duty for the temple, and that was all. There were old tales of mothers who presumed too much of a god and found themselves cursed with some twisted fate. Eula was no fool, and so kept her bloodline amongst those with mortal Blessings.

'Dautuna,' Ohba greeted her with a deep bow. Eulalia managed a brief nod of her head. 'Today is not the day to give us trouble.'

'I am no trouble! I am giving nobody trouble!' Dautuna, the Goddess of Fortune, spoke and set herself afloat. 'But I do not understand why we're going away. I do not understand why we're being asked to disappear and leave our home. We wish to stay here in the temple. This is our temple.'

Most of the gods lived out a great deal of their existence in the mashjor because it simplified worship; each tapestry was its own liminal space that was both bound to the mortal world and infinite. It also minimised the potential risk of a mortal beholding a god's volatile nature. There were some deities who could only be worshipped within an idol due to the nature of their godhood, but Dautuna had always swanned around with her followers. She'd folded herself down into something far smaller so that they could speak readily without any risk of madness.

Each tapestry could contain a being made from magic – a construct, a godling, or one of the dragons they all longed to protect. The holy men had already taken several of the dragons into some of the mashjor that were gathered on one side of the weaving room, but not without discussion. They could not take a dragon who did not want to be contained.

Eulalia's priest smiled in a small, sad way.

'There is an army outside of Muqdah.' He reached out and took one of the goddess's hands in his. 'An army that has not been defeated, headed by men who will rape and pillage their way through this city. They'll either burn our mashjor or they'll take them to their cities, and you'll end up a world away from us. I am sending you away with our people so that you can stay close to those who love you.'

She rippled and twisted away, her image shifting like a shaft of moonlight through forest leaves. No one had spoken the truth of it so frankly. The chamber grew quiet and Eulalia looked away, noting the holy men who had turned to listen to their anchor speak. Temple children lingered amongst them, the Child watching from beneath a loom. Eulalia swallowed.

'Why aren't you fighting?' Dautuna pressed. 'If there is a war to win, you should stand against it. You have the blessing of fortune and fire. You should not be running from them.'

Good fortune was why the elves had invaded. It was a treacherous thought to have, standing before the deity who presided over their great bounty, but that did not make it any less true.

'If we fight the war that you speak of, there will be no Svarnishmen left to worship you. If there is no one left to worship you, your power will wane, and it is my duty to ensure that does not happen.'

Dautuna cocked her head to one side, as if she was listening to a distant melody.

'The tides of fortune have changed,' the goddess concluded. Ohba opened his mouth, as if to ask a question, and then closed it again. Had Eulalia been more masochistic, she might have asked Dautuna what the deity had heard. She may be a holy mother, but she did not think herself a godly woman. If she were to put her faith in anyone, it would be in herself.

'Yes. If you could change them back, I would owe you many a tribute, but I fear that divine intervention may not be enough to save us from this.'

Eulalia blew out a long breath as Ohba spoke.

The gods weren't opposed to intervention, but there were some steps even they could not take. Dautuna brought fortune to the city and to all of Svarna; she was not what they would unleash upon an army. Most Svarnish gods had no interest in the active destruction of human life; it would have been an offence to their nature to speak the words and ask. There was a god of warfare and victory travelling around in a mashjor in the greater stretches of Svarna, one who'd been mounted on the palace walls. Had she been hung in Muqdah, Eulalia would have asked her to raze the invading army without a thought for her damned afterlife. She would have felt good doing it.

The Goddess of Fortune shimmered and shifted, growing smaller until she was even slighter in stature than Ohba. There was a plea in her eyes that flicked towards Eulalia and then drank in the vision of the dismantled loom chamber.

'I will see you again, Ohba,' she said softly. 'That is a promise. Your company is too pleasant to lose.'

A mourning quiet stretched out between them in which Ohba said nothing, only squeezed the goddess's hands within his. He had been born in the First Temple, had quite literally found his feet on this holy stone. He had once told Eulalia that he'd had his doubts about temple life. He'd had his moments where he'd fled into the city, to indulge in all of his base instincts, but it had been the gods that had brought him back. By comparison, Dautuna had called Muqdah her home for four hundred years; she would have seen Ohba through the entirety of his life. This was a farewell that neither were willing to admit to.

There was fear in the goddess's opalescent stare, of the uncertainty of the world beyond. Eulalia did not envy being so powerful and having no control of where one woke; Dautuna would have little say in where the caravans carried them.

Resigned to her fate, Dautuna turned and became ethereal. Her muscle and skin vanished into a flash of bright, cool light as she slipped away from Ohba and into the tapestry that had been woven for her centuries ago.

Her beloved had barely dropped his hands before there was an outburst of movement from one of the doors.

'Ohba, Bronnuq – there's someone down in the caravan dock!' Something within Eulalia twisted at the cry. They both turned towards the acolyte, jaws set in a similarly tense manner.

The young woman was a stranger to Eulalia, a grown temple child from another temple. Before Eula could even open her mouth to ask a question of her, she'd turned and disappeared from whence she came, with several following at her heel in a thrum of excitement.

'Little one!' Eulalia called, hating how shrill and nervous her voice sounded. The Child emerged from the throngs of people, trotting back to her mother's side. She reached out and tucked the girl into her side. Bronnuq's heavy gait and the tap of his staff announced him, his brows furrowed in confusion.

'There's someone in the docks,' he remarked simply. 'Let us go greet them. Warily.'

Together, they went. The remnants of a once great council of priests, Eulalia helping Bronnuq along, slowed by age. There were others, though, people pressing down to see who had come in their time of need. Eulalia could not entirely begrudge them their curiosity, but she could begrudge them her personal space. She peered out between shoulders and horns.

The temple docks were used sparingly for deliveries, built to accommodate both a small dragon and a host of wagons. When they weren't aloft, the Svarnish travelled in gilt caravans. The First Temple itself only had one caravan of its own, a great practical beast that required two men to operate. The temple had no need for more, as they rarely sent out anything from their home, apart from the occasional clutch of eggs.

There were more caravans in the docks, surrounded by young dragonfolk. Some of them were of the First Temple – temple children both grown and young, residents who must have come when they'd heard news of the invading force.

It was stupid to crowd into this place when death was knocking at their door. It was stupid of them to come without any protection greater than the renasci that followed them.

They're frightened.

The mob waded in slowly, pressing against the crowd that had poured out from the hallway. She braced herself against Ohba as the space around her collapsed inwards, and she was crowded by familiar people. Fidela reached out and clasped the small of her back, steadying Eulalia. Her priest had Rasyl tucked beneath one arm. As she watched, he took a stretch of his robe, looped it around, and tied it with a tug so that the boy was secure.

This would be one of the worst ways to die, as far as Eulalia was concerned. Crushed by a hundred people who forgot that she was amongst them.

'Make way, the holy mothers come!' Cuinu's voice carried over their shoulders. She was rarely grateful for his presence, but his barking tone had the right effect; the people split away. They poured out onto the docks, and the council of the First Temple pushed out into the central chamber. She loved her people, but they were stupid as sheep faced with dragonflame. They were not thinking. She needed to fix that.

'Grandfather?' The call came from an acolyte who towered above the rest, broad-shouldered and strong, his eyes bright with concern. His gaze found them amidst the crowd, and he broke away from those he'd brought. 'Grandfather!'

'Imamu?' Bronnuq broke free from Ohba's side.

'This is my grandson,' Bronnuq explained. The man had tears pricking the corner of his wizened eyes. 'Imamu, you have come to us.'

It was difficult to imagine that such a robust man had descended from Bronnuq, the elder wizened and bent like a tree that had grown into the flow of the wind, but Eulalia nodded. She let herself smile in some relieved way, unsure if elation or horror was the appropriate response. Bronnuq once had a daughter who had passed away some five summers back. Nemalia, a summer wind of a woman, who had flown through the First Temple on occasion but had largely written profound letters. She had sent wagons for Bronnuq to allow him to visit her until a round of feverish flu had taken her from the world.

'The army marched on Luodono first. We barely escaped them when the destruction began,' Imamu blurted. 'I knew they'd be coming here, so I took the caravans I could and I fled. I brought anyone I could.'

A construct stood behind him, his skin a deep, reddish brown; as Eulalia watched, the bands covering his body shifted over his skin, locking into a strange configuration. Renasci were bonded, as they grew, to a Blessed temple denizen. The denizen shifted through several states of being, depending on the task at hand. It was not hard to tell, looking between them both, whom this one had been bound to.

'You saw the army.' Eulalia spoke before she'd thought. The construct nodded decisively, but neither Bronnuq nor Imamu heard her as they embraced, clutching at each other with a ferocity reserved for family. She did not press it further, instead taking a breath and squeezing Ohba's arm.

They had seen the army, which meant that there was a chance that they might know who led it. Though others would not have thought to care, the difference between it being one of the Eschalion and Thurlow Thurlowe felt vast in Eula's mind. Eschalier, the sixth Eschalion, was formidable – the figurehead of his entire empire. Thurlow was a mad dog, a great deal of bark with very little bite. Stories had floated down from the north of how near to death he had come in trying to bring down Queen Taena's dragon. Calling down the dragon riders on Thurlow Thurlowe, the first of his name, would likely decimate his army, trapped as they were against the shields that surrounded Muqdah. Calling them down on the Eschalion was a much riskier manoeuvre.

She needed to take inventory, to see what they had before them. As lovely as the family reunion was, they could not linger any longer.

The caravans were ghostly. Beautiful things, spacious and elegantly supplied with everything one might need to live on the road. She counted three residential caravans, with in-built beds, and two that were meant for supplies. Those were the ones she paused before, staring up at the cavernous space within them and quietly trying to figure out how many people could fit within them. All the caravans lacked their original residents. The few strangers who lingered – no more than ten – did not fit into these spaces. They were not families, they were not travellers.

'I—these came from the Small Temple,' Imamu said, gesturing to the elegant caravans. 'The people who owned them fled well before the army's approach and did not return. It was our only way out.'

'And the dragons?' Eulalia heard Adil ask, though she was actively trying to ignore his presence lest she grow murderous.

Bronnuq's grandson exhaled slowly. There had been a nursery at the Small Temple. Eulalia's lips pressed into a line as she studied his face.

'You made it out,' she said. Eulalia reached out and grasped his shoulder. 'That's all we could ask for.'

She was no good at reassuring people – the right words always slipped away, like sand between her fingers.

'I brought those I could. The horses will be tired, but with a bit of feed, they'll be ready. I was casting protection spells on them the whole way out of worry that someone would see our caravan and try to turn the horses lame.' It was an intelligent decision, and if this man was anything like his grandfather, he'd be a talented caster.

'Someone, go get feed and water for the horses! Get some stable hands!' Adil called, sending two older temple children scattering into a narrow passageway that only they'd fit through. The horses would need efficient tending if they were to move again within the next few days, especially with the load they were likely to pile atop the wagons. She disdained seeing beasts caught in the throes of war – she'd say a prayer for them if she remembered.

There were other people who needed Eulalia's prayers, though. Eulalia looked back to the young Imamu, studying the concerned knot set into his brow.

'Nemalia had several children,' Eulalia said quietly, still watching him.

His expression wavered, like a flame threatening to gutter out at the mere mention of his siblings. Then he swallowed, and she watched the man strap some steel to his spine as he spoke. 'She did.'

She blew out a long breath. There was nothing she could say that would help that wound, as gaping as it was, so she settled on a quiet Svarnish farewell that they sent after those who'd left the mortal plane. 'The winds welcome them.'

Little else to be said, Eulalia retraced her steps back to the docks and joined the council, who stood watch over the proceedings. She wanted to say something to Bronnuq, longed to find something that could tell the grandfather how much she felt for him. Yet, her tongue seemed to tangle in on itself, her mouth running dry and cold. She reached out to him instead, and squeezed his shoulder gently. He looked at her with his grey eyes, searching for something within her face.

She could not tell if he found it there, whatever he was looking for. Yet, he leaned in all the while and clasped her face with one of his warm hands.

'We can send people,' Bronnuq whispered. 'With these caravans, we can save people.'

A chill ran through Eulalia, from the soles of her feet to the nape of her neck.

He was not wrong. There were only a handful of people travelling with Imamu. It looked as if the man had taken almost nothing with him and had bound them into one extended train to mitigate the need for handlers. It was an ingenious way to haul as many caravans as they could manage – she presumed that the wagons were stolen, but she couldn't bring herself to care. Someone had seen the danger that Muqdah and the First Temple were in and had come to help.

'Who do we send?' Adil asked. 'The whole temple couldn't fit into these caravans.'

The ancient holy man turned, releasing Eulalia to hold the hands of his younger companion. 'Many of us won't, but we can save the children. We can save our future.'

Once the stable hands began their work, the council walked Imamu and his companion down to the nearest quiet spot in which they could talk. The crowd that had gathered around them had dispersed following the excitement, though the newcomers lingered in the docks. Eulalia understood their uncertainty – even she'd be tempted to stay close to an immediate escape.

They were within the network of tunnels beneath the First Temple when the next blow came to Muqdah.

The earth shuddered. A tremor ran beneath their feet, a tremble that grew into a resounding rumble that sent Eulalia's heart spiralling into her gut. Rasyl began to cry – a high, distressed sound that she'd rarely heard from the joyous infant. She stumbled, thrown off balance. One of the renasci who had escorted them reached out and caught her with his iron grip, and she threw him a weak, thankful smile for his intervention.

'An earthquake,' the construct explained, unperturbed. 'It will pass.'

Yet, it made no sense – Muqdah had never experienced earthquakes. Other regions of Svarna experienced them frequently, but in the fifteen years Eulalia had lived in this sacred place, not a single earthquake had shaken it. Something dangerous was occurring out in the city, with enough force to shake the earth itself. Her hand clutched at the construct's shoulders so tightly that a pain shot through her wrist.

'Get us to the safest, closest chamber,' she told them. It was their job to do as the council bid, so the young man who held her nodded and lifted her into his arms. Another went to Fidela, put a strong arm around her waist, and scooped her up with little ceremony.

The group hurried through the halls, and with each step, Eulalia doubted that pushing forward was the correct move. She closed her eyes and desperately imagined the foundations of the First Temple holding strong. The distant calls of dragon cries sung down the hall, the sound of a primal confusion.

They were ushered into a small, low-ceilinged chamber with few trappings. Long benches were pushed against the furthest wall, and several rolled-up rugs rested against the other, little more than a storage chamber. The construct holding Eulalia released her once they were within, the earth still trembling, while Ohba braced against one of the far walls and clutched Rasyl to his side.

A bolt of magic ran through Ohba, a bright beaming pillar that shot out from the stone and into his chest. The golden magic glowed beneath his lean skin, pulsating three times before it seemed to flow back into Morouqdi's walls.

'He was aiming for the wards and struck into the earth instead,' Ohba explained. He blinked, and his eyes went a ghostly, Blessed gold as he stared into infinity. 'Our city stands.'

An abrupt pain shot through Eulalia's abdomen, down towards her hip. She let out a breathless, pained noise as she crossed to the corner of the room occupied by worship benches and slowly lowered herself onto the edge of a chair. Nausea overcame her in a wave, and she braced on her knees for a moment, breathing hard as her head swam.

'Something's wrong with Eula.' The Child spoke mildly, before she looked at Eulalia with those huge, dark eyes and saw the truth of the matter. Alarm flashed across her little face, and she broke apart a brewing argument between Fidela and Adil. 'Oi! Something's wrong with Eula!'

'Everyone hush!' Bronnuq shuffled over and knelt before her, his robes swimming around her ankles as he placed both hands upon her belly. She shifted her dress out of the way so that he could touch the skin beneath. He breathed deep and so did she, an exercise the two had done more than once. Eulalia closed her eyes as she steadied herself, shutting out the rest of the room. The space behind her eyes was cool and dark, a refuge from her flipping stomach. 'Breathe deep and long, Eulalia. Let me figure out what's going on with you and the babe.'

Once the nausea had eased, she opened her eyes and nodded.

He got to his feet laboriously, picking up his staff.

A ghostly image of her body appeared before her, floating in the air. It was full of colours, entirely indecipherable to her, but Bronnuq studied it with his brow furrowed. He said nothing, only adjusting his grip upon his staff and watching as the spectral Eulalia shifted and came aglow with different colours.

The grandfather of Muqdah was a user of silent magic. Many casters needed words of power to channel their internal Blessing, but with a Blessed heart, he'd grown so attuned with himself that he willed the spells into existence. A medical diagnostic spell of the scale he used was something Eulalia had never seen before. Nearly a century of nurturing goodness within himself had fostered powerful magic.

'I think you've just strained a muscle, Eula. The babe has not shifted yet.' Relief threatened to overwhelm her, but she looked at the knot in Bronnuq's brow and found that she did not believe him.

The shooting pain came again as she shifted, trying to rise and get her legs beneath her. It was enough to send her back down into the chair. 'You best not be lying to keep me calm.'

He appeared to contemplate saying something before turning his stare back on the diagnostic. 'There's a group of strained muscles on the right side of your hip, where you tend to lean your weight. The babe is not coming yet, but you are overextending yourself. The ritual will need to be done soon, lest your labour come earlier than we thought.'

That would take time that they did not have.

'The babe will come soon, though. Even our magic could only delay it for so long.'

To Eulalia's mind, there were only two real options. There was attempting to birth the babe immediately with an induction tea and hope, pray, that the army did not breach the gates before the labour was done. The mere thought was frightening. Eulalia did not want to be on a delivery table when the Eschalion army reached their temple. There was also a good chance that the tea wouldn't even shift her chances, considering how stubborn her first two pregnancies had been. Eulalia's eldest had come two weeks overdue, refusing to enter the world on anyone's time other than her own.

The other option was that Eulalia simply ignored the labour until after the army was dealt with. When the city was made safe, once they'd razed their enemies to the ground, she could be sequestered with Bronnuq and the holy men and birth the damned thing. But the longer they held off from calling the dragon riders, the further that option would slip from her grasp.

She squeezed her eyes shut as another pain shot through her. 'Fuck,' she swore. 'Fuck, fuck, fuck.'

When she opened her eyes, she was faced with a bewildered and deeply concerned room. Eulalia took a long breath and refused to look at Adil and Cuinu. She could not look at Fidela or Ohba, could not stand them, so she looked at Bronnuq. He had taken care of each of her pregnancies, had been the face that welcomed her to the First Temple.

'I'm so sorry about your grandchildren.'

He faltered. He had still been so settled, focused on her pregnancy rather than himself.

'I ...' Bronnuq searched for the words as the spell faded between them, opening and closing his mouth. He took in a long breath and blew it out, one hand shifting on his staff. 'I just hope they knew how loved they were. I wish that I'd been with them.'

With a trembling, stumbling sigh, Eulalia watched as a pillar of Muqdah crumbled. Sobbing desperately as he tried to turn away from her, Bronnuq folded against his staff, a river freed in him. His shoulders shook as he tried to speak and found only a choking, strangled cry. Eulalia reached out with both of her arms and pulled the grandfather of her heart into an embrace, gentle and unrelenting.

'They knew that you loved them,' she said. 'They knew. You loved them more than anything in the world.'

A pair of slender arms closed around them both, and Eulalia looked up to see Fidela fighting back tears, face pinched like she'd had a lemon placed beneath her tongue.

'The winds welcome them.' Fidela was the first to say the words in that room, her lip trembling as she clutched at Bronnuq's shoulders. Imamu came next with a fierce embrace that clutched them all together. Ohba, with his gentle soothing hum as he pressed inwards. Cuinu came, murmuring prayers beneath his breath, the name of each of Bronnuq's children and grandchildren rolling over them in a quiet tongue. Adil was the last. She barely felt him, a feather-touch against the mourning knot they had made.

'The winds welcome them.'

The farewell came again. It was all they could offer, even though words would fix nothing. All their farewells could give the living was the promise that they were not alone. The goodbye sounded different on each tongue, from whispering to quietly furious this had happened at all. Eulalia tried to discover that familiar fury within herself and found it sputtering, leaving nothing but grey smoke within her. All her energy, in that breath, was Bronnuq's. He needed it.

'The winds welcome them.' This was what the council of priests was meant to be. This was their family. They were supposed to protect one another.

Finally, a slim form pressed in between them, and the Child gently took Bronnuq's hands in her own. Eulalia saw the girl's blotchy red cheeks and streaming tears, a mirror of the grandfather's features – and something else. A fierce love in her young eyes, such righteous self-conviction.

'The winds welcome them.'

'And we will be able to farewell them properly when our city is safe,' Bronnuq said finally. There was a tension to the set of his jaw that Eulalia had not seen in her life. 'My grandchildren are unfortunately dead. We are custodians of a city that is living and in danger – there will be more dead to mourn when this is done.'

Eulalia trusted Bronnuq. He deserved their compassion, but he was deeply aware of the weight of his role. He saw each temple child as his own.

Several minutes stretched on for an eternity. The council of priests sat in the remnants of their grief. Then Eulalia, who always felt as if she played the darkest of roles in their number, became mercantile once more. The pain in her hips had eased, and she was acutely aware of how little time they had to waste. She pressed on.

'Imamu. We must know – who is leading the army? Did you hear whispers? Did they announce anything before they sacked the city?'

'It's Thurlow.' It was not Imamu who spoke, but the construct, Mosi, stood at the edge of the room. 'He announced himself over the Small Temple before he descended upon us.'

'Did you see him?' Ohba asked, gaze turning on Eulalia. He knew what this meant.

'He was not an Eschalion. The Eschalion have always been dark-haired and fair. The High Elf leading the army is blond, like the tales of Thurlow. Baked in the sun. He is Thurlow Thurlowe.' A sense of vindication rushed through Eulalia, turning her face hot. Her fingers tightened upon the bench where she sat until her knuckles had turned pale and sore.

'We can call the dragon riders down upon him, then.' Thurlow Thurlowe would struggle to contend with them in the open field – they had a real chance. A real, solid shot with Thurlow at the helm of the army. There had been stories of how the man had slowly gone mad as he'd combed across the country. The crimes he had committed were atrocious, but he'd suffered at the hands of Svarnish soldiers. He'd borne real wounds. He could die.

Cuinu snarled, his face having turned blotchy and dark in a sudden burst of rage. 'You opportunistic little—'

'Cuinu!' Ohba barked. It was a warning. Her holy man now had his hand upon his leg, where several blades were holstered. 'You'll watch your tongue, or I'll cut it out.'

'Why should I? I have served this temple for forty years. I have seniority on everyone here apart from Bronnuq. This bitch has spent little more than a decade serving Muqdah, and she does so reluctantly. Her squeezing out the voice of Svarna does not make her the preeminent strategist of this city. She's never even ridden a dragon!' His rage had grown unfettered and overwhelming as he set his glare upon Eulalia and saw her exactly as she was. 'Why should I watch my tongue for this foolish, useless woman?'

Eulalia laughed. If she had to claw her way through the mire of his foolish ambitions to do what was right for the temple, she damn well would. 'Because Ohba will cut it out,' Eulalia warned with a smirk. 'He just told you that.' A threat from her would mean little to a man whose rage was so heavily rooted in the superiority of his cock. Ohba, though, was the man who stood to inherit the power of this holy place.

Her words nudged Cuinu's attention away from her enough for him to realise the seriousness of Ohba's threat. She watched his conviction waver, watched the man falter as he stepped away. He looked at the council and grew painfully aware of how his outburst had turned their stomachs, how the Child had shuffled protectively in front of Bronnuq. How Fidela now glared at him as if a look alone could flay his skin from his flesh.

'She's done this on purpose, she'll take any opportunity to destroy the last of our dragons—'

'I am not here to throw our dragons to the slaughter. I was of the belief that the concern with calling the dragon riders was that there would be a merciless slaughter. Thurlow Thurlowe has struggled to contend with our dragons on the open field because they do not have an efficient way of slaughtering them in the air.' Eulalia kept her voice even, even if a sense of venom was leaking into her tone. 'If you dared to use that lump of mud you call a brain, you'd see that your argument has fallen flat. We have a chance. Let us use that chance, Cuinu.'

'Fuck you.' Cuinu followed this up by spitting at her feet and fleeing into the hallway like the coward he was. Adil took one quick look between them and followed, despite Fidela trying to hold him in place.

'Bastard,' Ohba muttered, bouncing Rasyl on his hip as he stared after them. 'Absolute fucking bastard.'

'Language.' Bronnuq patted the Child idly on the head, though he was shaking his head. 'I will go speak with them. I think it is quite enough that you have proven yourself to be in the right. If the slaughter of dragon riders was his concern, then logic should prevail, and he should agree to call them now that we know it is Thurlow leading the pack. That man is little more than an attack dog who's been let off his leash.'

It was a mean thing, to be so furiously happy in her righteousness, but the grandsire of Muqdah looked at her and smiled in his quietly approving way. In that moment, Eulalia was certain that he'd thought her right the whole time and had bided his time, waiting for the inevitable tipping point.

'Imamu, come with me. Your friend can watch the caravans.' Bronnuq waved between the two newcomers, and they departed the chamber together, the elder hobbling along on his staff as his grandson hovered above him.

Eulalia sat, bathing in the ridiculousness of Cuinu's outburst. It was one thing to disagree with someone's argument – they disagreed all the time – but it was another to degrade all that one had given to the temple. If that did not shift the needle in her direction, nothing would.

'I could kill him,' Ohba said this in the sweetest, calmest tone that he could manage as to not upset Rasyl. 'I truly could.'

He was close enough for Eulalia to reach out and pat on the side. Ohba was a physical creature, reassured by any kind of intimacy and physical touch that he could glean from those around him. The best gift he could receive when agitated was a hug, but Eulalia wasn't quite prepared to get back on her feet.

'Hold on to that sentiment in case we need it. Little one!' The call was all it took to bring the Child to her. She took the girl's calloused hands in hers and looked her intently in the eye. 'I need you to do something for me. I need you to go out into Muqdah and be my eyes, while the shield remains up. Look at the temples and people and be seen. Your presence alone will bolster the feelings on the streets. Make sure that they have not given in to madness.'

The people within the First Temple were nervous, but with their leadership splintering and unable to present a united front, how could they not be? She wanted to know that the rest of the city was not in shambles.

'Eula,' Ohba broke in. Eulalia gave him a sharp look and then turned back to the Child. She reached up and cupped her round chin with one hand, drawing her forward until they were mere inches from one another.

'And hear me when I say this, little one – if a single bolt comes down on that shield, you run all the way back to this temple without pause. You stay safe. Protect yourself like I would.'

The Child nodded dutifully, but watching her scurry off into the stone halls, Eulalia suspected that she may have lit a match that could very well grow into a wildfire.

Chapter Eleven

SVARNA

The Child wished she had been surprised by the priest's rage, but if she were being honest, Cuinu's behaviour was something of an open secret amongst the people of Morouqdi.

Everyone knew that Cuinu only honoured the women if it served him; the temple children had heard too many of his rants in their secret tunnels. The Child knew quite well what he thought of Eulalia, but to have people yell like that, explode in their rage, went against everything that the First Temple valued. It was disgusting. He was not behaving like an animal or a child – he was acting like an elf.

The Child turned a corner into a flat wall and hummed as the temple bricks shifted out of her way, allowing her into one of the service tunnels. They were the quickest way to navigate throughout the First Temple, only accessible to the temple children and the renasci who'd been born within the holy walls. She would have been a construct if they hadn't named her special when she'd been born. She wondered what it would have been like, to not have one foot planted in mortality and magic. She'd never know. The Child skimmed past several other temple children, shoulders brushing past narrow backs, and then off into the darkness once more.

The dragons knew that she was coming. The Child heard their curious chittering as she turned into the nursery passage. She did not pause, trusted that the temple knew her and would unfold before her quick feet. Brick unfolded like paper, creating a window the Child could fly through.

The nursery had quieted since their morning foray into the den. Once the sun roved towards the reaches of the sky, the dragons often roamed onto the temple roof, flocking to the warmth, sunning their wings, and allowing the great ball of flame in the sky to replenish their own fire. The Child had been caught on several occasions attempting to climb up and through the channels to join them – it was one of those things that she was not allowed to do until she was big.

Handlers and companions lingered around what looked to be a saddle that was entirely too old to ride, a once-great piece of Blessed craftsmanship. The Child sidled up to them as they chattered about the unfortunate state of the leather, tapping the shoulder of a familiar figure amongst the many.

'Will you help me?' she asked the construct inside the nursery, a dragon handler she knew as Uono. 'I need to take Kine to the sky.'

Uono took one appraising look at her high-necked dress, entirely inappropriate for dragon-riding, and cocked his head at her. 'You shouldn't be running around on your own, little one. Where is Eulalia?'

It was what they all called her, little one. She was almost a child and almost a woman, so she did not begrudge them the preference that she remain as they had always known her. Yet, it chafed at her want for freedom. To stretch her legs. To fly.

'Eula sent me.' Uono hesitated for a moment before he nodded, drawing her along the edge of the nursery. He led her in a semicircle, his eyes searching the dens until he settled on a point on the wall. He slipped a finger into his mouth and whistled hard, summoning out a small collection of young dragons who had piled atop one another in a small den as baby birds would in a narrow nest.

This was not exactly what Eulalia had instructed, but if she hadn't wanted the Child to take the skies, she'd need to be more specific.

'Kine!' Uono called, and from the clustered babies a young she-dragon emerged. Once the call was made, the construct stepped aside, leaving the Child to handle here. Kine was one of Idunn's children, a young she-dragon who glistened like the ocean. She was large enough to be ridden, but not so great that she'd been taken out of the city yet. The Child whistled idly for her and clicked her tongue twice, a code shared amongst the temple children. She held her hand out at thigh level, watching Kine carefully as she approached.

'Eulalia wants us to go see what's happening in the city,' she told Kine. 'I think she's desperate for eyes she can trust.'

The dragon clicked back at her, mimicking the noise that she had made. Kine lowered her head to the Child's level and hummed as she ran a hand over her scaled head. Heat flowed into her palm, curling around each of her fingers and drawing her forth. She allowed herself to fall into the heat, until she was hugging Kine's sharp nose, tickled by each breath the young dragon took.

She had wanted to ride the dragons more, but the holy men had been deeply nervous that she would take a slip and fall.

Uono and two other men brought a dragon saddle, securing it across the beast's barrel chest. Kine submitted to the saddling, lowering herself. The Child waited. Kine's eyes were ocean marbles, huge and piercing, staring straight through her as they always did. She was the only dragon that the Child had ever ridden – she had hoped to take Idunn to the sky, but the holy men had said it would only happen once she was grown and practised.

Once the saddle was thoroughly secured, the Child approached. She pressed her boot into one of the leather straps and used a loop set higher up in the harness to pull herself up. She flushed as Kine's heat radiated into her side, a cosy hearth.

There were two leather straps in the saddle. She hooked one over her chest and the other across her thighs, buckling them a touch too tight to ensure her security, before nodding. The Child placed her hands upon the saddle and whistled again, the call short and sharp. 'Fly, Kine.'

Kine let out a proud cry and spread her great wings. The ascent took the most work for a dragon; though they were built for the skies, they were not meant to have people on their backs. The saddle swayed as Kine leapt forward to gain ground. The Child's knuckles paled as she gripped the saddle, bracing into the straps that held her down. The saddle was incredibly secure, but there was always a hint of human doubt once one was atop a dragon – yet there was no feeling in the world that could compare once one took flight.

No longer an individual, small and mortal, upon a dragon the Child was something far greater than herself. She and Kine became a bonded being, sensitive to every breath or shift they took together. Kine spiralled around the nursery until they came to the top of the chamber. The dragon landed briefly atop the central pillar before she leapt off and launched herself into the sky above Muqdah.

The Child's heart took to the air. They swooped down from the nursery, the tallest peak, and descended into the throng of Svarna's holiest city.

A city unlike any other, it filled the horizon with temples, great and small. The alabaster stone was testament to the gods and the cardinal winds, each building a resting place for pilgrims to rest their weary heads upon holy land.

They flew past smaller squares that branched off from the First Temple and towards the cardinal square, one of the largest intersections in Muqdah with a huge compass at its centre. People whistled and cheered as Kine flew overhead. The Child straightened in her saddle, waving to the onlookers below.

The streets of Muqdah were full of movement. She perched Kine atop one of the great arches meant for dragons and watched. Renasci were out in force in the square, tending to great old saddles from a century long past. They were building structures around the edges of the buildings, tall walls that were bound to the pillars by hand. People hurried past the renasci without a glance, carrying bags and trailing children behind them. Holy men threw petal mixtures across their temple doors, chanting.

There was urgency in the swiftness of their steps, and the ways in which parents clutched their children to them. The holy men were not talking with that steady calm that she'd grown so accustomed to. There was a tremor in the heart of the city.

As she sat, the Child turned her eyes to the outer edges of Muqdah. Something dangerous that took root in the back of her mind. She was brave. She was the bravest and brightest of them all. She did not baulk when hard tasks fell into her hands. She was not frightened of elves. The Child whistled, short and sharp, and Kine launched herself back into the air. A great swing of her wings sent them upwards, a chorus of well-wishing floating after them.

The Child grasped the mast of the saddle, a long pillar that rested against a panel on Kine's back, and pulled it gently towards the outermost corner of Muqdah. The wind shifted as they tilted together, tangling its way into her hair and unravelling the braids that held her curls in place.

Eulalia wanted eyes. She wanted to see what was happening in Muqdah. There was no way she could have made it to the edge of the shields before her feet would have swollen up like soft cushions. Pregnancy did not seem a particularly pleasant ailment to the Child, considering how the body ached and complained as the babe grew. That meant that for Eula, the Child would be her eyes and her feet. She would look as far as Eulalia would have.

The city edge was devoid of people, presumably wise enough to flee deeper in when faced with the threat of war.

There was a mass at the shield. From the sky it was little more than a pool of water, a blue blot outside the city boundaries. As they made their descent, the pool grew and shifted before the Child's eyes. Thousands of people cloaked in blue, armour that glinted like a pile of silver coins abandoned on the pale land. A mass of people unlike anything the Child had seen ever in one place – she had seen people, she had been to city gatherings, but these strangers outnumbered even the largest festivals she'd attended.

The Child began to grasp what was facing their hallowed city – why fear now thrummed through the First Temple like adrenaline in the city's veins, why Muqdah's few remaining saddles were being drawn out of the dust.

She and Kine circled the area once. Her face flushed at the thought that, if the shields fell, if the invaders entered the city, the people she loved would not stand a chance against their might.

An idea bloomed like a deadly flower in the back of her mind. She whistled a circular sound, and Kine twisted, the dragon tilting until they both hung sideways in the air as they rounded back towards the city. The Child's stomach dropped as she sat suspended in the air, held to the saddle by the straps and her grip on the leather.

Rage – that was the feeling brewing in the very pit of her stomach. A churning darkness entirely unlike herself. Why were they not fighting? Why were her people hiding within their temples while the army was trapped in the open, with no shelter to protect them? She would need to be quick. Stories of the weapons they used to strike down dragons had carried down into Muqdah, that they were unwieldy and hard to aim. And Kine was faster than most fully grown dragons that went into war.

There was a great tower that held an elaborate astronomical clock with several faces, welcoming people into Muqdah. They circled behind it, levelling out so that the Child was upright once more as they rounded on the front of the city. She spied a man cloaked in gold amongst the throng, sticking out from the silvery-blue sea. The Child honed in on him, eyes narrowing, and perfect Kine found him too. The Child whistled a long call into the air, a melody that meant a great many things, but at its core meant go.

They fell out of the sky, the swoop of a predator. Together, they rocketed out of Muqdah's shields and dropped onto the Eschalion's army. A roar of surprise went up as they broke free from the shimmering dome, and people fled from them. Soldiers turned, desperate to escape, trampling those who were slower. Kine and the Child knew not to go to the ground. Dragons were creatures of air and fire – men dominated the earth, but dragons ruled the sky.

Their foray would have to be brief, quick, and devastating before the mass gathered itself to try and take them out of the air. As they dropped, the air grew sharp and metallic as magic swam and made itself true. That was the warning that came before dragonflame, a spiralling stone in the Child's gut that left her mouth dry.

Death came to Muqdah's door. Fire fell in a great arc over the elvish army, hundreds turned to ash in a single breath. Veins of wildfire crawled out from the initial scorch and caught on cloth, leaping from one armoured body to another like dry tinder.

They came out of the arc and turned sharply back behind the shield, flocking briefly to its safety. A chorus of screams filled the air, but they were swallowed by Kine's triumphant roar, a bone-quaking noise. The Child's heart roared along with her, demanding her vengeance to be known. This was what Eulalia wanted of the dragon riders; this was what should have been happening from the moment the invaders arrived.

Eulalia was right. Fuck the tenets of only acting in self-defence; let them attack those who intruded upon their sanctuary. The citizenry of Muqdah were not just human – they were dragonfolk. They should not fight what they are.

Together, they rounded once more on the army. A victory cry had shot up from the city, from those who stood witness to the Child's onslaught. This time, she aimed for the golden man, who must have been Thurlow Thurlowe. Kine's wings tightened against her great body, sharpening the speed at which they dove into the army.

Go. The gilded man did not run. That she had expected – Thurlow Thurlowe would not run from her. He did not believe himself a coward. He thought he could face a dragon and live.

They descended, fire and flesh and fury incarnate. The Child's fear fell away like water in the wind. Kine opened her jaw and poured forth dragonflame, icy blue and all-consuming. It hit a shimmering cloak of magic around Thurlow, and he vanished beneath the flame. Neither rider nor dragon faltered, knowing that shields could be pressed. Shields could be broken. Let it be Thurlowe, not Muqdah, who shattered this day.

Spears flew from the earth and glanced off Kine's hide. They would need something far stronger than that, and though she could see the heavy weaponry sat amongst the army, the panic Kine inspired had not yet abated.

They both knew that it would not last long.

Kine bore down on the gilded man and magic bloomed at the heart of the fire, a flicker of frost combatting the flame conspiring to turn him to ash. The Child's face twisted into something alien, a superior snarl.

A bolt spiralled overhead. The Child's gaze snapped to its source and found one ballista aimed at them, scrambling to be reloaded – it took several men powered by panic and the fear of death. The Child whistled, and Kine's jaws snapped shut. With a gale force beneath them, they rose again, and she twisted sharply to look down upon the army, hoping to see nothing more than ashen bones left. Instead, as the flame dissipated, there was the gilded man with a hot, red burn spreading across his pale skin. She could not help it – she laughed. It was a harsh, murderous sound as they drew up into the sky.

Legends could not be killed. You could not harm or pluck a lock of hair from their head. But Thurlow Thurlowe could be burned.

That was all Svarna needed.

Chapter Twelve

THE IMPERIUM

Being a bedworker who largely captured the attention of men, Nuru found many a challenge in her line of work.

The High Elf called Truls was not a challenge. He had been her patron since shortly after she'd arrived in the Imperium, not long after Nema's birth. It had been a risk taking him on when Taliesin, her healer, had told her that she needed to go easy on her body. Yet it was a risk that had entirely paid off. Truls' gold had paid for repairs to The Brass Wyvern done by Nords; it had paid for bail on more than one occasion; and it continued to pay for Andraste's nannying.

She could not afford to go without Andraste's services, and despite the fact she thought the Nord woman might quietly work for nothing, it was not in Nuru's nature to expect that of her friends. Nuru would not cheat her of that money. Truls was good for that.

Truls was the eldest of the Thurlowe brood and Taliesin's older brother, the hammer to his elegant quill. Despite the genetic disposition of High Elves and their usually willowy forms, he had turned out a brawny beast of a man, rippling muscles built from a century of training with some of the kingdom's finest warriors. He was a fairy-tale prince who occasionally walked into walls, forgetting that the entire world wasn't built for him.

The two spent several hours before their appointment shuffling through her wardrobe, trying to find clothes that would suit their outing.

'You can't go to the royal library in that,' he remarked, lounging across her bed. She was glad it was the largest of their beds, larger than even Takuma's. It had been a trade-off – he got the larger room, and she the larger bed. Truls would have looked absurd on anything smaller, legs dangling off the edge. 'You look lewd.'

She snorted, smoothing her skirts thoughtfully as she twisted in the mirror. Instead of the diaphanous, sheer dresses she usually wore to work in the Wyvern, she'd layered several linen skirts to try and fake a sense of modesty. Not that she really believed in such a thing. Modesty culture was a curious farce the High Elves took up – what sin was it to be proud of the skin their gods had gifted them?

Nuru had more modest clothes, but she never wore those to work. It helped create a division between her bedwork and her sense of self outside the boundaries of male lust. Men never wanted Nuru as she was – they did not want her pared back and dressed for herself, looking as young as she was. They wanted a caricature of a woman.

'Lewd? Firstly, that's never been a complaint before. Secondly – I covered up.' Nuru waved broadly to herself, as if that alone should explain it away. 'This is modest, Truls, as modest as we dress.'

'Modest for Svarna, maybe, but if a woman walked around the palace with that much cleavage, she'd be arrested for heresy,' he responded with a shrug. She contemplated a rebuttal and quietly smothered it. 'My mother used to walk around naked, but they thought she was chosen by god to be on this earth, so ...'

Truls' mother, Thalia, had been the last matriarch of the church and the closest a single woman could get to their gods. She had left her two princely sons in her wake when she died, though Nuru was yet to figure out which portions of Truls came from which parent. She propped a hand on her hip, levelling a look at the elf in the mirror. When she realised that he was quite intent upon a bowl of grapes they'd demolished and was not looking at her, Nuru turned on him with a huff.

'Unless you want to grab me a habit, this is what I'm wearing.' Nuru patted at her breasts protectively. 'I am still breast-feeding – I will not be held responsible for my cleavage.'

'No, but I might be held responsible,' Truls said blandly, 'and I don't like to take responsibility for anything. I thought this might be an issue.'

He clapped, and the magical focus in his ring sparked momentarily, summoning a bundle of fabric in the air above him. It collapsed into his hands, and he tossed it towards her. The cloak was a peacock-blue concoction with a deep satin lining, falling in scalloped waves as she unfurled it. She draped it over her, feeling as the fabric adjusted itself, shrinking to her dimensions.

Within moments, the cloak had picked nearly two feet of fabric off the floor and sucked back within itself, leaving an otherwise tailored cloak on her back.

'People will think I stole this,' Nuru mused as she twirled towards the mirror. It even had a golden cloak pin at the breast that she would have to sell, too gaudy of a thing to wear in the red-light district. 'I could never afford this.'

'Let them think you stole it, then.' Truls laughed, tossing a spare grape from his bowl up into the air and catching it in his mouth. He chewed thoughtfully as he hooked upwards onto his feet. 'It's charmed for warmth, for size, and it's yours for offering to fuck me in a library.'

She snorted. 'You're a true gentleman.'

Fucking in a library was a new one for Nuru.

She was a creature of comfort. She preferred intimate spaces, piles of soft pillows, and seafoam-soft blankets. It was what had drawn her to bedwork in the first place, when Takuma had explained all that he did. A bedworker of note could set the boundaries within their domain, dress it up as they pleased. Truls, in contrast, loved a little public debauchery. The Imperium was austere about its notions of honourable procreation, and lust for the sake of lust did not factor into that philosophy. Truls had internalised all of this puritanical code and decided he'd rather figure out what the fuss was about himself.

The stacks were monumental, a forest of bookshelves set so far from one another that one would feel incredibly exposed if someone came up behind them. With a little investigation, they decided that one of the research alcoves ran the appropriate line between risqué and criminal.

Sly giggling devolved into a muffled shriek as Truls hefted her atop the table, clapping a hand over her mouth and keeping the other firmly on her ass.

'You are hopeless,' he whispered.

There was a charm to Truls. He was no heavy-handed fool. He had dimples that appeared when he was feeling particularly devilish, and a way of making a woman feel like the centre of the known world. When she ruffled his hair, his curls sprung up boyishly around his face. He was a prince. He was not her prince, she could lay no claim to him, but Nuru could indulge in this fantasy for a little while.

'You are handsome,' Nuru whispered back conspiratorially. He looked like Taliesin in the soft light, if she squinted and imagined her priest with his hair shorn short. When he pressed his mouth to hers, she let her fingers slip into his silken curls. His hands roamed with expert efficiency, hiking up her meticulously layered skirts and grasping at her waist.

Truls was hefty in all regards. The first time he'd dropped his trousers, her stomach had flipped and churned as she'd tried to figure out what she was likely to do with it. Now, Nuru reached out and took his cock in her hands. She stroked him, listening to the way that his breath quickened. Not usually one for subtlety, he was doing an excellent job of keeping quiet.

It was almost meditative. Truls treated sex as almost a cursory activity, like fencing or feasting but with far less clothing. Nuru had once had very romantic notions of sex, nurtured by naïveté and youth, only to get married and discover she was quite ambivalent to the actual act. There was a fascinating psychology behind how two people bonded within the sheets, but her heart had never fluttered the way it did in books.

When he was as stiff as a man could be, Truls got on his knees. A woman had to be tended to, teased to arousal in the same way that a man did. She wound her hands into his hair, put one knee on either shoulder, and allowed herself to melt at the first swipe of his tongue.

It was not that she had agreed to Truls's many entanglements because he resembled Taliesin. In truth, she had met this prince first, all brawny muscle and wicked charm. Once she'd met her priest, the brotherly connection had simply been convenient. It was easier to forget oneself to pleasure when Nuru's hands were knotted in curls that could have almost belonged to Taliesin. She had spent a long time wondering how Taliesin would bed a woman. She couldn't imagine it would be anything like Truls. She imagined a true, genteel romance within the sheets.

But unadulterated pleasure would do, for now.

It hadn't always been so easy. When he'd first come to her, Truls had been overly confident in his own innate ability to pleasure a woman because nobody had ever dared to direct him. She had spent hours teaching him the angles at which he needed to hilt a woman to draw a breathless gasp, guiding him to the more subtle spots within that would send the hair prickling on the back of her neck. He was an apt learner once he'd discovered Nuru's critique helped him on more beds than just her own.

She allowed herself to soften beneath his touch, to crest – not just once, but twice.

Pleasure was Nuru's profession, and she was damned good at it.

After a brief, muffled session in the stacks, Truls left her to wander the library. Despite his show of the cloak, he never held any illusions about their relationship – she was a bedworker he employed and his brother's friend. They did not often talk about Taliesin when they were together, an awkwardness surrounding the topic. Though not so awkward that he was willing to sacrifice her company and her tongue.

Nuru found that she inspired one of two feelings in men. One was adoration – the excessive sort that allowed one to float through someone else's life unfettered by the expectations they thrust upon other people. It was men staring at her bare legs, remarking at what a pretty face she had. It was the intense looks, the way they lingered as she passed. It was men and their fascination with soft-skinned women with rosy cheeks that came from another world.

The other was aggression; Nuru had learnt that she inspired that at a young age. When she lived in the temple, she had often been shuffled away behind holy men and out of the way of strangers – somehow, they had all been acutely aware of it. It was something in the way that men sneered at her, the way they contemplated poking and prodding at her.

Both ended in fixation, the need to possess. She knew that was why Truls entertained her so much – some part of his elvish temperament had fixated on the thought of a woman who was anything other than suitable for his family's sensibilities. A Svarnish bedworker, with heaving bosom, intricately braided hair, golden chains and bangles that sung to her skin tone – even the ribbons she wore around her throat. It was a kind of beauty that the High Elves denied themselves. But that sort of adoration had its limits. She knew she'd reach her limit with him eventually, and if he caught her stealing from the emperor's library, that may tip the scales.

She'd best not get caught, then.

The royal library collection was predominantly elvish. A maze of towering bookshelves, it held the Imperium's history alongside anything deemed important by the scholars who curated it. It was a winding forest of tomes to explore within a sage-green chamber, their very own forest of knowledge.

Moreover, it was a feat of Imperial construction – there was nothing here that had not been constructed by magic.

It was not built for anyone of her stature. Nuru blew out a puff of air each time she had to climb a step. The tallest of the High Elves were nine feet tall, meaning everything was too broad for her, too high for her to reach easily. She was small for a Svarnishwoman, and was therefore tiny by comparison.

It was not the first time that she'd seen the library. Taliesin had walked her by it once in one of their rare outings to the family estate – he'd needed to talk to his sister and left Nuru in the library garden to do so. She knew what she was looking for. The Imperium prided itself upon the meticulousness of its cities, all falling within their heavenly design, so it was no surprise that they kept an extensive record of their work. Blueprints of all the Imperium were tucked away within these walls, where the High Elves thought no one would dare intrude.

Truls was certainly observing her from afar. It wasn't as if there were many eyes to watch them, with only the royal court and their families allowed within, but he clearly didn't want to leave her unmonitored. There were a few scholars in a distant corner, crowded around the table in a study room atop a long staircase, but they'd barely moved since her and Truls' arrival.

The archive was nestled away in one of the many gilded alcoves, hidden behind a counter. A collection of archivists came and went throughout the day, but presently there was only one senior archivist minding the collection. Nuru lingered behind an elaborate bookshelf, peering through the shelves. The archivist was an ageing elf – remarkable in his own right. With silvering hair and lined features, he must have been positively ancient. Nuru had never seen a High Elf grow so old; she'd presumed they just vanished into the ether when deemed no longer presentable to the Imperium masses.

His whispery form stood between her and the archives. She stood silently for several minutes, assessing how she would make her way in. Their plan depended on it – if she didn't get the plans for the Thurlowe estate, the others would have no way of navigating it.

Nuru had one way to easily gain access. The Blessing at her throat sat heavy, like a collar. When their caravans had first made the crossing from Svarna, she'd seen how they had treated those who practised open magic. They'd learnt quickly to keep their Blessings covered in those early days and to hide their most magical relics, lest they be requisitioned or told to turn back.

It had made her rightfully cautious. Magic was a tempestuous thing, though in her life it had proved too often to be an agent of bedlam. Yet, there was a reason that Takuma had sent her to do this – she was the most capable of it. She just had to think of the right words to say, and she had to think of them quickly, before Truls started wondering what she'd fixed herself on.

With a hard sigh, she emerged from behind the bookshelf and approached the archivist. The elderly elf was slow to notice her approach; Nuru quickly trotted across the polished floors, the soft, worn soles of her boots making little noise against the tiles.

'Excuse me, mis—' The archivist began to speak, but Nuru held up a hand, closing the distance between them.

'You are going to go fluff around in the shelves, as if someone mis-shelved twenty tomes and they're all very out of place,' Nuru said softly in Common. A tingling filled her throat as her magic manifested, her Blessing taking hold of each word as Nuru enunciated them. 'You never saw me. You never saw any Svarnishwoman in the library today, and you're quite certain that it's someone in that table of scholars over there that decided to be careless with the stacks.'

Nuru's magic took hold of him with almost no resistance. His eyes glazed over, and he nodded, turning and fixing on some random spot in the shelves before tottering off through a swinging door. She moved quickly, catching it as it swung back and slipping into the archives.

Within, the chamber overflowed with case upon case of small metal disks, each with a glimmering crystal at its centre. On the other side, tucked away out of sight from the royal library, there was a workshop full of empty disks and shelves of crystals. Nuru recognised the magic in the crystals; these had all been mined from a place of power. When enough magic was left to swell within the land, men could mine out physical manifestations of the power. They were treated as a luxury, a precious resource that would not always regrow. Where magic was most powerful, trees would sprout from the ground with crystal blossoms. In Muqdah, they had once enshrined those trees in alcoves and buildings, the holy men monitoring the harvesting to ensure that they never took more than the land could regrow.

Here, the Imperium treated magic like candy.

Nuru's hand flew to the pendant that hung between her breasts. She held it in her palm for a long moment, feeling the magic within it hum quietly in response to the sheer amount of magic surrounding her.

There was no time to linger. She picked a random disk from the workbench and slipped it within her skirts. She removed the package Takuma had given her and slipped it into the second drawer that lined the bottom of the workbench. He had not explained where the thing was meant to be placed, but he always took care in these things. For all of their shouting matches, Nuru knew better than to ignore him.

She ignored Takuma's guidance very rarely, in truth. She owed far too much to him and yet, Imamu had always brought out the worst in her. She and Imamu had been married, and so what had gone down between the two of them was private business. He should have known better to try and pry open their marriage bed, especially when that mashjor had been Imamu's bridal gift to her.

Once the package was appropriately stashed, Nuru disappeared into the archives, eyes scanning the shelves until she found the alphabetical markers. Under T, she began to search for the Thurlowe estate amidst the plethora of disks, trying to make sense of the inscrutable elven script. Surely, it fell under Imperium regulations – it had to be here. Did they really need to make archival scripts so ornate?

'Nuru?' a masculine voice called, freezing her in place. 'Nuru, are you in here?'

Shit. She stuck her head out from behind the shelf and spotted Truls on the other side of the alcove, leaning over the counter to peer into the archive. Unsure of what to do, she rose a hand to wave to him. There seemed no point in denying that she was here or hiding away amid the shelves. Nuru had known he was watching. She just thought she'd have longer.

'You're not supposed to be in here,' Truls said in a hushed voice, though he did not seem terribly alarmed. 'Like, at all. Like, we both get in trouble if anyone find you in there.'

Nuru calculated the risk factor against the tone of his voice, lips pressed together. 'Well then, get in here,' she said, surprised by how willing she was to take that risk. 'You stick out more than I do.'

He quirked a brow at her but, in a flash of energy, teleported into the archives with her. The air at her side was filled with the scent of lemons and fresh linen. Bless Truls and the fact that he did not presume the worst of her, bless whoever taught him that cleanliness was something to be valued and not scoffed at.

'What are you doing, Nuru?' Truls asked, peering down at her through his vibrant blue eyes. There was a reason that the Thurlowe colours were blue – some things persisted throughout the familial line, despite a distinct lack of inbreeding in comparison to some of their elvish friends. There was not a whisper of suspicion in his stare.

If there was one thing a marriage to Imamu had taught Nuru, it was how to lie when put on the spot. 'I wanted to see what was in here! No one was here, I thought it was just another part of the library.'

'Well, it is. Sort of.' He cocked his head to the side as if he were not quite understanding her, humming beneath his breath. 'They keep the plans for most of the empire in here, anything that's of enough importance for Eschalier to want to have a record of it.'

'Do you think you could show me where Taliesin lived when he was a boy?' Nuru asked, reaching out to squeeze his hand. Truls's Blessing tingled beneath her fingers, his magic itching to leap from him. When they had first met, Truls magic had been so acute that it had caused the hair on the nape of her neck to prickle. She entreated herself upon him with a pleading look. Pouting would have pushed it too far. 'He keeps telling me stories of how beautiful it was, but I didn't think I'd ever get to visit.'

'Our place, sure!' He leaned over and kissed Nuru quickly on the top of the head. 'You could have just asked, Nuru. I could show you home.'

She could have rolled her eyes at how sweetly stupid he was.

Truls was so overwhelmingly nice; it was the niceties of someone who had never been told no in his life. He knew that people did sometimes get in trouble, he was aware that he could lay witness to people being reprimanded for their decisions, but he was not one of them. He had never been one of them, coddled in the finest wool throughout his childhood and gifted the biggest swords that his little heart had longed for. He did not believe that he could make an incorrect decision as long as he was behind it. Together, they strode back within the archives, Truls taking the lead as he was prone to do. She tucked the cloak that he had gifted her over her head, feeling safer within the blue fabric.

'It should be, uh ...' Truls began before his thought lapsed, his eyes scanning the surroundings. He ushered her back through the archives, evidently reluctant to leave her where she might have been seen. 'Down this way. I've only been here a few times, but this archive doesn't look terribly different than the one at the Thurlowe estate. Ours is smaller, though, more religious. Mother wanted to keep some of the holy texts safe and close to her heart.'

'That's sweet,' Nuru mused quietly. He was very sensitive about his mother. She suspected that he had once been far closer to her than to the patriarch of the family. 'Do you miss Taliesin sometimes?'

'All the time when I'm at home,' Truls said. 'I'm just glad that he's happier in the church. His happiness is more important than father lording over him. There's a reason Nahia pissed off the moment she connected with the church.'

A brotherly sentiment that was almost out of place in the realm of Truls and Taliesin's otherwise complicated bond. There wasn't time to ponder it as Truls reached above her head and plucked a disc from its shelf.

'If I remember correctly, we just pop it on the base and ...' He snapped, setting the magical focus in his ring glimmering as it drew from his Blessing. As Truls channelled his magic into the disk, it set off a glow that mirrored his own; sparking to life, the crystal sent up a great image of an estate that darkened the archive. Translucent and bluish, it mapped out every room and corner of the Thurlowe estate in perfect detail. 'Ta-da! There's home.'

Nuru peered upwards, having to lean back to see it properly. Truls extended a glowing hand and waved at the hologram, shrinking it and drawing it down until it no longer stretched above their heads. She approached to get a better angle, fascinated at the see-through rendering of the Thurlowe home.

'I stay up here,' Truls explained, pointing to a corner of the vast estate. 'And Taliesin's room was up here, in this tower. My sister Nahia stayed down here when she lived with us. Somewhere that she could easily hop out a window and run off into the city when Father drove her insane. Isn't it impressive?'

There were veins beneath the earth, in the schematic. They all lead to the end of the estate, where the dome sat. Nuru tried not to fix on it, but she could not help it. It was as tall as the estate, broader than the library at a glance, a towering testament to the Thurlowe name. Nuru took in a breath, short and sharp, and said, 'Yes, it is. It's astounding.'

There was a shuffling from outside the archive and Truls startled, any pretence of relaxation dropped. He pulled the disc off the workbench and banished the hologram as he did, holding their blessed schematic. That is what they needed. 'Let's go. The grandpa is coming back.'

'I'll put the plans back,' Nuru said, realising that this was her moment to move. She reached out with her soft hands and took it from his palm. Her patron offered no resistance, though she kept expecting him to turn on her. Truls nodded, and Nuru dipped back towards the shelf, withdrawing the first disk from her skirts and finding the place where the Thurlowe schematics originally sat. She had to stretch upwards onto the balls of her feet to reach the shelf, balancing precariously amidst the royal archives. Nuru reached out and grasped the wooden cabinet to balance herself.

She dropped the blank disc into the open spot on the shelf, holding her breath until she saw that it was not about to topple forward. With a quick sigh, Nuru rolled back onto her heels and pocketed the Thurlowe disk. She fled back to Truls, who was waiting to pull her from the archives, barely making it under the glassy-eyed stare of the approaching archivist.

'That was too close,' Truls murmured as he helped her down the stairs, evidently at the end of his patience. He gave her a strained smile that she nearly wanted to apologise for, but Nuru kept her mouth shut. With her magic still filling her throat, tingling and hinting at an illusion of power, she decided it was far safer to choose a chastised silence. 'We should go.'

Nuru allowed him to shepherd her from the library. She watched the quiet myriad of thoughts that he went through, the nervous glances to ensure nobody noticed them too closely. He wound her through the maze and towards the servant's passage they'd used to sneak in.

Then Nuru saw the brothers.

They looked exactly as they had the night of Zuri's arrival – predatory.

The first was beautiful in an elvish way, but there was something flat behind the eyes, an insincere charisma that filled him. His silvery blonde hair shone in the sun, his hawkish stare burning through her as they approached.

The other appeared to the world with the elegant look of a cruel, hooked blade meant for disembowelment. There was no falsity to him, though, no sense of pretence. Nuru decided on the spot that if she had to contend with either brother, she'd pick the latter. She could contend with transparency, but the first was a different monster entirely. She had thought them both ghostly when she'd first laid eyes on them, but they were touched by the sun's warmth of daylight. Nuru offhandedly wondered if their mother had been Svarnish – a repulsive thought.

'Brother!' the first called jovially, and ice solidified in Nuru's gut. He was watching her; they were both watching her. 'Who is your fine companion?'

'Not for sale,' Truls responded shortly as he pulled Nuru gently towards him, wrapping an arm around her. She stood tucked against his side, watching as these titans sized one another up. 'A friend.'

'Interesting,' the second spoke. She knew she was not safe beneath her cloak when she heard his voice, as bitter as burnt sugar. 'I didn't know you shared Father's sensibilities.'

Something in Truls' wound up at the presumption. She felt it, pressed against his side, lean muscles winding themselves into knots as a fury swelled within him. His sword hand twitched.

'Don't presume to compare us,' Truls spoke, tone filled with a haughty disgust. It was as if he had suddenly rung a bell and become a true High Elf lord, one who'd sneer at her as she passed. Nuru swallowed.

'Don't be so sensitive,' the first teased. 'We've heard about you running around the red-light district. Everyone knows you've got your appetites – we don't judge.'

'You've got no grounds to judge after the shit you pulled in the guest wing.' With a huff, Truls pushed past them, though they offered little resistance. The brothers had prodded their tiger and gotten their fair share of amusement. Nuru glanced back as she passed. Their playfulness flattened to cold marble as Truls passed, their mirrored stares studying her until she was drawn entirely out of their reach. Truls took her out into the gardens and led her promptly to the Imperium streets, silent and tense.

'Who were they?' Nuru finally asked, when she felt like she could break the unsettled quiet.

'Those are my father's bastards. Llewelyn and Maldwyn.' It was only as Truls took an unsteady breath that Nuru realised that this was a flicker of fear on him. Her patron pondered momentarily before he turned, crouching until he was staring at Nuru directly. 'If they ever come to The Brass Wyvern, you refuse them. No matter what excuses they make, no matter the money they offer, you don't give them a moment of your time. Deal?'

She took her dusky hands and cupped his charming face, squishing it until his angular features were rendered soft. 'Deal. They look slimy, anyway, none of our bedworkers would touch them.'

This mollified Truls, but the words sounded anxious to her own ears. Something in her stomach flipped and turned as he nodded, taking her hands in his once more. Nuru was left with a singular thought as Truls walked her back to The Brass Wyvern, while his brothers' faces lingered in the back of her mind.

They know what I look like.

Chapter Thirteen

SVARNA

Eulalia's murderous intent was never aimed towards her children. However, there was an exception to every rule, and her eldest daughter had somehow sent her feral.

Two great waves of emotion crashed over Eulalia as she watched in horror from the temple entryway. One was fury, all-consuming and irrational – how dare the girl take her words and ignore them so blatantly, risking her life against a battalion. The other was pride. That was the worse of the two waves because she knew that, were the Child another, there wouldn't have been a breath of doubt within her that the person upon that dragon was the bravest person in Muqdah, the most powerful. But because that rider was her little one, she could not be proud of such a stupid thing.

Two things could be true at once. The Child's assault on the Eschalion Army was an intense show of Svarnish power, it was a great show of their might, and it was exactly what Eulalia had wanted to see in the skies above Muqdah. It was also a profoundly foolish, stupid thing to do.

When the Child landed, Eulalia just about climbed atop Kine and dragged her down herself. 'You—you purposefully disobeyed my wishes!' Her tongue stumbled within her mouth as she tried to find something in the Svarnish tongue that would properly articulate her frustration. Eulalia whistled and Zoraida approached, arguing with Kine in great draconic operatic. The Child hurriedly dismounted, clambering down to meet Eulalia, who grasped her dress and hauled her across the entryway.

'What have you done? What were you thinking?'

'It's what you would have done!' The Child's face was flushed, her eyes alight with the fire of her conviction. 'If you were able to ride a dragon, you would have done ten times what I did! You would have destroyed them!'

Well, that was a flattering thought. Eulalia bit the inside of her cheek, suddenly possessed by such violent relief that the girl was alive that bright tears sprang to life in her eyes.

Muqdah. A voice reverberated through the city, projected through the earth and the air. *I am your end.*

Eulalia instinctively clutched the Child's narrow shoulders to her, heart thrumming. Her eyes sought Ohba, catching a glimpse of his auburn hair and Rasyl in his arms. She made to shout but was interrupted by a sudden drumming. Zoraida's eyes snapped away from Kine and flew to her, the dragon sweeping through the crowd in great strides to shelter Eulalia and the girl beneath a broad wing.

Destruction comes to me as easily as breathing. If you stand against me, I will mow you down. I will hang your renasci and leave them to rot. I will cleave your dragons in two. If you stand against me, your city will suffer for eternity, long after the last child has bent the knee.

There was a pause, in which all of Muqdah dangled on a terrible precipice. Dragonfolk crowded together, Eulalia's kin clutching one another. She railed against the stranger's presence but found herself unable to block Thurlow from her mind.

But I am not a vengeful god. I am merciful. I am giving you the chance to surrender. A chance to live. The greatest of your warriors have fallen before the might of the Imperium.

For those who have been kept in the dark, let me remind you.

Images that were not her own flashed behind Eulalia's eyes. Streets covered in sheets of blood, horns snapped and broken. Resplendent castles frozen with ice, devoid of any life. A shining, golden dragon pinned to the earth by a great spear. Svarna laid bare and bloody in its ruin.

Bronnuq stumbled through the crowd and pushed around Zoraida's wing, Ohba clutching at him in an attempt to steady his gait. Eulalia looked at the Child and saw a ghost in her eyes, wavering and frightened.

'It's not real,' she told her child. She lied. 'It's not real, don't look at it. Don't.'

A woman who bore a marked resemblance to their once-queen, body splayed and impaled. Eulalia recoiled, stomach heaving as she stumbled away, trying to wrench herself free of the vice-like grip upon her mind. Ohba's arm closed around her shoulders and drew both mother and daughter towards him, as if to shield them from the horrors. Adil tucked himself within Zoraida's wing, eyes bloodshot and reaching immediately for them.

Free yourself of their fate. Surrender. Bend the knee. Live within the Eschalion's reign.

The silence that followed was deafening. Eulalia did not release the Child from her grasp, terrified that were she to let her loose, Thurlow would reach through the ether and seize her daughter. She took several heaving breaths.

The First Temple stood together, awaiting more words that did not come. When she looked around, Eulalia found that most of their kin were staring at where the council had gathered. She, in turn, looked at the men before her – stunned into silence.

'Project my voice,' Eulalia snapped. 'Let me talk.'

The council of priests looked between each other. Bronnuq was the first to nod, tapping his staff on the stone. Cuinu was the last, the temple's magic taking the resolution to him. All the temple needed was intent.

Golden light burst from the stones, circling the entryway as it struck each member of the council, before the Blessings of all Muqdah filled Eulalia, her veins alight with overwhelming awareness, as though emerging from a lifetime of darkness. She stared out from the temple – from every temple in Muqdah – and saw Thurlow's army refracted in her mind like shattered glass. Immediately, she tried to speak of the dragon riders, but found her voice caught, hooked in her throat by an invisible force.

Tears sprang to her eyes as she strained against the temple's magic. She could speak for Muqdah, but because they could not reach a consensus about the war dragons, the First Temple would rather strangle her than allow her to go against the council's decree. Such power within her grasp, only to be hamstrung by that same ancient magic ... the futility of it threatened to overwhelm her.

But she took a deep breath, finding her marble spine once more, and spoke to those who would hear her.

This is the sanctuary Morouqdi, the First Temple of Muqdah. We are the oldest hallowed ground in Svarna. We have nurtured dragon eggs since the first stone was lain in this city. We have known gods and strangers, and we knew the first Eschalion. Eschalier the First sat upon a dragon only because the first renasci allowed it. You are no Eschalion, Thurlow Thurlowe. You are the mad dog of the Imperium.

Eulalia stopped to take a breath, to open her eyes and behold the people who stood with her. Their faces echoed with hope, a resolution that she had not seen since the first bolt of lightning had struck. She swallowed hard.

I do not know how you have broken the wards that protect this city, but you have seen the might of one dragon, Thurlow Thurlowe, and you will experience a city of fire before this war is through. Muqdah has stood witness to the rise of the Imperium, and it will stand witness to its fall. We kneel to no man.

A cry rose from the city. It was not the wailing of the forsaken or the forgotten – it filled the sky like the very call of the gods. A thousand voices rose as one, a battle-cry.

A rumbling came from within Morouqdi. It was not the temple's magic or the quaking earth that Thurlow had beset upon the city – it shifted the winds like the tides of heaven. Idunn, the mother of Morouqdi's dragons, rose from her nest.

Her roar coursed through Eulalia, sent sweat beading on her brow. The sound poured out of Morouqdi, filling the sky above Muqdah and bringing all of their voices together in one great symphony.

Thurlow had but one reply.

So be it.

Anticipating one's doom was entirely different to feeling it. Hearing it. Watching it approach. The sense of security within the First Temple was slipping away, and despite herself, how pragmatic she'd attempted to be, Eulalia felt betrayed.

Women felt this. At a certain age, all girls were faced with the inevitable realisation that they were not as protected from the world as their naïveté had led them to believe. They were raised on fairy tales depicting the might of Svarna; they were the draconic daughters of Svarna. But that did not save them from men who snuck their hands up their skirts. From lecherous stares. Perhaps it had been childish of Eulalia to think, even for a moment, that Morouqdi could have been any different. Perhaps she should have embraced the war when it came, rather than try to escape it and prolong her own fate.

Her mind spiralled in the face of an inevitable doom. But she would not let the children feed off her distress. Eulalia allowed herself to step into that tempest alone.

She sat side by side with Fidela, keeping watch over the sleeping Child in a chamber deep within the heart of the First Temple. The stone above was a haven, solid, containing, allowing them to imagine their world was not unravelling entirely. Fidela was nestled into Eulalia's side, fresh from the bath, smelling of lilies and fresh oranges. Silence had consumed Eulalia all evening, away from the sky and the vanishing shield above Muqdah.

Their little dragon rider had refused to debate what she had done. She had shut down when Eulalia pressed, with that stubborn set to her jaw that meant that there was no point in arguing. Not knowing what to do with her, Eulalia had simply thrust Rasyl into her arms and dragged her away while they'd grappled with their incoming reality.

Bright, gentle Fidela was the only one brave enough to break this particular silence. She did so hesitantly, her fingers trailing over an exposed stretch of Eulalia's leg. 'She thought she was doing the right thing, Eulalia.'

The Child had done the right thing, which was why Eulalia was so bloody furious about it. She had done exactly what Eulalia had been wishing was done since the first bolt. But she was still a child. It should not have been her responsibility to defend their city. Only the ineptitude of the Council that had driven her forward – all but forcing a child to ride out was unhinged and unfair.

'Rage should not consume her at such a young age. Not like this.' She rolled her eyes and eased herself along the bed, sliding her legs behind Fidela's back and looking at the ceiling. 'She could have gotten herself killed, Fidela. When you have your first child, you'll understand – I would do anything to have her ignore her stupid, brave instincts and live a long life.'

Fidela climbed onto the bed, sitting on her knees and peering down at Eulalia. Her dark hands reached up and cupped Eulalia's face, and slowly, reluctantly, Eulalia allowed herself to turn towards that gentle pull. 'She is her mother's daughter. I'd think rage was inherited in the womb with you.' Fidela was the only person in the First Temple who may have been able to get away with saying that to her.

'She is Idunn's daughter. Dragonflame forges a person unlike any other.' The words came out flat and unconvincing.

Fidela blew out a long breath. 'I know you love your children, Eulalia.'

'Yes, I love my children.' Eulalia had that one thoroughly rehearsed. She groaned quietly, hand resting upon her rotund belly. 'I love all the children of the First Temple. That is our duty.'

Fidela rolled her eyes. Eulalia knew what she was searching for in her prying, knew why she was pressing Eulalia's boundaries. She had never discussed her motherhood with Fidela in this way because she'd spent years disconnecting herself from it. Fidela longed for Eulalia's approach to motherhood to not be so utilitarian, to find something soft and doting within her. Her fingers stroked the side of Eulalia's face as she bit her lip thoughtfully, looking between Eulalia and the slumbering girl across the chamber. Eula knew that she would not like where this conversation was going, but she made no effort to shift it, too tired from a lifetime's worth of battling.

'Why don't you call her by her name?' Fidela asked, daring to press where very few had in the fourteen years Eulalia had lived within the First Temple. She had not asked the question maliciously – it was not in her nature. Yet, Eulalia found her heart turning to lead at the mere thought of articulating what had hung over her for so long.

'Why do you think?' Eulalia asked, sliding off the bed and onto her feet. She shuffled over to where the girl slept, tucked beneath a woven blanket. 'I have no illusions of motherhood. I knew when I came to the temple what I wanted from life. I wanted to give my children to the temples, who would care for them better than I ever could. I didn't know what she'd become when I birthed her, only that she'd be a girl. Then she came out with her Blessing and the holy men named her theirs, the child of prophecy. She was no longer mine at all. I thought I'd have a moment before I passed her into the hands of the temple, to hold her, but they took one look at her and placed a claim upon her. She was never mine. Svarna claimed her from her first breath. The First Temple called her its daughter.

'But we were at war. The Eschalion declared war upon Svarna two years before I got pregnant, and we were in the thick of it, so we lost some of our privileges as people. The man who got me pregnant was lost to the conflict in the north. We had to come to grasp with some very hard truths. My truth was that my children were very unlikely to survive the elves.'

The Eschalion were not human to Eulalia. They were not dragons, who nested and hoarded and built community. They were death. They left the earth grey and ghostly in their wake. They had taken the girl's father, and they would have never even known his name.

Eulalia had not been terribly attached to the Child's father. They had been closer to a tryst than a real love affair, but he had been sweet. He had thought himself chivalrous. She never learnt what had happened to him, only that he'd taken his family caravan through the north to visit his grandsire and seemingly been ambushed. They'd found his beautiful caravan upturned, burnt through to a husk, the Eschalion sigil magically marked in the ground. Being informed of his death was Eulalia's earliest memory in which she'd understood, in some primal way, how terrible the world was about to become for them.

'I called her Nuru when she was born. Light, for the light of Svarna. Yet, she has never had the chance to be the girl that I'd named her for. She has only had the chance to be the chosen one – so acutely aware of her duty and the pressure that will be placed on her. Too smart for her own good, and twice as kind as I've ever been.' Eulalia sighed. She wanted so much from the world. She wanted to know that people were good and that they valued each other, that they valued the power of a community who stood for one another. She wanted justice. She wanted to know that some corner of the world was fair. Yet, she could no longer be disappointed. 'I couldn't bring myself to get attached to these children in that way. If I kept calling her Nuru, it would make her real in a way that I don't think I could bear. I've been letting her go since the moment she was born. I'm a terrible mother, Fidela.'

'You're a wonderful mother, Eula.' Fidela took one of Eulalia's hands in hers, squeezing it gently.

'And you are the best companion I could have asked for – but you are a liar.'

Chapter Fourteen

THE IMPERIUM

Here was something that Zuri learned almost immediately about Takuma of Svarna – he liked to talk.

It was his greatest strength and, perhaps, his greatest flaw.

Amidst the flurry of directions shortly after Zuri's arrival, Takuma had made the executive decision that she needed to have her horns fixed. They made him uncomfortable to look at, which was no surprise. They were deeply uncomfortable to have attached to her since they'd broken, and the cause of the piercing headaches that struck behind her eyes.

By the morning light, his barrage of conversation seemed subdued yet persistent. Having gotten very little sleep, he was distinctly rumpled and undone, whistling as they wandered.

She wondered if there was anything Takuma could do that would make him less attractive. Kicking a small animal might have done the trick. It was infuriating. He was obnoxiously good-looking and distinctly Svarnish, down to his full mouth and the cocky way that he tossed his hair when he caught a stranger's eye on their morning stroll.

The Travellers' Corner was comfortingly Svarnish. A square nestled into the heart of the Imperium, it was a short walk from the red-light district, placed along a flat road lined with trees whose garnet leaves shone in the sun. Caravans bordered the streets, the beasts that pulled them tucked into stables, swarms of Svarns milling about. How strange it was, to suddenly be amongst her own people after such solitude. Zuri found herself frozen on the road as her vision flooded with dozens of her horned kinfolk, dawdling through their morning routine in utter peace.

Takuma patted her on the shoulder, nudging her along and into the fray.

The caravans were pulled by great workhorses or oxen, depending on the master of the house. Zuri was struck by the look of two shining black beasts with braided manes and glistening eyes.

'The winds greet you, miss.' A well-dressed merchant with heavily silvering hair emerged from within his stall. 'How is it we've not seen you around before?'

'I've been elsewhere, I'm afraid. Away from family.' She smiled plaintively and was glad for the merchant knowing better than to pry upon the affairs of a stranger. There was no easy explanation as to why she'd been away from her kinfolk. 'You have such beautiful horses.'

'Well, it's nice to have you back with us.' The stranger gave a firm nod, and they continued on.

Once she was done admiring the stallions, Takuma shepherded her towards the goldsmith's caravan. He was another distinctly Svarnish-looking man, with horns so heavily adorned that Zuri was surprised his neck could support the weight. The goldsmith took one look at her twisted, broken horns and made a disapproving noise only ever truly understood by the children of Svarnish parents.

Training Svarnish horns usually occurred in childhood, when their horns were yet to be set in their shape. Though Zuri had been young when the bastard brothers wrenched them, they'd disregarded the proper methods. The horns should have been fitted into something harder than them and allowed to grow into the shape, instead they'd chosen a method far less refined. Zuri had no idea how one fixed the damage that had been done to them.

'This is going to hurt,' the goldsmith told Takuma. They were speaking around Zuri, as men were prone to do. She did not take much offence to it, in all honesty, as distracted as she was with the bustle of the Imperium.

'It will hurt more to live with her horns in the state that they are.' Zuri had seen Hotaru's horns, one twisted slightly and broken by force. There was no question of why Takuma could speak with such authority on the matter. 'Best we get them fixed now. The Brass Wyvern's paying for it all, so do what you must.'

Only then did the goldsmith meet her eyes rather than stare at her horns. She smiled at the man, unfamiliar with the expression upon her face. She wondered if it looked too much like she were baring her teeth.

They spent a great deal of time sitting while the goldsmith explained the significant work that would be done to her horns, given how badly they had been damaged. He would have to force her horns shut by taking his hammer directly to them before they could be set. He had not done so to a lady before – usually errant children who mistakenly twisted their horns in accidents – but he was certain the work could be done. They settled on spiralling whorls of gold that would accentuate the shape of her horns; when presented with the broken anklets for melting down, to his credit, the stranger did not flinch.

The cage fitted to her horns were clasped with force, Zuri's brows furrowed in a permanent knot. While he worked, she and the elderly man talked at length about the state of the world and the most interesting gossip amongst the Svarnish caravans, even though the names involved meant very little to Zuri. But, for a little while, she was allowed to feel as if she were a child once more, indulging in the gossip of her many aunties.

Takuma, however, wasted little time. He made a show of lingering within reach while they worked, but he did not remain static. Instead, he quietly roiled with energy, his emerald eyes never entirely on one singular focus. Words traded just out of earshot when Zuri was distracted in conversation with the goldsmith, a note passed to a red-headed Nord woman Zuri didn't recognise – but she could have sworn she winked at her as she melted back into the crowd. Takuma must have noticed her watching because he seemed to become even more careful after that, casually slipping his hand onto the waist of their next visitor and leading them out of sight while Zuri was distracted.

'It will be uncomfortable for some time, but you'll feel much better when it is done,' the man said – a common refrain that would be echoed again and again as he worked. 'It was a nasty lot, who did this to you. You won't find any of their type amongst us.'

Once her horns were finally set, the cage bound firmly and gleaming in Imperial gold, Zuri and Takuma wandered through the Travellers' Corner together. The little square was a distinctly Svarnish meeting place, but there was a plethora of snowy Nords also, their caravans carved with protective runes, selling living wreaths of evergreen branches that shifted beneath their touch. There was even a small bevy of northern elves with their soft, downturned ears akin to that of rabbits. Zuri had only seen a Northern Elf once as a girl. She was struck by a glassmaker's work, wind chimes shimmering like icicles in the sun.

'Why have you all travelled down this far south?' Zuri asked, after she had wandered over and spent an appropriate amount of time making appreciative noises at the displays of craftsmanship.

The glassworker was slight, with a head of cool, grey curls and spotted ears. It was impossible to say how old the stranger was, but crow's feet were forming at the far corner of the elf's eyes, betraying his centuries of life.

'Our arch mage, istr Signsif, is attending the dread mage's festival at the Eschalion's request,' the elf responded, a whisper of disdain on his tone. 'She is of such a status that she should not be made to travel alone – especially not within the Imperium's walls.'

The name meant little to Zuri, but she nodded.

'Not all arch magi are of such a temperamental disposition, you know. That poor girl is still at their beck and call, but she has never been so powerful that she has forgotten her manners.' As the glassworker spoke, his ears twitched and shifted in a decidedly distracting way.

'What's this party about, eh?' Takuma asked the glassworker as Zuri picked up a gleaming charm that looked like a snowflake made large. 'I know it's for the glory of the Eschalion and all, but they've got to have an actual reason for all this fuss.'

'You don't know?' The craftsman raised an elegant brow. 'Thurlow Thurlowe is claiming that the last of Taena's line has finally been felled. Only the gods themselves know if that's the truth or a convenient note in the Eschalion's grand rule.'

Something sentimental twisted in Zuri. Queen Taena was the last queen of Svarna, and she'd had five children, two of whom had been grown at the time of Svarna's fall. To think they'd been hunted down and slaughtered ...

Seemingly attuned to her discomfort, Takuma's vibrant eyes flicked to hers. He did not ask anything more of the party, but she could have sworn that she saw coin changing hands out of the corner of her eye.

He was working away. In the days that followed, Zuri realised that Takuma was always working away. There was not a moment between their morning and evening meals in which the gears within Takuma were not whirring. The dragon must have occupied his every thought, desperate as he was to give his companions the upper hand in an impossible heist. She decided, in that time, that he was utterly shameless about his thievery. He saw everything as a challenge.

He also pretended as if he had very little shame about his work, though Zuri had questions she dare not ask. Instead, she had taken to watching him from afar within the Wyvern, sitting in the laps of great men or with a woman in his. Performing for pleasure, he was transformed from the man whom Zuri was growing acquainted with. Instead of a gem, nestled in its setting, catching the light only when it pleased, he was much flashier when he was at play.

Zuri liked Takuma. She liked him far more than she was comfortable admitting. Given, that he was the first man that she'd met after her lengthy capture, however, and the role he'd played in her safety, she was trying to tamp down on that feeling. It was instinctive – of course she'd adore him. One simply had to be decent to seem the shining paragon when contrasted with the men that she'd spent the last decade with. And Takuma was a performer to his marrow, so conscious of how he was perceived and portrayed, that she found herself itching to scratch beneath the surface. The Takuma he showed her was more subdued than those delivered to the clients of The Brass Wyvern. Takuma the Whore, the brothel incarnate, was a flashy creature who found many ways to say very little at all. He eked out information from his clients, teasing secrets and sighs from them in the same breath as he drew laughter. He enjoyed being fawned over and placed upon a bronze pedestal; he enjoyed being fed fat grapes by elvish women. There was some game to it.

Zuri did not think that it was always a pleasure.

One night, she spied Takuma curled up in an alcove, whispering in the ear of a half-elf with a shock of snowy hair. Something about him was jarring to Zuri – his bawdy, raucous laughter so at odds with the Takuma who had spent his days caring for her. He could be raucous, she thought, but there was never a crass element to it. The way that the half-elf raked his eyes over Takuma made goose flesh rise on Zuri's arms.

'One of the service staff in the palace kitchens,' Hotaru remarked. Zuri never noticed the blue-eyed woman until she chose to speak. Zuri's eyes shot upwards to locate her shadow in the rafters. She was sitting with her legs tucked around a beam, swaddled in scarlet wool. 'They still lick the Eschalion's boots, but they're closer to nobility, so they think themselves special. Loose tongues, though. Must come with the submission.'

Hotaru spoke almost exclusively in Svarnish, Zuri noticed. She watched the Nords and the elvish lot, sharper-eyed than Zuri had given them credit for, and refused to allow her tongue to give her away. Zuri and Hotaru sat together in silence, watching Takuma be fawned over by a stranger until Zuri grew tired of the whole affair.

The first night that Zuri awoke screaming in the black of night, Nuru was first through the door. She took Zuri in her arms and settled her, swore to her that she was safe. Spoke to her calmly in Svarnish until her thundering heart settled in her chest, and then thrust a cup of hot tea into her hands.

The second night it was Andraste, the nanny, with her calloused hands and humming. It occurred to Zuri, that night, that she must not have been far from a wailing child, afraid of the elvish boogeyman.

'If I could just get a lock of their hair, I'd make sure they never slept peacefully again, you know. I'd keep them up every night worrying about the shadows.' Zuri did not miss the fact that there was a shadow that followed the nanny, twice as tall with spiny edges like a leafless tree. Everyone in this brothel had their secrets.

On the third night, it was Hotaru who was sitting across the room, watching her in quiet from the windowsill. The thief crawled into bed with Zuri and lay with her atop the blankets, a dagger held thoughtfully in one hand. Zuri had lain awake for an age that evening, winding Hotaru's curly locks into a half-dozen braids until drowsiness overtook her. Despite the sanctuary provided by The Brass Wyvern's painted walls, it was as if she could feel the nightmares approaching like a dark cloud upon the horizon as night fell.

Her horns may have been fixed, but the easing of the pain in her temples did little to eradicate the ghosts of the Thurlowe bastards. When she felt the storm approaching for a fourth time, Zuri did not submit to the terror. She climbed out of bed, wrapped in the soft quilt they had given her, and started walking.

Zuri had not slept well in years, a side effect of living half a decade with two narcissists who were also awake at all hours of the night. She kept waiting for one of the brothers to burst into her new home and drag her back through the streets of the Imperium. Every unrecognised shadow or shape took the brothers' form. She suspected that it did not help that The Brass Wyvern bustled at night, full of the ambient and varied sounds of bedwork. It would not be hard for them to come on silent feet through this labyrinth of sound and find her, tucked away in a quiet corner.

She avoided the central room of The Brass Wyvern as she went, slipping into the surrounding hallways. She passed the kitchen, the bustling heart of the Wyvern's fire, with a small crew of chefs and kitchen hands at any given time. Some of the girls doubled as labouring hands there, an easy way of strengthening the community within these walls. It felt good to feel the floor beneath her feet, to know that her Blessing could take her wherever she wished. The front of the brothel was shadowy, the lamps snuffed or turned down as low as they could without delving the hallways into pitch.

'I would kill them for you if I could,' Takuma stood in the doorway behind her, half-draped in shadow. He wore a hefty scarf over his shoulders that looked well-worn, his face marked by growing hollows beneath his eyes. 'I think plenty of us would sleep better knowing that they were in the dirt.'

'A romantic notion,' Zuri sighed, shaking her head. 'Yet I pray they die slowly and painfully, with none of us within their reach. Maybe from the pox.' She patted the spot beside her on the stoop. After a breath, Takuma dropped down next to her.

He spoke with conviction. 'I pray they die with a knife buried in their throat.'

What a passionate figure the old country would have made of Takuma, had he been allowed to flourish in a land of peace. With his beautiful face and his Svarnish pride, there wouldn't have been a man or woman reluctant to fawn over him. Zuri supposed that was part of his power. The world folds to a beautiful person in small ways, opens doors that aren't available to those less blessed in the face.

'Not working tonight?' Zuri asked, regarding his plain clothes.

He shook his head. 'Not with the rain coming back in. Feliks and I are keeping an eye on things – didn't want to risk any interlopers thinking the weather was cover enough to try anything.'

'You think they'd try something?' She had thought it her own nervousness, something absurd, but here Takuma was with his knife in hand.

'I don't know,' he admitted, and not for the first time, Zuri felt like he was keeping something from her. He was not lying, but there was something beneath his words that she couldn't get a proper look at. 'I don't know them.

I know High Elves, though, and I know evil men. That's enough to keep me wary of a night like this. Just don't go wandering into the night without one of us, will you?'

She nodded. She knew now why most of the lights at the front of The Brass Wyvern were snuffed. It was so that Takuma and his ilk could trap anyone who walked in the darkness, as if it would protect them. She wondered if Virnoi would be blocking a doorway if she glanced back, but the thought sent a shiver through her, so she didn't dare. She should not risk scaring herself so badly with her nightmares at hand – he cut quite the ghoulish figure in shadow.

Zuri was almost certain that the dark-haired elf was not entirely a High Elf. He certainly had the blood in him – his height gave that away – but there was a peculiarity to his features that felt distinctly foreign. There were several elvish tribes who varied greatly in shape and tradition, but she had never met them. Never known them. She could not have known how to tell a High Elf from a Northern Elf or a Wood Elf – she simply knew they were vastly unalike one another.

They sat together for a while with only the rain for company, staring out into the quiet storm. It was not the same as the apocalyptic downpour on the night of her escape. Something about the wash of rain was more temperate, but it quieted the red-light district all the same, each pleasure house having drawn back within itself. There were other silhouettes that lingered on the porches, likely having their own hushed conversations beneath the drum of the rain.

She'd never really known bed workers. She'd known of them prior to her captivity, but if any of the women in her caravan had worked in the profession, they'd kept it far from prying eyes. She wondered if all pleasure houses had the type of tight-knit community that The Brass Wyvern had.

'What is Feliks?' Zuri finally asked, after a good deal of consideration.

Takuma simply chuckled and shrugged. 'One of us. He's half Svarnish, that's all that really matters.'

'He reminds me of a black bear I once saw out the back of our caravan, sniffing around for food.' She raised her hands and tried to turn herself into a bear, curling her fingers into faux claws. She'd been far enough away from the animal that she'd been able to alert her family, but Zuri remembered how she had shivered when she'd picked out the dark shape from the forest, thinking of the children who wandered off from their parents when the afternoon grew long. She had sympathised with the thing, too, knowing that if it had not been starving, it probably would not have encroached upon them. 'Very cuddly looking, very big, very likely to rip off your hand if he decided you were tasty.'

'You're not entirely wrong,' Takuma said, a curious gleam in his eye. 'What caravan were you with? I know them all, you know. They all curse my name before they take their morning meals.'

Zuri found a fixed point in the road and studied that specific brick beneath the lamplight, gathering her blanket shawl around her shoulders.

'I was a caravan baby, born under the Meadow King – Dayo's father at the time. Our caravan was in motion before the fall of Muqdah, but when they picked up too many children to risk going back into the battlefield. When the Imperium announced they would take Svarnish refugees, they took the chance and migrated north. I think they let us in because the caravan was largely made of performers and healers. We were palatable.' Zuri's mother had told her that many of the caravans who'd appealed for sanctuary had been refused, despite the façade of refugee intake. They were lucky. It had allowed them to avoid the war. 'We were safe for a little while. It was nice. My mother was an acrobat, and my father was a performer – they were an act together. She was the one with the Blessed feet, the best tightrope walker you've ever seen. He had a Blessed spine, so naturally I popped out about as acrobatic as children can be.'

'The trouble started when Dayo's father got into it with some Imperial guards. He was more of a revolutionary than the Imperium had expected, a proper proud Svarnishman. He was just trying to protect his folk, but they didn't like that, of course. I remember the day he died.' Everyone in the caravan had looked up to him, including his son. Dayo had been forced to take responsibility too quickly – a gentle-hearted boy quickly hardened beneath an Imperial hammer. 'So, Dayo took up the mantle and the caravan tried to continue on as they were. But suddenly, we were not welcome in plenty of places because word had gotten out. They were trying to ice the caravan out of profit and watch its people waste away, defect to other caravans, but everyone was too loyal. We loved each other too much. We were family, and no one was about to abandon the new boy king. Dayo was barely sixteen.'

Zuri sighed. She wasn't sure how long that particular sigh had been trapped inside of her, waiting to be freed, but it had floated around the tomb of her body for some time.

'If it's painful, you don't have to tell me. I don't expect that from anyone.'

She patted Takuma idly on the leg and continued. 'Dayo brought us to this city, the true Imperium, when he heard that several merchant kings had gathered to talk – I think he was going to ask them for help. But the guard descended on the caravan. It was all bullshit. They claimed that we were harbouring an enemy of the empire, which we weren't. They started arresting people, and I saw Dayo knocked down and taken away, so I ran. I don't know what happened to my parents. I was such a caravan baby that I didn't even know how to find my way in a city, which is probably how the brothers found me.'

'I'm sure your parents are out there,' Takuma said after a moment. 'Some of the hardiest people I've ever met are performers.'

Her breath hitched, and she felt a lump rise in her throat. It was hope that she'd held on to for a long time that Maldwyn had taken specific joy in grinding to dust. She had thought there no place for Svarnishman amidst the Imperium, and here she was, sitting in an almost entirely Svarnish brothel, with people who had carved out their own corner of the world. Zuri swallowed, trying to quiet herself.

'But you were an acrobat?' Takuma continued on with a laugh, nudging her. 'That must mean you're very bendy, no?'

'I used to be.' Zuri laughed weakly as she stretched her legs out into the rain, testing how flexible her feet were. The priest, Taliesin, had done an astounding job in healing them – not a lick of pain echoed within her body. She suspected that he'd done more than just heal her feet that evening, as there were several old aches that had mysteriously stopped ailing her. The healer had restored something forgotten; she would have to thank him for that. 'I don't think you ever lose it entirely. I tried to keep stretching while I was locked up, hoping I'd be able to shimmy through some tiny window and out to freedom.'

'Do you still know any tricks?' Takuma asked. Zuri knew what he was doing, but she allowed herself to fall into the trap of it. She allowed herself to be cajoled, to soften beneath his teasing.

'Maybe,' Zuri said as she hopped up to her feet. 'Would you like to see one?'

'Absolutely.' He shuffled around to face her as she stood. Zuri discarded the blanket she had wrapped herself in, allowing it to fall soundlessly to the wood below her. It left her exposed to the cool air, but she did not mind it, the chill banishing some of the exhaustion that came with her scattered sleep. She straightened, touching her heels together as she balanced momentarily on the balls of her feet. The moment she stood with purpose, her Blessing took over, holding her aloft. She had never known imbalance in the same way that others had; the world had given her this much. If she had a foot on the ground, she would always find her centre of balance, the magic of the world anchoring her in place.

With a running start, she threw herself forward into a cartwheel. Zuri felt instantly weightless, a bird taking flight. Using her momentum, she did another and shifted her weight mid-air so that she was flipping forward on both hands. Zuri bounced upwards and landed on her feet – it was an otherwise simple trick, but still the first she'd attempted freely in a long while.

Takuma broke into a round of applause as she dropped into a deep bow with a flourish at the wrist. Zuri found she was smiling despite herself.

'Can you teach me how to do that?' he asked, hopping to his feet.

'I can try,' she said sceptically. Zuri trotted back to where she'd began the trick, sizing herself up beside Takuma. 'Your horns are a little vertical for all the cartwheeling, though.'

Takuma glanced upwards. His horns were elaborately curved in a way that she doubted was entirely natural. 'I suppose I would get stuck, eh?'

'Maybe. My father had big horns, but I never understood how he managed. He had to change every manoeuvre to adjust for how different his centre of balance was,' Zuri mused. 'Your arms are longer than your horns, though, so you might be able to do it.'

Together, they walked through the steps, and she flew through the tumble again and again, the shadows of the nightmare gone as her body trilled with freedom. She had stolen moments to practise in those accursed halls, stretching each muscle meticulously while the brothers had slept mere metres away, but it was wildly exciting to know that her body still knew how the work was done. There was not a flicker of fear that a hand was going to fly out of the darkness and seize at her, ready to reprimand her if things went awry.

'So, you and your wife started this place?' Zuri probed after a moment, thinking of beautiful Nuru and her soft, feminine curves. Takuma choked on several words, stumbling verbally for the first time since they'd met.

'Nuru—Nuru's not my wife.' He coughed. 'Don't get me wrong, we're close, but she and I are friends. We got each other out of a hard spot and started the business together.'

'Oh—' For a moment, Zuri was glad for the gloom, as it hid the flush that was almost certainly creeping into her features. 'I just thought—'

'Everyone thinks it. People think Nema is my baby, that I helped her escape her last husband just to marry her for myself. It's a selfish thing to think of someone. We're close, sure, and I won't deny that we rollick regularly, but we're not like that. She wants a husband who's going to carry her away to some country farm, where they grow flowers together and baby a herd of sheep – that's not me.' It was hard to envision Takuma that way, in a pair of patchwork overalls and a roughly hewn tunic. 'For a while, I wished that I could be that for her, but I like the city. I like movement. I like stealing away into places I shouldn't be and being a threat to society. That's not what she wants.'

She made a thoughtful noise and shuffled the conversation away from Nuru, reluctant to admit the source of her curiosity. Zuri had never been particularly good at flirtation; she hadn't had much of a chance to practise, but Takuma's voice was as sweet as thickened chocolate and his eyes were luminously blue.

'I always liked how crowded it was in the caravan. Being out in the fields was more unsettling than anything, just long grass as far as the eye could see. It feels like there's something sitting in the quiet when you're on your own out there.' Zuri had issues with all sorts of noise. If it was far too quiet, she grew unsettled and restless, anticipating that there was something waiting in that heavy weight over the world. Yet, when the world was far too loud, she withdrew – each murmur and shout made her want to throw herself into the void. Her father had once had a similar sensitivity, having worn a headdress that softened the world and made that great noise bearable. 'So, Nuru is not your wife, but you are family? Kinfolk?'

'Kinfolk' was a Svarnish concept. Family baked and bred by blood was important, but kinfolk – family made by time and the rivers of choice – could fuel a person's soul just as well. The bonds that one forged by their own hand could carry them through the world just as well as those that the gods gifted them. Takuma nodded emphatically, evidently pleased by the thought.

'Pretty much everyone here is. It started as just another pleasure house where we brought along other Svarnish folk. We both knew we'd be more comfortable surrounded by our own. But as time went on, everyone sort of galvanised around the house. There aren't many other places in this city where a Svarnishman can just exist. After a little while, we even figured out the guards would leave us be if we fed them a little extra coin on occasion, which brought in people from all over who had no interest in bedwork but needed a home. I didn't really mind that, it's just hard finding them the work. This place can only fit so many wanderers.'

'And Virnoi blew in with the wind?'

He let out an uncertain laugh, thrown off-kilter by the prod.

'Virnoi is an anomaly – but having anomalies is good, no?' In what Zuri thought was probably a nervous tick, Takuma extracted a knife from beneath his shirt and began to flip it idly over his nimble fingers. His brown hands were covered in rings of varying size and flourish, sparkling gemstones set in bright golds and warm, rosy tones. They were mostly real, she thought. 'One hopes for at least one pleasant anomaly to catch them off guard and keep them on their toes. He and Hotaru are my personal nightmares, to keep for myself.'

Hotaru, the other vivid-eyed denizen of The Brass Wyvern, who was constantly concealed beneath a blanket of worn linen and knitwear. Zuri had the distinct impression that The Brass Wyvern had heaped its hand-me-downs directly onto Hotaru, and she'd simply never made her way out from beneath the pile.

'That seems like a lovely family to have,' Zuri whispered. Takuma said nothing. He did not need to. He put away his knife, reached over and pulled her into an embrace that turned the whole world warm.

CHAPTER FIFTEEN

THE IMPERIUM

'Okay, so – here's the plan.' Takuma said, taking a long breath as he seemed to prepare himself across the table. Virnoi took up a carafe of summer wine and poured a glass for himself as he listened, his energy long since quietly burnt out. 'I've kept my ear to the ground, and I've been talking to some of Thurlowe's kitchen hands. We're going in through the playrooms. For his events, Thurlow Thurlowe hires out some help from the red-light district to entertain the elvish nobility he finds fit to keep company with. That's an easy way in for us – no one's going to question a handful of extra bedworkers when half the district is there.'

Nuru made an agreeable noise from beside Takuma. 'Taliesin says that his father is a fiend for women. When his wife died, he married her sister, who was barely of marriageable age by elvish standards. He has a roster of women who come in and out of that place at all hours, barely any regulars. It's a surprise he hasn't cycled through most of the city.'

'Not all of them make it out,' Virnoi sighed. He had arrived at his cemetery many-a-time to find their lifeless bodies, little more than girls with scarlet ribbons in their hair. There was a round of affirmative noises, though he suspected none of them realised the depth of the depravity they would be faced with.

'But we will because I've got this figured out.' Takuma shot Virnoi a look.

The mage shrugged. He flicked his wrist, and the projection of the Thurlowe estate rotated idly above the table.

'Nuru and I will go through the playrooms,' Takuma continued, 'masquerading as bedworkers hired for the occasion. It's the easiest way for us to go in, no one wants to think too hard about the flesh they're trading down there.'

'I'll go with you,' Zuri chirped. She was half-buried beneath several layers of blankets that Virnoi had woven himself, her freshly set horns now rimmed with gold that gleamed in the firelight. 'It will be easier to get me in as an entertainer, no?'

'Yes, it would be easier,' Takuma began, rolling his head in a circle as he thought. 'But I wouldn't write you into that role if you weren't comfortable with it. There are a few ways to get in through the kitchen and with Virnoi if need be. It is no real trouble.'

It was a horrific thought to Virnoi, to wrap her back up in the farce of pleasure after all she had been through. It would be no less horrific for Takuma, who did not much enjoy the work himself, but Virnoi refrained from saying anything. He sipped his wine. There was a dull ache in his arm from where he'd opened a vein the night before, and the alcohol would numb the feeling of it.

'We work on the ground,' Takuma continued. 'You, me, Nuru, and Feliks – to get the dragon unbound. There are things that we need to take care of. One, the dragon is fed in the evening, according to the wait staff. It is fed drugged meat, which is why it's unable to control the gas it's producing. It can't fly. They're going to give it one lesser dose because I slipped them some coin, but on the night, we're going to need to make sure it gets a hunk of untainted meat. It will need the fuel to start regulating its own body and be able to communicate in its right mind. Feliks, I think that one's going to be you.'

Virnoi thought that Feliks nodded in between frantic bites of a turkey leg.

'Back in Muqdah, the holy men would sometimes keep sick or hurt dragons sedated so that they were easier to care for. It's not unheard of, they're likely just trying to imitate the method that Thurlow would have seen during the war,' Nuru explained, waving her hands in the air. 'It's very hard to keep a dragon consistently under that sort of sedation. Their system burns through medication and toxins swiftly, with huge daily food intakes, so you have to medicate them with every meal. Otherwise, they'll just be back on their feet again.'

'Is the dragon sick?' Hotaru asked, piping up from beneath the table. She sat under there to eat, preferring to take her meals in a place with decent cover.

'We don't know,' Takuma responded. 'I wouldn't think so, considering how much of a show Thurlow is putting on, but none of the people I'm talking to know enough about dragons to say. Most of them haven't even seen it, only worked around the existence of the beast.'

'I really hope it's not sick,' Virnoi muttered. 'Healing magic isn't exactly my forte.'

Virnoi's forte was the magic of sacrifice and equal exchange. He'd spent years learning to turn his magic to any task, but it had its limitations.

'I hope it's not sick, too.' Takuma sighed. 'But if it can't fly, it should still be able to walk. With that magic book of yours, we should be able to figure it all out – we'll float it out if we have to, turn it into a cat or something.'

'Transfiguration doesn't work like that. You're not taking mass into account,' Virnoi responded. 'I will aspire to figure it out. This is what magic is built for.'

'Famous last words,' Feliks chuckled. A symphony of uneasy, good-humoured laughter went around the Svarns at the table, though Virnoi sensed only quiet from Hotaru. They were set upon this path, like birds upon the north wind, but Virnoi was less confident of their plan. Takuma flew through many a plan on gut instinct alone, and he often faced the consequences of those decisions. Virnoi did not know if his lover was prepared for the consequences of taking his Wyverns with him into the fray.

'So, one of us gets into the kitchens and either cleanses the meat or makes sure that whatever's getting sent does not reach the dragon. Feliks – most of those kitchen workers are Nords.' Feliks nodded, still busy gobbling down his meal. 'From there, we break away from the celebrations to go deal with the dragon directly. We go in, and Virnoi goes up to the top of the dome.'

'I can't undo the wards that are concealing the dome from the rest of the Imperium. That would take about a week of spellwork and enough active magic that it would draw the eye of the guard. The runes are hefty shit that I hoped would at least be beginning to unravel, but I went poking around the estate last night and there's no movement there. So, I'll use their illusory work as cover.' He extended a knitting needle he'd had resting on the table and motioned broadly at the top of the Thurlow estate. 'My plan is not to fuck with the dome itself. The top of it is made of Prismarium glass, which is resistant to physical destruction and magical tampering. Prismarium glass – prianieeria – was gifted to the elvish people by their god of plenty, Iliera, a deity who was sub-opted from Nord lore and adapted in the second Eschalion's reign.'

Andraste made a rude noise from where she was making a pot of tea. 'Illiera is Odrigg to us. She was a god of plenty, but her gifts were not infallible. My people never associated her with glass.'

'Probably because they made it up,' Virnoi shrugged. 'It wouldn't be the first time. Besides, the point – the issue with using prianieeria for anything is that it's the only part of the structure that remains unbreakable. It has to be attached to something, and this dome is attached to the building itself. There's an internal framework built to support it, reinforced with steel, that I could tamper with, but it's likely to be hefty and warded for stability because of what it's supporting. I could try unravelling the spellwork, but there will be a whole host of work on that tower – heat protection, tremor steadying, intruder wards. I don't want to have to worry about both that and working on the dome. If we're lucky, he'll have been lazy and paid another mage to place them on the estate entirely.'

In her chair, Nuru hummed. 'And why, exactly, have you been looking into elvish protective wards?'

'Personal reasons.' Virnoi avoided Nuru's stare by instead looking to Zuri. She didn't know him well enough to be suspicious of him. There were plenty of facets within the Eschalion's Imperium that Virnoi investigated because he had to. Driven forward by spite and fascination, he quietly pried into countless places he wouldn't have otherwise been permitted. 'My first plan was a displacement of the dome in its entirety. I know that sounds frightening in scale, but depending on the spellwork wound around the estate, they may have very little protection from temporal displacement. I take the top of the tower and put it in a different plane of existence for a short while, so that the dragon can fly free.

'If the illusory spellwork has been temporarily built into the building and not the dome, no one in the city should notice the dome's disappearance. From what I can tell, the illusion is not simply one that clouds the appearance of the dome. It fabricates the appearance of the dome entirely. If they've done it correctly, when the dome is removed from this plane of existence, it shouldn't even cause a visual blip.' Warding spellwork was a game of placement and purpose. There were a bunch of loopholes one could manipulate if they knew their way around the craft. 'But that plan presumes that they'll be capable of flight.'

It made a dozen different presumptions about the Thurlowe estate, based off Virnoi's working knowledge of the nobility and his own capabilities, neither of which were entirely dependable. His arcane focus, a book of shadows that he had inherited from his mother, held far more knowledge than Virnoi himself was privy to. It had a way of presenting him strange, niche spells just as he'd needed them, but also wrenching his plans out from beneath him.

There was no way of explaining all of that to Takuma without disclosing information Virnoi would much rather stay buried in the unmarked mental grave in which he kept all of his trauma. Instead, he did what he did best and came up with contingencies. 'So, there's a secondary plan. On the off chance that we can't get the thing off its medication quickly enough.

'Hotaru and I will come through an entry point high along the tower wall and into the main chamber. There's a tunnel at the very base of the tower, just beneath the chamber, that's broader than the rest. I'm presuming this is where they've transported the dragon through in the first place. It appears to be sealed off, but with a little magic and some firepower, we should be able to blow the wall open.' There were presumptions made of this plan as well. He was working off second-hand information and Takuma's guidance, which was usually well-intentioned but chaotic at the best of times. 'We blow the tunnel while everyone's focused on the festival and the revelry, levitate the dragon, and run like hell. I can't transfigure the thing into a size that we could carry, but I figure if we get out to the parade and the dragon is still sedated, I'll turn it into a float. Keeping something in magical stasis is far easier than teleporting a huge amount of mass at once.'

'None of those plans are exactly subtle,' Zuri spoke.

'It doesn't have to be,' Takuma responded, winking at the swaddled woman. 'Nothing about this has to be subtle as long as we don't get caught.'

'What do we do about all the noise? A silence spell of that size would draw too much attention,' Hotaru asked, having silently emerged from her hideaway while Virnoi talked. 'With the festival going on, we probably don't have to worry so much about subtlety. But if their estate suddenly falls to pieces above their heads because we blew out a structural wall, they'll probably notice the mage pulling it apart.'

'Have some faith, little crow,' Virnoi laughed, scooping her into his lap.

'And we'll have plenty of noise to cover us,' Takuma amended. 'While Zuri and I were down in the Traveller's Corner, I noticed several traders have brought in sparklers – huge, hefty fireworks that will turn the sky bright. The night's going to crackle with magic. We'll just be a whisper in comparison.'

'And what is the plan,' Feliks probed, 'if things go wrong?'

'If a few things go wrong … eh, we improvise. A plan is nothing more than that – a plan. It's an idea of how we're going to do this. If we have to flip some of the plan sideways to make it work, that's what we do. If things go terribly wrong, we run.' This was a common strategy of Takuma's while grave-robbing. If a tomb he'd disturbed happened to be the resting place of a lich rather than a skeleton, he ran. 'We have one night with one semi-feasible excuse to find ourselves in Thurlowe's estate without facing immediate arrest, but if things go south, we take care of ourselves first and the heist second. I want the dragon out as much as all of you do, but not at the expense of anyone at this table. Besides, if we do end up having to run, we'll be fine because we're Svarnish. There's not a single elf in the Imperium who could outfox us.'

'So, going from unsubtle to explosive,' Zuri remarked. Takuma nodded.

'There are more than a dozen different ways for us to get out of Thurlowe's estate,' Nuru said. 'And it's not very far before you're in the Golden Quarter, which Hotaru can attest has some pretty fantastic hiding places to hunker down until a storm passes.' She used the perfectly calming tone Virnoi had heard her employ to settle both Takuma and her babe. She had the capacity to wind any man around her finger given enough time, Virnoi knew. He'd watched her closely enough.

While he didn't know the particulars of it, Virnoi knew the signs that Takuma and Nuru had gotten into an argument. This wasn't particularly irregular for them. The pair loved each other fiercely and fought just as voraciously, far too alike to coexist without some warring conflict. Virnoi had theorised for some time that they'd actually both be quite bored if it hadn't been for how they jabbed at one another.

He hadn't pried into what their argument had been about, but he was certain neither had backed down.

'We are going to do all we can to get that dragon into the skies in a night, but if it doesn't work, if something fails—' Takuma spoke once more, stopping awkwardly as his voice caught in a peculiar spot in his throat. Hotaru stilled in Virnoi's lap, leaning up onto the table. Their lover's emerald eyes were shadowed for a moment before Nuru patted him on the shoulder.

'If one of us gets nabbed,' Nuru continued, 'the rest scatter. Takuma and I will get you out. It wouldn't be the first time we've had to bail one of our own out of an Imperial jail. If you have a weapon or anything stolen on you, ditch it before they drag you away.'

Virnoi had not been privy to these incidents, but he had heard plenty. One of the bedworkers had tangled with an errant guard, and Nuru and Takuma had taken to the streets with nothing but a handful of knives and Nuru's magic tongue. They'd walked their friend out of prison without issue, and the guard had never bothered anyone in the red-light district again. It had been a good measure of how much the pair could get away with in the long run.

'And despite any concern, you have me,' Virnoi said. 'There's only one mage of my calibre I know on this side of the Imperium that has anything close to my magic, and he couldn't do half of what I do with it. We'll be fine as long as we stay out of Thurlow's way. We get in, we get the dragon, we get out.'

Virnoi was far less settled than he presented, but it seemed to him that if he panicked, this semblance of bravery that had emerged within the shadow of The Brass Wyvern would fall apart at the seams. So he kept his mouth shut and free of doubt.

It was long after dinner and the rest of The Brass Wyvern had settled into their evening routine that Virnoi turned his mind away from their impending heist and instead to his lovers. He had indulged in this talk of dragons for long enough, and as intimate of a gesture as that was for Takuma, it did nothing for Hotaru.

Takuma had continued on when Virnoi had fallen silent, chattering away to his compatriots to figure out the finer details of this mess. Virnoi had retreated within his shell as he awaited a shift in the evening's agenda. There was always a shift when Takuma was scheming, for the man burned with so much energy that would need to be expelled before he could dare rest. Virnoi was often the outlet for such behaviour, hence his canny capacity to sense its arrival.

When it was only Feliks left, mulling over how much he could carry at a stretch, Virnoi nudged a dozing Hotaru from his lap. She had no tolerance for their hours, and living within the brothel had destroyed any sleeping pattern the woman might have developed in a normal home. She slept sitting, standing, or sprawled on whatever stretch of spare wood was unoccupied by clutter.

'Up on the table, little crow. Let me look at you while we have the chance.' Hotaru yawned but obliged, rubbing her eyes as she roused herself. Virnoi shot a look over at Takuma and Feliks, wrapped up shoulder to shoulder in the candlelight. When they did not sense what was occurring, he wrapped a singular knuckle on the table. As Hotaru hopped up on the table, Takuma waved Feliks away and sat stretched like a lounging house cat.

Feliks, wise being that he was, locked the door behind him. He understood the importance of privacy.

'How is your leg?' Virnoi asked as he knelt on the floor before Hotaru, unlacing those fine leather boots that Takuma had insisted upon. He tugged them loose, placed them both to the side, and began to roll up one of her trouser legs as he internally shook his magic awake. Virnoi had been born with a Blessed heart, though he'd had no awareness of it as a child. It was the source of all his magic, and was a restless, tempestuous, tired thing. It often required bullying to do the work that he required of it.

Beneath Hotaru's trousers lay what would seem to anyone else a perfectly normal-looking left leg. If one had the eye for it, though, they notice the discrepancy in the complexion. Hotaru was a fine woman, her body covered with the tiny scars, like a collection of memories, that marked a life's worth of shrapnel thrown at the undeserving. But her left leg was two shades too fair for Hotaru, the rest of her body warmed by the sun, and conspicuously lacking any scar to speak of.

This was, of course, because Virnoi had given her the leg. Hotaru had once fallen victim to an unspeakable tragedy, and Virnoi had expended all of his knowledge to right the Imperium's wrongdoing.

'A little light recently. I cannot tell if it's quicker than the other or simply confused somewhere in the ankle.' Virnoi kissed Hotaru gently on the knee as he traced a rune on her calf, his magic beginning to hum as it recognised its work. Diagnostic magics were primarily used by healers to pinpoint unseen ailments in a patient; but when he'd crafted the leg, he'd taught himself how to sense dissonance within the body. Within the framework he'd created, there was a whirring gear in her ankle that was overcompensating. Errant magic, when left without a hand to guide it, was often driven by this incessant need to improve upon itself, growing faster and stronger until it burnt out entirely.

This wasn't always a problem – a whisper of magic left by a lesser mage would have fizzled out into dust. But it was his love of Hotaru when he'd lain it within her marrow that had driven it forward, wanting to make their little crow faster on her feet than a Svarn was meant to be.

Hush, he admonished, tuning the stray whisper of magic into place, pulling it back alongside the impulses carried within Hotaru's body. It was to listen to her, not any echo of his own desire.

'Do you think we can do it?' Takuma asked the open air. Virnoi took a long breath and split his attention in two, between his humming magic and the man across the table.

'I don't think it matters.' Virnoi tucked Hotaru's trouser leg back into place and then sat, unwinding his shawl from his shoulders and draping it to the side. They'd try, even if the plan was half-baked and mad. All that would matter would be getting them out when it went haywire. 'But yes, I think there's a chance of success. Between your ingenuity, my magic, and Nuru's tongue, we've got a better shot than half the city. Even better that they won't be expecting us.'

Virnoi was a liar. He functioned in half-truths and the illusion of disclosure. He did not, however, consider this a lie. He believed that Takuma was very capable of stealing a dragon. What he didn't know was if Takuma would be prepared for what came after.

They didn't ask too many questions of one another. They would have hurt one another far too quickly if they'd begun, broaching topics that neither man wanted to speak of. There would be questions raised of Virnoi's parentage – not quite High Elf, but something transformed by his mother's heritage. The Wood Elves were a race of people who were secluded from the Imperium's strict societal structure; they roamed in the great forests, quieter than the wind, communicating only in hand signals that nobody had ever learned.

Virnoi's ears may have marked him for what he was, but Takuma had never spoken a word of it. Just like Virnoi had never raised questions regarding the Nordic patron of The Brass Wyvern, an old lover of Takuma's. If they maintained their boundaries, they managed a wilful peace between them.

'Don't count my Blessing out,' Hotaru huffed.

He rolled his eyes at her, staring up at her through his sheath of thick, dark hair that had fallen out of place as he knelt. Virnoi rose slowly, one broad hand cupping her waist, the other her pointed chin as he inspected her flushed cheeks and furrowed brow. 'Oh, darling. How I love you.'

Love was a tangled web of light that lay within Takuma's heart, and Virnoi the spider that had made his home there. Hotaru – well, Hotaru had surprised them both. Virnoi resolved to make the best of the time he had left with them and pressed his mouth over Hotaru's, tickled by the way she laughed into his touch.

Chapter Sixteen

SVARNA

The quarters of the temple children of Muqdah were located in the broader reaches of the temple. It took time for Eulalia to climb the halls from her own nest, waddling through to the western wing on feet that had already walked entirely too much that day. A woman who was days out from giving birth should have been resting on cushioned lounges, being fed a variety of candied fruits – not worrying about war. However, she imagined if she was unravelling, the children must be panicking.

It was customary that they slept in communal living spaces when they were young. Beds piled on every inch of stone, pushed into round gathering areas.

Bronnuq was there, his grandson in tow, making their way through the chamber together, patting heads and speaking words that she did not catch from afar. Imamu was counting.

'Children,' she called. A hundred faces turned to the call, eyes of grey and brown and black, full of a certain tremulous fear.

She knew all their names. She'd been here a decade; she had learnt them by the sound of their footfalls and the trill of their whistles. Atroxus and Petra and Hurthor and Ursoq, their siblings and cousins. Many of them had been birthed by the holy mothers, but in the wake of the war, there had been an ocean of orphans who'd fallen through the south. To make these orphans stronger, the holy men who were left had imbued them with magic, painted lines upon their shins and arms, and sung to the temple to bind them to the power that buzzed beneath their feet. They would be different creatures entirely from the renasci who were created within the womb – they would retain their pasts and their whims and their humanity. They would not go strange, but they'd be stronger and quicker. They'd always find their feet on Svarnish soil. They did what they could.

By contrast, when the children born in the temple grew to adulthood, they underwent one final ritual undertaken by the holy men to turn them entirely into the renasci that worked at the behest of the people. They were bound to holy men and given astronomical strength by the forging of molten magic beneath their skin, tongues twisted so they could speak to the earth itself. Nequit was merely two seasons away from making that final transition, and he'd taken to his oncoming role as a sentinel of the city with a bright sense of pride. He leapt to help Eulalia.

'What have they told you?' Eulalia asked the crowd of little faces, pulling a young boy called Yuoko to her side when he shuffled towards her.

'That the Imperium has come,' a girl of seven said. 'That the sky is falling.'

'I will not lie to you. I will not soften the truth, not now.' She felt so heavy. Eulalia took a long breath in and steadied herself as she blew it out, a breathing technique that Bronnuq had taught her some years ago. 'An army has arrived at Muqdah. An army led by Thurlow Thurlowe, an elf who I'm certain you've all heard whispered about when you were listening in on conversations that weren't meant for little ears.'

He was the boogie man to them, the shadow that lurked in the dark. The villain that had slain their blessed queen. The older children exchanged nervous glances with one another, while the young ones wavered, drawing strength as they clung to one another.

'Our plan is for all of you to be far from this place when he arrives.' There was a wave of protest, but Eulalia waited ever-so patiently until they quieted down once more. 'We may have been cursed with this war, but small blessings persist even in the darkest times. Bronnuq's grandson, Imamu, has brought us a caravan on which we can save many of you. The youngest of you will need to go. Anyone below thirteen without question, and their siblings – to try and keep families together. Those who are any older than that will be given a choice.'

'Nuru of Muqdah is your age. Nearing fourteen. She'll be leaving on the caravan with the rest of you because I want to see her live a long, pleasant life outside of these walls. I'd also like to see you all live to be older than even your grandsire, Bronnuq.' Nuru did not know this. Eulalia would figure it out. 'I won't force you to leave. We won't chase you out the door. But you must all understand, this is not your fault and this is not your fight. There is nothing you could have done to change this, but there is something you can do to save Svarna from this doom – you can live.'

Even looking upon them, she could not give them a total truth. She did not have to. As much as the council had kept the stories from the north to their own, Eulalia knew the children listened. They gossiped amongst each other when the adults slept, that could be helped.

The older children will not go, she thought. Not unless they had a younger sibling on the caravan; Svarnish sisters and brothers were nigh impossible to part. She could see some of the oldest boys set their jaws, having made the decision that would forge their paths as children made men. They would not be budged – but she wasn't trying to. They were about to send a hundred and thirty children away from the home that was supposed to be a sanctuary. She wanted them to understand why she'd dare betray them in this way.

'Muqdah's not safe anymore, is it?' This question was posed by a girl of sixteen, whose name had changed three times in the years she'd spent within the shelter of the First Temple. Eulalia thought that she was now known as Vishai, but that could have been a name already forgotten. When the temple children were left to raise themselves, they were given agency and control over what the world called them. They often asked Bronnuq to name them; some of the older children who were brought in from the broader world preferred to shed their past like an old, worn skin. 'This was supposed to be the last safe place in Svarna, but it's no different from anywhere else.'

'It should have been safe. If we'd done our jobs as adults, you'd all be safe.'

'This isn't your fault, Mamina, this is the Imperium!' Eulalia's heart clenched. She pressed her hand to her chest as an outcry broke across these children that had come to be hers, an outpouring of disagreement at the thought that the adults were somehow responsible for this. 'You couldn't have stopped this. You couldn't have.'

'What about your baby?' a boy named Darcei asked. She spotted him folded behind a bundle of blankets, face pressed against his sister's arm. Eulalia paused. She had not thought that they would worry about her, let alone her unborn child. She pressed a hand to her belly, glancing down at the absolute ocean of linen she'd had to don to keep herself even somewhat covered.

What about you? As long as she continued to walk the earth, so did he. She didn't know when this particular child had become a boy in the back of her mind. Another rosy-cheeked little boy to keep Rasyl company, someone who'd grow to be Ohba's shadow and maybe find themselves fond of their mother. What plans did she have to protect him? That feeling of helplessness that had been creeping at the edges of her defences began to claw at her throat, and Eulalia could only let out a tight, strangled sound.

'Eulalia's baby has to stay with Eula,' Bronnuq's creaking voice explained as he pottered through the crowd, carving his path slowly. 'But I'll do everything in my power to make sure he comes into this world a happy, healthy baby. One who'll be cared for by Eulalia's hands in just the same way you all were. Right after this, I'll be doing one last spell on him before he arrives, to make sure he's as safe as can be while he's still in her belly.'

That is a promise you cannot keep, she thought. He was grandsire to them all. In the way that only grandparents could, he settled them all with his magic words. He was trying to reassure all of his children, including her. She reached out and found their hands clutching at one another, squeezing as Bronnuq came to sit beside her. He allowed Imamu to take the Staff of Muqdah from him in a gentle motion that drew Eulalia's eye.

'Most of us adults won't be coming with you. It's our responsibility to defend this temple in any way we can and, to put it simply, there wouldn't be the space. We would rather save you from the Imperium than take your places ourselves.' They'd told the adult residents, the holy men and the other mothers, and hadn't given them much of a choice. If the holy mothers wanted to leave, there would be a place for them, but the caravan was supposed to be full of as many children as they could fit. There had been few objections. Unlike Eulalia, many of the other adults who filled the temple halls had resigned themselves to their fate some time ago. They would not have dreamed of stepping in on the destiny of a child.

'But you'll be alone. Who'll be here with you?'

'I have Eulalia. Eulalia has Fidela. Fidela has Adil, who has Ohba, who has Cuinu, who has me. The winds will keep us together until you catch the breeze back to us when this war is done. You'll all have to take very good care of my grandson.' Bronnuq's tone did not waver, did not betray any crumbling of his eternally calm front. 'Imamu is my eldest grandson. He's had plenty of experience taking care of his younger siblings, but they've gone to the wind. He misses them greatly, so I'm entrusting him to you all.'

The sea of small faces pinched and grew even more upset, some of them had sprung rivulets of tears. People who did not spend much time with children wrote them off as empty-headed, tiny imitations of adults. They thought them annoying and foolishly loud when they were, instead, endlessly surprising in the depth of understanding they had. They knew that their makeshift family were unlikely to survive the Imperium's arrival, but that they'd have something new. They knew that Bronnuq was already too old, too frail. They knew that those with titles were the first to fall when an enemy struck.

'You are all my children.' Eulalia laced her fingers together. 'So, I'm going to talk to you all as such. We are not your responsibility. No matter how much independence we give you all within Morouqdi, you are our children, and we're meant to take care of you. So I don't want to hear any screaming. I don't want to see a tantrum thrown or hear that any one of you is refusing to leave. I haven't always been a wonderful mother, but I like to think I have taught you all the importance of strength. If you believe that you are strong, that you can withstand this, you will all find a new home on the roads outside Muqdah. This temple lives in its people. As long as you're all walking and breathing, no army could ever take the magic of this place from us.'

Her words would have been harsher had it been a day earlier. She would have been far tougher on them had she had the energy, but it would have only worked on the older children. Little ones did not have enough of a grasp on the world to understand the weight of what was happening, only that they were being made to leave.

'You are Muqdah. You are Morouqdi. If this city falls, it may be gone in the eyes of the world, but it will carry on in you.' Her lip trembled, so for a breath she paused, pressing them both together to allow that tremor to pass. 'I need to know that you'll all be safe. For me.'

Eulalia collected her children and met Imamu and Mosi's caravan at the docks. Refugees had flooded into the temple throughout the night, each chamber and door filled with the dispossessed. Renasci idly directed them into the open halls, situating them as best they could with their resources stretched. The Child's assessment of the city folk had not been incorrect – they were scared, but they were filled with the unsettled calm of a people who had expected this upheaval. When the war had begun on the bridging border that Eulalia had once lived on, people had been truly panicked. Several decades on, these were folk who'd watched their doom approach them slowly.

The few renasci that were familiar with riding were saddled and secure when they passed by the nursery. Eulalia paused when she saw Uono riding his ruby-coloured dragon, her tread lapsing. A quiet certainty grew over her. This was the last time she'd see him. She sensed the hot wind of death and stared, a despair beneath her sternum snatching away a breath. Uono was a construct who was several centuries old. He'd been exempt from most of the calls for soldiers and riders because he'd been deemed entirely too vital to Muqdah. But not this day. There was a hard set to his jaw and his brow, the look of a man who would not be dissuaded.

She was ashamed that she had not thought of him, in all of this. Of the few dragons suitable for any sort of warfare, Uono would be amongst them.

The plan had been settled for Bronnuq's grandson and his companion – as the army entered the city, they would leave under the cover of the chaos. The roads outside the city were open, so they had decided that their safest path would be to wait until the majority of the Imperium's army had flooded into Muqdah and left the roads empty. The youngest temple children had been tucked into their caravans, bundled in wraps and clothes, accompanied by their siblings or those who would care for them. Imamu watched over them all, pointing people to wherever there was free space and watching the hallways.

'The shields will be entirely down soon. They'll be making their way into the city,' Imamu warned them as he approached, his voice low and even. The city beyond the temple was eerily quiet, the air filled with the distant rousing of the youngling dragons and the singing birds that filled their gardens. It felt wrong that they should sing, not possibly knowing the hellfire that was about to flourish within the city walls. 'Mosi's out watching on the road so that we can time our exit – they shouldn't suspect one construct amongst the many. Especially with the few that are up on the dragons.'

'This is my boy, Rasyl,' Eulalia said. Her voice caught for a moment, hitched uncomfortably as she unwound Rasyl from her side. He was little, but not so little that he did not understand that a farewell was occurring. It was early in the morning for him to be unbound from Eulalia's side, and he writhed uncomfortably in the cool morning air.

Bronnuq's grandson looked at her for a long moment, not comprehending why she was handing him her babe.

'You'll take care of him. He likes yoghurt and bananas and shlarva. He's often happy, but when he does cry, he usually just needs to be close to someone.' She thrust Rasyl at him again, insistent, her chin dimpling as his dewy eyes stared out at her. He was a babe, but he was not foolish, he looked up at her face and knew in his tiny heart that something was deeply awry.

His face wrinkled and twisted, cheeks growing red as he let out a wailing cry. Every bone in Eulalia's body screamed to pull him back against her side, but she knew that if she did, she'd never be able to put him down again. She would be entirely unable to relinquish him to the wind. Instead, she shifted him in her hands and took a step forward, pressing him into Imamu.

It was an admittance of defeat for Eulalia. In the night, a shore within her had collapsed, and her resolve to keep her children by her side had been rendered hopeless.

'Just—just, please, take care of them. Teach them our language. Make sure they know what our temples once looked like.'

Fumbling, Imamu put his great hands around her boy and shifted him towards his chest. He was not practised at holding children, so Eulalia reached out and guided his hands until he was bouncing Rasyl on his side, just as Ohba would.

'You should come with us too, miss,' Imamu said. He broached the topic gently, genuine concern shining in his eyes. 'Ma'am. Venerated mother. You should not be here so pregnant, anywhere in the world would be a safer place to give birth.'

'I—I can't.' She took a breath. 'I won't. My Ohba, he's the anchor of the city. He's bound to Muqdah. He can't leave, and I can't just leave him behind.'

A good mother would have climbed on the caravan with her children and left, any man be damned. She had never been a good mother.

Though his mouth opened to speak once more, no words left Imamu's mouth. He seemed to know there were no objections that he could make that would dislodge her from this decision that she had not made herself and already overcome in the night.

'Bronnuq won't come with me,' Imamu said. 'It seems I have come all this way and I won't even be saving my grandsire, the one thing I'd been hoping to do.'

'When this is done, we will come find you.' She reached out and brushed the shoulder that Rasyl was not resting against, squeezing gently. 'You know he'd never leave Muqdah. He thinks of this place as his home, us as his wards. He's been here for fifty years.'

'I should have known. Anchors live and die in their temples.' Even when they had long since passed along the role, this was a broadly universal truth. It was difficult to disagree upon that.

'Give it the day,' she pressed. Eulalia would not live to see gentle Bronnuq die in war. He would die in his sleep, with his grandchild at his side, if she had any say at all in it. 'Have some faith in his magic.'

Yet again, the lie fell tangled and flat in the air between them. It was not a moment in which one could begrudge her lying, so instead Imamu nodded and continued to bounce Rasyl to keep the boy quiet. The fact that Bronnuq had passed on the staff of Muqdah quietly, without any fanfare or noise, said volumes about how he anticipated the day would end.

Here came the difficult part. Leaving Rasyl would be heart-wrenching, but it would not break her. The boy could not fight. Eulalia turned to her elder child, looking at the girl and waving her towards the caravan.

'You too. I do not pick favourites – if I am sending one child off to live, I'll be sending you both. You should not be here for what's to come.' Her delivery was too nonchalant, yet somehow too tense. Eulalia winced at her mishandling of this, but it was not as if she had any guidance. Abandoning one's child, even to another, was something that left a wound on the soul far deeper than any blade would ever be able to reach. 'Stay with this caravan, and when this is done, you can come home. But you can't stay through the fighting.'

The Child stared at her, a knot of confusion forming beneath her brows.

'No,' the Child said, steeling herself. It was a visible stiffening that went from the top of her tiny horns to her feet as she realised the weight of what Eulalia had thrust upon her. 'I won't.'

Eulalia swallowed. 'Nuru—Nuru, you have to go. You can't stay here.'

That was not enough to shift her stubborn girl. Of course not – not her little one. The bravest temple child in all of Svarna, who mounted a dragon and laid waste to an army that should have struck her out of the sky. The girl who'd been reared from birth to believe that she was the heart of the city, that she would bring about an age of good fortune to the people of Svarna. She'd try to root herself to the foundation of the First Temple if she thought there was a chance it would change the tides of morale.

'I won't leave you. I won't leave everyone. They all depend on me! They all look to me to know that the world is good!' It was, perhaps, the only true outburst that Eulalia had seen from the Child. She'd thrown tantrums as a babe, stomped her feet as she'd grown, but never had the girl gotten angry like this. She was a bad mother, to have let the holy men convince this girl of her own importance. To let them tell her that all of Muqdah weighed on her tiny little shoulders. 'And the world is good! The world is great! People deserve to know that. You're just staying here to die, and I won't let you!'

Like bellows upon a fire, her daughter's outrage fed Eulalia's frustration, her fury, into a hot flush that climbed into her cheeks.

'You don't make decisions for me.' Eulalia could hear herself, terse and clipped, but she could not stop. She seized the girl's face in a hand, cupping her chin to force eye contact. 'You are a child. It is my responsibility to protect you. I am protecting you by putting you on a caravan that will escape this war. Muqdah as you know it will not exist when the elves are done with it, but you can still be you. You can still be a beacon for those you travel with. Go, take care of your brother.'

They were not a loving pair. They attended to one another, but more often than not, they kept each other at arm's length. They shared a vital need for independence. This was what they were supposed to be – not mother and daughter, but arbiter and plaintiff. Who were they if they were not violent, if they were not fighting one another to fit a role that the world demanded of them?

Eulalia thought, for a moment, that the girl might cry. It was almost enough to make her drop the subject entirely, but her distress hardened into a petulant submission. The Child wrenched her face away from her, the Blessing that caged her throat aglow with rage, before she strode past her and climbed unceremoniously to stand at Imamu's side.

'If you die, my ghost is going to haunt your ghost,' the Child swore. 'You'll never get rid of me.'

'When you love someone, you carry them beneath your sternum for as long as their memory lives on in you.' Sentimental words were slow to come from Eulalia, the painstaking process of pulling blood from a stone. She could make anything happen within herself, though; she could force herself to be anything for her children. She had made herself a mother. 'I'll be carrying you with me until we see each other again, little dove.'

She reached for the girl, crossing the great chasm between them, and pressed a kiss to the Child's forehead. Turning to her beautiful Rasyl, she touched her nose to his hair and allowed herself to breathe his scent one last time before she stepped away. She farewelled them quietly before Ohba took her hand, and they made their way back into the heart of the First Temple, Eulalia fighting back the downpour of tears that would undo her if she surrendered to the tide.

Then, just as expected, the storm broke over Muqdah.

Chapter Seventeen

THE IMPERIUM

Nuru was not sure why she waited until the brothel was quiet and unassuming to leave.

She tried not to think too hard about the fact that Takuma was lounging around in Virnoi's room. He would have come with her, had she asked, but would have stopped her entirely if he'd had even an inkling of where she was going. She could ruin the entire heist in an afternoon if she wasn't careful, but Nuru, being nothing if not stubborn, wouldn't think about that. She would think about nothing.

Her tumultuous marriage had taught her many things, one of which was that not thinking was a skill. If one could remove themselves from conscious thought entirely, the world floated past without true worry or concern. So, Nuru had become good at not thinking. She did not think as she holstered Nema on her body and tied the wrap that would hold her there.

It was easy to slip away. It was always easy to slip away if Takuma's eyes were not on her. She'd grown up smaller than most of the other temple children in Muqdah, mindful of her footing in a world where she hadn't truly known her place. She no longer demanded the attention that she once had, and small children became small, soft-spoken women who could disappear within a sea of larger folk. The Imperium was a levelling force in the world. People with glorious pasts were commonplace beneath the Eschalion's reign.

The Imperium, being the belching, broken, dreadful city that it was, carried her away. She strolled with Nema out of the red-light district and up to the main promenade, through the broad marketplace that took over the Nords' Corridor in the afternoon. She ensured that she made quite the show of taking a scrawled shopping list and a woven basket, tucked on one arm. It would be an easy excuse to use if Takuma questioned where she had gone. She'd used it before, and though he could always tell when she lied, he did not always fight with her about it. They both understood that to keep their sanity, they had to keep their own secrets.

La Pietà's Cathedral was a reverently built structure that shadowed the poorer corner of the city, joined with the quicksilver tower that spiralled upwards and watched over the city. The church had claimed it a show of charity from their matron goddess that the church should be built where the beggars could attend service. It may have seemed a more genuine notion if the statues that welcomed people within had been gilded in actual silver.

The church and its elegant steeples called to her, and she let her feet pull her along, knowing the path by heart. She would have plenty of time before people began to question her absence, which meant that Nuru could savour the open air.

While she loved The Brass Wyvern – she had to love the Wyvern for all it had given her – she'd begun to wonder if the walls had grown tighter. Sometimes, she felt as if the roof was likely to collapse inwards and trap them all in the Imperium, never to be embraced by a Svarnish wind again.

The square that preceded the church was covered in a shifting carpet of ivory birds. At some point, one very smart bird had figured out that if they lingered in the square long enough, an upstanding member of the church would feed them. That one bird had then realised that if they brought along a friend – or several – the parish would take pity on them and free themselves of any leftover food. The hustlers in the city had then wizened up to the potential for a quick coin, which meant that young elvish faces now dotted the square – attempting to sell off small paper bags of birdfeed to those who wished to entertain themselves with the decidedly domestic avian flock.

But of course, each of these hustlers took one appraising look at Nuru and decided there was no need to try and peddle their wares to her, that she was obviously destitute. It suited her fine. These birds were all fat and happy, anyway.

As she approached, the shadow the monolith cast swallowed her. In this corner of the Imperium, there was no place one could hide from the far-reaching sight of the priestly tower. Nuru squinted up at it momentarily, lips pursed. The tower was where Taliesin lived and slept, where he watched the world. She had an irrational, all-consuming hate for the secrets that it held.

Nema burbled happily on her chest, enraptured by a bird taking flight. Nuru sighed and stroked the top of her head, soothed by the feather-soft curls that sprung from behind her budding horns. 'Yes, yes, we'll see Taliesin soon.'

She had been the one to argue they shouldn't involve Taliesin in the heist because of his familial disdain. The longer she had sat on the thought, the more it bothered her – she'd lain awake thinking about it. She did not keep secrets from Taliesin. Once someone had seen a clear view of your nether regions throughout the course of an intensive and troubled birth, the idea that anything should be secret could be done away with. It was no surprise that Nema loved him – he'd brought her into the world.

The cathedral itself was a testament to elvish craftsmanship. Light did not simply exist within these walls, it sang. Stained-glass panels lined the outer wall, stretching away above her head. Each was their own master work, fragmented arrays of colour catching any sunbeam that dared greet the day, sending broad shafts of multicoloured light into the aisles.

Still refusing to think of anything at all – how furious Takuma would be with her, how the guilt would chew at her – Nuru walked.

Someone needs to know where you've gone if you disappear. Someone needs to know to take care of Nema.

It was quiet enough here to shake herself from her stupor, to allow herself to think properly about what she was doing. She stroked Nema's head all the while as she lingered in the mammoth entryway, letting her motherhood bind her in place. Before she'd become with child, several summers after she'd departed Muqdah, Nuru had spent entire years untethered from the world. Out of step with time and the strange people that could not have possibly understood the depth of what she had lost.

She had not wanted children. Bringing a horned child into a world where Svarna stood occupied by the Imperium was not a wise or kind thing to do – not when they'd grow up scorned, unable to speak in their ancestral tongue without compromising their safety. She hadn't had a choice with Nema. By the time that she'd escaped Imamu, there was no healer that would have handed over an abortifacient when she'd been so far along.

Nema was a blessing she had not wanted. Nuru had plenty of those. Every day she spent with Nema, Nuru wondered what the world would look like for her when she was grown. For now, her daughter kept her grounded in a world that she'd once been transient in. Nuru had to keep them both safe.

One long breath.

A second, longer breath.

Nuru turned and trailed down the great aisle at the heart of La Pietà, drawn by the sound of someone telling a story.

There he was. As elegant as a swan, he stood surrounded by his own flock of elvish children. As ever, he wore his signature blue, the colours of the priesthood that allowed those who saw him to know he was a beacon of mercy. Taliesin was such a beautiful man – his light hair shone with a soft, rosy overtone in the sunlight that bathed him. She lingered from afar, listening to the swirling tones of the elvish language as the sound carried along the polished stone.

She'd never learnt elvish. Nuru had tried – she'd picked up bits and pieces out of necessity, but she'd found the sentence structure peculiar. The shape of the words confused her tongue, which had only spoken Svarnish and the Common Tongue in her youth. Perhaps as a girl, she'd resented the idea that she must learn it or fail entirely at thriving within this foreign country. She could have listened to Taliesin speak for an age, though, to the great passion with which he told stories in his native tongue.

Not wanting to interrupt the story time, Nuru found an empty pew and sat on it with Nema, who had recognised Taliesin's voice and grown wide-eyed.

'Nuru?' Taliesin called. The entire brood of ducklings had turned to stare down the aisle, curious eyes peering at her through the pews.

Decidedly embarrassed, she could do nothing but wave. She had not meant to interrupt them – she would have sat through the session quite happily. It would have given her more time to reason away Takuma's inevitable frustration.

He spoke for a few more moments with the children before calling for someone else, which summoned another pointy-eared priest, who took up the duty of storytelling with a similar enthusiasm.

'I wasn't expecting you, Nuru, it's such a long walk to La Pietà from the Wyvern.' A long walk that Taliesin made regularly, without a hint of complaint. Taliesin shuffled down the pew, dropping down beside Nuru. He reached out to clasp her hand and that was all it took for Nuru's despair to melt away, to allow Takuma to be forgotten, even momentarily. 'Is everything okay? How is little Nema?'

Little Nema had begun to squirm the closer the priest drew, and was now grasping at her mother's blouse.

'She's fine,' Nuru huffed as she loosened a fold of the wrap and plucked the babe out. It was a second-nature switchover; Taliesin took but a moment to take Nema in his arms and begin to bounce her idly. The babe, delighted to be back in the arms of her favourite person, gurgled with delight. 'We both wanted the walk. With how busy the city has become, I wanted to see what the revelries were about.'

The Imperium was gearing up for a city-wide celebration, almost at the last moment. If there had been any formal announcements about Thurlowe's party, she had not seen them, but people would take any excuse to celebrate at the empire's expense. It wasn't as if Nuru would have been able to read it had they plastered proclamations on the city walls, unless they'd put a picture of Thurlow Thurlowe on every poster. Taliesin lowered Nema into his lap and bounced her on his knee, allowing her to clutch at a finger.

'I wouldn't think too much of it,' Taliesin said cheerily. He had to know. Even if his father hadn't mentioned anything, there was no way that Truls would have allowed his brother to stay ignorant about a party of note. 'Though there are some fantastic candy-makers setting up booths near Pietà's House of Midwifery. They should be giving away caramels for nothing, if you wanted a treat.'

'I'll go past on the way back.' Nuru nodded. She did not know what else to say to him, so the two sat together in a sensible quiet.

Some people, when faced with quiet, must fill the void with chatter of all kinds. This chatter varied vastly, but was often meaningless, prompted by an overwhelming sense of awkwardness. Taliesin and Nuru had no such qualms. They sat often on their own, with nothing but Nema's half-shaped words to disturb that soft blanket of silence that swaddled them. She felt a wash of relief roll over her when she realised that he would allow her to do it once more, even if he kept looking at her anticipatorily.

Perhaps he knew her too well.

The Church of La Pietà was supposed to be a herald of mercy. The patron goddess, Kyrie, loomed over them all. A pale statue that towered at the furthest end of the church, preceding the entry to the priest's tower. She was not distinctly elvish nor Svarnish, simply a willowy woman with a sheet of silken hair and a great halo made from Prismarium glass that sent vivid splashes of light arcing outwards from her crown. Nuru had read the stories of Kyrie; her midwifery, her motherhood, and how she had cared for the great serpent that had shaped the world. She was a variation of a Nordlund goddess, much older than the Imperium, but the heart of the story remained the same. That was the nature of stories – a thousand different mouths could speak the words, yet one could still hear the echo of the first in a stranger's voice.

'Is something the matter, Nuru?' Taliesin prompted gently, his tone so profoundly kind that it made her heart ache. The words that she'd been trying to speak tangled in her throat. 'I do not wish to presume, but you've got quite a concerning look about you today.'

He'll try to stop you, a voice within her warned, one which sounded far too much like Takuma for her liking. You know he can't understand what this means to you.

She ran a hand against her ear to ensure that she was not wearing the charmed earrings they used to communicate from afar. There were few of those within The Brass Wyvern's vault, but they often used them on busy nights to keep an eye on the many corners of the pleasure house. She'd donned the jewellery last night but had been mindful to put the earring away before leaving, so that Takuma could not reach her.

But she could see it in Taliesin's soft, blue eyes. If he knew that she was walking into danger, he would do everything in his power to convince her that the cause wasn't worth the risk if it meant putting herself in danger. Another voice rose within her, one that felt far more like her own. It was gentle. It was honest. You do not lie to Taliesin.

'I can't tell you exactly what it is,' she admitted. 'Takuma would not forgive me, I think, but I would not forgive myself if I did not tell you. It's trouble.'

His eyes never left hers, but he nodded. She reached over and gently ran a finger from the top of Nema's head downwards, tapping her lightly on the tip of her nose.

'Svarnish business, I guess?' His tone was perfectly polite, but it sounded about as close to exhausted as Taliesin ever grew. They had used that excuse in the past to keep their secrets, and Taliesin had truly tried to respect it, knowing Svarnish business had already been imposed upon too much in the world's recent memory. She struggled to find the words to smooth the worried line between his brows, but her voice failed her again. Instead, she found herself staring up hopelessly at his beautiful face.

Perhaps Imamu was right. He had called her selfish when she'd told him that she could not bear a child, that her body would not survive such a laborious thing. He'd called her petty. Perhaps she was selfish now, too, dancing around the words as if it could absolve her of being a liar.

'Svarnish business – and with everything going on with this big party, it's all a lot. I had to convince Andraste to work a night I'm almost certain she'd rather have off and pay her a little extra for her trouble, which leaves my purse strings tight for a few days.' Nuru watched him intently as she spoke, placing each word carefully as if she were stacking dominoes between them. 'The core of the Wyvern won't even be at the establishment for the evening, so we're trusting Sabtha to care for the place while we're off at work. Everyone's feeling antsy.'

She was not telling him exactly what they were doing. She was not breaking her loyalty with Takuma, only trying to let Taliesin in on the secret. A sharp realisation snapped together in the beautiful man's face, his hands gently holding hers in place. He would hold her in place if she let him, and Nuru indulged him. If he'd asked her to leave with him in that very moment, she would have thought about it. She might have agreed. Nuru was consistently taken by surprise by how far she'd fold for him.

'If you need help taking care of the Wyvern, you'll let me know,' Taliesin said. All of those words atop one another meant many things that could not be honestly said.

Nuru smiled weakly. She was so relieved that she could have collapsed, fallen on the tiled floor until the sun rolled down over this great city and the priests would have to carry her out to clear the pews for the evening mass. She could have kissed him for all that Taliesin saw, even when Nuru's mouth ran dry and cold and left her unable to articulate the truth. She leaned slowly against him, their bodies resting upon one another.

Though he could not reciprocate the motion, bound by protocol and Kyrie's immense stare upon their shoulders, he did not draw away. His priest's cloak folded and welcomed her, and a gentle counterweight greeted Nuru as Taliesin's form bowed back against her as she allowed herself a moment of respite.

'Maybe no help just yet, but would you keep an eye out for us on the night?'

Chapter Eighteen

SVARNA

As the shields of Muqdah fell, inch by inch, breaking apart from a singular crack in the sky, the temple shields rose.

The strongest magic in the world was sacrificial; this was known by any Svarnishman worth their salt. Things of importance sacrificed near a vein of magic would gift the wielder a profound amount of power for them to use as they pleased. It was how they nourished the land when famines came – a scaled egg or pound of flesh for the betterment of the community. They were creatures of togetherness. Sacrificial magic almost certainly shouldn't have been undertaken in a panic and required a methodical, often slow approach. Eulalia supposed she could forgive them for that.

Ohba radiated Blessed light as he worked. It was impossible to tell how much he was juggling within the city, but he was sweating, dusky skin gleaming in the lamplight. She had never known the toll of spellwork in the way that her companions had, but she'd watched the effect it had taken on them. She'd seen perfectly competent mages collapse when they sank their teeth into a spell that overcame them.

Bloodletting was considered the most selfless of the sacrificial arts. Those who did not want to involve a third party would give up parts of themselves to secure what they needed from the world. That was why Ohba took a dagger to his arm now, the one that he often wore at his hip. The shining knife slipped through the flesh of his arm, as easy as silk, leaving a river of crimson in its wake. He left a trail along the great entryway of the First Temple, smudging it into the stone as he went.

'Eula.' His voice was distant.

She smiled weakly. All of her smiles felt weak of late. 'You should rest.' He would need a few hours of sleep before the army came. The holy men woke before the sun broke its fiery path into the firmament and had exceptionally long days. She was certain that sleep would not come to them, even if they found themselves exhausted beyond reason, but it would do them both some good to try. 'You can't work yourself into the ground before the army even arrives. We'll need you tomorrow. Who's got a healer's drink?'

A holy mother could ask for anything from the holy men, and they'd find a way to supply it. It was mere moments before someone produced a brewed cup that she held out to Ohba.

The substance inside was fragrant, took hours of work, and would help him replenish his magic along with anything he'd happened to give up while reinforcing their temple. She hoped that it was only blood and that she would not later discover he was missing a spleen or a kidney or some other non-essential internal organ that Ohba had decided was worth sacrificing for the temple shields.

She wouldn't have been opposed to the thought of an organ sacrifice were it not for the severe lack of healers they had to attend to potential internal bleeding. They would need him on his feet in the days to come, and recovering from that specific injury was a long-winded thing.

'Drink,' Eulalia demanded. Ohba nodded and nursed the cup, taking sips as she watched him down the potion. Healers often thrust them into her hands while pregnant, ensuring all the while that not a drop went unconsumed. She knew very well that dosages mattered in magical medicine, just like it did in the practical.

'There is blood of the voice at the front of the nursery, to stop entryway by those who'd mean Muqdah harm, and to preserve the life within. A small amount of heartsblood in Idunn's hideaway – it won't be enough to shield her, not that she'd need it, but I'm hoping it will be enough to preserve an egg or a hatchling if it comes to it. Arms for the door in an effort to hold them closed.'

As if responding to Ohba's rolling words, the shimmering door shifted colour in Eulalia's peripherals.

'Is there more work to be done?' She looked around at their exhausted faces, drawn tight and tired by the force of what had already been laid. There would be wards activated and lain on every external door and window to stop any outsiders from crossing into the temple, and it would have taken their host of holy men to ensure that the sacrifices were made safely.

'Not without sacrificing a person entirely to the cause, which we're not doing.' Eulalia quirked an eyebrow but said nothing. There was a discontented murmuring from the holy men – evidently the topic had been discussed, and a decision made that they agreed upon. She did not wonder which side Ohba was on, being the best and kindest of them all. He would never sacrifice one of their own in this sort of magic; he would consider that a sort of selfishness that they could not recover from. Eulalia found herself far more on the side of the disgruntled, but it would have been an impossible task to take a blade to those who were willing to put in the work for the temple.

It was a shame Cuinu was not in sight, though. She could have made good use of that man for such a ritual.

'I do need to rest,' Ohba conceded. 'If we can.'

She nodded and, with a familiarity born through years of companionship, he took her arm and they walked. There was a tenderness to the way that she made sure to avoid the freshly healed slit in his arm, and a strength in which Ohba ensured that Eulalia had someone to lean upon. The ache in her tired feet was so familiar that it had become a part of her, like all the pains of motherhood that Eulalia had adopted into her state of being.

The temple vibrated with anxiety. Several of the younger children had needed to be sequestered because they were unable to stop crying, and Eulalia had entrusted the older children to care for them in the way she could not. By the dawn, they'd be packed onto the caravans, on their way to a freedom that was a little more peaceful than what they had in this temple.

'Tomorrow, Fidela and I are going to handle the two dissenters,' Eulalia explained softly as they walked.

'The city defences will buy us time.' Ohba patted her hand gently, unfazed by her plan. 'You know, Nuru was brilliant out there. I've never known a child as brave as she was on Kine.'

She smiled weakly, her tread pausing. He stopped and looked at her, measuring Eulalia in his own way. The feeling that was fighting to swallow her was a strangely melancholic beast.

'She was brilliant. She was better than any of us.' That was the Child's lot in life. She had more to say. Yet, for the first time since this had all begun, there were no words to speak; her tongue twisted in on itself and was still. No one would have believed it, but Eulalia, the iron mother, was losing her nerve.

'You're exhausted, Eula.' He said it only after a long breath, making some quiet presumption of her silence. She had never known what Ohba had thought of her, only that he'd been the most forgiving of her hot temper. When she'd arrived as a girl, belly swelling like the moon, she'd snapped at everyone and had no patience for the ritual of holy motherhood. That would never have precluded her from becoming one – a woman's temperament did not disqualify her from the sanctity of the temples – but it had sent men scattering in her wake. But not Ohba.

She was not tired. She very well should have been, but the child within her was unsettled and thus, Eulalia was painfully awake. Ohba guided her forward, down to the chambers she shared with Fidela, and she succumbed to his magnetic pull. They stopped as they came eye to eye with Adil, who had found his woman despite her actively trying to avoid him for a sparing handful of hours.

Fidela's dark eyes met hers fleetingly before she dragged Adil to the room that led off from the children's, closing the adjoining doors silently behind them. Eula had never known much of their relationship, other than it was tumultuous and that Adil was likely the father of Fidela's child. The young woman wasn't certain, for which Eulalia applauded her.

Instead of allowing Ohba to fuss over her, she took to unwinding his excess layers and placing the linen carefully on the stone. He had complained once of how sacrificial magic took its toll upon him, leaving him dizzy and winded. Eulalia was only pregnant, she had not been bleeding herself out for the sake of their holy land.

So, here was the thing about love.

It had a way of sneaking up on the hardened. Eulalia had never thought herself likely to fall in love after her first man had fallen; ever since, she'd found romance an objectively painful thing to behold. The thought that a person could see the world falling apart and still go out of their way to cut flowers for someone they held dear was ... objectively heartbreaking. So Eulalia had cut out the romantic part of herself. She had decided that weathering the world on her own was the only option.

But then there had been patient Ohba, who had seen a woman made from wind and thunder and found a mother. Found Eula beneath her armour and kneaded out someone who loved her people. Who loved him. There was Fidela, who had found a lover in a stranger. There was gentle Bronnuq, immovable as stone against the storming waves of her temper. They had seen all that she was and what she was likely to become, and had pressed her.

She fucking hated them for it, if she was going to be entirely honest. Had she not cared about them and this city so much, she might have fled with her children in tow and left them to the wolves. She could have been far safer. Instead, she was standing with Ohba waiting for the world to come crashing down upon their heads.

'I'm going to kill Cuinu tomorrow,' she said quietly. She could no longer hear Adil and Fidela, which meant that they could no longer hear them.

'Good.' Ohba nodded. 'He's overstepped time and time again in his mother's place. She should have been here, guiding the way of the First Temple – not him. We should have never allowed him to take a seat on the council when he had barely made it into the priesthood.'

Neither wanted to speak of what would come tomorrow. The reluctance lay thick on Eulalia's tongue, but she had to press on. There would be no slowing; there would be no backing down from the war when the shield finished its slow descent into nothing. Each decision was final. She carefully placed another stretch of linen to the side before she turned back to Ohba, studying the man she'd spent years striding beside.

Bloodletting had grown more common as the war advanced, necessary to save any who returned wounded and reinforce the magicks that protected Muqdah. Sacrifices made to try and protect a city that was slipping from their grasp like water between tightly knitted fingers.

'If the gods are good, we will be able to save this city,' Eulalia said. It was a lie. She was a terrible liar; she managed it with none of the same conviction that would keep her sane otherwise. The gods had nothing to do with the predicament they were in.

'Damn the gods,' Ohba muttered, taking her face in his hands. It was then, before the apocalypse, that he stole his first kiss from her.

He was bruising and hot with magic, chest radiating enough heat that another would have drawn away from it. She did not find any pain in his ferocity – they had always been far more similar than they'd ever admit. He was the most Blessed of holy men, built from dragonflame and passion. She had no magic, no power, nothing but her claws and her teeth. To admit they were the same would be to admit that the mean could inherit Muqdah and rule just as the anointed would. The holiest people she'd ever known were the harshest, had the most calloused hands.

Her hands tangled up into his reddish hair, raking it free from where he'd bound it.

How she had longed for this. How she had ached for him. She dragged him back, and with one spare hand, he closed the adjoining door to the room in which the children slept. He came for every breath, taking kiss after kiss as if he were afraid that she would be wrenched from him if he let her go. She pulled him hard against her, gripping him roughly as he pressed her into the corner. His thigh lodged between her legs and hitched upwards, drawing a sharp gasp from her. Gods, how it felt good to be touched.

It was only once there was nowhere else to go that Ohba allowed them both a moment to breathe, resting his head upon her shoulder. She found her slender arms wrapped around his broad shoulders, her hands trembling as she tried to press every inch of her holy man against her. As if she could memorise him, imprint him upon her so that he might live on in her memory of this moment.

'We don't deserve this,' he murmured. 'Nobody deserves this.'

That melancholic murmuring lingered between them for an eternity. Had she been a lesser woman, this was the moment in which Eulalia would have departed this world with her love, in some quiet attempt to escape the destruction that was sure to come. Had she been a coward, she would have taken her children with her, foreseeing the truth of what was coming to their door.

Something in Eulalia broke beneath Ohba's hands, and she found hot, hateful tears in her eyes. She recoiled from the feeling, from this sudden wilting weakness within her, and she stared upwards at the roof, trying to burn away that dangerous river. She had not cried in years, and she would not start now. If her children were going to make it to the other side of this war, she would need to be strong, stronger than she had been.

'Ohba—' She reached up. Eulalia lifted his head with both of her hands, and when he turned, she pressed her mouth to his.

There were no words that night, no gods. Only Eula and Ohba and the promise to keep living.

The Imperium's mere existence is the practice of meticulous control. They keep their most gifted spellcasters trapped in towers, where they will be educated in only the respectable schools of magic. They ban necromancy from the masses because the Eschalion are deemed the only people who should wield such power. They allow the colonies their gods, but only when wrapped in Elvish packaging, peddling their values. They control everything.'

– Avantika istr Signsif, Iskildr's High Mage.

PART TWO

Chapter Nineteen

THE IMPERIUM

Virnoi did not know where Takuma had bought the garb of an elvish whore monger, and frankly, he didn't want to think about it too much.

All he knew was that this corset shouldn't have fit him as well as it did. From the jewel-toned, billowing sleeves to the contrasting embroidery, there was no reason for the Svarnishman to simply incidentally have this in his size. The only thing that settled Virnoi was that he'd been allowed to keep his bones, disguised by the work of a fine jeweller as dangling earrings and ivory cuff links at his wrists. Bones are crucial to a necromancer's safety, the most efficient way to defend oneself.

The entire Imperium was alight with many a celebration, vibrant banners bearing the insignia of the Thurlowe serpent wreathed by roses. As they walked, they saw it again and again, the feathered serpent that represented a dynasty of elvish justice. It was Thurlow Thurlowe's day, and the whole world swayed to his will. Stalls packed the thoroughfares as they slipped through the Imperium, crowds spilling out onto the street; no one really knew why they were celebrating. They only knew that Thurlow Thurlowe wanted to party. It was all the excuse that the Imperium needed.

Fuck the Imperium, fuck the silks, fuck the Thurlowes. This tight collar itched at him, and the garish colours turned Virnoi's pallor sallow. He could feel every seam digging against his skin, the heavy jewels weighed down his pointed ears. He wanted to tear himself out of his own skin and be entirely anew, but there was a job to be done. Fuck the whole fucking parade.

There were two processions of guests. One at the front of the Thurlowe estate, full of the nobles and the puritanical types. It could not be forgotten that Thurlow's last wife had been Thalia, the head of the church, and he still had plenty of sway within La Pietà. Priests and cardinals came in their many-coloured cloaks, swathes of blue carrying themselves along the shining road, the sisters trailing deferentially behind in their lilacs.

Virnoi and his lot gave them a wide berth. He hurried his Svarnish companions along to avoid drawing the eye of the church – not a single cardinal had spoken out against the sacking of Muqdah, despite several centuries of allyship with the holy city.

They never spoke up about anything, La Pietà, which infuriated Virnoi's failing sensibilities. He did not have many morals left in his body; he'd abandoned them long ago, but even his rejection of them left wreckage behind. Virnoi tried to school his features into something less disdainful, knowing that he could not sneer at them while dressed like a whore monger who'd go to an evening service. They did not join the holy men and women, that was not their gambit, as they could not pretend to be amongst them. Instead, they joined the second procession of entertainers and help meant for the evening's fun.

'All the less reputable help are supposed to be going down through the back entryway to draw less attention to themselves,' Takuma had explained. So, Virnoi took his companions through the gardens, down along the narrow paths with their flowering trees. One High Elf amidst many and his ducklings in red, following in a neat line at his tail.

There were plenty of brothels who'd been approached to supply skin for the event, most of which were smart enough to refuse the request outright. Thurlow Thurlowe had the reputation for ruining his playthings. Takuma was under the assumption that no one had approached The Brass Wyvern to be involved in the event. Virnoi hadn't yet figured out how to fess up that when a High Elf had shown up requesting to purchase a handful of girls, Virnoi had possessed the man and sent him off in a fright. This had been long before there was any talk of a dragon.

Only recently had Virnoi connected those specific dots, not thinking much at the time about another lecherous elf in the Imperium trying to pretend like slavery was not outlawed. Fuck the fucking High Elves. They always asked for girls.

They were all the same. Golden-eared pricks who benefited from merely existing in a country they'd monopolised. The land was not theirs; it had been the Nordlund before the High Elves had descended from the north. The irony of him fitting right in amidst the rabble was not lost on Virnoi; all it took was a corseted vest and a set of silks for him to look like any other High Elf. The only remnant left of his mother was the slight difference in the shape of his pointed ears.

The Wyvern workers were draped in plain cloaks to present a front of relative modesty, but the sheer layers of red linen that poked out from beneath gave them away. A shimmering cloth had been draped from Zuri's horns, not only to mark her as an entertainer, but also to conceal their shape. Takuma had arranged the fabric with painstaking care, which was why it had taken them so long to leave the Wyvern.

'Delivery,' he remarked blandly. He waved back towards the Wyvern workers lackadaisically, not lingering on one person for too long. This was not a game he'd played before, but the last thing he wanted was a pretty face catching the guard's eye entirely too quickly. 'Where do you want them?'

'Working house?' the first guard asked, straightening when he met Virnoi's stare and saw a glimpse of the animosity that lay within. Virnoi had seen enough lords in his life to know the look of nobility, the sense of reproach that noble sons had for any sense of labour. It made sense that an estate of such esteem would have noble brats guarding it, that they would limit the mere chance of common folk crossing into these royal halls. Thurlow Thurlowe thought himself one of the Eschalion, even if he did not have the gall to say so out loud.

'The Stuck Pig,' Virnoi said. The name had the effect they'd hoped for, and the two guards chuckled, glancing at one another. He managed a lazy smile, rolling his eyes. 'I didn't pick it, I'm just the ferryman. No one really cares about the name of the place as long as the women are pretty.'

'How many of them will be working?' the other guard asked, and Virnoi took a deep breath, resisting the urge to jab at the fact that the Imperium should have taught its children to count to four. He was supposed to be one of them today, as inane as they were. The guard peered past Virnoi's side, presumably looking at one of the lot. Virnoi would have guessed that it was Nuru. It was almost always Nuru; she had a face that drew the elvish eye. She complained about it regularly.

'Four bodies on the table, requested by one of the lords of the house above,' Virnoi said with an upwards jerk of his thumb towards the castle that towered over them. The more he spoke, the slimier he felt. He would apologise for this all, later, if he got the chance. He would have to scrub himself raw to feel like himself again once this was all done. 'Apparently one of this lot is a family favourite.'

The second guard turned towards Hotaru and asked, 'What about the little one? She's got such pretty eyes.'

Hotaru stood in a fine cloak with a scalloped edge that he also did not recognise. Her curls had been bullied and braided, leaving a river of dark curls down her back but keeping the majority of her hair off her face. The young woman's Blessed fingers were hidden beneath supple leather gloves that Virnoi had bought her some time ago, but she'd never worn, preferring her tired fingerless ones that were hidden in her cloak. It was entirely unlike the little thief to remain so polished. She was covered from her neck to the tips of her toes, the absolute antithesis of the prostitutes that followed.

They'd dressed her like that on purpose. He should have guessed that it would have made little difference.

A chill ran through Virnoi, sinking deep within his gut and anchoring itself there. He turned and cupped Hotaru's chin with one hand, tilting her head back until she was looking up at him. He kept his grip otherwise gentle as he stared down into her eyes. If gods of the forest existed, the ones his mother had told him of as a child, they had taken the finest saplings and wound them together to make Hotaru. They had taken tourmaline for her eyes, pressed the flush of lily petals into her cheeks.

'One of mine,' Virnoi said, unsmiling. 'Lay a hand on her, and I will skin you.'

The second guard swallowed, and Virnoi let the words hang in the air for a moment between them before he smiled, dropping Hotaru's chin. He looked back at both guards and continued on simply. 'Now, where do you want them?'

The first guard was finally wise enough to open the ledger in his hands, fingers skimming over scrawled lists of names. Virnoi watched through narrowed eyes, knowing that this was something he could easily falsify. Only a whisper of magic, but it would have been a waste. If the guards sensed that someone had tried to tamper with the guest list, then it would set them on alert. He needed them to think nothing was properly awry.

'We've got nothing listed for The Stuck Pig,' the guard said – which made sense, given The Stuck Pig was a brothel that didn't exist. It was a name that Takuma had picked because it was almost comically common, something that could have been reasoned away by the work of a cheeky tavern owner or a brothel madame. It was purposefully lowbrow. A bedworker saying that they worked for an establishment like The Jade Peacock or The Ivory Pearl conjured an image that lingered with a man. People paid no mind to someone from The Stuck Pig.

'Well, I brought them all this way on the order of your Thurlowes.' Virnoi took particular care while enunciating the name, rolling his eyes. 'It's not my fault that your people don't have the books together. I'm doing as instructed.'

'Sir, we're just doing as we're told.' Of course. The cry of the incompetent. No one was ever actually in the wrong, simply following a hard set of orders that they bent whenever they thought they weren't being watched. The fun thing about incompetency was that all it required to get them to fall into line was a little bit of trouble.

Virnoi cast a glance backwards, finding that his eyes rested upon Nuru. They had their own way into this event with her, laced up in that corset. He made up his mind slowly about what to say next. High Elves never rushed their words – those of greater importance set the pace in the conversation. He was supposed to be the more influential one, these two guards merely grunts amongst the litter. When he spoke again, his tone is utterly scathing. 'You want to run off to Truls Thurlowe and tell him that his favourite whore isn't going to be at the celebrations?'

The first guard began to speak before the second elbowed him hard in the side. He leaned in and muttered. 'We don't want to piss off the golden child by leaving his woman out here.'

Smart men. A silent exchange was had between the guards as they stepped apart, words exchanged only through the peculiar stare they gave one another.

'They stay in the playrooms. Help don't go any further than the kitchens,' the first guard said, his tone firm. Virnoi smiled at them, trying to channel Takuma's charm. He wasn't a fraction as charismatic as Takuma was, but the charade probably suited the character that he was supposed to be.

'That was the right decision, boys. Pleasure dealing with you.' He slid backwards to usher the Wyvern crew in ahead of him, though Hotaru never left his side. He'd given her directions in The Brass Wyvern while they were on their own. Once his little red ducklings had passed, he herded Hotaru in with his cloak, following them down a narrow hallway that led to a dressing room behind a curtain partition.

The Thurlowe estate had not gone to the brothels of the red-light district, Virnoi realised as he regarded the sea of varied horns. They had gone to the caravans; there were only a handful of faces in that dressing room that were not Svarnish. Virnoi sucked in a sharp breath between his teeth, realising what lay before him. The others found familiar faces amidst the bunch, greeting friends in the clusters of Svarnish folk that had arrived before them.

He was not sure if this sight unsettled his friends as much as it did him. High Elves did not associate with Svarnishmen, not en masse. That means that Thurlowe's household went out of its way to recruit this lot. Virnoi drew back into a quieter corner of the room, the only place where he won't risk bumping into someone. He could see the stares he was getting, distrustful glances from the collection of bedworkers and performers who were preparing for the evening.

Distrust was something he'd grown unused to after his months at The Brass Wyvern. He'd been there since last winter, meaning that it had taken them nearly an entire cycle of seasons to stop considering him as 'other'. He regretted not objecting to the costume now – he knew Takuma had reason enough to take advantage of his High Elf blood, but that didn't make it any less uncomfortable for him.

'Takuma!' a voice called from within the group, and Virnoi saw his paramour slip through the crowd to clap hands with a man that he did not know. As he watched, Takuma leaned in and exchanged a few short words before turning on his tail and slipping back to where they had clustered, shrugging out of his own cloak as he went. Garment hooks lined the walls of the room, cloaks and bags crowding the walls. The cloaks that the Wyvern workers were wearing were so plain that it would not matter if they were nicked. They were meant to be abandoned; plain, linen things that they had no attachment to.

Takuma looked like an elvish caricature of a Svarnish prostitute – all golden netting and sheer, red linen – and he had dressed his women to match. As the proprietor shrugged out of the cloak, he was a sight to behold. The trousers were made from several layers of shifting, see-through fabric that left very little to the imagination. Virnoi struggled to maintain eye contact with him, skimming over the rest of the crowd instead. Takuma was not armed beneath the costume, which concerned him deeply, but Virnoi put his faith in his ability to defend himself.

Nuru had been afforded some form of protection, at least. She wore a corset laced tightly with several blades tucked in the back, in reach if she needed self-defence. It left her heaving bosom bare, accentuating the Blessings that wrapped around her throat. The only true coverage she had was in the thick, top layer of her skirt, hiked up to expose a bare leg. One thigh was wrapped in a gold chain with a hefty charm dangling from it in the shape of a tiny dragon.

Zuri was the last to unfurl from beneath her heavy cloak. They had truly done all that they could to make the woman unrecognisable, painted in shimmering bronze body paint that matched the golden frame that crowned her horns. Trousers made from sheer panels of fabric were laced at her waist, her breasts bound in a knotted top that was secured to a shining ring at its centre. Her face was not hidden, eyelids and cheekbones swiped with the same paint that accentuated the sharp planes of Zuri's features. It turned her into a goddess of war.

'You look beautiful,' Hotaru breathed, evidently in awe. Zuri's focus broke in a moment, and her lips pressed into an embarrassed smile as she fiddled with the ends of her braids.

'Thank you,' Zuri said in Svarnish, briefly meeting Virnoi's eyes. He swallowed.

He had not missed the way in which Takuma had been staring at Zuri since her arrival at the brothel – like he was discovering the north star. Almost everyone was falling in love with the woman, Nuru remaining as the only one-way street amongst them. It had been some time since someone had caught Takuma's attention the way that Zuri had, though. The last paramour he'd taken on had been Virnoi.

The elf didn't have a jealous bone in his body. He was just quietly trying to figure out how to approach this new person, this new attraction. Or if he could approach it at all – and now was decidedly not the time. Virnoi shifted his attention back to Takuma.

'Are you good to do the work?' They were not about to speak freely surrounded by so many ears, so Virnoi picked his words carefully. All the pomp and condescension of the High Elf façade was entirely lost now; he could not maintain that specific level of obnoxiousness for particularly long.

'We're always good to work,' Takuma said with a shrug.

The Brass Wyverns took one another's hands slowly until they were standing in a circle, with Virnoi watching from just out of arm's reach. As he watched, they took a deep breath in unison and pressed a kiss to their companions' hands. It was such a simple, intimate thing that twisted a quiet knife in his ribs that had been slipped there some years ago. He could not begrudge them all this sense of community, but he would never be a part of it as Takuma or Nuru were. They were made of something far different than he, and they knew it. They quietly left him out of these rituals, these whispers and intimacies.

He could have had a family that had these rituals, could have known a people who embraced him so. But his blood had betrayed him in some deep way and made him an omen of bad fortune instead, leaving him without a family to call his own.

A word was spoken between them that Virnoi didn't bother to hear. It wasn't for him. If Takuma had ever noticed how far away Virnoi floated when he felt far away from them, he never quite showed it. They kept their secrets to themselves and remained inscrutable, to their detriment.

Hotaru turned first towards him, eyes bright and sharp. She was quick to part from the circle and trot back and catch his arm. There was not a person in the world that trusted him in the way that Hotaru did. Takuma trusted no one entirely, but Hotaru threatened to make him an honest man with how readily she'd follow him into the abyss.

She was brimming with excitement, fiddling with her rings and rolling her weight around on her boots uneasily, as if readying herself for flight. Hotaru was faster than any of the Wyvern workers, having perfected a quick disappearing act with years of avoiding the Imperial guard.

He was not sure what to say when she joined him, so instead he patted her on the top of her soft head of curls. Every time he looked upon her, his eyes were drawn to her broken horn, an unfinished shape that had been snapped halfway down its length. She had never given him any explanation for how the horn had been snapped. Some stories were too painful for even them to tell.

Takuma and Virnoi did not mince their words. His vibrant eyes scanned Virnoi once, up and down, before he patted him on the chest.

'We'll see you later, big boy.'

Well, that was that. He nodded and turned on his heel, passing his usual companions and crossing into the narrow passageway that led into the playrooms. He cast a sparing glance down at Hotaru to reassure himself that she was following at his side, not faltering or falling behind.

The playrooms were a sprawling maze of velvets and gold fringing, brimming to the edge with empty tables and questionable wall mounts that gleamed in the golden lamplight. They were the perfect height to be reached by a High Elf, which set a chill through Virnoi. He could not honour the feeling, instead drawing them both through several empty rooms. The Svarnishmen were clustering around the entryway, reluctant to press forward past anything but that initial room, which gave them plenty of space to work.

'You stay with me,' Virnoi muttered to Hotaru. 'If anyone tries to sneak a hand up your cloak, you say the word *fermare*, and I will handle it.'

If anyone tried to slip a hand up her cloak, they'd likely find the veritable armoury they'd strapped to Hotaru's back.

Chapter Twenty

THE IMPERIUM

Hotaru kept close to Virnoi's shoulder as he ducked within one of the booths that lined the playrooms. He was mindful not to rush, to draw too much attention to himself.

He did not say much. That was Virnoi. They did not trade needless words, not after so long in one another's company. He grasped her shoulder, and she only hesitated for a breath, knowing the repercussions that would come with fighting his magic. Hotaru willed herself into his grip as they vanished in tandem.

She hated this so much, mostly because of how confused her mind became when she was incorporeal. Virnoi's magic was a great, otherworldly thing that extended far beyond himself – Hotaru could not even deign to understand how he saw the world. She simply had to trust that he was not going to lead them directly off the nearest cliff. She found that when she passed through a wall, she could still feel the twist of her stomach and the uncertain twitch of her hands. She knew from many of these leaps that she should not consider the reality of the walls they passed through, how the building was made from brick and wood and how manifesting midway through would most certainly be the death of her—

Consider: a ghost. A ghost who passed through the world without ever feeling the bounds of the physical world. Unfettered from mortality or worries about how they would slip and fall if they placed a foot wrong. They did not even have feet. They just were. Spectres were a real threat in the world they lived in, and she could just be another.

They landed with a hard thud together, Hotaru first and Virnoi right after. Her stomach whirled unsteadily as the mage brought them both back to a corporeal state. She was built for climbing, for feeling the hard ground beneath her feet. She was not meant for this type of magic – that unhinged people from the bounds of gravity. She and Virnoi had practised it on occasion, but the first time he'd tried to float her, Hotaru promptly emptied her stomach over a rug he was fond of. It took all her strength not to do the same again.

He pressed a finger to his lips, and she steadied herself, pressing a hand over her mouth to quiet the sound. He waved a hand in the air, and the shadowy tome that Virnoi often pored over manifested from nothing, called without a single sound. Hotaru did not hear the magical word that he spoke next, but the familiar chill ran through her all the same. Magical words were not always spoken for the purpose of being heard.

A bubble of quiet ballooned out from where they stood, softening the sound of her breath and her shifting boots. She exhaled hard, swearing between her teeth, and was unsurprised when the sound did not leave the bubble. Virnoi snapped the book shut, and it turned to smoke, dismissed for now.

Time to go. He spoke quietly, directly to her mind rather than aloud. She, Takuma, and Virnoi had taken up the earrings that would allow them to speak with one another.

Virnoi led the way, and Hotaru's quick feet scurried after him. High Elves were so immensely tall that they had no real concept of pace. They did not understand how quickly someone like Hotaru, who usually enjoyed being the shortest person in the room, had to work to keep up with their freakish spider legs. She loved Virnoi, truly, but no one had any good reason to be so damned tall.

She tried to keep an eye on her surroundings as she went, but the tunnels had no true variation to them. They passed by a break in the wall and found the same white tunnels carried on forever, broken occasionally by a doorway or a standing guard. Further along the tunnel, the guards grew more frequent, eyes following them with the mild concern that one did an unleashed dog.

They stared at Virnoi far more than they did Hotaru. That was why they'd dressed her as she never would have on her own. A Svarnishmen dressed as a servant was almost always a creature who'd already been defeated by the weight of the empire. As long as they were not questioning their presence, the pair would press on. She did not know how Virnoi knew where to go, but she kept close to him.

Eventually, they passed a partygoer, dressed in dark peacock feathers that flared out in a great dramatic ruff at the top of the woman's short neck. High Elves found the most creative way to cover themselves, to look both modest and gaudier than any sin they committed in the red-light district. Further along they found a cluster of partygoers, one of which was a sister of the church in a glimmering cloak, all being ushered along by a servant who looked flustered. He spotted Virnoi and Hotaru lagging even further behind.

'We've got some stragglers!' the servant called. He waved hurriedly at them, cheeks flushed and tone shaking. 'Please hurry along, we have a schedule to keep.'

The group of elves who had lingered behind did not pick up pace. Virnoi and Hotaru sped past.

Several elves stood out from the crowd, but it was the woman Hotaru eyed. The one who stood slightly removed from the other peacocks. She was not as willowy as the Imperial elves and the shape of her ears was more delicately pointed than her peers, wrapped in a fur that was brilliantly white to Hotaru's eyes. Whereas the Imperial women largely wore their hair up, this woman's hair fell in a crimson swath that spooled in the fur, leaving the distant impression of a bloody pelt. Hotaru stared because she was wildly beautiful and wearing little cloth beneath the fur. She'd never seen an elvish woman expose such décolletage.

Northern delegation, Virnoi spoke in her mind. He was amused by her distraction – Hotaru didn't know what else he'd expect from her. She had a weakness for beautiful women. *They're no friends of the Thurlowes. She's a consort to the prince, little crow. I don't think she shares your tastes for the fairer sex.*

'Welcome, welcome!' a booming voice called down the tunnel, so loud that it had to have been enhanced by magic. She hurried down the hallway, having to walk far quicker than Virnoi to keep pace with him. As they drew down the tunnel, the voice shrunk and grew more human – and far more irritating. 'We are in no rush, but we do have a schedule, so hurry along so we can get to the exciting part of the night.'

Thurlow Thurlowe was built like a taper candle, slim and steady; instead of flame, his crown was made of copper. His coral hair fell in a silken sheet around his angular features. Hotaru had only ever seen depictions of him from afar, printed in papers and scrawled caricatures – none had been favourable. Watching him from mere metres away, she could see how his sons were an echo of him. He had given Taliesin his fine bone structure and brow, given Truls the reddish tint to his hair.

'I know you've all heard rumours about this grand project of mine. This addition to my estate that I've kept under the dark cloak of secrecy, under magical lock and key – what have I been doing here?' His voice, in contrast to his elvish glamour, ground against Hotaru's ears like salt against stone. She was reminded of an off-tune whistle; an instrument ancient and rusted. 'I have organised this party for you, my dearest friends and denizens of the empire, to show you myself.'

'So why isn't Eschalier here?' someone whispered conspiratorially above Hotaru's head. There was no way that the lord could not hear them if Hotaru could; the High Elves were not subtle in their gossip.

'You know Eschalier hasn't entertained Thurlowe in years.' Eschalier, the reluctant emperor, had retreated slowly from the public eye before Hotaru had ever arrived in this city.

She clung close to Virnoi's side, twisting until she had found a gap between shoulders that revealed the frosted glass behind Thurlow's back.

'I have done what no elf has done before. I have hatched a dragon.' Thurlow paused for dramatic effect and was rewarded with a disbelieving murmuring from the crowd; a lady tittered nervously. 'I took the knowledge that we gained from our assault upon Svarna and I have done something that even the Eschalion have failed at. I have brought dragons to life in the Imperium. In our kingdom.'

A ring on his long-fingered hand glowed, and with a flash of magic, the frosted glass cleared.

Hotaru didn't even see the dragon at first. She was too interested in the way that the window rippled as Thurlow pressed its hand to it, shifting. Prismarium glass did not do that. The whole point of Prismarium was that it was resistant to any and all magic – it made no sense. The window had to be made of something else, and as she mentally tore through a list of potential building materials, she found herself decidedly lacking for knowledge. She peered up at Virnoi, tugging slightly at his coat to try and draw his eye.

I see it, Virnoi said along their mental tether. *I'll figure out what it is once I get to work.*

An awed chorus rolled over the crowd as she strained onto the balls of her feet, brows furrowed as she tried to see the thing that they'd come all this way for. The habitat beneath the dome was rimmed by a pool of crystal-clear water with an island at its centre. It was covered in tall trees whose foliage branched out into great olive-green domes, and a thick brush that grew close to the earth. This was the one corner of the Thurlowe estate that had been entirely unrecorded in their plans, entirely flat and blank in the latest stages of the construction. The Imperium demanded records of everyone, but it did not demand they be up to date, especially not when the person they were asking records from was a prolific war criminal.

That scared most people.

Then the trees shifted, parted by a great body that was hugged by titanic wings. The dragon was a sight to behold, a creature unlike anything that Hotaru had ever seen. This was disregarding the fact that the only dragons she'd ever seen were in tapestries and picture books. It was built not from the earth, or gnarled tree roots like Feliks – this was a being of pure magic. Intangible, ephemeral magic.

Its scales were huge, layered arrowheads that shimmered as it prowled, changing colour from ivory to moss green as it made its way around the island. Once it had reached the end of its unseen path, it circled and paced back along that same route with its cavernous wings half-extended as if threatening to take flight merely by moving. She knew that it could not fly. It did not matter.

Hotaru's heart began to drum thunderously, threatening to break free from her chest in the panic that descended upon her – that dragon could not be a hatchling. It was a titanic beast, craggy and scarred on its side. Virnoi had told her an old story about how he'd seen direwolves from afar as a boy. How he'd seized with fear, how his body had known that if he'd crossed those beasts, they'd be able to tear him limb from limb. She now knew that ancestral fear. That dragon, that mesmerising thing, could turn them all to ash if the window before them fell. She wouldn't have blamed it. Not when it had been trapped in this hovel.

The wave of awe that fell over the elvish crowd transformed into riotous praise, and Hotaru's mind collapsed into a mental heap as she listened to their amazement. She knew that Imperium elves were arrogant. Their great weakness was their overconfidence; she simply hadn't thought them quite so stupid. It was like watching someone lie down in front of a bear.

It cannot breathe fire now, little crow. Breathe. Had Hotaru been holding her breath? She sucked in an unsteady breath regardless, following it with another for good measure.

She laughed. It was a peculiar habit she'd taught herself when faced with an astronomical sense of fear – Hotaru made herself laugh. It did not matter if she truly made the noise, she forced herself to giggle soundlessly at the sight before her. Hotaru believed that it tricked her brain into thinking that there was not an imminent danger at hand. Necromancers tricked and cheated the body all the time, and she could do the same. So, instead of being afraid, she found a hilarity where she should have found only horror.

Like clockwork, the laughter dulled the intense panic threatening to overwhelm her. The High Elf nobles were all far too preoccupied with the dragon to notice the muffled laughter in their midst.

'You've outdone yourself,' one elf proclaimed. 'This is a victory for the Imperium!'

'How much for the first egg? Will it be able to produce one?' Dumb question, one dragon on its own can't produce another. 'What about a whole clutch?'

There were peculiarities on the dragon's form that Hotaru began to track. The space between its chest and throat was swollen, a fat apple caught mid-swallow. There were long gouges of discolouration along its rib cage, where the scales no longer changed colour and instead remained a colourless ivory. As it strode around the habitat, it shot out bursts of hot air that bent the world in its wake, but not a hint of flame. Takuma's intel had been correct.

'This is barbaric,' a feminine voice was the lone dissenter amongst the crowd. Hotaru twisted and saw that several elves were staring incredulously at the beautiful redhead, whose brow was twisted. 'Do you not all realise this? I know you feel as if you have to ooh and aah at this man like he's a petulant child showing you his new toy, but that dragon is a sentient, magical being. Keeping it in a cage is a wild act of slavery.'

Perhaps Thurlow did not hear the unsettled noises that rolled through the crowd, the vague murmuring and sway of a crowd made deeply uncomfortable by the woman's words. Had the words not been true, they might not have dislodged the temperament of the crowd so easily.

'Avantika,' Thurlow responded, drawling out each syllable of her name. 'You do like to protest, don't you?'

'You are keeping an incredibly intelligent creature in a cage, ridding it of its freedom of choice. I thought slavery was meant to be illegal in your grand Imperium, wizard.' Wizard was said with a decidedly smug sneer. There were politics beneath the insult that Hotaru did not understand, but she knew that Thurlow was bristling, the barbed words landing exactly how she had intended them. Virnoi's hand came down on Hotaru's shoulder, drawing her closer.

'The slavery of the humanoid is a crime.' The arch mage stated the law as if it were self-evident to everyone attending. The ruling that outlawed slavery in the Imperium had not specified the humanoid, Hotaru knew. The emperor's wording had been wildly forgiving for the victims of magical transfiguration and the Wood Elves, whose appearance had lain into question their status as humanoid for several centuries.

'So, the Imperium ignores the sentience of magical creatures and beings that do not look like them.' The redhead drew her fur up around her shoulders in her haughty motion, dangerously well-articulated. This was a woman whose words would not be easily misconstrued.

'Does Iskildr even have anyone living up there, besides a handful of you freezing elves?' Thurlow laughed, so dismissively that it irked even Hotaru's temper. Iskildr was the kingdom of the Snow Elves that sat to the north of the Imperium, uncertainly allied with the Eschalion. They were so foreign to Hotaru that she had never factored them into her worldview, having never even met a Snow Elf before. 'I thought your lot were slowly dying up in that arctic wasteland.'

'Enough people for you to feel the need to invite my beloved to this farce.' There were a couple of muffled gasps at the stranger's brazenness, and the crowd's opinion turned quietly against the outspoken redhead. Hotaru felt it like a shift in the air; they were turned towards her with the hint of scorn in their stares. She and Thurlow were now sneering at one another, all polite facades gone. 'You are lucky not to face him on this fine day – it is no wonder that Eschalier wants nothing of your ways in his age. You'd sow ruin amongst us all with this idiocy.'

Thurlow's great, pointed ears flushed a scarlet red, and his mouth gaped for something to say. Hotaru could have laughed, as it looked like he'd been struck upside the head by her words.

Avantika laughed – it was a feral, mocking sound. 'You need not escort me out, Thurlow, I know the way.' Despite her protestations, the guards shouldered forward all the same. The delegate gathered herself with the poise of a queen and barely acknowledged the shadows at her shoulders, chin held high as she strode away from the crowd. Hotaru stared after her. Elegant from every angle, outclassing Thurlow's awkward mannerisms a thousand times over. 'Enjoy the savagery while you can!'

Not all elves have an Imperial sensibility, most just don't have the willpower to get involved in it. Avantika is notorious for this.

'For the rest of you, the party awaits in my home!' Thurlow glossed over the scene as though nothing had happened. 'The ballroom has been filled with the finest entertainers of our great kingdom, just for my beloved guests. Enjoy the festivities, allow yourself to indulge in my wealth, and know that with every day, our Imperium grows greater.' He waved them onwards and was assaulted by people at his shoulder, who were ready to beg for an ounce of favour in the hope of attaining a dragon egg. It was not an orderly finish in any means, people crowding around the great viewing window to watch the trapped dragon while Thurlow strode away, presumably to bask in the warmth of his sudden adoration.

A man like that could only be adored by what he did for others. For his country. He was not fluttering around this city being fawned after because of his personality.

Virnoi did not warn her. When most eyes were turned away from them, he said something low beneath his breath and sunk them both straight through the floor. She gasped, her mind whirling, and when she opened her eyes again, they were standing outside the Thurlowe estate. Knee-deep in a flower bush, she heaved as she dragged herself out of the plants and into the garden grass. Out here, festivities were in full swing, partygoers from the Golden Quarter spilling into the estate drunk on their own laughter and the bubbling atmosphere.

Her ears tingled, her stomach twisted, and Hotaru found giggles spilling from her lips.

'Is this magic?' she asked, as she was almost certain that this laughter was not her own. Hotaru had been possessed by fear mere moments before, and suddenly, her unsteady legs were the subject of every ounce of humour in her bones. Her necromancer regarded her, and his striking features were twisted with an extra wide, bemused smile.

'A blanket, atmospheric charm to make the world a little lighter, little crow. Seems it works quite well.' The world was an awfully pleasant place. Virnoi seemed to her an intensely handsome figure in the cut of dusk as he took her face in one great hand and peered down at her. A quiet chuckle shook his shoulders, his expression blossoming into a boyish grin that lightened the hollows beneath his eyes, allowed his cheeks to look fuller and softer. 'Your eyes are as bright as sapphires in this light.'

The universe stopped, slowed, bloomed before her eyes. Hotaru swallowed as her laughter spiralled down within herself, quieted by the intensity of Virnoi's stare. They had both been taken off guard by the charm. When her laughter softened, Hotaru found she could focus on why they were here. She reached up with one gilded hand and swiped his arm away, repressing an embarrassed laugh.

'Flattery will get you everywhere, any other night. We've got places to be.'

Virnoi winced, rubbing at his brow for a moment before he righted himself. 'Yes, little crow, we do. I didn't realise your joy was so contagious.' When he reached out again, it was for her shoulder instead of her face, and he tore the world open for them both once more.

They did not leap directly up to the tower. Virnoi's magic had its limitations, and the greater the jump, the more likely they'd draw the attention of the guard keeping an eye on magical signatures in the area. Thurlow would hopefully be preoccupied with his entourage of hapless followers. However, their map had not come with a list of his staff who carried spellcaster Blessings; their only intel on that front was that Nuru believed Thurlow wouldn't hire someone who couldn't cast a basic spell. To try and avoid detection, Virnoi took them onto the lower roof of the grand Thurlowe estate.

The tower that held their prize was lain out beside the central family estate. It was joined to both halves through the spider's web that lay beneath the earth, which had not seemed to be a purely Thurlowe invention. The channels ran far into the Golden Quarters – for what purpose, Hotaru did not deign to consider. The Brass Wyvern need only worry about how it could serve them. The roof of the hall beside the tower was broad and flat, so far above the earth that for a moment Hotaru imagined them both as low-flying dragons soaring over the Imperium.

Slowly, Hotaru turned on her boots. The tower lay before them, soaring upwards into the heavens, the fallen night reflected in the crystal dome that crowned it like an impenetrable mirror of the heavens.

'Time to get climbing,' Virnoi remarked, his eyes turned upwards. 'Put that leg I gave you to good use.'

Virnoi's wonder was softer, more restrained than hers, but she saw it gleaming within him like a geode. Hotaru grinned at him, the thrill illuminating her angular features with her own sense of youthful joy. She stuck her tongue out at her companion before bursting into a run, trotting across the roof with a bounce in her step.

'Bet you can't beat me to the top!' she shouted, the wind whipping at her cloak.

Chapter Twenty-One

THE IMPERIUM

The number of Svarnish folk in Thurlowe's estate made no sense.

Even if this was the dread mage's spiteful way of grinding down an already exhausted people, it still felt more malicious than that. Had Nuru been welcome amongst the caravans, she could have gone to them, asked each one of them what conversation had happened to draw them into the Imperium. It felt ill-fated to see so many of their own in this place, like a school of silvery fish stranded in the middle of the sand sea, flapping and wheezing as they slowly cooked beneath the hot sun. A place they had no reason to be.

She didn't doubt that Takuma felt it too, the peculiarity of it all; they had spent years living in the Imperium with only a smattering of horned folk passing through their lives. Most of those who had stayed for any great length of time had worked at the Wyvern in some regard. They knew them all. But people in this crowd knew them from before their city life, and that was decidedly a terrible thing. Nuru and Takuma had robbed their caravan and fled. Nuru didn't care if they saw her as a kin traitor – she had no ill will towards them – but they were still at risk.

'If we do this tonight,' Nuru muttered, 'and we leave all these kinfolk within reach of the guard, we're going to cause a massacre. They'll be scooped up, imprisoned, and they'll disappear forever – it'll be pure chaos.'

'I know,' Takuma hissed, adjusting the sash Nuru had at her waist. Her temper flared in the back of her mind, his sharp tone feeding into the frustration that already lingered there. He had this horrible habit of sounding dismissive when his gears began to turn, churning away to try and find them a way out of this predicament.

She reached out and they clasped one another's forearms, their great eyes locked on each other, onyx and emerald quietly panicking in tandem. 'We'll need to get them out and into the city when it happens.'

'I know, Nuru, I'm thinking.' She huffed but did not press. They were barely back on solid ground; this was not the time to pick another quarrel. Nuru knew the cogs in Takuma's brain had begun to churn the moment they'd noticed the diaspora of people flooding into the Thurlowe estate. 'Why would Thurlowe invite so many Svarnishmen into his midst? He's asking to get robbed.'

'The children of Muqdah, working for their pleasure whilst he unveils the literal dragon he's managed to trap? It's perfect for them. He rots our culture and makes us privy to it.'

Thurlowe was using Svarnishmen as decoration. Waving around his dragon and their people to drape over the estate.

The Wyvern workers were lingering in the dressing room uncertainly, trying to gauge the temperaments of the other Svarnish folk and what they were here for. Nuru was certain that plenty of their kinfolk here weren't bedworkers. They looked out of place in what should have been a familiar setting for those who worked in the field. They lacked the signature slashes of red and dressed in clothes that would take time to remove or creased easily. People paid for bedworkers for a variety of services, but skin and discretion were involved in nearly all of them. If one walked out looking like they'd had a roll in the hay, it defeated the purpose.

It struck Nuru that many of these women had likely been coerced in some way to attending this estate tonight. That thought birthed a black chill in her gut, a sudden bead of rage that was far greater and older than herself. She heard her mother cursing in her memory, spitting mad.

She took a steadying breath and let out a puff of shimmering air. She'd already been on edge, and this development was all it had taken for her magic to sing to life. Her Blessing sat around her throat, begging to be freed, begging to be put to use.

'They won't say anything to us,' Takuma murmured as they slipped through the dressing rooms, Zuri in tow. 'Half of them would love to cross Imamu and get away with what we did, they just don't have the balls to do it.' After stealing a merchant king's wife, a caravan, two horses and a good bag of coin, Takuma had quite the reputation. Before that, he had been known amongst the caravan folk as Imamu's silver-tongued thief, but he was not the sort of man to settle for making a name for another. He was always going to strike out; Nuru was just glad she'd factored into his plans.

Takuma was making this excuse as they rounded the corner into the playrooms and were faced with Mosi lounging at one of the central tables, one arm lazily stretched around a bronze-skinned elf.

'Well, shit,' Takuma swore.

A lump the size of a walnut grew in Nuru's throat.

Mosi was the preeminent bedworker amongst the Svarnish ranks, and had he been floating around in the old country, he would have been the closest thing they had to a courtesan. He'd gained his reputation by working his way out of the war and into the Imperium, willing to entertain homosexuality amongst his clients before the Imperium had relaxed on some of its stricter laws. It had won him the coin and respect to walk in most cities undisturbed, even in the clothes of the holy men who came before him.

'I suppose that answers who's the authority of the evening.' It made sense that if Mosi had been roped into this whole affair, others would have come. It also meant that Imamu would be lurking somewhere, potentially through a magic thread that joined the two men. Mosi was a big boy and allowed to wander out into the Imperium on his own, but Imamu and Mosi were an authority amongst the caravan folk. They had come out of Muqdah, founded a caravan amidst the heart of the war, and kept their people safe.

Something in Nuru's heart twisted painfully, deeply sentimental.

Mosi looked like a creature of the night, as though he had taken a starless sky and draped it across his tattooed skin. Silver rings gleamed on his fingers, creating a metallic gauntlet across his knuckles, matched by the broad bracelets that donned his wrists. Everything about the way he presented himself served as some form of armour, a uniform that he donned to distance his work from his true self. It was no wonder that any man with the interest went stumbling over themselves to lay a hand on him.

'Feliks, Zuri, go to the kitchens before the entertainment of the night sets in.' The unlikely pair shared an indecipherable look before they nodded and fled into the velvety maze. Zuri was rightfully suspicious of Feliks. He had been an interesting and bizarre acquisition for the brothel, to say the least, and he continued to surprise them a little at every turn.

Once they were out of sight, Nuru glanced at Takuma and jerked her chin towards Mosi. His emerald eyes flicked between them both as Nuru turned, having decided already that she wanted to greet their old companion.

'Nuru, don't—'

She looked sharply back at Takuma, venom on her tongue. Whatever he saw in her features was fierce enough to steal the words from his tongue and snap his mouth shut. Nuru would not be told what to do about a man who had once been her friend. She reached out, took Takuma's hand, and marched them both up to Mosi's table.

'Mosi,' Nuru murmured.

'Nuru,' Mosi said her name, the intensity of his stare never wavering. He spoke in Svarnish then, sparing a glance to his companion. 'You've made a dumb decision coming here tonight.'

'Seems like we're in this particular idiocy together,' she responded lightly.

To say that her and Mosi's relationship was complex was probably understating the matter. One could take every thread in a tapestry and knot them together around the singular lodestone that was Imamu and that wouldn't even be half of it. Mosi was looking at her as if he didn't entirely believe that she was here, his river-grey eyes drinking in every ounce of her as she approached. The last time they'd lain eyes upon one another, she'd been fleeing into the darkness with a babe in her belly.

She fell into Svarnish talk with a familiar ease, as easily as she breathed. Nuru looked at the High Elf beside Mosi and smiled easily, the smile that she lent all patrons within The Brass Wyvern to put them at ease. 'I am so sorry for the intrusion, sir. We're old friends who have been living a world away from one another.'

'Oi, Aloysius, give us a moment, will you? Find us some drinks, I haven't seen Nuru here in years.' There was no mention of Takuma because the two men had been at odds with one another in every breath they'd traded. They'd worked together and forged the occasional unsteady alliance, but bickered aggressively all the while.

'The talk I tolerate from you,' the dark-skinned elf said with a gentle laugh. 'You want summer wine?'

Mosi made an affirmative noise, and at her shoulder, Nuru could sense Takuma's disdain. She shook her head as Aloysius rose, refusing an unspoken offer as he passed. She'd never taken to the drink, having been too young at first and then having Nema tucked on her hip. Takuma had a hard rule of not drinking while he worked, but like many of the best men Nuru had ever known, Mosi had a vice. She did not generally hold it against him – the war had left its scars on them all.

'Seems like a relaxed mark,' Nuru remarked as her eyes followed the elf across the room. Aloysius was dressed in dark, muted tones and lacked the many layers of clothing that she'd grown accustomed to seeing on elves. It was almost tame of him, to dress in a tight silk velvet without almost any embellishment.

'He's an architect, not some stuffy noble with a complex.' Mosi didn't move from where he reclined. 'Pretty sure that Thurlowe invited him as a matter of custom.'

Architect. Someone had to have designed this thing, of course – it was almost reassuring that Thurlow wasn't smart enough to put it together himself.

At her side, Takuma squeezed her hand twice. She wrinkled her nose as if something had tickled her senses. This was how they'd learnt to communicate when words would betray them; small motions and expressions, things other people wouldn't think much of. Mosi would see the signs like a dog saw the hints of a rabbit in the brush.

Once she was certain Aloysius was far enough away, she slipped onto the chair opposite Mosi. Takuma, her eternal companion, leaned up against the back of the chair.

'They're renting you out to elves now? Has Imamu lowered his standards so much?' Takuma probed. It was not how Nuru would have started the conversation – they could use Mosi. He was good and strong, a better warrior than any of them.

'Imamu wasn't given much of a choice – even he can have his arm twisted.' Mosi snorted. 'Did y'all raise your standards? Looks like you might actually have clients with money for once. Better than the swine you'd pick off the streets.'

It was an interestingly superior stance to take for someone who'd joined them on the streets. Most Svarnish bedworkers were nomadic, living on the road and floating amongst the network of inns and taverns that covered the elvish Imperium. They had little choice – property law across the broader empire was slow to update, even in allowing Svarnishmen to hold temporary residence in Imperial property.

'What sort of establishment picked you two off the street?' Mosi pressed, eyes glinting. He was not asking for himself, Nuru was quite sure of that.

'The Preening Peacock,' Nuru responded simply. It was not a real establishment, but in the years they'd spent nurturing the reputation of The Brass Wyvern, she'd developed a mental roster of fake brothels to claim that they worked under. As far as most were concerned, The Brass Wyvern did not exist, an alleyway rumour about a pleasure house manned by beautiful dragonfolk. Such a place could not exist within the Imperium, so it was written off as an urban myth. The High Elves would have liked to pretend that there was no place for Svarnish bedworkers in their brothels, but in truth, Nuru and Takuma could have worked at any number of places on their strip. There was a growing appetite within the population for Svarnish flesh, and they could have made their coin a dozen different ways in the course of the day.

Takuma made a rude noise. Mosi scoffed. They both knew quite well that Nuru was lying, but she didn't care. If she left the two men to it, they'd come to blows in a heartbeat. Takuma would swing first because, of course, he was Takuma, but that would be the end of the discussion. In truth, she had no qualms with Mosi. He had sat and watched them leave on the shadowy evening they'd fled Imamu's caravan, hadn't raised a finger to stop them.

'Do you know what's going on here today, Mosi?' she slipped forward and into the seat opposite him. 'What did they tell you?'

It was conspiratorial enough a motion that she saw her once-mentor switch gears, the slope of his shoulders softening as he folded forward, lacing his fingers together. This was the Mosi that cared for the caravan and for them, the listener. When he spoke, it was in Svarnish, his tone steady and unreadable to anyone who'd dare to listen.

'They didn't tell us much. Imperium guards came with one of those diplomats and told us that Thurlow Thurlowe was throwing a celebration on the anniversary of Muqdah's fall. If we didn't send workers to help fill out the night, they were going to stop giving the caravans the generous allowance of passage into Imperial cities.' The look on Mosi's face was enough to tell Nuru what they'd thought of that.

A celebration of the rape of Muqdah. Nuru tasted iron and realised that she'd clamped down on her own tongue. It was like she'd been swallowed by a black pit, Mosi's eyes on her all the while. She reached out across the table, and he gave her his hand. They stayed like that for only a second, with Nuru squeezing his calloused palm, before they broke apart. She shook her head. 'He can't do that.'

Mosi would have argued. He and Imamu would have never given into that claim. They would have fought tooth and nail, both men from Muqdah who'd watched it fall.

'That's what we thought. A few of the kings got together and spoke. None were willing to risk it. Most of the big trade cities are Imperium-based, so they figured what was one night compared to continued trade in an empire they forced us to join?' He rolled his eyes, the disdain in his voice thick. 'I told them it was stupid, but the kings had a fair point. If the Imperium stops us from trading in their cities, they cut the legs out from underneath any Svarnishmen who made it out of the old country.'

'Pretty much all the cities are theirs nowadays,' Takuma muttered. That had not always been the case – for centuries the Nords had held sovereignty over their largest holds, cities, and towns. This was their land, after all. But with time, the Imperium had eaten away at the old laws. It was a rotten thing.

Many of those who'd gotten out of Svarna had been adamantly against living beneath elvish subjugation. If they could not trade in any decent city, though, most caravans would be forced back into the ruins. There they would have had to truly watch the elvish nobles fluttering about their old palaces and temples, turning everything into a fascination.

Of course, the kings folded. They were proud but transactional creatures, they were survivalists. They kept their people alive and with full bellies so that the old country could carry on in some small way.

'They have a dragon,' Nuru whispered. 'That's the real celebration, Mosi. They finally have their own dragon.'

Speaking the words aloud made them real. She watched as the realisation struck him, his grey eyes flicking over to where Aloysius lingered metres away. An architect. Mosi's eyes narrowed. 'How do they have a dragon?'

'Don't know for sure – best guess is that Thurlow stole an egg during the pillage, and it's taken this long to get everything together. It's not like they would have known how to hatch it.' Nuru wrinkled her nose, unsure of Takuma's assessment of the dragon's arrival in the Imperium. Dragon eggs were notorious for taking extensive time to hatch, but they could generally not be triggered to do so without the presence of an adult dragon. It was why dragons like Idunn had ended up settling in the nurseries for years, watching over any egg that passed beneath her gaze. The dragon that Zuri had described to them didn't sound like any hatchling Nuru had seen. She studied Mosi. 'Does it really matter how Thurlow Thurlowe has a dragon?'

He stopped, picking up one of the drinks that Aloysius had left on the table and swirling it before lifting it to his nose and inhaling deeply. His hand trembled as he did.

'I guess not. They took enough from us, why not dragons? Next thing we know, there will be renasci running around the Imperium.' A ballsy thing to say for one of the few fully fledged renasci that had survived the war.

'We're going to free it. Tonight. Everyone needs to be ready to run when we do. That's why I came to talk to you. Are you the guardian for tonight?'

'No, I'm not,' Mosi inclined his head to Nuru. 'That would be your husband. How do you intend on getting a dragon out of an elvish stronghold?'

'Don't worry about it,' Takuma said. 'And she's his ex-wife. They're not married anymore. Don't suck his cock any harder than you already do.'

The older man did not dignify that specific barb about Imamu with a response, simply shooting Takuma a long look. In their youth, that look had often come before a well-aimed swipe at the top of their heads. Determining that Takuma was out of his reach, Mosi crossed his arms and stretched backwards into the lounge. 'No, I think that's actually something I should worry about it. Especially if you're the one handling it – Takuma, have you ever seen a dragon?'

'I don't need to have seen something to be able to steal it,' Takuma said in a barely contained snarl. 'I'm not a total amateur.'

'You're not a master thief, either. You're a fool with a tendency to get ahead of yourself, which spells death where dragons are involved.'

'He has me,' Nuru cut in. 'And we have magicks of the old country, so we'll do fine.'

This was an ancient argument they did not have the time for. She reached out across the table and took Mosi's hand in hers, dragging him insistently. Mosi could play this disinterested figure all he wanted, portray a façade of a man who wanted to prioritise only his caravan to soothe Imamu's ruffled robes. But the time for pretence was over.

'Nuru,' Mosi began uncertainly. She shook her head.

'Bickering about whether we should be stealing something helps no one. We are doing this tonight, and you are either going to help us or stay out of your way. I will not permit you to hinder us.' It did not fail Nuru that she was using the same tone of voice that she did when trying to gently reprimand Nema or manage conflict between the youngest Wyvern workers. 'We could use your help, though. We—we could use an extra pair of hands on the ground, and you have always been someone I'd want on my side in a fight.'

She could not blame Mosi for anything in her life that had gone awry. He was the sort of man who toiled in the eternal dark, who'd rather have sold his skin than put another person in a guillotine. As she clutched his rough hand in hers, Nuru stared at him with huge eyes that implored a thousand pleas upon him. If he was here, her escape from Imamu was already at its end, but that did not mean this night needed to end here. He wanted to stop them because trying to steal a dragon was a foolish, grand thing that no one in their right minds would have attempted, but those were the sorts of things The Brass Wyvern excelled at.

People who thought like normal folk did not buy a brothel in the heart of enemy territory. They did not make themselves spectres.

'When the chaos starts, you will get everyone out, won't you? You'll take care of everyone.'

After a long, pensive moment, Mosi sighed. 'Of course, I will, Nuru. You need not ask.'

Chapter Twenty-Two

THE IMPERIUM

It hurt Zuri in a tender place to be amongst so many Svarnishmen and still not have the freedom to simply be with them. She recognised the shape of these shadowy halls as she and Feliks traversed the crowd, and her every muscle buzzed with a fear that she could not control.

'Aye, girl, you are a vision in red,' a soft-cheeked woman commented as Zuri passed. Zuri found she could do nothing but smile, her tongue dry and her Svarnish caught on her tongue. She reached out and brushed the stranger's shoulder affectionately as she slipped away. It did not seem to matter to anyone here that they did not know her, or that she'd not been with her people. She was Svarnish all the same.

'They're not lying,' Feliks remarked idly. 'If Takuma wanted you to blend in, I don't know why he put you in that.'

'It's all a performance, no?' Zuri shrugged.

'Or he just wanted to look at you in it. He likes rope on his women.' She snorted – had it been from someone else, the comment could have been almost salacious, but Feliks spoke with a docile, nonplussed tone that raised no hackles. It was factual. She had only been with them for a matter of weeks, and she was somehow adopted without question into the realm of Takuma's women. She wondered who Takuma would count amidst that number.

They turned out of the playrooms into a hallway, separated by curtains. She let Feliks lead the way, his broad form half blocking her.

'Can you even speak Svarnish, Feliks?' she asked once they were separated from the crowds. There was something terribly intimate about the narrow, velvety hallways within the Thurlowe estate – they could not hold two elves abreast, meant for only one and their companion or a flurry of servants.

'Some.' Feliks shrugged. He had a glint in his eyes as he looked back at her, a shine she had only seen from beasts in the night. 'Not all of us have the luxury of growing up amongst those who speak the tongue.'

'Yes, that would be why you don't speak Svarnish,' Zuri said with a smile tugging at her lips. 'You are Svarnish even without the tongue, Feliks, I'm not questioning that. I'm more curious about what you're made of.'

In one of the most utterly bizarre moments of Zuri's life, Feliks' mouth did not move, but he spoke to her in the dark, his voice emanating from somewhere lower in his body. 'Keep asking questions, then. You'll figure it out eventually.'

A shadow fell over Feliks' shoulders, cast by elaborate drapery from a nearby alcove, and his image changed. It was hard to look upon, a shadow so dark that her eyes struggled to discern the shift. For one moment, he was the Feliks that she knew; then he was not a he at all. His shoulders narrowed, his bulk slimmed out, and he gained the swell of breasts. He shook out his hair, now a luscious mane of auburn falling to Feliks' now slender waist.

It was Feliks. He had the same angular cheekbones and squarish jaw; his eyes sparkled just as they had mere moments before. He was Feliks, he was just now also a woman. He winked at her, totally unbothered by the incredulous look in Zuri's eyes. 'Everyone loves a pretty woman, don't they?'

Everyone did love a pretty woman. Zuri was no exception. He was also almost entirely topless beneath the shawl he wore around his shoulders. Zuri's attention shot down for a half-second and then back to Feliks' face, still disbelieving of the strangeness that stood before her.

They arrived in the service kitchens, which were a third of the size of the lord's personal ones. There were several kitchens in Thurlowe's estate, small and large, with all the kitchens ready to be in service at all hours. But the lord of the manor couldn't tolerate his servant's food preparation happening alongside his, so this was relegated to daily usage and for play nights. That was all information that Takuma had gleaned from his chatting away to the Thurlowe servants – it did not surprise Zuri that they'd divulge this information in some roundabout way. Not when the rakish, vivid-eyed bedworker had been the one asking.

The service kitchens were steaming, crowded with fair-feathered Nords and harried elves. They barely glanced at Zuri and Feliks in their entryway until a servant swung around a corner, needing to pass. Feliks swung sideways to let them pass, and Zuri followed suit, suddenly uncertain of her performer's garb amidst the alabaster brickwork.

This was a lot of people for Zuri. She had been easing into groups in the Wyvern, growing more accustomed to noise and chatter, but there was so much movement here. Translucent vegetables simmered in huge pots, pale meats roasting in smoke chambers, servants blowing off steam about the evenings and their errant affairs. Zuri knew this of service staff; they adored the privilege of complaint. Her mind shifted through each conversation, searching for something of note. They were here for a purpose – Zuri could set her mind on that and weed out the chaff.

It would distract her from a dark question that loomed in the shadowy corners of her mind. Had these been the people who fed her, while she had been trapped in Llewelyn's wing? Had all of these people known she was here? She had known that, at the very least, a handful of cleaning staff and very likely a chef or a cook of some kind had been aware of her, but not this throng of staff. An ancient knife twisted in her gut, provoking a spat of venom in her psyche. Llewelyn would have taken great pleasure in knowing that everyone in his father's estate comprehended he had a prisoner trapped within its walls and that they were not to intervene.

There had been people changing her linens, bringing her meals, and making sure that she was not starving herself. Zuri had tried to leave her food abandoned when she'd been learning how to navigate her life beneath the brothers' boots. Death had been preferable to life away from the plains and her parents, but being force-fed was worse.

She was not a fantastic shadow. As Zuri followed Feliks around the edge of the kitchens, she drew the gaze of strangers. Dayo had always told her that she was a beautiful girl. She had not been one for vanity and yet, now, it was as if there had been some minor shift in the world. She had gone from a ghost – an echo of a caravan, of her father – to something of note. When had that happened?

'Oi,' a brusque voice called. Her head snapped towards it and found a snowy-haired man wearing an apron over his servant's garb. A Nord through and through with eyes so bright that they glowed, two tiny full moons within the man's skull. They were startling creatures to look upon. 'You dragon folk aren't supposed to be in here – scat, will you?'

The reprimand was half-hearted. Zuri bowed her head weakly, casting a glance back from whence she came. Feliks, remarked upon for his brilliance at blending in, did not pause at all before he spoke. He shifted slightly to block Zuri's body from sight – this costuming truly cast her as an outsider amidst them, though Feliks' outfit was not far off. He was in similar silks to Takuma, albeit with less adornments, muted red fabric wrapped over his fair muscle.

'She's just looking for oil. Special request from one of the knife-ears for the festivities, he wanted … lubrication.' It was an absurd explanation to Zuri, but Feliks said it with that same nonplussed, unbothered tone that he always had. He was a convincing liar – it appeared as easy as breathing for Feliks. She suspected that his heaving bosom now helped the cause. 'Thought the easiest fix would be olive oil. Can we take a spare bottle for the freak?'

If the chef noticed anything awry, she could not tell. His face softened, hard stare turning warm as he appraised them a second time. He struggled to drag his gaze away from Feliks, for which Zuri was somewhat grateful. She may have been raised a performer, but she had not been a spectacle in some time. If she was never leered at again, she would be content.

Finally, he asked, 'Where are you from, girl?'

'Down on the snow run near the black valley,' Feliks responded. He swung his auburn hair over his fair, freckled shoulder. 'Near Breidrkald.'

'One of my cousins lives out that way.' A smile warmed the Nord's features, though it did little to appease Zuri's apprehension. One could warm up ice with sunlight, but it did little more than drip, it remained wrought with frost. Distractedly, she supposed that they found the Svarnishmen just as unsettling. Zuri had never seen a pure-blooded Nord until she'd been in the heart of Eschalion territory.

'Everyone has a cousin out that way.' Zuri's companion threw her head back and laughed, a melodic, boisterous sound. This dazzling persona was a hearthfire that drew every eye in the room, so different from the quiet, imposing brawn Zuri knew. The man chuckled, and then the two traded words in an old tongue, one that Zuri did not know. Nordish was rough and quick, spoken from the back of the throat.

She understood what he was doing, though. There was trust inherent in sharing a mother tongue with another who spoke it. Feliks had marked himself as trustworthy in mere minutes. It was dangerously easy.

After a short conversation that seemed well-humoured enough, the two languished in a pause before the chef shifted back to the common tongue. 'Didn't know things were starting up so early. There are bottles on the back wall, take one and if you need another, come back – gods forbid the bastard wants to cover himself in it.'

Llewelyn had been a lean beanpole, long-limbed in all ways. The intrusive thought of his bare ass covered in olive oil was a violent punishment that Zuri shuddered away from.

The Nord looked at her dead in the eye and tapped his chest with a fist. 'You bedworkers are stronger than any of us. Certainly, stronger than me. I'd be lopping off limbs all over the place.'

Being otherwise entirely comfortable in her silence, the world skipped a beat as Zuri registered that this relative stranger was speaking with her. He was looking at her, but she was not expecting him to genuinely see her, tucked behind Feliks. She blew out a breath and shrugged, trying to feign a level of friendliness that felt strange. 'If I could, I would.'

He chuckled at her before directing his attention back to Feliks. 'You should come back down to the Frost Quarter when you have a spare evening. You'd be welcome, sis.'

Feliks nodded towards the cook as he and Zuri hurried towards the back of the kitchen. The rack on the back wall was an enormous thing, shelves stacked from floor to the ceiling with oils and spices, featuring great bottles containing floating mushrooms that, to someone who'd spent her childhood foraging, looked distinctly inedible. The far end of a shelf, at eye level, was piled with haphazardly tied bundles of flowers. They seemed out of place, the staff's effort to salvage what beauty they could from the world.

She did not know the word for olive oil in elvish or Nordish, so she looked for a substance of the right consistency and trusted that Feliks would find it if she could not. She glanced at him briefly as they ducked around a pair of bickering waitstaff.

'You are a menace,' Zuri hissed in their mother tongue.

Feliks giggled. Zuri was struck by how Svarnish he was, despite how his colouring leaned into a snowdrift. There was a roundness to Feliks' nose and a fullness to his mouth, a high angle to his cheekbones that were meant to carry into the horns that crowned him. The gods had painted him up to vanish within the Nords' land, and yet it mattered not: he was a dragon beneath the skin, just as she was. She reached out and clasped Feliks' hand with her own and, for the first time, was entirely at ease with him. He responded in unbothered, perfectly articulated Svarnish. 'I quite like this form.'

'You're quite pretty.' It was a total understatement of Feliks' beauty. His beauty was a trap, meant to entice and entrance; he wore womanhood like a black wreath of belladonna.

'I'm quite good at being looked at – I think you'll also find I'm quite talented at not drawing the eye at all.' Zuri understood Blessed magic. She'd carried power in her feet since she was a babe, had seen how it had carried her through the world. The magic that Feliks bore was unlike anything she'd ever seen, so she did not object or raise any of the litany of questions demanding some form of answer. 'Let's get this meal sorted for our friend, shall we?'

A slab of meat sat at the furthest end of the service kitchens, sitting on a low, hand-drawn cart before a hatch door framed in streaky, dried blood. Zuri wasn't familiar with the practice of butchery, but she was certain it had to be almost all of a pig, sans the legs and head and curly tail. Or a portion of a cow. If this was the dragon's regular meal, there had to be a slaughterhouse of livestock somewhere purely for this purpose.

Feliks casually shoved his hand into the guts of the thing.

'You concern me,' she remarked.

Feliks looked at her and the grin he gave her was wolfish and sharp. 'Then I haven't lost my touch.'

Zuri turned backwards to the maze of cookware and flushed-faced workers, uncertain, only to find that their presence had been totally forgotten. The cook had turned his attention back on the simmering collection of pots sitting before him,

'Oi girlies!' another voice cut through the kitchens, words slurring. Zuri turned sharply and eyed the drunken elf wandering in through a narrow doorway. She quickly smothered the urge to sneer at the man. A flicker of uncertainty crossed Feliks' face. Zuri waved him off as she strode to meet the swaying elf. Feliks needed to work, and if he was as excellent at turning away the human eye as he thought he was, he would be fine on his own. She suspected that mysterious gender-bending shapeshifters did quite fine without babysitters.

Despite her disgust, Zuri knew how to handle this man. She stopped before him, craning her head upwards to meet his gaze. He loomed over her, crowding forward until she could smell the liquor on his breath.

'Yes?' she said.

'What are you doing out of bounds, doll face? All you horned folk are to stay in the playrooms, where you belong.' Boiling the Svarnish identity down to their horns was something that only a Svarnishman truly had the right to do. An elf calling them horned folk was half a step up from calling them goat people, but it had a real pretence of respectability beneath it.

'My master deigns I walk wherever he allows me in these halls,' Zuri remarked blandly. She kept her voice low and even, sensing that chef's presence in her peripherals. It was easy to flatten the light from her eyes, mimicking a stare she'd learned from the two men who'd once been her captors. They had responded best to her when she'd mimicked them; she suspected that this elf would be all the same. 'As you are not him, you have no say over my movement.'

'Your master?' The elf remarked incredulously, his eyes flicking downwards towards her ankles. She lacked the shackles, but Zuri didn't think it mattered. 'Who is your master?'

'Master Llewelyn.' Dropping Llewelyn's name had the desired effect. He rolled back, his eyes skating over her once more as he reassessed the woman who stood before him. Llewelyn may not have been a true son of the family, but his reputation had leaked out from the familial vault, corrosive and never-ending. This was the type of worm who'd think great things of Llewelyn – they'd take his venom as aspirational. 'He is not a fan of drunkenness or infringement upon his property, so I suggest you step back.' It was a gamble, but, emboldened by the way that the stranger was stumbling for words, she stepped one boot forward and leaned on his foot. 'Or else I might mention your horribly lopsided face to him and how you were disgracing his father's halls. How about that?'

Zuri had never been a soft woman. Her father had not taught her to be polite to men if they made her uncomfortable; her mother had told her not to quiet herself for the sake of another's voice. Even as a girl, she had been sharp and sullen-mouthed, with no instinct to smile to comfort someone else's temper. It served her well. She was not built to bow.

Her Blessing, powered by nothing but her rage, tingled in her feet. The copper base in her boots warmed, the magic leaping downwards into the conductive metal.

'You're a mean thing,' the elf hissed. 'Of course, you'd be his.'

She sneered. In a quick movement, she swept her boot across the tile and brought it down directly on his boot, leaning her full weight on his toes. He was too proud to draw away and instead bristled back at Zuri, eyes narrowing.

'I'm not just mean, I'm cruel. What do you think belonging to Llewelyn does to a person?' She felt a knife twist in her soul. Zuri leaned in, never tearing her gaze away from this stranger's. 'What do you think that does to a woman?'

The elite, Zuri had learned, like to pretend as if they were all very above the debauchery of their friends while still gleaning invites to the cabal. There were men who had known where she was, a wraith living in the shadowed halls of this estate. They had known which chains had bound her, and though they may have occasionally snuck her a sympathetic look, a scrap from their plate, they'd never stepped down from their gilded pedestals to intervene on her behalf.

Why should she have spared a thought for them?

'Bitch,' he hissed. Zuri grinned, fierce and daring. If he was going to swing, he would swing and be faced with the threat of Llewelyn. The omnipresent threat of Llewelyn the mean. Anyone who knew him and had half a functioning brain would know that they'd be wise to avoid erring on the wrong side of his temper.

Over the stranger's shoulder, Feliks bounced idly, drawing Zuri's eye. She removed her boot and scoffed. 'Keep walking before he sees fit to teach you about the glory of the Thurlowe clan.'

In that threat, she felt the spectre of Llewelyn within her and the scars he'd left. She heard his imperious tone, and she swallowed, afraid that she'd find ice creeping onto her tongue if she allowed any more frost to claw its way within her dragon's heart. The stranger snarled and pulled away from her, scurrying through the maze of workers carelessly as he disappeared from the service kitchens – Zuri wondered idly why he'd been there in the first place.

She turned and found Feliks standing, as busty as ever, clutching a bottle of olive oil so large he could balance it on his hip. The butcher's cart was empty of meat, and Zuri looked from it to Feliks, bewildered by his feral grin. 'Good eating, eh?'

She had absolutely no idea what Feliks was, but Zuri had no intent of being ungrateful to whatever gods had forged him.

Chapter Twenty-Three

SVARNA

Eulalia lingered in the soft grey haze that shrouded the tender hours before dawn, watching Ohba sleep, cherishing the softened creases around his mouth that only the sanctuary of slumber could deliver. She crystallised this moment in her mind, in the hope that she could hold it through whatever was to come, before she reached out and roused him with a gentle press of her hand to his cheek.

They had work to do.

Cuinu had to fall.

He would not bend or fold to the city's needs. He would not see past his own pride. So he had to fall. If she were at her full strength, Eulalia would gladly do it with her bare hands – had envisioned it in detail many a time, in fact. It was just a matter of making it happen, while she looked and felt like she had swallowed a watermelon.

The earlier stages of pregnancy were manageable; she could feel the alien shift inside her when the babe fluttered, but the broader stretches of her body remained stable. Strong. It was this season before childbirth that sent her legs quivering, her feet swelling into great balloons, that had her afraid of the slightest of slips. No, she could not take a brawl with Cuinu in this condition – however gratifying squeezing the life out of his smug neck might be.

Eulalia wouldn't have to fight him, though. She simply had to find him.

A flurry of dragons took flight as Eulalia and Ohba emerged into the cavernous lungs of the First Temple. She counted seven. Only three of them had riders, but as they went, the greatest of them flashed his wings like a sheet of rubies, and she knew that Uono had taken to the skies. There was no guarantee those that did not bear riders would fight alongside the bonded pairs, but it was a flicker of hope. The raising of a flag.

Other dragons crowded around the nursery doors, watching the chaos that was unfolding.

The eldest temple children, those who would grow into renasci given a year or two, flew between the rooms on bare feet, attempting to care for the clusters of kinfolk that had fled into the First Temple for sanctuary. Ruhim shouted directions from atop a pillar, urging people to move further within their great walls. Earthquakes and apocalypses were frightening, but the temple could withstand them – as long as the elves stayed outside their walls, they would be safe here. The city could fall. The temple would stand.

One hand clutching at Ohba's shoulder, they descended into the madness.

An arc of holy men stood watch at the main entryway, murmuring amongst themselves. Most bore staffs of their own, artefacts they could use to channel what magic they had. They were all Blessed creatures, beloved by their gods and gifted with talents beyond Eulalia's imagining. A pair of renasci stood within the shimmering shield that protected the temple from what lay outside it, untouched by the protective magic.

Someone had been waiting for them. Fidela, lacking almost all her jewellery apart from two bronze horn caps, was dressed in a deep olive green and boots that were meant for work. She looked as if she had slept very little, greyish hollows hanging heavy beneath her dark eyes. She had been lingering on a pillar stand when they approached, watching the crowd that twisted around the First Temple's halls.

'The winds do not know where to carry their people today,' Fidela called.

'The winds of war are more chaotic than those that came before,' Eulalia responded. They could wax poetic about the winds for hours; Eula suspected it was the Svarnish birthright. 'I don't think any of us can pretend to know what the winds have dragged to our door.'

Ohba crossed to where Fidela stood and helped her down from her perch, the two sharing an unsteady look.

She had needed Ohba last night, but she needed Fidela now. She pressed a harsh kiss to Fidela's mouth, felt how the younger woman embraced her in response. The two were companions in their marrow, and with doom staring them down from afar, they had to find some little stability in what lived between them. Neither were built for fear, but none who walked the world were immune to its effects, sending their hearts thrumming and guts spiralling into the darkness. It was their resistance to it that mattered.

'He has not moved,' Fidela hissed. She would have breathed steam and spat fire for all the frustration that she held in those hands' full of words. It was a strange thing to see, coming from someone who'd always seemed so soft and sumptuous to Eula. Eulalia shook her head. 'We argued through the night, but he is scared, Eulalia. He's scared of seeing Svarna's ruin, and he thinks the war dragons are the last of their kind, that there will be none left if they are struck down.'

'Then we will move him. Better Svarna's ruin than ours.' As long as they lived, Svarna as they knew it could walk with them. As long as Nuru and Rasyl sat on the caravan, full of temple children and those who'd brought them into the world, Svarna could be what they believed it to be. 'Cuinu first.'

Above, in one of the nursery windows that watched over the First Temple, a dragon crooned to the chaos. The two women drew away from one another, though Eulalia found herself reluctant to let go, hands lingering on forearms, eyes stuck on one another.

'I love you,' Eulalia admitted. 'I truly do.'

Fidela laughed, the sound harsh and as bright as the morning sun. 'Do not say goodbye yet, dear Eulalia. Let us live to see another day.'

There was work to be done, and they both knew it. They kissed each other again, this time on each cheek, before Fidela disappeared into the crowd. She would not go far. Eulalia's dark eyes followed her as she circled to the sentinels standing watch at the main entryway, holy men in their jewel-toned drapery and their set jaws. Cuinu stood amongst them with a quarterstaff in hand, silent and greyish in the wake of the distant fighting that would roll towards them.

'Eula—' Ohba spoke her name at her side, such an intimate sound in this crowded place. His voice wavered.

'We do not say goodbye yet,' she responded softly. 'We live to see another day.'

He took her face in his hands once more and kissed her with more love than she'd ever known. It was Eulalia that untangled her body from his, cupped his cheek lightly before she nodded. She could spend the rest of her days kissing him, could have died a peaceful death in his arms, but that was not what Eulalia was meant for. She was meant for violence.

Eulalia stepped away, taking several long breaths to temper herself. She located the bellows that lived within her chest and settled her stare on her enemy as she walked, pushing away a vague discomfort in her hips. In her feet. The hint of nausea that threatened to crawl its way back up her throat if she paid it any mind.

She had thought that the flame that drove her might have quieted. That she might struggle to summon it now that she'd surrendered her children to this war. Yet, she caught a glimpse of Cuinu and her fire overwhelmed her in one sharp breath. With Nuru no longer at her side, there was nothing to quash Eulalia's fury. She pressed through the shifting crowds and tapped one of the holy men in line on the shoulder, stepping around him once he had backed away.

'Let's end this mummer's farce, Cuinu. It's time for you to fold.' Eulalia drew herself to her full height, straightened her spine to look down imperiously at the utter coward that stood before her. The holy men who flanked him, friends of them both, pressed gradually away until he was left on his own amongst the many. 'Look at our temple. Look at our city! The shields have fallen, and still, you stop us from calling in the dragons of war. Still, you claim that their lives are more important for the legacy of Svarna than our own. You disgust me.'

The uncertainty in his gaze hardened and shifted to disbelief as he listened. His eyes frantically turned on the crowd, pleading for some sense of understanding.

Discussions amongst the council had always been a private affair, but why should the people not know which councillor had betrayed them? Why should Cuinu not have to answer for the fates he condemned them to? The stunned silence of the crowd was replaced with a venomous sense of murmuring, their talk rolling between tongue and ear, echoing the accusation that Eulalia had levelled like a javelin at her compatriot.

The two were never going to be friends. Their blood ran too hot, and they both believed in their own superiority as people of a holy inclination. They could have been allies if they'd been better at bending to the ways of the world. Yet, there were parts of them both that were built of steel and stone, two countenances that could not yield lest they break.

'How—' Cuinu began, his face burning red. 'How dare you pin this on me. How dare you—'

'It's beginning to sound repetitive, this rant you have.' She found no joy in this, no sense of vindication. She sought only to resist the destiny, the death, swarming to greet them. 'You've set this city to slaughter for your own pride.'

'I am a servant of this city!' He roared, the people around him scattering even further to get out of the way of them both. Dragons emerged from the nursery to investigate what was evolving between their stewards. 'I have done nothing but protect it, you venomous cunt. I will defend it against this apocalypse, even if you will not!'

'I am doing what needs to be done. If you were interested in the sanctity of this city, you'd understand that.' This was no longer an argument that Eulalia cared for. 'I think you'll live just long enough to regret the path you've taken. I pray the winds take you.'

He swung his quarterstaff, turning on Eulalia with a snarl, but in his fury did not notice Fidela emerging from behind him. As he lunged, Fidela leapt forward and shoved him, sending him off balance. Ohba came down on Cuinu like a thunderclap. He did not have to wield a weapon to win such a fight, not with Muqdah's magic coursing through his veins. Staff met strong forearm and was thrown to the side, Cuinu's grip broken by a sharp twist. Eulalia stepped back to protect herself.

Her holy man struck Cuinu just below the ribs, up and into his diaphragm to knock the wind from him. Ohba was gilded in his own magic, golden and bright, a sacred fury within him.

'We could have saved this city,' Ohba muttered.

Eulalia's opinion alone was not enough to turn the tide of the city against Cuinu. She was, perhaps, the least loved of the holy mothers, the harshest in her judgements. Ohba was beloved.

Her dark eyes roved the crowd and found them staring past her, fixed on the two men. There was a shock and revulsion, but there was also anger – an emotion she had not sensed in her kinfolk since the queen had died. If she left Cuinu on his own, they may have torn him apart for her. It was a deadly thought. She wouldn't have had to lift a finger, wouldn't have had to engineer an execution that vindicated her point so publicly. But she could not wait for the people of Muqdah to find their taste for violence.

'Our gods no longer walk amongst us. The winds no longer know where to carry us, for there is no safe haven in Svarna. So, if you will not try to bring justice to Muqdah, Cuinu, I shall forge it myself.' She rested her fair hands on her great, round stomach and found herself steel and marble, utterly immovable. There was little woman left within her, just a hard frame and the flame that consumed it. Cuinu was doubled over, wheezing, as Ohba and Fidela drew away from their victim.

Eulalia rose a hand to the sky and whistled once, short and sharp.

Zoraida had been waiting for Eulalia's call. She landed with a thunderous echo as people screamed, shouting and scrambling to get out of her way. The First Temple was colossal, but it had not been this full in all of Eulalia's residency, which meant that Zoraida ran the risk of injuring far more people than they both wanted.

They only wanted one.

Zoraida's shadow fell over her in rippling waves of heat, rolling through the air and singing to Eulalia's assuredness.

Cuinu regained his breath as he stumbled back, his rage swallowed by fear – a sudden awareness of how far Eulalia would go. How deep her convictions ran.

There was fear in his eyes – what a delicious thing.

'You cannot command a dragon,' he spat. His venom now trembled, lacking that almighty arrogance that he had learnt to sharpen his knives upon. 'You cannot.'

She should not have had to. Eulalia did not falter. She looked at Cuinu and found only violence within her. Where her heart should have been was a barbed, twisted thing that had found its target.

The air around them both wavered and swam with the heat that was growing within Zoraida's gullet. Eulalia's senses were flooded with the smell of dragon, the gas that Zoraida produced that would turn into a wall of fire at the slightest of sparks. In that consuming violence, she saw herself.

'I do not deign to command Zoraida,' Eulalia said. 'I have simply informed her of your folly.'

Honest words were more traitorous than any command she could have given Zoraida.

Cuinu had the good sense to run. He attempted to charge back into the crowds that had filled the temple, scrabbling and stumbling. But one Zoraida's strides matched five of his, her speed enough to steal air from Eulalia's lungs as she passed. Eulalia knew that a flicker of fear could turn a dragon around on its handler and tamped down on her primal instincts. Her conviction did not fail in the face of her own mortality.

In his panic, Cuinu crashed into Fidela, not hesitating to shove her into Zoraida's path.

Eulalia's fiery rage went ice-cold, as any reason left within her spiralling into the abyss.

'Not her!' Eulalia screamed, the shriek cutting through the clamour of the crowd. Two renasci appeared in a blur from within the clusters of Svarnish faces, one catching her before Fidela could hit the ground, the other sweeping them both out of the way.

The she-dragon launched over Fidela in one great leap, disregarding her entirely, and landing hard on Cuinu's back. Her titanic foot slammed the man to the ground and pinned him there.

Eulalia's hands had balled the linens of her dress up and threatened to tear them to shreds. God, how she hated him. 'Finish it.'

Zoraida lifted her talons, permitting Cuinu to stand once more.

Then, she crushed him, and the man once known as Cuinu snapped like a bundle of dry twigs, his mortal form no match for the draconic vengeance that was upon him. His skull shattered like a boiled egg beneath her jaws, his abdomen torn open. Eulalia, who had brought this down upon him, did not look away.

No one in the city of temples had anticipated a great priest being devoured like a rabbit in a wolf's snapping jaws.

But Cuinu had never been great. He'd barely been holy.

The she-dragon tossed his body into the air and then turned slowly on her haunches, chewing slowly and methodically. Flesh and bone were ground to nothing as Zoraida stared back at Eulalia, with that intimately familiar look in her eyes. Mouth full of gristle and gore, their vengeance enacted, Eulalia's mind whirred and turned like she herself was a construct waiting for some nebulous command to set her to action.

Her whole body trembled, the hairs on her arms prickling. She took a step and thought, for a breath, that perhaps her body would give up on her.

'Fidela.'

Eulalia rushed forward. Fidela, despite having stared death in the face mere minutes before, did not appear nearly as shaken as Eulalia felt. She crossed past Zoraida and embraced Eulalia fiercely, arms closing around her shoulders. 'Eulalia.'

Had she had the capacity for it, Eulalia would have cried. For now, she could only savour the feeling of flesh and blood beneath her hands and the fact that Fidela was still here, alive and able to embrace Eulalia. That Zoraida had been wise enough to know the target of their fury. She held a moment longer, savouring the life between them, before untangling herself from Fidela's grasp.

'Where is Adil?' she asked. Only half the work was done; they still had another stubborn priest to catch.

They would learn later that Adil, hearing the commotion from afar, had embraced the fear that they'd all felt in the wake of Eulalia's rage and fled.

Chapter Twenty-Four

THE IMPERIUM

Any bedworker in the Imperium worth a grain of salt knew their escape routes before the work began.

So, while the party commenced, Nuru scouted. Takuma lingered in the main chamber, gauging the developing temperature of the pot they'd stepped into. She kept her head bowed deferentially, eyes away from those who loomed over her, which meant that she was largely left to her own devices. That suited Nuru fine, given she was almost utterly at odds with her own people on some level. Nuru could feel the whispers spring up between her kinfolk, those who knew what she'd once been.

Wife, girl, merchant queen. There were no real merchant queens – it was a patriarchal title – but that was what she'd once fancied herself. When marriage had just been a bond and not the shackles weighing her down beneath its waters.

It made sense that she was at odds with these strangers. They bore similar features, similar horns, similar hurt, but Nuru had committed a cardinal sin by fleeing from her marriage with a growing belly. She'd committed the sin of abandoning her community to strike out on her own, to wish for something different from what the Svarnish had put upon her shoulders. In her absence, Imamu would have spun his tales and made a friend of every person who laid eyes upon his bronze caravan.

He was here. She knew that. Mosi was here, and so Imamu was also; one did not go without the other. Goose flesh rose on her arms at the thought, her mind reeling and stumbling over how to possibly avoid him.

So, Nuru cased the joint, just as she had a hundred times when she was younger.

The plans stolen from the archives seemed largely accurate. Thurlow had built himself an opulent brothel in almost all respects, tucked away against his estate – twelve open rooms that ranged from display rooms to a communal engagement chamber that was decidedly devoid of people when Nuru circled through. She'd much rather it stayed that way.

Once Nuru made it to the very end of the playrooms, marked by an immense mahogany door, she was left with the unsettling reality that this space held the capacity for at least one hundred and fifty men – and their playthings, of course. That was a lot of men. These sorts of places were almost never populated by women. Women had their carnal sins, they truly did, but they preferred to indulge them on more intimate stages.

But these spaces were not designed with the workers in mind – they had every amenity meant to comfort an elvish titan. Huge, cushiony chairs and tables that were set higher to accommodate their height, harnesses and swings hung from the roof – so tall that Nuru thought that even Feliks would struggle to reach them. Her jaw clicked thoughtfully.

She would have to tread very carefully amidst this lot once the High Elves swanned in, expecting service with a smile – and they'd stolen a dragon.

There it was – that flicker of cold, ancestral rage. She smothered it again. She needed to keep herself under control. There would be time to scream and rant and vent her magic into the void when this was through.

She circled back slowly, counting whips and shackles, subtly jiggling the handles of the playrooms and feeling for their locks as she went. They were not magical or special – Thurlow Thurlowe still valued some level of physical craftsmanship. Nuru turned through the perimeter of one of the performance rooms and walked carefully along the collection of booths that sat against the walls, mentally tracking how long it would take to traverse the space.

They would have to get everyone out. That was a lot of people to consider for, even with Mosi's promises.

'Nuru,' a voice muttered. Before Nuru could say anything, a hand reached from within one of the alcoves. An iron grip seized her forearm and she wheeled away, spitting, but couldn't resist the sheer strength that drew her in. 'How dare you.'

Her husband, the bronze bull of the caravans, stared at her through utterly disbelieving eyes. He was gilded, now, shining in the low light – twice as beautiful as he was in her memories.

She shouldn't have been thinking about him. Shouldn't have wished Imamu into existence because he had found her, had somehow been dragged through reality itself by her hoping he was within reach once more. Nuru swung out with her spare hand, snarling, and struck him not in the face but in the shoulder.

'You vanish into oblivion with my babe in your belly and a caravan full of my riches, and you expect me to treat you with kindness?' he snapped. He would not let go of her arm, she expected, afraid that Nuru would vanish into thin air.

She had no words; instead she railed against his grasp, striking him again. 'Nuru—Nuru!'

He did not quite shake her, but he gripped her shoulders and held her, staring down at her.

'I can't do this right now,' she said. 'I can't, I can't do this with you.'

'You don't have a choice,' he growled. Nuru could have struck him for how he spoke to her, but instead she simply turned her face away, pressing her lips together. 'Where is the babe? Did you have her, have you left her?'

His hand slackened enough for Nuru to pull herself away, and she stumbled across the booth, climbing onto the chairs to put as much distance between them as she could.

'I didn't abandon her.' She tolerated a lot from the world, but she would not have anyone question her parenting, not when she'd twisted the world around their broken family to give Nema something good. 'How dare you—how dare you. You told me I had to have her, and then by the time I could find an abortifacient, it was too far along. I was too pregnant, and taking it would have risked us both. Your babe is perfectly safe.'

They may have been at eternal odds with one another, warring beasts locked in an endless struggle, but to question her motherhood was a deathly insult.

'You left us,' he hissed. He was wise enough to keep his voice down, not wanting to draw the elves down upon them. He was far more furious than she could navigate in the middle of this particular job. 'You left your caravan—and you left me. What was I supposed to think?'

Her husband's frustration with her had always been a loud thing. When they had their smaller disagreements, they'd devolved into shouting matches, preferring to scream into the open air than give in to their spouse. Their caravan had made jokes about the married dragons and how they'd danced, but they had steered clear when their voices softened to whispers or their stares hardened to ice.

'You were supposed to think about what you'd said, Imamu.' Her voice dropped to a growl. 'You were supposed to think about how you'd treated me. Are you telling me we have been apart for years, and you haven't looked inwards, not once?'

Of course, he hadn't. She'd tried to convince him at the time, spent weeks pleading with him. When he set his mind upon a thing that he believed was the truth, impenetrable walls went up in Imamu's mind. It served him well in all manners of business – he was brilliant when trade was involved. Yet, everyone who'd founded that caravan was a walking interpersonal disaster, bonded by violence to one another and totally unable to handle an adult conversation without imposing their own agenda.

'Nema.' The name had not meant to hurt, but it fell with the weight of a blow. The hardness in his features crumpled and wavered. For a moment, Imamu was almost an echo of the young man who had saved her in Muqdah, who had given her a home. 'Her name is Nema.'

'After my mother?' he asked after a long breath.

Svarnish families often named their babes after those they'd once known. Bronnuq had been one of the kindest people she'd ever known. Her memories of what once had been her home had faded throughout the years, worn away by time, but the people would never leave that spot in her sternum that ached before dawn. A litany of names and faces that lingered, awaiting the day that Nuru saw them all again.

Nuru was painfully aware of the growing sound in the playrooms as people filtered in; but if she tore away from him now, they'd never speak again. This conversation was too important to sacrifice it to the greater agenda of the evening, not when their job had not truly begun. If they had been in the dragon's den at that very moment, perhaps Nuru would have insisted that they spoke another time, perhaps she would have run.

But she had been longing for him, had she not? She'd felt it while lost in the quagmire of the Imperium robbery; she had thought of him. He would have known what to do better than she did. It was not beyond her to think that her Blessing had made this conversation a reality.

'I don't hate you, not enough to rob you of that. I just couldn't be with you. I couldn't be what you asked for.' She'd thought of so many names when she'd been pregnant, but Nema had stuck, turning the bizarre shifting in her hips into an infant. 'Your daughter's name is Nema.'

'I—let me see her, Nuru.' It was a plea. A plea followed by a long breath, a lift of the chin. 'It is my right to see her. Don't you want to see Rasyl?'

Her stomach flipped. It wasn't—she hadn't meant to leave Rasyl. She just hadn't been able to take him with her. Renasci were bound to holy men, and as her brother had grown, Imamu had been the only one at hand who'd had the magical prowess to maintain his power. They couldn't live as normal people, renasci – they needed someone, or they would resort to hibernation if there was not enough magic in the world to sustain them. Nuru, having no holy training of her own and no real grasp on her own magic, had not wanted to watch her sweet brother turn to stone when he was away from the flock.

So, she had left him and felt terrible for it. She had missed him every day, but it had been for his betterment. It had been so he could live. 'You are horrible.'

'We are both horrible,' Imamu responded coolly. 'That was why we fell in love. We are horrible, scarred, temperamental beasts who hoard people like the dragons we are. Let me see my child.'

Takuma would kill her. If he had come upon them in this moment, he would have known how she was about to betray a core tenet of their work at The Brass Wyvern. Their plans stayed tucked away within the Wyvern, between the ears of those who could be trusted. Brilliant, frustrating Takuma despised Imamu. He had been left entirely unable to understand why Nuru had loved Imamu, why she had considered walking into ruin because that was what the caravan had needed of her.

He did not understand how she could love a man who asked so much of the world. When she hung the portraits of her two men together in her mind, it was funny how similar yet so vastly different they were from one another.

Nuru would never be able to share that thought with Takuma.

'Thurlow has a dragon.' She let the words free. 'From the size of it, there's no way that he's hatched it. He's stolen some youngling from the war and trapped it. We're here to free it.'

Imamu said nothing. He took a long, deep breath and studied her with his disbelieving brown eyes, searching for deception in her face. She jutted out her chin and set her shoulders, watching as the realisation rolled over him, as he realigned all he knew of the evening.

'You're here to steal a dragon?' Her ex-husband asked. His scepticism stung; there once had been a time in which he'd never dare to doubt her. They had been a team, the inseparable founders of the first caravans that had found ground within Eschalier's Empire.

'Yes. You always talked about how I was shirking my duty by not using our power for the greater good. So here I am. Stealing a dragon.' She rubbed her face before she took another proper look at him, cocking her head to the side. 'Why are you here?'

'Because a squadron of the guard showed up at one of the caravan circles and tried to muscle their way in on our women.'

Nuru hissed. Caravan circles were the only safe spaces that the displaced Svarnishmen from the south had in the new world, several of the merchant kings joining their great trains to allow their people to mingle. Nothing was sacred in the Imperium, but she had thought that there had been small efforts made to not intrude upon their communities. As long as they knelt for the Eschalion, what did their customs matter? Imamu glanced away from her, avoiding her stare almost meticulously.

'It would have been another massacre, so I stepped in. I got women who knew the reality of what tonight was supposed to be, who were strong, and we came to appease the Imperium.'

That made more sense.

What Imamu did not understand – and could not because he was a man – was that the evening would be a massacre, regardless of whether the women had volunteered. They would be groped, objectified, and taken to bed by men who they couldn't have possibly consented to, who they would not be paid for. This night could not be allowed to go on.

Some men tried to understand it, how long silences in unmade beds and the spinning psyche could scar a woman for the rest of her days, but how could they? They were not the ones who'd bear the children of strangers, of men who didn't understand that anything other than yes should be considered a firm no.

The men had come – they had not abandoned their women to this fate. But what would be left when the night was done? How would they handle women who carried that sort of pain?

'This is bad,' she murmured. 'This is very bad, Imamu.'

'I will mitigate what damage I can. That is all we can do.' Imamu was not reasoning with her. He was talking to himself. They knew each other well enough for him to know how objectionable Nuru would have thought this night. She didn't blame him. She blamed him for many things, including the fall of their marriage, but he and the Merchant Kings had made many hard decisions that kept Svarna alive in the Imperium's reach. They had been men thrust into a level of authority no one had anticipated, many of which had just been merchants. Tradespeople. She was not sure the decisions she would have made in their wake would have been any different.

A stolen dragon and its kinfolk, all at risk of burning to ash in this great furnace of a city. Nuru reached out and squeezed his arm, drawing him back from his nervous affirmations. 'If you help me, I can help you.'

'You cannot save them all, Nuru. You can only take care of your own. If you can save that dragon – a dragon freed would be wound enough on the Imperium's pride.' He was adjusting his grip on the staff of Muqdah, great gilded hands fidgeting nervously. He had never broken that habit in all the years she'd known him. 'That will be something.'

That was where, fundamentally, she and Imamu disagreed.

'I'm not asking you to join the job, Imamu. I'm just asking that you watch as the night progresses, and when I need your help, you intervene. Just as we once would have. Just as you would for another.' Perhaps it was mercantile of her. To think that she could use him when she had already stolen so much from him. 'And I will give you an opening to get our people back into the city, away from these men. Then, when all of this is done, we can talk about Nema.'

Hope sparked in his eyes at the mere mention of her name, an intensity turning on the thought of his child like a hawk preparing to swoop on an unsuspecting fish.

'Whatever happens tonight will be enough of a distraction for you to escape with the women.' They were going to carve the roof off Thurlow's estate. The chaos that would follow should have been more than enough, and if it wasn't, she'd create more. If she couldn't create more, if her own magic failed her, she had Feliks. She had Takuma. They would figure something out. That was what they did. 'I swear it. I will not leave them here.'

In the end, Imamu trusted her loyalty to their own more than he judged her misdeeds. Neither had enough time to linger on the decision; with each wasted second, the night was continuing without either of them.

'Fine. I will do what I can.' That was all she asked. The two nodded at one another, minds elsewhere, before Nuru drew away from him and went back to the curtain that shielded the alcove. She threw it back and found that the playrooms had been thrust into a full-blown celebration, Nordic kitchen staff flocking to the tables with great trays of food. Her senses were flooded with the sweet, cloying scent of summer wine.

'We will conquer this night together, Imamu. We were once good at this.'

As she stepped down and into the throng, Imamu spoke to her back, suddenly regaining the avariciousness of the man that she had once married. 'Where is my tapestry, Nuru? Where is Victory's mashjor?'

She barely glanced at him as she fled into the elvish throng, and for a breath, she was an echo of the girl who'd taken Kine to the sky of Muqdah. The brightest and the bravest dragon rider, who felt no flame or fear.

'Where it must be, dear husband!'

In her trailing path through the rooms, Nuru had thought she was quite successful in her attempts to avoid attention as the celebration flourished. Lingering against the walls, Nuru was surprised to note elvish and Nordlund bedworkers had been recruited for the night – a barely tasteful mix. Elvish noblemen were reclining in the plush setting, picking at their food and chattering excitedly about many things. The fresh pick of women who were flowing through the rooms, the great ball above, the *dragon*. Everyone was speaking of the dragon. She would see the dragon soon enough, so Nuru did not linger, instead keeping her eyes tucked down and herself close to the walls. Navigating through these rooms was not so different to navigating around beasts. Stepping out from cover was almost asking to be seized up or swept away by the greedy, so instead Nuru simply pressed on.

She had been about to return to Takuma's side when she was stopped once more from the shadows.

It came from the booths. Those private alcoves set into the walls that were proving quickly to be her doom, complicating what should have been otherwise simple.

'Miss,' a voice called. Distinctly accented by the elvish tongue and distinctly masculine. 'My, aren't you a fine woman.'

There were plenty of women the stranger could have been speaking to. Yet, her instinct told her, without question, to whom the shadowed man was speaking. She should have been suspicious when she turned inwards and found it unlit, draped in the shadow of the half-drawn curtain. It was too dense to be natural, but Nuru wasn't thinking about glamours and spells – she was thinking about Imamu. Contemplating their night.

'Perhaps,' Nuru responded. She turned into the darkness, setting a hand on her hip as she fell into a familiar mask. 'I've been told as much before.'

'Would you come here? So I can get a better look at you?' Now was not the time to refuse a customer or draw more attention than was necessary to herself, so she took up a light-hearted tone of an amused bedworker, flattered to have drawn the eye of a prospective client. Her raven-black eyes slid momentarily towards the room in which she'd left Takuma before she focused on the velvet-lined booth.

She stepped up onto the first stair and then the second. He would not get a better look at her in this darkness, so it seemed to her that he wanted to get her within his reach. Yet as Nuru peered down at this stranger, the thought wasn't totally objectionable. The stranger was sharp-shouldered and angular, the ghost of a handsome man.

'Closer.' The man said. There was magic beneath his words, something that swayed her gently. Nuru logged her knowledge of it in the back of her mind, held it there while she stepped upwards again into the booth. 'You really are ravishing.'

Maybe men weren't always so bad. When they were charming, it softened the hard edge of her armour. Nuru turned away and drew the curtains closed at her back, humming a forgotten tune quietly as the air shifted around her. Magic that had been cocooned around this booth swirled and peeled away, lifting the gloom that had been shielding the person within from sight.

She shifted back on her heels, still maintaining her tune. The stranger's face flickered and shifted, some illusion unwinding before her eyes. It was several breaths before the stranger was rendered recognisable. Candlelight that had been shuttered by magic flickered and swelled back into existence, filling the booth. There, sitting in an iridescent halo, was her priest.

'Taliesin,' she hissed, her face warming. 'Are priests allowed to be flirtatious?'

'I wasn't acting as a priest.' He at least had the good sense to look embarrassed before the severity of the situation overtook him. She had lain the bait for him to follow her into this party, though she was yet to entirely understand why. Keeping him in the dark simply felt like too much of a betrayal of the relationship they'd built in the space between them.

Truls had always been the golden boy of the family, a man who'd never had a flicker of doubt about the glory of his ancestry. Taliesin was the flickering, curious son who'd always pressed against the constraints of his station – perhaps a natural evolution from being the second son rather than the first, the child who did not hold the armour of an inevitable inheritance. That was how he'd ended up in a delivery room an age ago, staring down a heavily pregnant Nuru in the midst of a furious wave of contractions. He was the one who wanted to save the world.

She must have paused, watching him too long, because Taliesin's already furrowed brow deepened further with concern, and he shuffled over in the booth. 'Come here, Nuru. Are you okay?'

There wasn't a flicker of doubt in Nuru. She floated further into the booth, tucking her feet beneath her as she climbed onto the lounge. Taliesin twisted to look at her properly, making a concerted effort to avoid her bosom and keep her eyes upon his. She found it quite endearing how much he persisted in his attempts to maintain his innocence and nobility, as if a moment of slipped modesty wouldn't have been utterly endearing.

'I'm okay, Taliesin,' she said, the polite thing to say. The look in his eyes was more than disbelieving as he reached out and grasped one of her hands, squeezing firmly.

She squeezed back. 'I'm sorry you came all this way. You are truly the kindest man I've ever met, to come all this way to check on me. You are too much.'

He shook his head.

'I can get you out of here, if we need to. I can get everyone out if I need to – you can keep my father's money, I don't care. It matters more to me that you're safe.' Nuru puzzled over those words for a moment before the realisation of Taliesin's assumption flew over her.

She couldn't help it. She had been so prepared for a fight, bursting at the seams with magic. At the thought that she had been here working for the elder Thurlow, Nuru threw her head back and laughed. The sound was half hysterical, for the thought of touching Thurlow Thurlowe alone made her skin crawl. The other half was relieved that this was how Taliesin would have handled it, with such unyielding understanding.

'Oh, Taliesin – no.' She took his beautiful face and cupped it in her hands. Nuru had to sit up on her knees on the booth lounge to be even close to level with him, and he had to lean downwards. 'I would never – and I do mean it – I would never work for your father. I promise you.'

'…Thank you,' Taliesin said after a lengthy, bewildered pause. 'That is truly a Blessing. But if you're not here working, what are you doing here? You can't dally with my father, Nuru.'

'Taliesin …' Fuck the Svarnish code of secrecy, he deserved to know. He had come all this way to try and keep her from danger. He was as good as family. 'I'm not working for your father. I'm stealing from your father. He has a dragon.'

Chapter Twenty-Five

SVARNA

They found Adil in one of the prayer chambers.

Eulalia did not miss the fact that Fidela took the lead when they grew closer, darting ahead on swift feet.

Elves, in every experience that Eulalia had with them before the war, had a very clear concept of love; they believed that it was sacred between spouses. They believed, quite strictly, that only two people could live within the holy love a marriage provided. This worked well enough for them. When she had lived on the border, she'd traded with many an elf in a perfectly happy marriage with an entirely appropriate amount of children.

Svarnish love was something else. One was supposed to love all their kinfolk as family because they had been made from the same flame, built from the same dirt and magic. One was not supposed to restrict their love if they felt something calling at their soul. This meant that plural marriage and extended family units were prolific, and often the pleasure of the soul was prioritised over creating the new scion of a dynasty.

Procreation was a product only of marriages between those who'd found themselves comfortable enough to know that child-rearing was for them. The thing about loving someone who loved another was that, to do it truly, one had to kill all possessive instinct within them. There was no room for jealousy or possession or darkness; love for another was not something that a person could control or bully.

Fierce, beautiful Fidela had always loved Adil. From her first day at the temple, she had lain her eyes upon him and seen something that Eulalia had not. Now, everything he was hinged upon what Fidela had seen ringing with some sort of truth. Otherwise, they'd have to kill him.

She didn't want to kill him. If she murdered Adil, she would take something from Fidela. Something they would not be able to repair. She could not possess Fidela, could not make her ambivalent towards Adil.

The prayer chambers were a quiet, luminous place of worship that had somehow escaped the flood of people that had rolled in throughout the night. They were small and numerous in number, a maze of coloured glass that set the world aglow in rainbow light. They were not akin to the rest of the temple, with its spacious roofs and towering architecture – these chambers were quiet and cloistered. The magic that had forged this part of the temple had turned the world soft and pillowy, protected it from the chaos of the city.

Prayer was not supposed to be a spectacle. The gods enjoyed their spectacle – that was what the great loom was for, the offerings left before them. Prayer was an introspective thing, a conversation had with oneself. These rooms had been built to give dozens of pilgrims a moment to gaze upon their own reflection, shone a hundred times through the dragon-glass of Muqdah.

'Adil!' Fidela cried as she turned a corner, disappearing within the labyrinth.

He had sought sanctuary in prayer. He was still rising from where he had been kneeling, swathed in ivory cotton and cloudy sunlight.

Adil had a gentle face. Eulalia had always thought that of him. His soft, sloping features always stood in stark contrast to Fidela's pixie-faced ferocity. He had a sheath of chocolate curls that were usually bound tidily, but they'd been left wild in the wake of Muqdah's doom.

'You need to change your mind on the dragon rider dispute, now.' Please. She would not beg him. She could not. She had already debased herself too much, had already killed one today. 'If they're sweeping from the north, there is a good chance they've stopped at the Small Temple to find survivors. But that conflict is over – this one is yet to find its resolution. This one can still be saved.'

She did not know what was left at Luodono, but they'd had a far greater ratio of renasci to people. If anyone had survived, they would have them to rely on. Muqdah needed more.

'You are an exhausting woman,' Adil said. He spoke as if he were threatening to collapse upon himself at any given moment, a man who'd turn to dust entirely if they pressed too hard. 'You wish to save us so badly that you'd throw others to the wolves.'

'Of course, I want to save us, Adil.' Eulalia pressed a hand to her belly. 'I don't want to give birth in occupied territory. I don't know what they'll do to the children, or to us. Do you think they'll let us live, Adil? Me and Fidela? Do you think they'll let anyone who wears their horns with pride survive this massacre?'

He was no Cuinu. Adil did not clutch his convictions close to his chest; he was not jealous or pig-headed. He wanted to believe that he was taking Svarna down the path that was the least bloody, that might allow the country to come out of this intact. Adil still believed that path existed. He looked at her with his great, coal-black eyes, and he did not take her as a viper. It was such a revelation to her that she opened her mouth to speak again, only to find her voice had betrayed her, that it had gotten lost somewhere in her chest.

'My love, you have to change your mind.' Fidela placed one hand over his, and in the other gleamed the flash of a blade. She did not wield it with intent; she turned it quietly around in the air with the familiarity of a hunter who'd butchered many a rabbit. It was an almost airy motion. Even holding such a thing in a place of prayer would have made their ancestors utterly incensed.

'Fidela—' he began, but the words were soft and sorrowful, quieted only as Fidela took her spare hand up to cup his face. She kissed him on the cheek.

'Eulalia wouldn't kill you,' Fidela whispered. The sound carried around the room, bouncing off crystal and glass until it was as loud as any of Eulalia's words. 'But I would, Adil. You know that. For all the people out in that city that need us to care for them. They can't talk to the temple as we always have. Our queen may be gone, our council small, but we're here. And we must continue to be here, Adil. We must continue to watch over this beautiful city. For them.'

'Fidela.' It was Ohba who spoke the woman's name, gentle and plying.

'No, Ohba.' She looked back at him, but her knuckles paled on the hilt of her blade. 'Eulalia has been fighting for us since the moment the Eschalion's army arrived at our doors. She has tried to drive us, encourage us to do the right thing for our people, and we ignored it for entirely too long. We let Cuinu and Adil misuse their patriotic compassion, let them ruin our chances of getting out of this unscathed. Now we have to commit to controlling damage when we can.

'Have you ever been in a city that's under some sort of siege? That's been attacked? Because I have. I came from a little city just south of the capitol.

One of those places where nobody, other than the people who lived there, remembered the name, but simply flowed through the town on the way to somewhere else. We didn't even know the army was coming until it was upon us. Let me tell you – desperation does hard things to the human psyche. I watched people trampled trying to get out of the way of warhorses and blades. I watched people lock out their own family in the hopes that they would live. I won't watch it happen again. I won't die to Thurlow now.'

Whatever fear or uncertainty had initially driven Fidela had fallen away, like brittle leaves from the tree, leaving only the winter bark and sharp-edged branches.

'Then ... we'll call for the dragon riders.' He conceded so simply that, for a moment, Eulalia did not register the words. He was not shaken by her threatening his life any more than he was shaken by Cuinu's murder or the doom falling upon them. The fact that all of this could stare down upon him, and he still stood steadfast, while his companions unravelled at the seams, was a miracle unto itself. 'You never told me that, Fidela.'

She blew out a hard breath. Her hands were shaking hard as she sheathed the weapon at her side. The two embraced tenderly, their foreheads coming to rest gently upon one another. She might have been hysterical, but Fidela laughed for a moment, a breathy, soundless motion that could have transformed quickly into a sob had she not clamped down on the feeling. 'I didn't want you to look at me like some sorry tragedy. This whole country is turning into one.'

What god had Svarna crossed to have been cursed into this spiral? Who had reached out from the heavens and decided that they could take so much from them?

'Adil.' Eulalia's voice found its way up and out of her throat. 'You want to make the call for help?'

'No. I wish for you to make the call for help.' The First Temple, sensing the shift in the council's decision, answered with a hum through the brickwork. The foundation sung to those who lay their feet upon it, and Eulalia's feet tingled as the magic crept out from its hiding spots, emerging from every crack and crevice to see the work done. In the quiet gap that lay beneath the distant din, Eulalia felt a drumming in her ears, sending her mind spinning as she tried to grasp at the rhythm that the world would demand from them.

She could see the world. She could see all of Svarna in its vast glory, from the endless plains of the west to the white-barked forests of the east. Each temple was joined to the First and those that had fallen, ruins left in Eschalion's wake. She reached further across the expanse of her grand country and delved deep into the Imperium, the thought alone enough to call her to the Eschalion. She saw a monarch sitting beside a fallen sigil, his collar encrusted with jewels and the bloody darkness of grief.

Eulalia could see the wind. The way that it flew from one corner of the land to somewhere else entirely, through the towers of their holy city and down to the far sea.

In the winds she found the dragon riders. They were not numerous, spread far and wide from one edge of the world to the next, but they were there. She seized upon the knowledge of them and found her voice.

This is Moroudqi, the First Temple of Muqdah. The words rung from every temple signal, humming through miles of open air. *Our city is under siege, assaulted by the dread mage Thurlow and the Eschalion's army. We are a settlement of women and children, of those who were not called to war because we were too frail to fight. We will fall before long. This is the last call before our eternal silence; if you can bear fire or a blade, come and fight for all that is good. If we are not saved, know that in our final moments we were thinking of you all. You are the only saviours we have.*

Faces turned towards the sound of her voice, hundreds, if not thousands of them. Eyes and ears searched the endless firmament and found Eulalia's voice, her call from the ends of the earth.

If there are war riders left in Svarna, Muqdah needs you.

She was drawn back from the great world with a tug, a pull on an invisible thread that she had not known was attached to her. It pulled her away from the skies and the temples that she would never see again, from the people she would never know. From the Eschalion in his stained-glass tomb, back to their steeples and their love letter of a city. She saw their city from the Small Temple, where Imamu had watched the world fall apart. Flame pouring through the streets, answering the deafening ring of battle.

Eulalia fell into her body as the world fell away, shattered fragments of an atlas her mind had never been meant to hold all at once.

'Eula,' a voice called. 'Eula, come back to me.'

Ohba. By the time she had made it all the way back to herself, she discovered the cost the temple's power exacted on those who were not truly faithful. Eulalia, utterly exhausted by carrying more magic than the world had ever meant for her, collapsed.

Chapter Twenty-Six

THE IMPERIUM

If the architect had been fawning over Mosi, he should have been a dammed easy mark for Takuma.

It was just a matter of getting Aloysius away from the other Svarnishman, somewhere secluded. There were plenty of private rooms – this entertainment wing was meant for bedwork and blood. Thurlow Thurlowe would have been remiss not to include at least a handful of soundproof, padded rooms that could be locked from the inside. So, Takuma just had to get the architect into one. Without Mosi.

Considering that Mosi had taught Takuma all that he knew of seduction and bedwork, this should have been an easy task.

Mosi was quite the teacher.

Takuma had contemplated a hundred things as they approached this day, one of which being how they were going to get into the dragon enclosure. Several chambers connected to the habitat, that were little more than blank rooms on the schematic yet still all marked as magical passings – doors that needed a specific incantation cast to draw someone through. It was perhaps a bigger problem than he wanted to admit, but Virnoi, in theory, should have been able to figure it out.

However now, the architect for this glorified prison had stumbled into his lap. He'd never have to admit to Nuru that he had missed something – or had been wilfully ignoring it in the hope that someone else would figure it out.

Elves who hired Svarnish bedworkers weren't particularly special. Often, they were entertaining some fascination, a shallow fixation on the exotic. Broadly, they wanted to fuck something as far from their parents' respectable sensibilities as they could.

This Aloysius was something else. It was clear he was fascinated, certainly, but he hadn't quite reduced Mosi to an exotic plaything. The High Elf was fawning over the man, plying him with drinks that sat barely touched, pressing him with question after question. He was getting very little response as Mosi who, devoid of his usual charm, chose to respond through his teeth.

'You're scheming,' Nuru mused quietly in Svarnish as she circled back through the room.

'Architect,' Takuma muttered. 'Have you seen your husband yet?'

She rolled her eyes, but said nothing, which distracted him, and he flicked his eyes to her. Nuru knew how to mask better than almost anyone, but there was a stern line to her brow that was almost imperceptible, a tension in her jaw that gave her away.

Nuru was worried.

Maybe if they hadn't argued over the tapestry, she might have admitted to it. Takuma hummed thoughtfully, tapping his foot against the carpeted floor.

That struck him as odd – why would someone carpet playrooms? Cleaning bodily fluids out of this plush carpet had to be unpleasant. He supposed that Thurlow Thurlowe had never had to concern himself with the manual labour involved in their cleaning.

'Do you need him?' Nuru asked, still speaking Svarnish.

'No,' Takuma said. 'But I want him. It would fix something for me.'

As if speaking it into existence, the words called Aloysius in from afar. The High Elf hopped to his feet and floated back towards the bar. Takuma did not wait more than a breath before he prowled towards that glinting corner of the chamber, trailing behind a cluster of Svarnish performers to cover the purpose with which he walked. Leaning against the polished bar top mere moments before the architect approached, Takuma lounged out, watching Aloysius in his peripherals.

Prim and proper, lacking all the pomp of nobility, he waited for the bartender rather than call him over. Takuma blew out a long breath – he almost felt bad for the stranger. Almost. He had still designed the dragon's cage; he could not be afforded much of Takuma's sympathies.

'You picked out Mosi personally?' Takuma asked airily, tapping at the glossy wood.

Aloysius stalled, seemingly not realising Takuma was addressing him. Takuma turned his emerald-green eyes on his mark, gaze skating over the dark clothes and pinched brow. Plenty of places in those robes for the architect to have hidden a blade or weapon, but a magical focus was a different thing.

Takuma saw no hint of wand or staff, nor a glimmer of a Blessing. There was an unspoken confidence with which Blessed folk tended to carry themselves, well aware that some higher power had deemed them special simply for existing. The architect laughed nervously, rubbing at his mouth.

'I guess,' Aloysius admitted. 'I'd seen him around and heard of his reputation. He's fascinating, isn't he? I guess you already know that.'

Takuma made an affirmative noise in response, unwilling to trust his tongue to lie on that specific front. He and Mosi had a long, tangled history.

'He doesn't seem that interested in the night, though. Perhaps I'm just not good company.' The architect was *nervous* – how that tickled Takuma. He was nervous that introverted, silent Mosi was not talkative. *Are you sure you meant to hire him?*

'I guess I may be a bit of a bore when compared to his usual clientele.'

There it was – a chink in the armour for Takuma to slip beneath.

'Not at all,' Takuma said, leaning towards Aloysius. It was easy to reach out and brush a hand over the elf's, lingering over soft skin, entirely unmarked by labour or battle – just like the broad majority of elves who passed through The Brass Wyvern. 'I think you're plenty interesting. You're an Imperial architect, are you not?'

'Something like that – the Thurlowes used one of my designs decades ago to create an enclosure, and they sort of just kept me on the books. When they needed a new one, it wasn't terribly hard to draw it up for them. I don't do much actual work for the Imperium.' Aloysius did not draw his hand away from beneath Takuma's. Instead, the two spent a long moment watching one another from along the bar.

This was easy prey – this man wanted to have someone falling over him.

'You and Mosi have known each other for some time?'

Mosi was not drinking. He was *watching*.

'Years and years.' Takuma flashed him a dazzling smile, one that he had perfected through years of practice with Nuru. 'The stories I could tell you about that man, they'd make you blush.'

'Which stories?' a quiet, familiar voice asked. Mosi had abandoned his booth and approached on Takuma's blindside, too damn stealthy for his liking. He looked between them, his face schooled with a gentle amusement.

'Oh, you know.' Takuma rolled his eyes. '*Stories*. Stories from when he wasn't in such high demand. All of that love blows up the ego after a little while.'

This was a statement that was palpably false, especially where Mosi was involved. It mattered not. They were in a profession that thrived on deception.

The two Svarnishmen shared a long look, beneath which there was a quiet question that Mosi could not answer. They were both tightly fitted beneath their respective masks, though Takuma had still seen enough.

It was precisely because they'd known each other for so long that Takuma had at first been caught off-guard by Mosi's presence here. Mosi's obvious disinterest in his butter-soft client led Takuma to conclude that it made no sense that Imamu had come to this event. There was no amount of Imperial gold in the world that could have dragged them this far, which meant that there had to have been a shift in the conversation.

'I think I'd like to hear those stories,' the architect said, closer to Takuma's ear than he had been moments ago. The trap snapped around the elf in that same breath, drawing hard and tight. Looking up at Aloysius, Takuma allowed his grin to grow toothy at the suggestion. At such proximity, Takuma's eyes did most of the work for him. It was why Imamu had shuffled him into the bedworker trade to begin with – a Svarnishman with vibrant eyes drew attention.

'Aloysius,' Mosi mused. 'Shall we find somewhere quiet to kill some time? Takuma can always join us for some excess excitement. It doesn't look like he's got anything better to do.'

The two Svarnishmen exchanged a glance, and Takuma quirked a brow in question. In a motion that anyone else would have dismissed, Mosi raised a hand to his earlobe and rubbed it. That was that.

Mosi took the lead, linking arms with Aloysius and drawing him away from the bar. Takuma found himself smiling despite himself as he watched Mosi switch on that inimitable charm, a subtle transition to make sure that it was not jarring. He leaned in to whisper to Aloysius, who had to stoop a significant amount to draw close. Takuma followed as they wound their way to the back of the main chamber, which branched off into the private rooms.

Nuru's gaze connected with his only for a moment.

The private rooms were carefully crafted, with expansive round beds and padded walls. Takuma ran his hand over the wall beside the door, feeling the fine grain of the velvet and the firm insulation beneath. As he slid the door shut, the sound of the brewing revelries fell away, and the world grew silent and small. The soundproofing sent a chill wind through Takuma, Zuri's face flickering in the back of his mind, that terribly damaged horn she'd had upon her arrival. Perhaps she hadn't been reserved when it happened because nobody had been able to hear her screams.

When Mosi pulled the architect into a kiss, the man melted. Takuma saw the feral edge to the motion, how Mosi's hands were perhaps a little too firm on Aloysius's cloak.

It was a distraction. Takuma strolled along the perimeter of the room until he found a compartment set at his eye line. He popped it open with a quick flick of his wrist and, just as Takuma had hoped for, there lay any tool of debauchery a bedworker could hope for. Vices and switches and a broad feather duster, clamps and cages and *silk rope*. There it sat, neatly set on a hook, length enough to tie up even a gangly High Elf. He grinned to himself as he heard the snapping of the buttons at his back, fabric being discarded unceremoniously at their feet.

He took the rope and tucked it into the waistband that sat against his back. The costume left little to the imagination, but it was so distracting that Takuma was certain the architect would not notice. Not when Aloysius's hands were tangled in Mosi's hair like the elf was clutching for air. Takuma knew that Mosi had a unique talent for making people feel as if they were the centre of his whole world. *What a farce.*

Waiting for an opening, Takuma prowled, keeping his back turned away from the pair all the while – not that they noticed.

The bed was circular, but it was meant to have people bound to it. He brushed his leg along the frame as he walked, waiting until he felt something hard and metallic before he drew away. Meanwhile, Mosi had efficiently gotten Aloysius down to his underpinnings; exposing broad stretches of bare skin, with barely a hint of magic beneath it.

'Perfect,' Mosi murmured. 'Tell me, Aloysius, what does Thurlowe have tucked away under all the Prismarium?'

'It's just some dragon,' the architect admitted sheepishly as Mosi's strong hands pushed him onto the bed. 'A silly thing to try and keep, really, but the lord would not be denied.'

'Just some dragon,' Takuma echoed, his temper flaring.

Mosi climbed onto the bed, straddling the architect and pressing him down. The door, which Takuma had left open by a crack, barely made a noise as Nuru slipped inside. When Aloysius's eyes threatened to turn, to draw towards the shifting surroundings at his shoulder, Mosi leaned in and kissed him fiercely. It was a bruising thing to look upon, meant to seduce and to harm. There was not a gentle bone in Mosi's body – Aloysius was getting exactly what he'd paid for.

Takuma had little more than a moment to move. He dropped down and looped the rope through the bed frame, securing it with a hard tug, before he tied down the architect's forearm. Aloysius was sharp enough to sense the snare closing around him, feel the spring of the bear trap as it threatened to snap tight and crush him within its jaws. Takuma twisted to look as Mosi clapped a hand over Aloysius's mouth, his whole weight bearing down on him now.

Important things a bedworker should learn to stay alive – how to tie a man down in a minute. Faster, if possible, while not worrying about how pretty the rope looked. After enough years in the industry, Nuru and Takuma could tie down a full-grown man in forty-five seconds.

The poor elf was bright enough to struggle but, as bewildered and horny as he was, he didn't stand a chance.

The knots would need to be secure, but they could not be too constrictive – when Aloysius was found, it would need to look like an embarrassing carnal entanglement. Embarrassing enough that the elvish nobility would prefer to just sweep the mess away into some shady, skeleton-laden closet.

'Nuru—' Mosi spoke her name, sighing as he stared down at Aloysius with a look that bordered on apologetic. In contrast, the look in Nuru's eyes was flinty and unforgiving. Her Blessing began to glow, the golden cage encircling her slender neck, shimmering as she took a long breath.

'Aloysius,' Nuru said, her words taking life. 'You will be calm and silent. You do not believe we're going to hurt you.'

As she spoke, her words came out iridescent and amber, the magical light looping into an echo of Svarnish script as it left her parted lips. A tingle ran through Takuma, but the magic was not meant for him and did not affect anyone other than Aloysius. The words sank into Aloysius's skull and his eyes glazed over, an unnatural calm falling over him as his muscles grew slack. There were very few people that Takuma had met in his life who could resist Nuru's magic.

To this day, people joked that Nuru had a Blessed throat – something suitable of her standing as a bedworker. The truth of her Blessed voice was far more formidable.

Nuru cocked a brow in silent question at Takuma as Mosi climbed down from the bed.

'What spells protect the doorways to the dragon's enclosure?' Takuma asked.

Nuru took a long breath, staring down at Takuma while she worked her magic once more. It had always been a methodical process for Nuru, and not without effort, a fire within herself that she had to stoke, fickle and flickering if not fuelled by the fervour of emotion. She felt little for the architect, so she had to bully the magic into her throat for this. She turned on Aloysius once more.

'Aloysius – tell me. What spells protect the passages that lead to the dragon?'

In a daze, the architect's eyes rolled between the three dragonfolk. He could not help but talk, his voice burbling forward against his will.

'A patronymic stopper spell.' Aloysius's eyes grew hazy and golden, Nuru's magic compelling the words from him. Part of the architect was resisting in some small way, his words stilted and cold as a golden bruise spread over his eyes. Nuru's brows knotted in confusion.

'Pat-row-nym-ick?' she voiced the word, her Svarnish lilt tripping over the term. 'What does that mean, Aloysius?'

'A patronymic is a name derived from the name of a father or male ancestor. When the term is used in relation to spell work, it refers to a spell tied to male ancestry and fatherhood – the only people who can pass through those doorways are Thurlowes or those touched by Thurlowe.'

If Takuma was any less determined, his heart would have spiralled away into his gut. But he would not fail. He swallowed the dry feeling in his mouth.

'Aloysius,' Nuru muttered. 'Go to sleep. When you wake, do not remember us or this conversation.'

The architect collapsed on himself, eyes lolling shut. The three Svarnishmen sat there for several lengthy breaths before Mosi, the oldest and sharpest of the trio, muttered one word. *'Fuck.'*

Chapter Twenty-Seven

THE IMPERIUM

'You didn't know about this?' Nuru rounded on Takuma, her heart thundering beneath her sternum. She had been terrified that Takuma would somehow discover her transgressions, her quiet breakaway from the Svarnish code, yet here he was, throwing them all into a job he had not even prepared them for. It was a hell of a security measure for them to miss. 'How did we not know about this, Takuma?'

'The Imperium doesn't require its nobility to register every single ward placed on their property!' Takuma threw his hands up in the air. 'I knew there was something there, but I didn't think it would be this. That's a stupid fucking security measure, who would do that?'

'Thurlow Thurlowe, evidently,' Mosi said, pinching the bridge of his nose. 'You have to pull this job.'

'Shut up,' Nuru snapped, decidedly more opposed to the tone with which he said it than the actual thought of withdrawing and reassessing. 'That dragon will be free tonight; I just want to know why we didn't know. I want to know how a tomb robber and a necromancer somehow missed this.'

Her magic trilled through her, flaring in every shadowy crevice of her body. It filled her with such boundless energy, amplifying the flutter of anxiety that had been rising in her ribs. Nuru's mind raced, trying to fit this security measure into the plan they'd sketched out. They had gone out of their way to avoid involving Taliesin, not wanting to drag him into this mess, but now they needed a Thurlowe.

'We knew there were wards, but not the specifics!' Takuma was flushing up to his ears as he stared at Nuru. He was doing exactly what he did when trouble began to rise, throwing up a defensive wall. 'Virnoi can't figure out everything from afar, we knew that we were going to have to improvise a little.'

'This is some intense improvisation,' Nuru huffed. It was not an impossible problem, though – she was stringing their options together. She turned on her heels and strode to the head of the bed, crouching beside the slumbering elf. Nuru's emotion made it easy to draw her magic forth. 'Aloysius, does the Thurlowe have to be alive to activate the spell?'

Without opening an eyelid, the architect mumbled. 'That was not specified in the spellwork.'

'Aloysius, go back to sleep.' That left them with distinct options. Nuru stood over him for a moment, still clutching her skirt. She felt the heavy weave beneath her fingertips, tracing the worn threads that hugged her waist and allowing them to ground her in place. It would all be okay. They would do what they had come here to do. 'We cannot just pull our people from this mess. We have a mage working on unravelling the safety wards on the dome, he's going to crack the thing like an egg. The job is in motion. The dragon will be freed tonight.'

They weighed one another up, Mosi and Nuru. They were two dissimilar people who had loved the same man, and may still, in their own way. They'd once strategized and schemed together to bully Imamu into being gentle, even when the world had answered them with nothing but desolation. Nuru suspected that was why she saw some distant decision made behind his dark eyes.

'We can't kill a Thurlowe,' Mosi said after a long moment. 'The Imperium would never let it go. Every Svarnish man, woman, and child would be shaken down.'

'I don't know if my magic can hold a Thurlowe.' Nuru let her skirts go and wiped her hands, striding over to smack Takuma over the back of the head. At least understanding of why she was swiping at him, he made no effort to get out of her way. 'I've always had trouble with casters, and their whole family practically breathe magic. I can only ever convince Truls to do little things that he'd probably already be amenable to, I haven't held a Blessed person like that since I was a girl.'

'Maybe we try and if it fails, we murder them?' Takuma said.

She didn't particularly want to murder the Thurlowes. Truls was well-meaning and was single-handedly going to put Nema into a good school with his coin. She was infatuated with Taliesin, her lovely priest. If she murdered Thurlow Thurlowe she was dooming everyone she knew, as well as any hope of The Brass Wyvern's continued existence. But there were other Thurlowes, those who may not have shared their father's name but most certainly shared his propensity for lovely, Svarnish women.

It repulsed her to even think about. She had seduced more men than she could count, become fluttery-eyed and enraptured any man who'd paid her mind in The Brass Wyvern. Nuru could catch the eye of a lustful man. But something had gone fundamentally wrong when the world had made the Thurlowe brothers – in all her years working, she hadn't met anyone with such a dead, flat stare. She could not risk exposing Zuri to them once more. If they went this route, it had to be Nuru in their sights.

'The bastards,' Nuru and Takuma said in turn, with vastly different levels of glee.

'We could kill a bastard,' Takuma said. 'He's got plenty of them, they're all over the Imperium.'

'I'm still opposed to that,' Mosi countered. 'But bastards are better than full-blown Thurlowes. If we can catch one, and if we're not caught the moment they're slaughtered. These elves are funny about their own – the worst of them is still better than the best of us. They'd still see us hang for it.'

We. The word hung between them, an unspoken agreement. Mosi would join them and Nuru was thankful for it – elvish murder was not something she really wanted to consider. Nema would not be able to grow up fat and happy and unbothered by the world if her mother were hung for crimes against the Imperium.

Nuru had plenty of crimes against the Imperium logged beneath the walls of The Brass Wyvern, but they were all permissible things: thievery and unlicensed bedwork, the quiet way she and Takuma managed their unruly clients, a tolerance of blood magic, errant use of their personal Blessings, incorrect registration of her personal Blessing with the local magister. None of those things truly mattered by the Imperium's standards. They did not threaten the ruling class.

Murdering a silvery-haired Thurlowe, on the other hand, was more than a threat. If they were discovered having even the power to seize control of the mind of someone as prominent as a Thurlowe, they'd all likely disappear into a nameless royal prison.

Mosi would never allow her to go to prison for such a crime. He knew that she was a mother. After all, the last time the two had lain their eyes upon one another, she'd been quite pregnant and intent upon escaping her husband.

Imamu, despite his feud with her, would not allow her to rot in an elvish prison on principle.

'If we're to do this,' Nuru said, after a long moment of consideration, 'you're going to need to talk to Zuri, Takuma.'

Chapter Twenty-Eight

THE IMPERIUM

No curse word in the elvish tongues could articulate Virnoi's frustration when Takuma sent him the echo of the architect's words.

They had known wards were layered throughout much of the estate, but a patronymic was stupidly complex and arguably needless in almost every usage he'd ever seen. It required the blood of anyone currently tied to the patron in question, and the spiritual essence of any Blessed folk in the mix. That was not an easy thing to draw from a person without crippling their magic for an entire season, which was why it had fallen out of fashion around the same time that the church had banned blood magic. Thurlow had been married to the head of the church, yet here he was, using banned practices to safeguard his pet. His prize.

Virnoi wasn't particularly surprised – abusing banned practices was quite normal in the Imperium – it was just that it was a pain in the ass.

Could we just kill a Thurlowe? Takuma asked. It echoed an old conversation they'd had when they were both heady on a good deal of alcohol and pleasure. They'd been ranting about the Imperium and its nationalists, those who believed with their whole being that the war on any culture that was not elvish was truly for the betterment of the nation. The sentiment of it had boiled down to one simple, question.

Why can't we just kill these fucking people?

Virnoi snorted. Takuma was the more bloodthirsty of them.

If you do, the protection ward on the roof will shatter and alert Thurlow to our presence. He wasn't entirely against the idea, but the risks involved made him wary.

The protection ward was a common household ward that was placed on most of the houses in the Imperial city. It meant that if any resident of the house was harmed by an intruder, the magic would alert the head of the home.

This was by no means a foolproof security method; though, with a bit of fiddly spellwork, one could disrupt the ward and disconnect it from the household. His mind turned to it – he had been so focused on the wards surrounding the dragon den that he had not considered the protection ward, presuming he would not have to cause bodily harm to a Thurlowe.

Could you possess a corpse to walk down to the passageway if we did?

Takuma, if you bring me a corpse, I could make it do a Fiorcren jig into the dragon's mouth. Of course, I can walk it to the door. A hum of amusement ran along the mental thread that joined them. Virnoi sighed and pressed a hand to his mouth. *But I don't know if I can protect everyone from an extended battle with Thurlow Thurlowe, so kill the murderous instinct for the moment? At least until we've done the job that needs doing. Give the man over to Feliks, and he can keep his head.*

His companion in almost all endeavours huffed. Virnoi did not have to see his face to know that Takuma was rolling his eyes. *I'll try. I make no promises for everyone else. Can you see how many Thurlowes are on the grounds?*

He nodded to himself, pulling his focus from the conversation. He sought Hotaru and found her bright, blue eyes peering over the rim of the dome, their conversation having caught her attention. She pulled herself onto the roof and trotted over without a flicker of fear at the sheer height of their perch.

'Takuma's killing a Thurlowe?' she chirped.

'Not yet.' *Yet* because it seemed like an inevitability to Virnoi. *Yet* because, despite all of their work, Thurlow Thurlowe had the resources of an empire at his beck and call. Disconnecting him from those would be the wisest thing they could do. *Yet* because Virnoi had seen the darkness behind Nuru's eyes when they'd discovered he really had a dragon. Even if the murder did not happen that night, Takuma would take a knife to the royal tree eventually if the opportunity kept presenting itself. Virnoi wouldn't mind culling the Thurlowe tree, but it was not a task one accomplished while trying to steal a fucking dragon. 'Watch me while I cast. If there's even a spark of peculiar energy up here, draw me out of it. I'll be poking around where I shouldn't.'

She nodded dutifully and crouched as he summoned his tome, leaning against the dome to steady herself. Virnoi focused his intent into the tome, bringing each of the Thurlowes to the front of his mind. He pictured them wandering aimlessly through the confines of their home, and with a sharp motion, he bit his thumb hard enough to draw blood. Three drops of blood fed to the pages would set his magic to work.

The church may have banned the practice, but Virnoi had not been raised by god-fearing folk. Small sacrifices made great changes when committed correctly.

'*Trouvare*,' he murmured before falling into his own mind, pulled away by his Blessing. He floated within the void for a moment before he found himself standing in the Thurlowe playrooms. Untethered from physicality, he drifted, surrounded by churning flames. Each flame, varying in height and hue, stood as the ghostly representation of someone below. A willowy, maroon flame lingered at the back of the room beside a spirit that twisted in on itself peculiarly – Zuri and Feliks. That made sense. Virnoi sifted through the energy as he drifted, aiming his intent as one would steady a bow.

Thurlowe. *Thurlowe, Thurlowe, Thurlowe – trouvare.*

There were five Thurlowes on the grounds. The first was in the tunnels, escorting a cluster of flames down the tunnels. This spirit was thin and towering, its pale whitish-blue form burning with uncanny uniformity. He filled the space, crowding everyone with his insidious air. Virnoi kept his distance, lingering at the end of the otherwise empty tunnel. He had been here and did not have to wonder where in the Thurlowe estate it was.

The second Thurlowe was in the entrance hall. The spectral flame was clustered by other candle-flames, but he did not simply burn – he crackled and swelled with every breath. Virnoi tasted petrichor as he drew closer, wet dirt and rainwater as his body tingled. Truls Thurlowe was a commanding presence in any state, it seemed, and Virnoi was not one to trifle.

Trouvare. Show me the others.

The third and fourth were together. He named them in his mind, knowing them from afar and up close. The bastards were twin flames who mirrored one another, one dark where the other was light. One cool when the other burned oppressively bright. Together, they were difficult to look upon. The pair migrated through what Virnoi assumed were servant corridors, trailing down to the playrooms. He blew an ominous wind on their backs, knowing that they were not skilled enough casters to sense who threw a chill at them.

Who was the final flame? That should have been all the Thurlowe babes on the grounds. Virnoi reached for the fifth presence. It slipped away from him like smoke, intangible between his fingers.

Descending into the mud of the world, the path to the final Thurlowe was a gradual and uncomfortable thing, a contest against Virnoi's focus. They were trying to hide away in plain sight, that much was clear. He might have folded when faced with such fog, had he not been a petty, spiteful mage. But there was nothing that Virnoi believed he could not do, with enough work. He bit the inside of his cheek and tasted blood, sharp and metallic. *Trouvare. Reveal yourself.*

His tome did the work where he could not – an errant presence floated at the back of his mind, almost a nonentity, lacking the personality a magical focus ought to have. The spectral hands of his mother guiding the tome. He felt her tugging at the edge of his cloak as he sought for the final Thurlowe, pulling him along like a child who'd wandered from the path.

Without ado, he was standing in the playrooms once more, surrounded by the same collection of spectral flames. Virnoi twisted in place. There was no difference in those that were here, the same crowd that he had passed through only moments earlier. He wandered through the space, studying each person with a more discerning gaze. These spirits either did not notice his passage or they wilfully ignored him, too preoccupied with the unfolding debauchery. *Come out, come out, wherever you are.*

The spirit in the booth had not been there on Virnoi's first pass, he was almost entirely certain of that. The strange being swelled and changed like a flame catching on dry tinder. It grew larger than any spirit that Virnoi had seen in the Thurlowe estate today, taller than Thurlow Thurlowe. It was hulkingly broad-shouldered, with long and wavering claws in place of hands.

It was a rare moment in this plane that made Virnoi wish to withdraw, but the look of the thing set his body alight with fear. Nothing had frightened him growing up in the forest, be it bears, direwolves or great elk; he'd understood their natures. He knew why the bears threatened elvish encampments when food grew scarce. He knew why the direwolves thought their hunters strange and snarled if they drew too close.

Virnoi did not know what this thing was.

'I do not have the time for you, Virnoi,' a familiar voice spoke, cutting through the dull thrum of the spirit world like a howling dog in the night. 'Leave me be.'

With a flicker from the spirit flame, a wave of the spirit's wrist, Virnoi was thrown back into his body. He blew a sharp breath through his teeth and swallowed the blood left in his mouth.

Priest.

He and Taliesin were at odds with one another on several fundamental magical and empirical ideologies – it was not good that he'd appeared out of the ether to interfere tonight. There was no way that he was ignorant of the job they were trying to pull off. It was too strange to see him descend from the priestly tower and go somewhere that was not the Wyvern.

The grave digger reached within himself and found that mental thread that ran between he and Takuma, the Svarnishman waiting patiently for a response.

Takuma. You've got the brothers on their way down to the playrooms, the princely brother in the entrance hall, the father still doing escorts, and the priest in the library. Is the priest supposed to be here?

It was unusual for Takuma to show alarm. His heavy layer of composure usually suffocated any emotion that would break his perfect façade. Yet, it rose now, a new flame that would burn through his cover if not smothered immediately. *The priest is not supposed to be here. I'll handle it.*

Virnoi nodded, returning his attention to the wards.

He sensed blades leaving their sheaths far below his feet.

CHAPTER TWENTY-NINE

SVARNA

'Up you come, Eula, now is not the time to sleep.'

A candle-flame flickered in the void.

She was suspended at the heart of a great darkness, the voice drawing her out. It unrolled the great petals that held her in place and freed her limb by limb. She did not mean to resist, but she pulled back against the call, pulling away from that place where the light had shifted. An echo of pain rippled through the mud and the stone to where Eulalia lay, threatening to pull her apart. The earth was eternal and silent. It would crush her if she pulled the wrong way, making her immortal within the stone.

'Eulalia, please come back to us.' That voice came again, earthly and simple – not the eternal presence that held her in place. She sought the source of the voice, but the light that it brought vanished alongside the sound. It danced out of her way, a quiet heat, a shard of joy, avoiding her gaze like a child playing a game.

Mother of wolves, a voice called from the void below. *The bearer of the shattering. The inferno. You have called for help, and you shall receive it.*

Eulalia yearned to look down, to pull away from that pain that burned above and move towards that resounding call. An unseen force pulled her along that string, bound to her by human hands. By someone she knew.

The darkness below surged upwards, opposing the pull of the world above the black. It swept over Eulalia, as thick as mud, clogging up her lungs and coating her bones with ash. Turning them to dragonbone. She coughed and seized, feeling the distant echo of pain once more. The earth swallowed her whole, sucking away the light and the sensation and turning her to clay. There was no resisting such a force, and for a little while, it was comforting to be a part of something so great that she need not think of anything else.

Auburn hair swept through her peripherals, the memory of calloused hands pressing upon bare skin. Flame burst into existence in the void, exploding into a deafening cacophony of light. It burned away the earth, turned the void to blinding sunshine. She was entirely real again, her aching feet and her burning skin. That same mortal voice cut through the eternity, clipped and irritated now. 'Eulalia—snap out of it.'

That did the trick. She leapt into herself, the black earth burned away by the great fire. Bronnuq was peering down at her, the deep grooves of his face twisted in concern. She let out a soundless groan and attempted to shift her head, only to realise that one of his hands was supporting it and gently keeping it in place. Eulalia stilled as the elderly man lowered her slowly onto something soft, pressing his lips together.

'I've got you,' he said. 'The temple dragged you down within the earth when it gave you the magic to make that call. It's going to be a bit of a process to fully bring you back. People without Blessings aren't meant to make that sort of descent.'

She would have nodded, but the base of her skull felt as if it had been reinforced with hard clay. Bronnuq pulled away, raising his hands to hover above her as he summoned a soft, radiant light into his palms. Eulalia felt him draw back pieces of her from that darkness and fix them in place. Sensation returned slowly to her mortal coil, tingling and pulsing quietly in response to Bronnuq's magic. He grumbled above her, tutting disapprovingly as he worked. 'That call should have been made when we were all together. It was a horrible mistake to put it upon your shoulders.'

Eulalia lay until the whole of her body had returned to her, raking through her most recent memories. When she felt her feet again, she attempted to move, wedging her elbows against her sides to push herself up. Her teeth clenched, a peculiar weakness grasping at her shoulders and making her tremble. She persisted, unperturbed by her body's complaining. Two gentle hands helped her upwards. She found Nequit watching her with eyes marked by worry. Her mouth was dry as fresh cotton; she tried to force herself to swallow.

Her grandsire's hands came down upon her stomach and his magic hummed in her skin. It sank into that alien life she carried within her, to where that flutter had begun a season ago.

She realised, all at once, that she had fallen. She remembered the sensation, Ohba's distant shouting. Anxiously, she fumbled with a hand on her belly and let out a breath when she was still full. She was too pregnant to have taken a fall at all. She'd seen other women in the past have their babes cut from them after an accident – it was no pleasant affair.

Bronnuq smiled weakly at her, a small attempt to reassure her. 'The babe is okay. Whatever magic the temple sent into your body must have shielded you both, because Ohba said you hit your head quite hard.'

'How long was I gone?' Slowly, Eulalia was wading through the greyish haze that Bronnuq had pulled her from. Enough time had passed for her to be carried back here from the prayer rooms.

'Not long. Half the morn.'

A bestial panic clawed at her feet, threatening to clamber up and seize control of her. Half the morn was much too long, especially when they were at war. Eulalia slammed down on her fear. She was still alive, Bronnuq was still alive, and that meant that the First Temple was still standing. Plenty of things could have happened in her absence, but the felling of a city was not one of them. She took a long breath in and blew it out, steadying herself as she fought to feel like herself once more.

They'd brought her up to the nursery. The chamber should have been a sanctuary but was entirely unsettled, the younglings huddled and shifting in their alcoves. Idunn was half-risen at the back of the temple, surrounded by her children. Zoraida had returned to her perch in the windows between this nursery and the great entryway, her spiny tail swaying from side to side.

Eulalia sat, unable to make any sense of the temple's magic. She studied the severity of Bronnuq's brow as he knelt with his hands over her stomach, lips pressed together into a hard line.

'The dragon riders haven't come.' It was the only conclusion she could draw from his expression. There was still plenty of time for the call to work. It had to work.

Bronnuq shook his head. 'No. The skies have been empty of all but our own. Uono was struck by several bolts, but he was an inferno as he went down, so he certainly took some of the army with him.' Eulalia stopped, her turmoil falling away. Too much could happen in a morning. It didn't matter that he had been a construct, Uono had been someone's son. He had cared for their dragons, played with the temple children on the quiet days, and grown into a man within these walls. He was theirs, and he'd gone to the wind while Eulalia had been trapped in the dark. There was no time to panic. There was no space to panic. They'd lose more of their family before this day was done. 'The winds welcome him.'

'The winds welcome him,' she managed. The phrase echoed through those that surrounded them, carried from mouth to mouth with a nervous tremor. Eulalia wondered for a moment who had birthed Uono, who had cared for him. She wondered if he'd had a lover. It was a shameful thing that she did not know, that she'd never thought to ask. She forced herself onto her feet with Nequit's help. She was getting steadier but allowed herself to lean on him, not quite trusting her legs.

She had done what she'd fought for. She'd made the call. It was not some magical fix, but it had shifted the karmic needle, had sent her voice out to thousands. The eyes of the world were turning upon this cataclysm – people would see the horror inflicted upon them.

'Some of the men were discussing trying to mount Zoraida to take her to the sky. She was saved from that fate only because they were about to lose an arm or their life over it.' Bronnuq spoke quietly, and Eulalia nodded. That sounded like the foolishness of men. Zoraida was not a dragon who could be swayed; she'd be far more dangerous to their adversaries without a rider strapped to her back. 'Those who can do so are fighting, Eulalia, and they are fighting hard.'

Something beneath his words set her on edge. His tone was entirely too gentle as he updated her on all that had happened in her absence. Eulalia studied the side of his head as Bronnuq kept his eyes forward. The more aware she grew, the further he drew away from her.

'Bronnuq.' *You best not be lying to me to keep me calm.*

'You went into labour when you fell,' he admitted quietly. 'At the very least, you had several contractions. I've used a stasis spell to delay it, but that will only last so long. That babe is coming, whether we're ready for it or not.'

Shit. She swallowed, glancing down at her belly. Stopping labour as it begun was a last resort of the holy men, an eversion of the natural order. Eulalia had only ever seen it done when they were trying to buy themselves time for potentially complicated and long labours.

'It was going to happen eventually,' she said. A lump formed in her throat. It was inevitable that the babe would come, but some part of Eulalia had still hoped she'd make it through this without a newborn in hand.

'Eulalia—' Bronnuq stopped. Took a breath. Reached out and grasped one of her hands as he pulled her through the great door that led out of the nursery. He had not been lying to her, but he was omitting the worst of it.

On the other side of Ohba's wards stood the elvish militia, lining the entryway in their shining armour. Armed with spears and swords and their own sense of profound magic, they formed a towering wall that blocked them from the rest of the world. 'They arrived in the last hour. They're stopping anyone trying to flee through the streets from reaching the temple.'

Eulalia looked past the wall of Imperium flesh into the further reaches of their home. Svarnish dead littered the temple garden that stretched out into the city. Bodies draped in soft linens, holy men and renasci fallen together. The gleam of betrothal caps amongst horns betrayed a woman; the narrow shoulders of another telling of a temple child. The more she looked, the more young ones she saw on the ground.

Temple children had stayed to fight, but they'd also tried to flee back to the First Temple, thinking it their sanctuary. There was even the corpse of a youngling dragon amongst the lot, its neck cleaved almost cleanly in half. Their beautiful gardens had been desecrated by death and ash. Perhaps Morouqdi had not freed her yet. The rage that she felt was an ancient beast, rearing its mighty head and sending a rumble through the temple that turned the eyes of kinfolk to the earth.

'Zoraida,' Eulalia hissed. Zoraida did not have a clutch of eggs that she was guarding – she would not be rooted in place like the matriarchs who nested. The she-dragon descended from her perch in a single, silent leap.

'Eulalia,' Ohba warned. She pierced him with a look and saw him withdraw whatever objection he had been about to vocalise. She stepped forward on her stilted gait and the sea of people parted, hundreds of dark eyes turning upon her. Some were bloodshot and furious, others were wet with the tears of the heartbroken. Eulalia had broken her own heart when she'd put her babies in someone else's hands, knowing that they would likely grow beneath the rays of a different sun. All that was left was that black void.

Zoraida poured out of the temple and leapt onto the elvish wall, crushing several soldiers as their spears failed to pierce her hide. Her jagged maw opened, and the courtyard lit up with a river of dragonflame. It poured down over the poor souls stuck beneath her and, as the mortal body was likely to do when met with such flame, they folded. The magic shields they'd tried to swathe themselves in buckled and blew apart.

The flame worked two-fold, incinerating the elves and the bodies of Eulalia's kinfolk that laid fallen in the courtyard, turning the world grey as the corpses darkened and then took to the breeze. Svarnishmen were meant to burn when they died. They did not bury their dead but turned them to ash, truly returning to the earth from whence they came. In one fell swoop, Zoraida brought both a fiery death and honoured her own.

The elves who'd escaped Zoraida's initial assault scattered, rearing back with the fear that people were supposed to have when faced with a dragon. She and Eulalia cleaved a path. They broke the human wall apart like a sledgehammer, and in the city Eulalia saw those who were awaiting sanctuary emerge in a frightened panic. She saw children.

'Ohba, go!' Eulalia shouted and Ohba flew, snatching a holy staff from the construct at his side. He passed the shimmering shield and took two renasci with him, his form bathed in the holy light of the temple. He struck down one elvish warrior, bringing the staff down hard upon their knees, shattering bone with an almighty crack. Another came at him, the flames having half-fused his armour to his body. Ohba took that staff to the man's skull, and it burst apart.

There were more soldiers coming – they would need to move quickly.

'You lot, go! Your anchor is out there fighting to save those people. Bring them within!' She was no general or commander – Eulalia did not understand where this certainty came from. The remaining renasci left looked to her momentarily before they poured out into the courtyard, creating a passageway lined by their bodies. Eulalia stopped before the door, eyes fixed upon the frightened faces trying to flee into Morouqdi. 'We stand strong, or we die like dragons!'

A collective holler went up from the renasci, a unified cry. As more elves flooded into the courtyard, the temple children met them – children who'd been born in these temples, who'd grown to be Svarna's greatest resource. Each had grown, not loved by one but hundreds, by the greatest village they could have asked for. They were warriors forged from the magic of their country, so strong that they did not carry weapons, and they would die for the family that they fought for.

With an opening broken in the wall, that family was coming in a flurry. The first that Eulalia saw was a woman with her hair wrapped in blood-stained linen, a babe clutched desperately in her hands. Two of Morouqdi's renasci pulled her towards the door, and she ran, cheeks wet, directly into Eulalia's arms.

'I thought we were dead! There are so many dead!' she cried as Eulalia held her, shifting to the side. Temple children followed her, those that came from different temples, their features worn by fear and grief. Two were helping an elderly holy man, a girl with a great slash of scarlet marked upon her shoulder and her brother wielding a stolen sword. They each touched Eulalia as they went, grasping at her arms and side, to embrace her in some fierce sense of thanks. There was not a thing in the world that Eulalia would not have done for these people.

She should have stayed to reassure them, but Ohba was still outside their sanctuary, fighting for his life. Instead, Eulalia took to giving orders. 'Everyone to the tunnels! War has come to Muqdah, but the earth provides – we have stores to last for years, *go*. There are healers within those walls. As deep as you can go, create space for others who may come!'

They were wise enough not to stop, to run from the stink of blood and dragon in the air. They helped one another along, a cluster of holy men breaking from those who had been standing sentinel in the main chamber to guide them down within the ground. They would be far better at reassuring words than Eulalia; they knew how to lie to people.

'Everyone back!' The cry came not from her. Eulalia's eyes snapped back to the battlefield. Though the renasci were fighting well, elvish reinforcements *were* coming, and these soldiers all wielded bespelled weapons. The magic cleaved through flesh, despite the hardening rituals done before these children had ever been born. She watched a soldier sink a curved blade into one of her child's shoulders, a dark poison spreading rapidly beneath his skin.

That was not why the call had been made.

A sliver of gold had broken through the clashing figures in the distance, the sun casting the figure aglow with light. She narrowed her eyes, squinting, and found that the gilded stranger was wearing a blue robe beneath it – the colour of dove feathers catching the sky. Eulalia swallowed.

'Ohba, come!' Their rebellion lasted mere minutes, as the denizens of Morouqdi fled back within the safety of its walls, wounded and marked with the blood of the empire. Ohba held desperately to Zoraida's horns as she leapt through the windows far above the doorway with one powerful flap of her wings and, as she descended back onto the stone delicately. The she-dragon deposited him on the stone with a toss of her head, and Eulalia limped over, her gait stilted and tight. His perfect skin was marred by blood and soft, pink tissue torn from another.

'You did that,' he murmured. 'I was—I was scared, like a fool.'

There was a whispering death in his voice. Eulalia pulled him into a haphazard hug; she needed him to right himself before another decision was made in the temple. Eulalia could not let the anchor of their city fall to pieces when they still had the rest of their lives to spend with one another.

Frantically, her eyes sifted through the crowd. All were fixed upon her, regarding Eulalia with a reverence that she'd never seen in another.

Finally, her eyes met Fidela's. The woman's eyes were raven dark and hard-hearted, and Eulalia knew why. She felt a symphony of fear sing in her marrow.

Thurlow Thurlowe had arrived at the First Temple.

Chapter Thirty

THE IMPERIUM

So, Nuru's frustration with him might have been a little deserved.

But some things even he could not anticipate – overwrought blood magic as home security felt like an absolutely absurd obstacle. He wasn't an amateur. He'd robbed wealthy elves before, climbed straight through their windows and fled without ever raising an alarm. Takuma had kept his head low to the ground and listened to his thieves recall dozens of jobs. No one had ever survived robbing Thurlow Thurlowe, so he'd had no additional information. No leads. Just whatever the kitchen hands were willing to whisper, whatever information they'd gathered as a crew.

Perhaps he was making excuses for himself. He had promised Nuru that if there was anything the Wyvern needed to know, he'd hand-deliver it to them. He had failed at that, but he would fix it. He'd never caused a problem that he hadn't eventually repaired in some small or great way.

That was a little bit of a lie. It didn't matter. What did matter was both speaking to Zuri and figuring out where the fuck the thorn in his boot, Taliesin Thurlowe, was. Doing all of that with Mosi as his shadow would be another beast entirely. He was intimately familiar with the way that Mosi watched the world and how, now that he was on their backs, they would not lose him. It was Mosi who'd first caught Takuma thieving from Imamu's caravan, who'd noticed the clutches of bread and handfuls of fruit he'd been taking from their stocks. It was Mosi's fault that he'd been dragged into Imamu's caravan in the first place. Though he was grateful for meeting Nuru, for escaping from beneath the Brass Bull's thumb, he would hold that grudge against Mosi for as long as he lived.

Several metres from where they'd left their unconscious architect, Takuma stopped. He turned to Mosi, giving the surroundings a perfunctory look to make sure that Nuru was not listening in some shadowy corner.

'We're not friends,' he snapped in their mother tongue. Mosi did not flinch or show a flicker of surprise, he simply stopped mid-stride.

'We do not have to be friends for me to want to make sure you don't get thrown in an Imperial prison.' Mosi sighed, but his voice was entirely too even, inhumanly steady. 'We were once friends. At the very least, we once travelled in the same caravan. That's enough.'

'You were always such a loyal dog. If someone threw you a bone *once*, you'd follow them to the ends of the earth.' A spiteful venom crept into his voice that he did little to hide. People had been looking at Nuru like she'd murdered her firstborn rather than escaped a toxic marriage. Takuma was never going to be beloved by these self-righteous fools, but Nuru needed them. She would never even get a chance to defend herself on the tilted stage that Imamu put them all on. 'Run along, Mosi. I don't have a bone for you. The best thing you can do for me and Nuru is to stay out of our way.'

'Takuma—'

'Stay here. Make sure that your people get out. Imamu has made it very clear to the world that we are no longer *your people* to worry about,' Takuma sneered. He could have bitten Mosi's head off for presuming that he was welcome in The Brass Wyvern at all, that he'd just be allowed to walk with them without proving himself to be anything more than an errant lapdog. 'If people come out running and screaming, covered in dragonflame, maybe then things will have gone so wrong that we might actually need your help.'

Words were a weapon as fierce as any blade, and his were honed to be particularly cruel. Mosi's chin rolled upwards like Takuma had swiped at him, his stony eyes narrowing, and when his hands fell loosely at his sides, Takuma knew that he would not follow him any further. He had kicked the hound and scared it off. Instead of lingering on any regret, Takuma turned on his heel and strode away from his former mentor. Nuru could say what he wanted about him pushing Mosi away later – for now, he had enough on his plate.

In his core of cores, he knew that Nuru had snitched. She'd given up the ghost to Taliesin because she found herself incapable of keeping a secret from him. That was why the priest had broken a lengthy family feud to attend the evening's celebrations. Takuma did not believe in random chance throwing people together in such a way. It would have been too convenient, too simple. One didn't break a family feud on a festive whim.

One problem at a time. He would try to speak with Zuri first.

How long do we have until we can enter the dome? He sent that question along the mental thread that joined he and Virnoi.

It'll be ready soon. If you can start getting everyone in position, I would, because they've just dropped the meat in the enclosure for the last group of guests to see the dragon feast. Once they're gone, it should be as easy as unlacing a corset. A thoughtful, conspiratorial pause. *I think he's waiting for the emperor. There was a lot of chatter about Lord Eschalier not attending the event, but I can't sense him on the grounds. You just need to get us a Thurlowe to walk through the patronymic.*

Yes, because that was a simple task.

Easier to walk through a patronymic ward than to try and undo it. He didn't disagree.

The long-limbed woman they called Zuri had found a perch. Takuma wasn't entirely sure what to make of the sight before him. Aerial shows were not an unknown thing amongst bedworkers and brothels, but to find someone with the talent was a rarity. Zuri hung from the ceiling, tangled artfully in the vibrant fabric, body twisted into an elegantly arcing shape as she twirled. She kept herself aloft entirely through the strength in her lower body.

Nearby, Feliks kept watch, standing as a broad-shouldered man, left alone due to his bearing. That was half of why Takuma liked him so much – he walked like a sentinel. People took one glance at him and promptly decided that he was not worth bothering. It was a small blessing that Takuma wasn't entirely sure Feliks had understood until he'd learnt how oppressive the male attention could be.

'Like what you see, boss?' Feliks asked, winking across the way. Takuma wrinkled his nose in response but found no lie that would fly from his tongue in convincing dismissal. Of course, Takuma liked what he saw. He may be thrice as resistant to seduction as the standard man who walked the Imperium cobble, but he was still a man.

Zuri remained a scantily clad woman who scratched at the peripherals of Takuma's masculine sensibilities, demanding a response. A response he could not honour.

He whistled once, quiet and quick. Her dark eyes snapped towards him, and he waited expectantly, watching as she untangled one leg from the silks and then the other. He had not asked her to do any of this; it seemed to Takuma that she was flexing within the reaches of this place that had once been a cage.

'Catch me,' she called down. She only gave him half a breath to respond before she slipped from the silks. He was grateful for his quickness and the years he'd spent hefting Nuru around as Zuri's weight fell into his arms. He held her for several seconds before he let her down, though he could not draw himself away from her entirely. He rested his hands upon her waist, blazing warm at her proximity. Zuri spoke in Svarnish, her tone light and airy and entirely unlike the woman he'd been hosting within his walls. 'Are we moving?'

'Not yet. Soon. There's a problem.' A problem Takuma should have pre-emptively fixed, but had somehow entirely missed. The thought left a hard, uncomfortable lump in the base of his throat. He had brought his Wyverns into this mess, and he had not even prepared adequately. He was a fool. 'There's some messy spell only permitting entry into the dragon's den to those who have Thurlow blood. So, we need to acquire one of the brood to get us through the door. I'm not betting my money on us convincing the little princes.'

Taliesin was a thought. He likely would have taken them through, but Nuru had a whole heap of affection for the priest, and implicating him in this was a complicated matter.

They needed to work within their capabilities. Svarnishmen could only rely on the Svarnish, and even then, they could not rely on everyone. His time in Imamu's caravan had taught him that – the fact they'd all been born in the south did not make them all dragonfolk. He had never sung to the winds, had never felt flame within his heart, and he was distinctly unlike the holy creatures who'd emerged from the ruins of Muqdah. He could only trust the flesh and blood humans amongst them. He could trust her.

'You want my bastards,' Zuri remarked. She was entirely indecipherable, any vulnerability shuttered away behind a curious mask. Zuri's assurance was peeling away his personal panic, and inspecting whatever she saw within Takuma. He had no idea what she'd find there – perhaps it wasn't for him to know. 'Llewelyn and Maldwyn.'

Her bastards. They were her tormentors and her bastards to kill. He had promised her that if she wanted them dead, Takuma would find a way. That was his way. If she wanted to be the one who drew the knife, he would arrange a quiet room in which she could comfortably wield it.

'One of them. You can pick. It would be easier if we could work on the fly, but I would not force anything upon you.' There were ways to split a pair, to lead one off and entrap the other. He and Nuru had run plenty of jobs on strangers, wielding flesh like a scarlet flag before an ox. Never to kill, not intentionally, but all that changed that equation was a weapon in the dark. 'Nuru would be doing the work, or Feliks, or both. You wouldn't be in their way.'

He couldn't do it. Putting himself in front of the brothers would encourage too much aggression; they'd both been itching to murder him when he'd faced them on The Brass Wyvern's steps. Takuma was intimately familiar with the look of a man who wanted him dead. You work in the beds of men who paid for discretion and access to the body of someone they'd not be seen in the daylight hours, and hostility became a knife's edge upon which to dance. A game. Takuma preferred playing that specific game on his own.

'The brothers are here. They'll be right on top of us shortly.' Zuri blinked at him. 'If you want an out, I have an out. I can have Feliks take you from this estate this very minute, and you will never have to see those men again. We can finish the night and meet you back in the Wyvern.'

Silence lay between them, thick on their tongues.

'You can't finish the job without the extra hands.' She spoke carefully, meticulously rolling through each syllable in Svarnish. 'You said that this was already a small crew for a huge job, but that we'd manage. You won't manage without Feliks and me.'

Zuri had been paying a good deal of attention to their plans, even though she'd said almost nothing throughout the discussion.

'Then we don't finish the job tonight, we come back another night. Another day.' It would be a waste of Virnoi's magic, and they'd have to cover their tracks so that Thurlow never felt a whisper of their presence, but it could have been done. On a night not like this, he might have been able to slip within on his own, but he'd have to wait longer. It could have been seasons before they'd get another chance like this, and it would not, unfortunately, fix the issue of that patronymic. It wasn't as if Thurlow were about to take the spell down.

Zuri shook her head. 'We won't have as good of an opening.'

She was right. She had proven to be right about a good deal of things that Takuma on his own would have misjudged. He did not respond to her fair assessment, keeping his eyes on her with his brows furrowed. He did not know what it was to be so sincere, so certain. Not with the ease that Zuri had.

'That dragon got me free. The only reason I made it to The Brass Wyvern is because it broke that vent open.' She spoke the words quietly, nodding to herself all the while. 'I won't leave it behind. Not a second time. We do not deserve beasts that would go to such great lengths for us if we would not do the same.'

Ah, the nobility of those who were far better than he. Takuma would not have been anywhere near as inclined to such generosity if he had faced what Zuri had. He did not know if they deserved dragons. The dragons had never done anything for Takuma other than gift him his horns, and they'd proven to be a whole lot more trouble than they were worth. Yet, he supposed, with some consideration, that the dragons had brought him Zuri. He valued his people well enough to add that to his narrow list of Blessings.

'I'll help you get my bastards – Maldwyn can be killed quickly, if need be, but Llewelyn ...' Her hands dug into Takuma's shoulders, fingernails cutting tiny crescent moons in his skin.

'He suffers,' Takuma finished. He did not know exactly what Llewelyn had done to her. He did not need to know, he didn't ask, but it was not hard to imagine. If it was a story that Zuri wanted told, she might tell him one day. But he was familiar with the flash of thunder behind Zuri's eyes. There were stories from the bed chamber that he'd never told another. He held crimes against his person and his community in the back of his mind, plotted his vengeances for years at a time as he lined up his knives. There were so many people in the world that would remember him when the time came.

'The most abyssal rings of hell would be too kind a place to send him.'

He was quite sure that it was in the nature of the Svarnish in this age to keep a furnace of rage burning within them. Nuru was so saintly about the way that she treated those who'd slighted her that Takuma found himself doubting his own temper at times, but that had always been their lot in the world. If they were both tempestuous hurricanes, there would be no quiet in The Brass Wyvern. No one would have been able to stand them.

'Are you certain?' Takuma asked, finding himself deeply reluctant to throw Zuri in the path of darkness once more. 'You have been through enough. A dragon is arguably far sturdier than you are. That thing can take a beating.'

She pursed her lips, and then her enigmatic expression broke, replaced with the type of magnanimous smile that should have been inscribed on the cover of a storybook. Zuri rose upwards onto her toes and pressed a kiss to the top of his head, sighing. 'You are sweet, but we must all conquer our own monsters, no? I can't just enlist a shining prince whenever there's an evil king who needs felling.'

'I wouldn't mind.' Takuma was a scoundrel. He robbed tombs and the rich simply to prove that he could. He ran The Brass Wyvern only because the duty had been thrust upon him, not because he'd wanted to be in charge of taking care of a cadre of Svarnish bedworkers. He was the prince that Nords talked about in tavern tales, the ones that ravished the local maid and then stumbled into a lich's den. He was hardly a shining prince. 'But I can't move you, it seems, so you're with us today.'

Over Zuri's dark shoulder, Feliks and Takuma shared a look. The fair man's features were composed in a mask of idle boredom. It lacked the edge of urgency that preceded trouble, but Feliks was decidedly impatient, which meant that they may have lingered for a touch too long in place. They were drawing the eye of the patronage. Takuma nodded, and his perfectly monstrous bruiser trotted away into the velvet labyrinth, returning mere minutes later with Nuru at his side.

Priest. The thought of Taliesin pushed through his inexplicable bout of complex emotions. He studied Nuru, her crossed arms and how she was biting thoughtfully at her lip. Takuma should have hunted the priest, pinned him down, and figured out what Nuru had told him. None of his other Wyverns would have snitched on the job – they all minded their tongue and didn't tell their friends. Nuru had Taliesin, and considering the lengths she'd gone to for her last bull of a husband, he knew the limits of her love and the lack thereof.

But was it worth it to press the matter, when pressing Nuru tended to end in them walling one another out entirely?

As frustrating as the thought was, he slowly severed the thought of Taliesin from the current wheels that were in motion in his mind. He could harangue Nuru afterwards for her folly if Taliesin decided today was the day of foolish intervention. Nuru was a mother; she worried whenever she put herself at risk because of her toddling babe at home. She was allowed to be a little frightened.

He clicked his teeth together before mustering up his most dazzling, most distracting smile – hoping that they would not read the uncertainty in his features.

'We have two dogs to catch and a window opening. Let's go get them.'

Tension eased off Nuru's shoulders as Takuma herded them down the hall. He kept his eyes on her back as she led the way, a sense of purpose taking over her stride. They took to a single-file line, with Takuma at the end and Nuru at the front, following a predetermined path they'd marked on the tavern floor. He needed to believe that some part of their plan was working, that he had not botched this entirely.

Their way to the dragon was through one of the greater playrooms, which was now full of people. There was a bridge between the main estate and this one, which broke off into the network of tunnels that led straight to the dragon. One by one, they wound their way through the evolving debaucheries. As he picked his way around a particularly rotund elvish lord who had a Svarnish woman he could have *sworn* was a baker, he had to swallow the sympathy in his throat. The only thing that was protecting him from being groped heavily was the church's grasp on the Imperium and the conservative claws it held on its men. Most all of them were plenty attracted to the handsomer sex, but they'd rather not exhibit it so boldly amongst their own.

There was nothing in the church's writing that said homosexuality was written off entirely, but there was a heavy implication about the general purpose of marriage being procreation that really fucked with the men. The wives, in contrast, were quite shameless about their ladies-in-waiting and their dearest friends. The dichotomy was something that fascinated Takuma because he had never been a woman, so he'd never been able to understand how they functioned so vastly differently.

Nuru had stopped. She looked back over her shoulder at him with her doe eyes, lips parted uncertainly, before she shook something from her shoulders and pressed forward.

All the hair on Takuma's arms stood on end, and he was struck by the feeling that his gut was swivelling, demanding that he get out of the way. He hissed between his teeth, frustrated that he could not warn them, instead reaching out and grasping Zuri by the wrist. Her eyes flicked back to him, head cocked in question.

A low popping sound danced through the air, quieter than the man speaking at his side or the Nord's calling from the kitchen. He pulled Zuri back towards him as the world split apart. At the end of the chamber, Thurlow Thurlowe stepped through a magical tear, and his two bastard sons stepped through the door that had sat closed the entire night.

It happened too quickly for Feliks to grab Nuru, who'd walked right into the arch mage of the Imperium.

It was not Takuma's night.

CHAPTER THIRTY-ONE

THE IMPERIUM

Nuru, who did not long for an immediate death and the derailment of their plans, wound her foot back from its mistaken place on Thurlow's boot.

He stared down at her, his bright, bluish eyes narrowed, as if he could not quite see her well enough from high up on his perch. She swallowed, her mind stumbling with her errant feet – before Nuru could think clearly, she dropped into an imitation of an elvish curtsy. She'd been taught it once and seen it many a time from afar, one hand clutching her skirts and the other pressed to her waist. Nuru didn't know if she should have been staring at her face or bowing her head, so she picked the safer option and kept her head low.

'My apologies, my lord. I should have watched where I was going.' She *had* been watching where she was going. He had somehow managed to step directly into her path like a foul breeze. Her hand stayed tight on her over-skirt, fingertips finding some sort of calm in the familiar thread work and weave that lay there.

The Wyverns had melted away at her back. She could feel their presence in her peripherals, disappearing into the crowd, and she did not blame them. If one of them went down tonight, the others would have to press on to get the work done.

She couldn't go down. Not with all she carried.

'Yes, you should have.' There was a dark sneer to his tone. She kept her head tucked tight, pointed downwards and away from him. He went to step around her but, despite how fervently she was willing him away, he stopped. Two other elves joined him, darkly dressed and entirely too familiar.

The bastards. Of course. That would be just her luck. If Thurlow Thurlowe did not recognise her, they most certainly would. She could navigate one or the other, Thurlow Thurlowe or his mean brats, but she could not manage both.

Without word or warning, Thurlow dropped down to Nuru's level.

Thurlow Thurlowe had not aged nearly as well as he should have. He still held the mark that she had left upon him, but it had not healed gracefully. The side of his face was a patchwork of ageing scar-tissue and fresh skin, so bright that it was stark and odd in contrast to the rest of him. His scalp had never recovered entirely; Kine had burnt the hair from a streak in his scalp so thoroughly that it was still bald. Fair, copper hair grew in uneven sprouts that he'd attempted to conceal with an elaborate gilded headpiece.

Maybe she was her mother's daughter. Laughter burbled up in her throat, and she had to slam down on her hysteria, swallowing her voice. She did not rise from the curtsy, entirely frozen in the station.

'Have we met?' he asked. The hair at the nape of Nuru's neck prickled and rose. His tone had dropped from reproachful to curious, feather-soft to her ears.

She shook her head, pressing her lips together as if she could stop her magic from slipping out. Thurlow Thurlowe tilted his head at her as if it would allow him to focus, his eyes aglow with magic. The thought that this man, of all the people in the world, had been gifted a Blessed Heart provoked a rise of venom in the back of Nuru's throat.

A decade had changed her quite significantly. It would have changed anyone. But Nuru had fallen through the years, fighting constantly in an attempt to regain her wings or pull herself out of this bizarre trajectory that saw her as a passenger within her bones. She had softened out from her time as a dragon rider, her face and figure rounded out, and she'd learnt to bind her hair atop her head rather than wear it loose.

She would not have recognised who she'd once been if she'd come face to face with her former self.

Looking upon Thurlow's hard blue eyes now, she knew very well she should have run. There was a greed that gleamed within him, gaudy and bright, and it would demand an answer from its host. An action.

He was *looking* at her – looking at her in the way that only men can look at a woman, peeling away her clothes and jewellery and quietly rearranging her in the back of his mind. She could see his memory trying to close around her.

'You're quite pretty, aren't you?'

'Yes, my lord.' She'd never been one for false modesty. Nuru's fist closed around her skirts, but she did not rise, even as her legs burned from holding the curtsy. She would not give him a reason to strike or turn that malice on her in front of the crowd. They were watching, not so drunk as to not pay attention. The chaos that had surrounded them had softened in some sly, telling way.

What stretched on between them next was something entirely unspoken. As the two stared at one another, both poised in their own way, Nuru unfolded within herself. She took a long breath and let her magic bleed out from the spot in her throat that she trapped it, a golden flame she'd kept snuffed within herself. She would not survive a fight with Thurlow Thurlowe without her Blessing uncoiling. She grew hyper-aware of her body, of the strength in her arms and the wisp of each breath as it left her. Of every small sound she wished to make, and how her voice would unmake the world if she let it free.

As her magic worked, she felt cool, like she'd been carefully dropped in a brisk river. It washed away her nervousness, drowned the echoes of the past that called for vengeance. It left only Nuru, staring up at Muqdah's doom.

Thurlow, in turn, was judging her quietly, sizing her up like a dog would a marbled slab of meat, trying to figure out how easy it would be to make her disappear without those sitting in the butcher's shop taking note. There was some other undercurrent of malice that coursed through his veins, far deeper than desire, but she could not crack open his eggshell brain and pick it apart, so she ignored it. She could not deal with the unknown.

She drew away just as his hand snapped out, as quick as a viper strike. His hand missed her throat but grabbed at her dress instead, catching her bodice as she tried to pull herself out of his reach. Nuru opened her mouth and then clamped it shut as she was hoisted off her feet.

She could unmake the world. Or she could allow him to unmake his own.

'I do know you,' he hissed. That hysterical, ridiculous laughter burbled up in Nuru again, but the wind went out of her as he wrenched at her dress, and it snaked shut at her ribs, cutting off her airflow. Her hands gripped at his forearms, clawing at the silk sleeves he wore. 'The little spitfire herself.'

With her magic roaming free within her body, she could hear the quickening of his breath and the quiet curtain that had fallen around them as Nuru was hoisted into the air.

'Lord Thurlowe, it would serve this night well if you'd remove your hands from my wife.' Imamu's tone was heavy and authoritative; this was the voice he wielded amongst the merchant kings and the unruly. He was a velvet blur in her peripheral, and she twisted to look at him, gazes connecting before Imamu turned on Thurlow.

'This is your wife?' Thurlow asked, his voice dripping with utter disbelief. The tip of Nuru's flailing feet hit something hard, and she managed to leverage herself up enough to breathe. A tingling hit her shield of cool magic, and she knew that it was Imamu's work, some spell that he'd conjured without breathing a word.

'Bound by blood.' Imamu was not lying. Their marriage had been old-fashioned in a way even the standard Svarnish patriot would not have deigned to be – they'd gone into ancient magicks to shape their bond. 'She's a good woman.'

'She's fit for service, then.'

'My wife is not a bedworker,' Imamu said, his voice softer but still unyielding. 'We have done everything that was requested of us to enable the continued existence of the caravans within the Eschalion's Empire. My wife came to oversee the night, not to work.'

'Surely you can make an exception for one night, for our grand celebration.'

'Don't you think you've asked enough of us?' Her ex-husband took a long breath and the platform beneath her toes expanded, shifting upwards to give her a steadier ground to sit her boots upon. 'You demanded that the caravans attend this party as a show of *diplomacy* between the Eschalion and what is left of Svarna. We came, despite knowing how much of a farce this would be. My people here are risking life and limb to provide your entertainment. The least you can do is put my wife down.'

'Where in Svarna did you both hail from?' It was a taunting question. She rubbed at the tender places on her chest where the dress had dug too deep, shifting away from Thurlow and into Imamu's side. She had often disappeared within him when she'd found herself too scared to face the world, but she simply needed a moment, needed to be readily out of reach of this lord.

As she caught her breath, she felt it. Thurlow's magic roved over them, searching, skimming through them as it tried to pick them apart. Searching for a mistruth to leap upon.

Imamu had yet to take his eyes away from Thurlow, jaw clenched. To the unknowing, he would not even look like a mage, simply a man stepping in on behalf of his wife. She hoped he was wise enough to keep his magic tucked away until the last second, when they would truly need it, that he knew her well enough to know she hadn't spoken for a reason.

'Father?' a melodious, deeply concerned voice called. 'Father, what are you doing?'

Bless the Church of La Pietà for allowing a man like Taliesin to flourish, bearing the grudge that he held against his father. Thurlow swung towards the voice as Taliesin emerged through one of the adjoining rooms, swathed in a glimmering blue cloak. There was a glamour magic surrounding him that made him look as if he were wearing a mantle of starlight, the cool halo cutting through the warm haze.

'Taliesin?' Thurlow paused, his malice leaving him in a confused wave. His eyes glanced between Nuru and his son in a sharp, harried way. 'What are *you* doing here?'

'What is all of this, father? I came with Eschalier and Nahia. They'd heard of some party happening here tonight and dragged me along.' The name *Eschalier* snapped Thurlow like a bowstring. He grew flushed and unsettled, his hands suddenly smoothing his elaborate robes.

'Eschalier's here?' he asked, bewildered and apparently intent on not answering the question of what he had been doing. Nuru's eyes slid to Taliesin's and lingered for a moment as the priest nervously shifted his weight.

'Yes, Father. So is your daughter, *Nahia*.' Her name seemed to leave no mark whatsoever on Thurlow's psyche, other than a shadow of reproach that felt very non-parental in nature. 'What is all of this?'

'Don't worry about it, Taliesin, it's just a bit of fun,' Thurlow said with a wave of his hand. Nuru took in a deep breath, contemplating spitting venom once more, but now was not the time. 'Eschalier is *far* more important. Come with me to greet him, we'll fetch Truls from the celebrations upstairs.'

Thurlow Thurlowe released Nuru and swept away, though his eyes fixed on Nuru as he passed – though the colour and shape was reminiscent of Taliesin's beautiful stare, they were nothing alike. The patriarch of the Thurlowe clan held no glimmer of humanity within him, just a deep glacial ice that held regard for nothing but itself. She did not care. She was not afraid. She'd seen the ice for what it was, still scarred by the fires of Muqdah. Ice that shifted and melted could be vaporised.

Nuru glared balefully at his departing back. She stole a look at Taliesin and found his eyes fixed on her in turn, full of worry. He flicked his finger, and the echoes of pain that were working through her body dissipated, cleansed by a soothing wash of magic.

I'll watch him, Taliesin said, through a narrow magical connection they'd forged earlier that day. *Please, Nuru, stay safe.*

He's seen me now. As long as he knows my face, safety is uncertain. Which meant that Nema's continued safety had slipped away from her in one evening and fallen uncertainly into the abyss that sat beneath the strings of fate. *I will call for you when I need you.*

He was entirely too smart to nod, always acutely aware of how many eyes were on him. Taliesin turned slowly and followed his father. Just before Thurlow disappeared into the more noble reaches of his home, he stopped. He turned towards the two dogs that followed at his feet and leaned in, spoke some quiet words to them while he stared at her and Imamu out of the corner of his eye.

'No,' Takuma said as he pulled her away from Imamu. Zuri appeared from within the throng of skin and silk, taking her hand, dark eyes staring over Nuru's back. Any humour or seduction had bled out of Takuma. He now looked every bit the rogue, vibrant green eyes flinty. As he drew her back, his hand brushed along her shoulder and slipped a blade out of her corset. 'You need to run.'

He hadn't been able to hide his blades on his person, so they hid them in a corset that was already reinforced with steel. It hadn't been hard for Nuru to make the thing, just tricky to figure out which blades would fit within the panels without digging into her. Takuma bent over to look her directly in the eye, drawing her out of the shock she'd been trapped in. 'Nuru, *go.*'

Zuri grabbed her hand, fierce and strong, and the two women ran.

Chapter Thirty-Two

SVARNA

Thurlow Thurlowe had come to Morouqdi, in all his gilded nonsense, and was about as intimidating to behold as a cooked hen.

That may have had something to do with the fact that he was cooked. Beneath his very pretty, very decorative helm, his skull was bubbling and swollen in the most peculiar patchwork that Eulalia had ever seen. Kine's dragonflame was still trying to strip Thurlow to the bone, but sheer spite was keeping it from sloughing off in huge stretches. She knew what was happening – there had been enough burns in the temple in Eulalia's time. Thurlow was trying to heal the damage as it happened, mitigating the damage to his flesh, rather than allowing the fire to work its course and heal the burn left behind.

If he'd been healing a run-of-the-mill campfire slip, it would have worked.

Eulalia was struck by the sudden question: how had he come this far if he didn't know how to heal the simplest of burns? Svarnish children were taught the nature of a draconic burn the moment they were old enough to comprehend the danger of them. How had he come all this way through their grand land and not figured that out?

'I would like to talk,' he said in impeccable Svarnish. The great hall had fallen grossly silent, transfixed by his emergence from the violence. 'This massacre – all of this – can still end. Let's sit down together and talk like men of our station.'

Eulalia's eyes flicked from Bronnuq to Ohba to Adil, the holy men who had not yet heeded her warning to flee but were quickly wizening up. Fidela shook her head, a keenly unsettling motion when her eyes bore such fear.

Those who'd lingered flooded from the door in waves, disappearing into the further reaches of the temple, unwilling to face the arch mage of the Eschalion's empire. They would be safer in the tunnels.

That left only the guard of the First Temple and its guardians.

Thurlow waited, his lopsided features the picture of patience. Eulalia was no fool; her body would not be so tense if she had the upper hand in this conflict.

A whistle broke through the quiet, a dragon call by a handler or a rider. The whistle swooped downwards and trailed off warily. Her eyes snapped to the maker of the sound and found Adil, his hands cupped around his mouth. Their whistle tongue was an insular practice that Thurlow could not have picked up without being raised amongst dragons, and Adil had put it together. He was warning them to be wary, to walk with caution.

Thurlow's eyes narrowed. It was a tiny shift in his expression, but Eulalia had spent too long levelling problematic men not to take note of it.

One couldn't force a dragon to do anything, so the first holy men had devised a language of suggestions. You did not tell a dragon to take flight, but you could urge it to, ask it kindly. You could ask a dragon what the wisest path was to take and trust that it knew better than you, which it almost always did. The most insistent term in Svarna's whistle-tongue was *you have to,* which could be attached prior to any melody to try and impress one's agenda upon another.

When Bronnuq whistled weakly, it was the last thing that Eulalia expected to hear from him. You *have* to. They had to. They could not sacrifice the chance to save lives – if he was willing to speak with the temple, they may as well listen.

She opened her mouth to object and snapped it shut. *No.* Instead, Eulalia shook her head, whistling one shaking, repeating note. A sentiment that amounted to an absolute refusal. No one in the temple should have stepped any closer to Thurlow than they were at that given moment. He looked like a hapless fool, but he'd slain their queen. He'd taken their royal city and struck through their wards. His appearance meant nothing in the wake of the fact he would lay waste to the world, and not even his master would stop him.

The others were wizening up quickly, and there was a chorus of objections that rose from the other holy men. Eulalia stepped backwards once and then again, finding herself possessed by her own doom, convinced that if they chose to negotiate with him, it would be the end of them. They could hold out within the further reaches of Morouqdi if they closed the doors properly – it would take a while for Thurlow to strong-arm his way through. If he'd broken the eternity shield, he would come for their personal work with time. They did not owe him a conversation, a negotiation.

Someone reached out and squeezed her arm. She flinched and was met by Nequit's young stare, the determined set of his jaw. Eulalia had not even noticed him at her back, but she gently pulled her arm free of his hand and looped it around his shoulders, pulling him into a tight embrace. The boy did not resist, allowing her to hold him as if that alone would rid him of his fear. She did not have her babes, the ones that she'd birthed, but Eulalia still had her children. There were still children in Morouqdi that looked upon her and saw the one of the only mothers they'd ever known. She was frightened, but they were children trapped in this nightmare. There was no reality in which she could fathom how terrifying that must have been.

Eulalia could not run. She could not give into fear.

'Go,' she whispered to him. Nequit pulled away, looking at her with a tense sort of horror. 'Down in the council chamber, hide there. I will come find you in the tunnels.' With the conversation occurring between Morouqdi's guardians, Eulalia trusted that her words would be lost beneath the noise.

He was not saying anything. The look in his dark eyes was one of a total refusal.

Eulalia pressed again. 'Take as many as you can beneath the earth with you. Any stragglers that will listen – trust me.'

He was still shaking his head, a tiny jerk of the muscle that was more instinctual than conscious. Beside herself, Eulalia did not manage a smile, but she ruffled the hair between his short, round horns and pressed her face there. She had not known that she'd been blessed with so many wonderful children until it was entirely too late to appreciate them. As she spoke, Eulalia did not know if she'd ever see him again. 'Listen to your mother, sweet boy.'

She prayed that he did not notice how she shook. Finally, he turned and fled on quick feet, weaving his way through the crowd.

Only once Eulalia was certain he'd vanished into the earthworks did she force herself to face this infinite darkness. A strong whistle cut through the stilted conversation, and this time it was Eulalia's man who called for attention. He was repeating Bronnuq's sentiment with more force. *We have to.*

Being one of the only people Eulalia paid true heed to, it settled any further argument they would have had. Ohba was the anchor of all magic in Muqdah, a man who had literally bled through the night for the sake of his people. He was not someone who'd choose to negotiate with the army had he seen a better option. Out of the corner of Eulalia's eye, she caught Fidela shaking her head – but Ohba was not looking at Fidela. He was staring at her.

I want to live, Ohba had said, staring down into the earth as if the temple would have saved them. *I want us to live,* he'd said when he'd pressed a kiss to her collarbone. The look in his eyes could have written epics about the tragedy that had brewed within them, this fallen love that they would not get the chance to play out together. She and Ohba would never be married, never have the chance to enjoy simple domesticity. That was not their lot in life.

With a trembling sigh, Eulalia surrendered.

Ohba of Muqdah closed the space between them and took both of her hands in his, skimming his thumbs over her unmarked skin. He lifted them and kissed them both before he pressed his lips to the top of her head. He stayed with her for as long as he could, five whole eternities, before he gently released her and turned away, his shoulders were set in a hard line, raised an inch higher than they should have been. The sentinel of Morouqdi was afraid.

'We will speak with you, Thurlow Thurlowe,' he called. 'The council of Muqdah convenes.'

Perhaps Thurlow expected more to emerge from within the gathering, for there to be some grandeur to their procession, but the trio of men went first. Though Ohba should have taken the central role, it was Bronnuq who shuffled into place with the ease of a man who'd sat in this role for most his life. Adil and Ohba flanked either side of the temple grandsire. These men had been both her dearest friends and the bane of her existence, which was what pushed Eulalia to step forward. Thurlow looked down upon them with the distant expression of a person who expected the world to bend to his whims.

Thurlow settled in place, blowing out an exasperated sigh.

'It is good to see that someone can see reason in this blasted place.'

Something froze Eulalia in place, and she resolved herself to watch this from afar. If they needed her to negotiate, they would call her forth, but Eulalia would not approach her death willingly. If Thurlow was going to reach through that shimmering shield and take her, she would scream and kick and claw his eyes out before the last breath left her. She would pour hellfire upon him, that strange black magic that had allowed her to bring desolation upon the courtyard.

'No more of your people need die. The whole city will not kneel, but this temple, the First Temple, it is a symbol of Svarnish prosperity. I could allow your city clemency for your surrender.'

Was this offer any different than his initial threat of violence? To Eulalia, this seemed nothing more than a courteous rearrangement of words. Her lip curled in response.

'If you'd truly thought that there was a chance to avoid violence, you would have already offered it to us from afar instead of bringing your army within our walls and slaughtering our women and children.' She had expected Ohba to speak, but instead came Bronnuq, his voice steadier than it had been in years. The elderly man cleared his throat, patting his chest, before he continued. 'Why would I believe that you would call back your men from the slaughter when you did not attempt to negotiate with us before you struck? You're a warlord, not a diplomat.'

'You are observant,' Thurlow drawled. 'I'll give you that much. But you have lived long enough to know the nature of these compliments. If blood is not spilt, then no one understands the consequence of disobedience. The Imperium is the almighty authority, and we must be heeded. Had you simply allowed us into the city, knelt to our rule, none of this would have happened. You call me a war criminal, say that I have slaughtered your people, but it's your own fault. You can't pretend that you weren't warned.'

'I do not know if you failed to understand the nature of this city, but Muqdah is otherwise empty of warriors. Soldiers were sent to the army gradually from all over the country, and when they failed, the men here who did not have duties fell in battle, just as those before them had. There was no one left in our city to fight, only those who'd been fractured by this war.' Bronnuq did not rise to the jabs, the barbs that Thurlow threw in the hope that he would get a reaction. 'No one in this city stands at fault for your corruption. You have lain siege to a city occupied by women, children, holy men, and renasci, those whom your Imperium does not consider human. So, in your histories, they will not be listed in the death toll. We holy men are non-violent healers and midwives. The women are mothers of our nation. And the children were too young to answer the call for soldiers. Anyone fighting you in the streets was a warrior before their time, who will lay a bloody mark upon your soul when they fall. I suppose you don't care for that, though, do you, Thurlow Thurlowe? You are drenched in the blood of the innocent.'

'Your city,' Thurlow began, 'is a city of *dragons*. That is what history will remember. It will not remember you, who stood so steadfast in your advanced age, or the woman who called for help. It will remember that I took the grandest dragon city in Svarna and gave it to the Eschalion.'

'Your people do not understand our dragons well enough to write the history of them.' Ohba cut into the discussion. His soft voice was seething with despair – she was not sure if she imagined it or if the temple truly carried his voice further than it should have, sending his words spinning along the stone. 'That is why you're here, isn't it? The Eschalion wants our dragons. You High Elves have never seen magic in the world that you did not want to possess – you think you can take a dragon, like a toy.'

'I think I can take anything.' The whining tone at the back of Thurlow's voice evened out into a hard confidence. 'There's no country in this world that can stand against the might of the Eschalion.'

She had been so distracted by her own fear that Eulalia had not noticed Fidela's absence amongst these holy men. Her eyes tore through the crowds, hunting for Fidela. She should have known when she had not stepped forward, had not been prepared to breathe fire through the door to defend their home. She was not the type to run.

'Do you know the institute that you are attempting to oppose?' Thurlow continued. 'You are the furthest south of all of Svarna, nestled away in this great sanctuary. Most of you have probably never seen the Imperium in all its grandeur. You stand against the empire of all empires, the great machine. Our institution was the one that created the empire of prophecy, Fíorcre. We strike fear in the hearts of all hellish creatures who live within the dark—'

He kept talking. Eulalia was no longer paying attention; she was acutely aware of when a man simply liked the sound of his own voice. A dark shadow shifted on the far wall of the temple beneath the great windows. Zoraida had answered another's call and slipped away. Fidela had a spear grasped in one hand and as Eulalia watched, Zoraida lifted one wing and allowed the lean woman to reach out and grasp at the underside. It was as close as another had ever gotten to the she-dragon without losing a limb.

She did not say anything – any distraction would give Fidela away. The point of whistling had been to keep what secrets they could from their invader; it would be entirely foolish for her to speak and betray the work that had already been done. Eulalia was many things, but she would never be a fool, not in a fight. Yet, she could not watch Fidela make this mistake.

She whistled Adil's first tone into the air, quietly, that same trailing melody. *It's a trap.*

Thurlow Thurlowe was still waxing poetic about the Eschalion's dystopic grasp on the world; he did not stop at the sound of her soft whistling. Fidela looked back at the sound, the two women eyeing one another across the grand hall of Morouqdi, Eulalia begged her to return with the despair written in her bloodshot eyes. Fidela held steadfast in her conviction.

Eulalia wanted to run to Fidela, to hold her in place, but that was never her station in life. She was no hypocrite.

Eulalia's vision swam as Fidela pulled herself up against Zoraida's side, tucked neatly beneath a wing. It took one great leap for both woman and dragon to make it to the windowsill, and one more for chaos to shatter the façade of negotiations as they landed hard on the stone. Screaming filled the air, frantic shouting in elvish. Eulalia was left blind from within Morouqdi – she stumbled along the chamber to try and catch a glimpse of the council outside, a choked sob falling from her lips. She pushed people aside until she stood before the grand doorway, Adil's eyes turning to her in question. Thurlow had whirled to meet the shadow of death that had dropped upon him.

A river of dragonflame poured out onto the stone, Zoraida breathing short bursts of destruction upon the world as she tore through these toy soldiers. Thurlow spoke a word that she could not understand, and frost bloomed in a great wall around him, only to be decimated a moment later by the sheer heat of Zoraida's power. Several spears glanced off her side, thrown by frightened men from across the courtyard, and Eulalia's dragon roared. She reached out and grasped Adil's arm, the world awash with water, her face bright and hot.

'Fidela,' she gasped. Adil went horribly still.

Thurlow spoke again, words stolen by the almighty drumming in Eulalia's ears. The spear he summoned was a cool, hard ice with a jagged tip. He threw it upwards as Zoraida reared at him, about to bear down and slay the arch mage before he could even step foot within Morouqdi's wards. His weapon struck upwards with sharp force and pierced straight through the she-dragon's throat as Thurlow drove it downwards, into her chest, a horrid grin of utter delight on his face.

Eulalia had never heard that gurgling within a dragon, that ugly sound that came up for Zoraida as instead of withdrawing, the she-dragon leaned hard into the spear. Her claws came forward to swipe in the air, mere hand-spans away from rending Thurlow limb from limb.

The arch mage of the Imperium was so preoccupied with the dragon that he did not notice its rider tucked within the wing. Fidela dropped from her vantage point, half awash with flame, the edges of her skirts smouldering. Spear in hand, she charged forward, a harpy of Svarna.

She lunged, and her mortal spear broke through the half-formed shield of frost, both of her hands white-knuckled upon the grip. But it did not pierce Thurlow's skin – the tip of the spear brushed against Thurlow's armour, forcing Fidela to a stop.

A wintery spear, its icy blade honed so fine that it bore the look of glass, shot out from the shield and punched through Fidela's ribs. Another took her through the gut, piercing her swollen belly. Someone screamed as an elvish bolt impaled Zoraida, launched by a titanic javelin that had been dragged within Muqdah's walls. Fidela had frozen, her eyes growing distant as her hands trembled. The elf reached out and knocked her spear from her hands with a disinterested swipe of his long arm.

'A shame,' Thurlow sighed. 'You would have made an excellent war bride.'

Fidela was shaking, a tremor that began in her hands and worked its way through her body.

With a tiny flick of his index finger, another spear cut through the swirling magic and pierced Fidela through the thigh, cleaving apart her soft flesh. She stared up at the High Elf, her features full at first with an uncertain fear before they hardened. Fidela crafted her own death mask with the furore of the godless as she spat the blood flooding her lungs upon Thurlow's silk robes.

Eulalia braced against Adil, unable to steady her legs beneath her. She sobbed darkly, unable to stop the shuddering that had overtaken her.

'Fidela,' Adil called weakly, to nobody. He called her name again, but Fidela was breathing hard, her hands grasping at the spear planted upon her chest. Eulalia closed her eyes for long enough for the world to become level and whistled one low, harrowing note.

The world burned at the temple doors as Zoraida, with her last living breath, answered the final call. There was a whisper of a smile on Fidela's features as she was engulfed in dragonflame, rendered to ash as the inferno licked at Thurlow's shields. It climbed up along the warded doorway, threatening to burst through Ohba's wards. Then, with a final crack, Zoraida fell silent and still, departing this world to keep beautiful Fidela company on the northern wind.

Devastation blew a hole through Eulalia as dozens of voices called out, crying for the life of a holy mother and the promise of victory that she had carried on her back. She had braced herself for Ohba's loss, knowing that he would be thrust into this war, but Fidela was good. She was better than Eulalia. She had cared for the child she was carrying like mothers were meant to. She had seen the good in everyone, even hopeless Adil. Even Eulalia, who had been so enraged with the world that she'd frightened all. There was no right world in which Eulalia outlived Fidela – Fidela was good, but this world did not value good.

'I guess that would mark the end of diplomacy,' Thurlow spoke, his voice taking on an excited trill. 'Let it be known that your people struck first.'

She turned back to where the warlord stood, to find him drawing a pendant from within his cloak. As he clasped it in his hand, brandishing it at them, Eulalia realised that it bore the image of a curled dragon with the night sky at its back – a royal seal.

'Get back!' she screamed, her voice hoarse. There had never been any doubt in Thurlow's mind about how he would enter Morouqdi or if he would be able to pass through the shields at all. He had never wanted them to surrender; he would have never compromised. He had been him playing with his food, knowing that he already had a knife. Bronnuq had guessed that the death of Queen Taena had something to do with Thurlow's breaking of Muqdah, and he had been right. *Of course, he had been right.*

Thurlow Thurlowe, the doom of Muqdah, punched a hole through the ancient magick of the First Temple's wards.

Chapter Thirty-Three

THE IMPERIUM

Zuri fled with Nuru into the pale, perfectly ivory tunnels, the web beneath the Thurlowe estate.

Her heart thrummed and panicked, galloping in her chest like a frightened beast at the thought of the bastards at their back. She was with Nuru – she was not alone, so her fear could not take hold of her as it once had. She had honed her fear into a fine tool to drive herself towards freedom. It was a strange thing to reach for it only to have it slip away.

Her dark eyes slid to Nuru and knew that it was her. This bright-eyed woman, in all her certainty, who had watched over her as she dreamed, who had lied and covered and believed in all that Zuri said, had somehow managed to steal that fear away from Zuri. Simply by willing to run with her instead of abandoning her to the wolves.

In a sense, it was a betrayal from the world above – her monsters were hers; they were meant to be her tormentors. It should have broken some universal rule to let them loose on someone as sweet as Nuru. But she was quick, and she did not drop Zuri's hand, instead pulling her along. Zuri was possessed by the thought that they were children, charging away from the terrifying shadows that lived in the basement, but the world had betrayed her before. It would betray them again. That was the nature of the Svarnish condition after the death of their last monarch.

The tunnels were deserted of people, empty stretches of alabaster that seemed so stretch into eternity. Their footsteps clattered along the stone, echoing down those endless walls. They had both worn hard-soled shoes meant for work instead of soft slippers, and they felt deafeningly loud.

'Stop,' Nuru said, pulling at Zuri's hand. She circled slowly with Zuri, eyes scanning the walls. The Blessing that encircled her throat was radiating light, as golden and radiant as the sun, casting a warm halo that sung to her dusky skin.

Once she had decided something, she pulled Zuri with her to the wall and placed her spare hand against the brick, letting out a breath marked by the stress of the chase. 'Show me the way.'

The words came out in a hazy, bright tangle of light that rounded itself into Svarnish script. It was verbal spellcasting turned corporeal. If Zuri reached out a hand and ran it through the air, she'd feel wisps of smoke slip across her skin. She'd seen people speak magic into existence all through her life; it was a common technique to focus the mind and make conjuring easier rather than drawing from nothing.

Something strange happened then, something which Zuri did not quite understand. The stones beneath their feet shifted, ever so slightly, the way that long grass moved when shifted by a tickling breeze. The Blessings in her feet tingled, and she found herself hopping instinctively from one foot to the next, wanting to avoid the magic that was in action. It was as if the whole world around them was reaching out to answer Nuru's call, alive and swimming amongst them.

'How much magic do you have?' Zuri asked aloud, amazed.

'It may not answer me.' Nuru shrugged. 'This isn't my place to command.'

Zuri wasn't sure about that. She could feel it shifting, carrying her words like an echo through the earth. A light broke through the cracks between the brickwork, tentative at first, before it burst up like a sprite from the ground. The bauble of radiance shot down the tunnel.

Nuru grasped Zuri's hand, and they were running once more. She wondered for a breath if Takuma was behind them, if her brothers had cut him down, and then the wind carried the thought away. Takuma could handle himself.

The light turned sharply and shot into the wall, illuminating a collection of bricks. They followed, and though human instinct pulled Zuri back, Nuru did not hesitate. The wall unfolded like a thick piece of paper, revealing a maintenance chamber stocked with basic cleaning supplies. The door was narrow but wide enough to fit them, revealing a slim chamber. Nuru pulled them within, and they pressed into the empty space.

She'd taken shelter in one too many maintenance chambers lately. Some part of her fate seemingly existed in mopping equipment and buckets.

'How much time do we have?' Nuru whispered. 'How long do you think they'll take?'

'I don't know,' Zuri responded. 'When they chased me, they'd sometimes delay, just so that I couldn't anticipate their arrival. To make themselves more frightening.'

It had worked, but their games had been played in the dark, tangled up in the shadows and gloom of the estate halls. She imagined it would be quite different in the stark, white void that they found themselves in.

'So, we have a little time. Especially with Taliesin in the way.' Nuru nodded, pacing back into the chamber and circling back. Perhaps Taliesin would be enough of a deterrent to slow them. They were bastards, unnamed by the Thurlowe tradition and instead given names by their mothers, but they wanted to fit in with nobility. That was why they dressed the way they did, why they attempted to demand some sort of respect from those that surrounded them. 'Llewelyn is a caster, isn't he?'

'Yes. Trained in some magic school in the north. Maldwyn is as well, but his magic only ever took to *plants*.' Despite them waiting upon assailants to burst straight through the wall, the words brought a snicker to Zuri. For all his cruelty, the causality of fate had given Maldwyn nothing but the power to sway plants. Not being an exceptionally creative man, that magical pull had almost certainly limited his cruelty to what he could do with his two hands.

'Plants?' Nuru responded, a smile creeping onto her features. 'His magic is *plants?*'

'That's what the hound was made of outside the Wyvern, the one they were chasing me with. Those hounds of his are good creatures, drawn from the forest and the lost spirits of dogs who died there – it's just a shame that he's the one who made them.' Zuri had cared for those creatures because they were not responsible for their masters, but they were animals who answered to some unseen tether, who had not known that they'd ever died. They thought their feed and their care came from Maldwyn, so they answered only to him, even if they'd take a pat from Zuri. She'd only ever called one of them to heel, having spent enough time sleeping on the estate floor with his favourite pet. 'He would have made an excellent estate gardener.'

'*Zuuuuuri,*' a familiarly perfect, smooth voice sung through the walls. Nuru straightened as Zuri's bravery spiralled downwards, somewhere into an abyss that lived just below her ribs. His voice was crisper than it should have been, as if Llewelyn was calling her from a mere arm's length away. All it took was his voice to conjure a spectre of Llewelyn in this tiny chamber, and she found herself fixed, too frightened to look over her shoulder and find him standing there. '*I saw you.*'

'He's enhanced his voice to pass through the walls,' Nuru explained it away. At least she could hear it too, and Zuri was not hearing things like she had been in The Brass Wyvern. 'It's probably easier for a Thurlowe to do in this place. He almost certainly can't hear you.'

The hound. It was snuffling and scratching at the wall, which she could hear through the brick and stonework. Maldwyn had one trick, and he'd use it to the end of his days.

'I won't let anything happen to you.' Nuru took both of Zuri's hands in hers and guided her to the side, tucking underneath one of the shelves with her. 'Takuma and I made you a promise and I intend to keep it. Those men out there did something terrible to you, and you should not have to face them – not when they scare you like this.'

Children were not meant to face the monsters that lived under the bed, no matter how brave they were. She swore that she was brave, but she looked down and realised she was trembling all the same, like a willow branch in the wind. Nuru studied her intently for a moment before she drew back, patting her hand as she turned that intense stare upon the wall through which he'd entered.

'Zuri, block your ears and stay down.' Zuri slammed her hands over her ears, pressing her knuckles in to drown the sound out entirely as Nuru's Blessing grew bright once more. The bricks peeled away from the door, parted by a mere finger-touch. The woman opened her mouth and spoke, and while Zuri couldn't make out the sound, she saw it again. Sapphire blue fire lit the room, bursting from the tangled light that had flown from Nuru's mouth. As the brick peeled back, the heatless fire flew to fill the space, pouring out into the open hall.

As the bastards drew away from the entryway, Nuru strode to the door. She looked at Zuri and smiled, princely in her bearing, and then disappeared into the hall. She caught a glimpse from where she crouched of her fleeing down the hallway in a flurry of silk and gold, followed swiftly by the familiar blur of two men she'd grown to memorise. The hound's thunderous gait followed, its great dense form pounding against the ground as he flew past.

Time slowed in the moments that followed Nuru's disappearance as Zuri realised what had been done on her behalf. She willed her feet to move, to rise from where she was, but hit an implacable surge of fear. She could not think of Nuru, so she instead thought of The Brass Wyvern. Of the safety within its burgundy walls, of the thief who'd crawled into her room with a knife and guarded her like a jealous dragon upon its hoard, of quiet murmurings spoken in the dead of night. She thought of Takuma's fingers laced with hers, and how little Nema had stared at her in wonder, gurgling away.

She thought of Dayo. Kind, compassionate Dayo who had watched the world fall to pieces. She had never been able to contend with the bastards on her own, in chains, but her feet were light. She was a free woman. She was Zuri of the Long Grasses, and she was not alone.

She was free. Zuri took one step and then another, emerging from beneath that shelf where Nuru had tucked her. Her Blessed feet had taken her this far, and she trusted them, more than the quiver of fear in her gut that Llewelyn drew. Her feet were hers, and they'd survived broken glass and beatings, taken every scared step that carried her this far in her life.

Zuri felt the whisper of a breeze, coming down through the tunnels, and she ran. The metal disc in the bottom of her boots rung out every time they hit the brickwork, the sharp ring of a gong. She must have been in hiding for longer than she'd thought, for she could not see Nuru or the brothers in the halls, but she could hear them scrapping. She followed the sound down a stretch of alabaster hall to a fork and twisted sharply on her heels, catching a glimpse of Maldwyn's back and the snapping hound.

Nuru's muffled voice was swallowed by an anomalous silence.

Zuri had not entirely understood the purpose of the boots when Takuma had given them to her. The whole costume had seemed to her a bewildering misdirection, a visual charade. The little cloth that she wore would not protect her like armour, but it was tied so securely that her breasts barely shifted as she ran. With each sharp step, the magic in her feet sparked as if conducting, provoked by the movement. True magi used magical focuses like staffs and wands; these boots were just a different way to focus her Blessing. To give her some of the power back that she'd lost within these walls.

'Maldwyn!' The cry came from her as an explosion, a battle cry that she'd nurtured for years within her ribs. Zuri would take the lesser brother first, and then Llewelyn. Being chained to these men who made her crawl had hardened her and frightened her, but it could never have stripped back the marks of her parents. Of Svarna.

Something was wrong. She could not see Llewelyn and Nuru around the corner, but she did not doubt they were there, blocked by the Thurlowe guard dogs.

She whistled sharply between her teeth, a mimic of Llewelyn's own dog call. The hound's head snapped towards her, leaves that were curled inwards to resemble ears flicking. It did not snarl or snuffle, it simply stared at Zuri with its transparent eyes, cocking its head to the side. Zuri paused, her conviction wavering for a breath like a bright candle in the breeze. He had all the hounds his magic could muster, but it was always this one at its heel. Maldwyn had raised it, given it life and form. Zuri wasn't sure that it would betray Maldwyn for another.

'Go,' Maldwyn commanded. His eyes narrowed as the hound hesitated. The beautiful thing looked at its master and then to its old companion and whined, confused. It *whined*.

He drew the spirits of his hounds from real dogs. That sweet, stupid amalgamation of plants had felt something when Zuri had lain beside it. They did not deserve dogs. He certainly did not deserve his dogs. He did not understand how dogs loved people; they were simply tools to him.

Maldwyn snarled in frustration and whistled sharply, an ugly rage swamping his features. Zuri bared her teeth at him – with her magic threatening to spark into a wildfire, she could withstand anything.

She was proud of how long the hound held out, resisting the push of magic, but then the beast lurched forward. It was going to do its job, whether it wanted to or not, because it could not help the nature of its existence.

Her teeth clicked together. Three quick steps forward to meet the hound, and then she leapt into the air, into a hard pirouette. The magic that had been threatening to spark in her foot exploded, summoned by the intent behind the movement. Zuri had not had the chance to dance since she was a child. Now that she'd grown, there was a darker slant to it.

Her foot slammed into the hound, and it flew, undone by a Blessing that had never been used to kill. The beast was thrown into the wall so fiercely that the stone cracked as its mass hit the stone. Plants were sturdy things and the writhing vines that comprised its frame did not bow or break, but the knot of flower petals beneath its strong ribs fluttered and stopped. It quivered within its ribs. The hound went to rise and struggled, legs collapsing. Zuri knew Maldwyn well enough to know that his creations could feel some semblance of pain, a needless thing he'd added only so that he could punish them.

She was light-footed as she floated back onto those copper discs beneath her boots, feeling the sensation of the earth steady despite all that had changed. Zuri sighed.

'Please, stay. He is not worth dying for.' Her Blessing unfolded as if a star had leapt into her body, burning bright in the narrow cage of flesh and bone that made her. All the brothers had ever asked from her magic was a dance or a trick; they'd never had any real interest in testing her power. They had not thought a Svarnishman capable of holding anything of note, especially not a girl who was as slight as a whip and lived in a caravan renowned for its docility.

Maldwyn clapped his hands together as Zuri turned on him, not to applaud but to activate his own Blessing. The array of silver rings he wore on his fingers sparked and lit up, casting out long rays of cool light as he summoned a pair of blades to hand.

Bitter, mean laughter filled the air, and Zuri realised that it was her own. She whistled a winding tune, listening to how it found its way along the stone until it hit a sudden wall of silence. With her mind ablaze, she could almost see the thin wall of magic that was responsible for swallowing the sound. Silence protected most anyone from magic that was cast through the mouth, which was how plenty of spellcasters worked. It was how Llewelyn worked. As long as she could not hear Nuru, she could not hear Llewelyn, which meant neither side was casting a spell and their fight would be entirely physical.

Nuru was armed. They would have Takuma and Feliks at their tail.

And so, Maldwyn and Zuri fought.

Chapter Thirty-Four

THE IMPERIUM

Nuru's magical signal lit up the back of Virnoi's mind like a bonfire in a black night. Hotaru, tied to him by that mental web, saw it from her perch above the city.

Perhaps it was selfish of Hotaru, to look at this world from on high and drink in this vision while her companions worked. Yet, she'd gone from cutting her teeth on the alleys of this great Imperium to standing upon the tallest of its towers, and Hotaru, for one, thought she deserved a moment of victory upon the nebulous waves of fate. From all the way atop Thurlow's estate, the Imperium stretched out like the firmament itself. A velvety dark canvas covered in tiny arrays of light, radiating from their little corner of the world, spiralling out like clustered fireflies that blinked in and out of existence.

She had always preferred her city at night. The daylight was too harsh and bright, illuminating every ugly flaw in the world and burning down upon their sins. There was space to move when dusk fell, to breathe between the bricks. Standing atop the sky, Hotaru pondered that perhaps she knew why the High Elves maintained this haughtiness. If she'd been born to see the world from so high, she might have believed other people to be lesser mortals as well.

She pressed quietly along that mental thread and into the back of Virnoi's mind as he lifted himself out of his spellcasting trance. The spell that had burst to life in their web was most definitely Nuru throwing some sort of offensive curse out at someone, but Virnoi had no idea what it was.

Are you with Nuru? Virnoi asked Takuma. When their mental threads were bound together, the sound bounced around within the back of her skull like they were calling through an empty chamber.

Takuma's voice came back, harried and clipped. The sound of the stressed, of someone dealing with something that had gone horribly awry. *No—we've got trouble.*

Hotaru straightened slowly, climbing to her feet. There was a storm forming far beneath her feet, something that would upturn this stretch of beautiful fireflies.

She had climbed down a little from where Virnoi was working to get out of his way and was instead seated on what she believed was the Thurlowe observatory, or perhaps their library. She hadn't been particularly interested in memorising the parts of the estate that they weren't poking their heads into, it wasn't as if she'd ever step foot in there.

Had she not been with Virnoi, climbing at such a height might have frightened her. Yet, she found her way up the wall on sturdy boots, hands finding grip on the latticework they'd used to mount a titanic climbing plant on the side of this tower. There was no plant in this city that wasn't augmented by the magicks that surrounded the Imperium, and so she was quite certain that it would hold her. They had to grow the plants thicker and stronger when they made them so large, and she was not particularly large.

She scrambled atop the dome to find Virnoi flipping through his dark tome, his features the picture of quiet concern.

'I can't reach Nuru,' he said as she approached along the edge of the dome. 'She's too walled in for me to connect with her.'

Virnoi, Hotaru and Takuma had become an unlikely unit in their time together who, as a trio, worked as one. That was why they trusted each other enough to press in upon one another's minds without a violent rejection or any sense of mistrust.

Hotaru blew out a long breath. 'Send me down.'

Virnoi's eyes slid over to her and lingered, as he took entirely too long to respond. 'I'd rather not.'

'You can't keep me out of danger on this particular evening.' Her hands checked beneath her cloak, patting knives and blades that she'd meticulously strapped to herself hours ago. Almost all of them had chips of bone in the hilt that matched those on her cuff, crafted by Virnoi for her hands. 'Our holy mother is in danger. You can't go, so send me down.'

It felt less like a jibe or joke when she said it that time. *Our holy mother.* Nuru cared for them all, she watched over their nightmares and their meals and patted them on the head when they'd done a good job. Virnoi was still thinking at great lengths before he spoke, so Hotaru pressed.

'If Takuma isn't there to defend Nuru, and she's had to use her magic, something is wrong. You know that.' Nuru had barely used a breath of magic in all the time Hotaru had known her. She had certainly felt the draw of it – her Blessing had glowed as bright as any lantern when she grew frustrated, but she was always so exceptionally quiet in those moments. For an age, Hotaru had thought that Nuru's Blessing was passive.

The snow-white tunnels came into focus as she adjusted her eyes, turning from one corner of the world to the next.

Leave no witnesses was Virnoi and Takuma's mantra. Corpses weren't a problem when they had a necromancer at hand, but disappearing people were a mystery in the Imperium's great search for balance. Hotaru slipped out a scarf from beneath her cloak and wrapped it firmly around her mouth and nose, securing it at the back of her head.

Having Blessed fingers made Hotaru a fantastic thief. It did not make her fantastic in a fight; that had all been the hard work, years spent drilling with knives of all varieties, with bare hands, turning battles into fascinating games that Hotaru had excelled at. Living on the cobble had made her fierce, and being gifted a new life with her fresh leg had ignited a flame in her that was fanned by a sudden will to live. A will to fight.

She flipped back the cuff of her jacket and checked the charm-bracelet that sat against her slender wrists. One of the charms, a bronze bear, floated upwards. It pointed straight down the hall, twitching slightly from side to side as she watched. *Nuru.*

Hotaru took flight down the hall, charging towards two guards stuck in idle conversation. Two small throwing knives slipped onto her gilded fingers. She waited until she had the right angle and threw the knives, once and then twice. They sunk into both necks. After a long-held breath, the knives drew themselves out of the men and floated back to Hotaru's outstretched hand. Having buried themselves to the hilt, it took only a flick of her wrist to clean them.

Blood poured from the guards, a swath of crimson threatening to flood their suits, before the world shifted and the blood simply sucked itself back within their wounds. Both men straightened and marched backwards to the other side of the hall. Another sentinel at Virnoi's behest. Corpses weren't an issue when a thrall could be managed. A necromancer could hold several thralls at once, and if one wasn't concerned in holding that thrall for a particularly long time, it took no time at all to dump their bodies somewhere that nobody would care.

She kept running. She let that narrow thread tugging at her wrist guide her with an unwavering faith, knowing that Virnoi's magic was uncompromising. There were three more guards in her way, but they fell just the same. She aimed for the skulls because it compromised their brain with how deep the daggers went, killing any meaningful function and leaving the space for Virnoi's necromancy to take hold of them. He called it vacating a body – a quick shift of a soul so that there was less of an argument on the way in.

Hotaru rounded a corner and found Zuri pinned to the wall by the fair-skinned elf, Maldwyn. He had thrust a blade through her hip and held her down with one arm. He did not look so good. His ribs appeared to have been caved in on one side, and his leg had been broken jaggedly. Zuri lashed out at him with one leg, wildly trying to catch him with her boot. She was snarling at the elf, unflinchingly leaning into the blade, barely a flicker of pain on her beautiful stormy features.

'Dead or not dead?!' Hotaru shouted down the hall. There had been an understanding made between Takuma and Zuri, but she hadn't been made privy to the particulars. Just because she and Takuma were bound at the brain did not mean she pried.

'Dead!' Zuri screamed and spit blood in Maldwyn's face. Hotaru drew a mean knife from its place at her ribs, thin and with a jagged edge. She pressed a kiss to the pommel and threw with her Blessed fingers, trusting the way that the weight fell away from her. Maldwyn tried to escape, with a moment's more warning than Hotaru's other victims, but with a severely broken leg he didn't have far to go. With a hard *thunk*, the blade sunk between Maldwyn's ribs, piercing his side and diving deep to tear open his lung.

Don't take him, she told Virnoi. She felt his magic recede, lingering there like a dark shadow. This one did not deserve an immediate death, to be ousted from within his own body without the knowledge that he was dying. Hotaru did not recall the knife with a flick of her wrist, instead leaving it to tear at Maldwyn's insides as she closed the distance between them. He staggered and capsized, hand slipping from the blade stuck in Zuri. His lung was collapsing, wheezing as he struggled to draw a full breath. Hotaru's blade would leave the bastard with mere minutes on this earth, which meant that they would need to move quickly.

'Zuri!' She flew to the woman, wrapping one arm around her to ease her weight on her wounded side. Hotaru was not strong like Takuma or Feliks, but she could help.

If you want her to be able to walk, remove the blade. It was not a want, Hotaru needed her to be able to walk. She grasped the blade's hilt with one hand and pulled it free in one sharp tug. Zuri gasped, her fingers digging into Hotaru's shoulders, but she did not scream. Blood rushed forward to fill the space the blade had left, pouring down over her leg. *She'll bleed quite a bit.*

'Nuru will be able to fix that,' she said, a frantic edge to her voice. Taliesin would have been Hotaru's first choice for a healer, but Nuru was a tight second. 'I think.'

Hotaru removed the scarf that had hidden her face and wrapped it around the top of Zuri's leg, tying it tight and quick. She did not know which knots would be the most secure, but she let her fingers work until Zuri had three ascending knots, from her thigh to the high point of her hip. It would staunch the bleeding, but there were worse things they'd have to deal with later. If the blade had sliced into the ligaments that joined the hip and the leg, Hotaru would need to hope that Nuru's magic could reconstruct muscles entirely.

'Are you with me?' Hotaru asked, cupping Zuri's face with one fierce hand. 'I can't do anything about the pain right now, but I need you here.'

'I'm here,' Zuri snarled. The two women stared into one another's souls before they drew apart, Hotaru carefully removing her hands from Zuri's body. She took out the largest of her knives, one of Virnoi's hunting blades. The hilt held not only a sliver of bone but was instead lain through with it, carved ivory swirls depicting a rearing stag on one side and a wolf on the other. Hotaru nodded towards the brother that Zuri had called for the death of.

'This is yours.' Zuri tested the weight of the weapon in her hands, unfamiliar with it, before her hands closed tight around the hilt. 'He is not mine to kill.'

There were some karmic vengeances that could be enacted by the world at large. It was funny when a villain of this largely dark world slipped and fell down a well, but when someone killed a dog, it was the wolves' right to call for blood.

She walked slowly over to where Maldwyn had fallen, rasping and struggling to claw his way along the stone. If his brother knew what was occurring, he did not care, not bothering to intervene from around the corner.

Zuri kicked him down with the weaker leg and then stepped across his shoulders, crouching down and grasping his hair. If Zuri had any final words left to say, they burned beneath the silence of that moment, beneath her laboured breathing and her tight grip on the blade. He did not deserve another borrowed word from her tongue.

Zuri brought the knife down and then drew it sharply across his throat in a jerking motion. Blood sprayed out on the floor of the pale tunnel, and she dropped his head hard back onto the stone, which provoked a sound that made even Hotaru wince. Skulls weren't meant to take like that to stone, but it didn't really matter with his death upon him.

Zuri and Hotaru pressed around the corner. The silence beyond was enveloping.

It's a silencio spell. A mage-killer. A mage would die today, but from the looks of what was unfolding before them, Nuru would not be the fallen one. The venerated holy mother of The Brass Wyvern had taken their jokes about climbing High Elves quite literally. She was on Llewelyn's back, the golden chain that had been secure around her thigh now wrapped tight around his throat. He was attempting to claw and swing at her, but Nuru was using her comparatively slight bearing to her advantage, dropping down and dangling out of his reach.

'Holy shit.' Hotaru was thoroughly impressed. She reached out and took her blade back from Zuri.

'We need him alive,' Zuri said, biting the words out from beneath gritted teeth. Hotaru looked at her, a flash of amusement in her blue eyes.

'How do you propose we do that? Any bright ideas?' She was good at felling people. Being the shortest of the Wyverns, she wasn't exactly about to wrestle a High Elf to the ground. Zuri had killed her chances of doing so when she'd been run through with a blade. Hotaru lifted one boot in the air and took a quick, sharp breath. Virnoi was doing important work – she didn't want to take him from that and then delay their access to the dragon, but she wasn't sure what other options they had. '*Ferm—*'

Feliks dropped from the ceiling in the middle of the ball of silence. He plucked Nuru off Llewelyn's back, and when Llewelyn flailed wildly around to face them, he swung hard. One solid hit up into the elf's diaphragm knocked the air straight out of him. Grasping at Llewelyn's clothes with both hands, Feliks threw him hard into the wall. The silence was the perfect cover for a battering. He raised the High Elf above his head and flung Llewelyn to the ground.

Mages were fantastic in a fight when they had the advantage. Once a bruiser was involved, mages were only as useful as their physicality. It was a weakness of the Blessed to think that their magic would protect them from all woes.

As he slammed Llewelyn's head into the pavement, the bubble of silence flickered and burst, the stretch of tunnel raucous in comparison to the deafening quiet. Feliks was breathing hard, his chest heaving, but his features were a dark façade of joy. A great white grin split his fair features, but his eyes held an endless rage.

'Stop!' Nuru shouted, and Feliks did not continue for a moment longer. He dropped the mage, hissing frustratedly before pushing him onto his back, pressing his boot against his chest to hold him down. The once perfectly handsome Llewelyn was now wet with gore, nose twisted and broken, his mouth covered in blood. He managed a weak sneer as Nuru stepped forward, crouching down so that she was staring directly into his face. 'Llewelyn Thurlowe, *freeze.*'

Nuru whispered the words so softly that they did not have to all cover their ears, but Hotaru felt her magic work, tingling in her ears as it tried to take root. She shook it off like a distant static, swallowing the sudden flood of sharpened sweetness in her mouth. Llewelyn did not stand a chance, his whole body tightened in place. He glared balefully upwards at the soft-faced woman, but could not lift a finger, tied down where Nuru's magic saw fit.

It had taken two days of spying on The Brass Wyvern for Hotaru to decide that she'd never want to get in Nuru's black book. Takuma's black book involved a litany of petty justices and inconveniences, Nuru's black book tended to resolve itself in people quietly disappearing from the streets. Choking on their drinks and falling blue-lipped to tavern floors, hearts stuttering at the most incidental moment. Mothers were, without a flicker of doubt, some of the most frightening people that Hotaru had ever encountered.

'Are you okay?' Takuma asked at her back, sending Hotaru leaping out of her skin. She whirled on him with a snarl, slapping him on the shoulder for creeping up on them. 'Fuckers threw some guards at us before they went after you to keep us occupied. I had to lose them. It would have been pandemonium, slaughtering them upstairs.'

A pause as Takuma looked over Nuru and Hotaru, and then to Zuri he added, 'You've been stabbed.'

That was one way to bring them down. Though Hotaru's blood was still pounding, she looked down at Zuri's hip once again and saw her slick dark skin. Hotaru's adrenaline was dropping quickly and as she spiralled down from her massacre into herself, she was finally seeing the severity of Zuri's wound.

Zuri took a narrow, trembling breath and staggered. People who used their Blessings frequently and with skill were often shielded in a web of their own magic, protected from pain and ailment. It was why Hotaru had once made herself such a prolific thief. When she had thieved, it had quieted the feeling of the rot that had been festering within her body, as her Blessing embraced every bone and muscle within her form. Thieving, twisting things idly between her fingers, had allowed her body to ignore the fact that she was dying. It had kept Hotaru on her feet.

Zuri was about to grow acutely aware of her own mortality. That was going to hurt.

'Breathe,' Hotaru told her. 'Breathe deep, lean on me.'

Pain like that in the leg was terrifying for someone who valued being on their feet. Takuma made the call that Hotaru had stalled on, distracted by trying to keep Zuri standing upright. 'Nuru!'

There was a flurry of footsteps as Nuru approached, but Hotaru did not tear her eyes away from Zuri, still grappling against her largely bare skin for grip. There was no way for Hotaru to grasp her and to not feel vaguely uncomfortable with what she was pressing against. She breathed in time with Zuri, trying to make sure that she was taking long inhales and not sending herself into a fit. Nuru pulled them apart, firm hands pushing Hotaru to the side so she could access her leg.

'I don't know the anatomy of a leg, my magic is only as strong as my knowledge, so I can't promise that it'll work—' Nuru pressed both of her hands onto Zuri's hip, dark eyes huge as she looked to Takuma from guidance. 'I'm not a healer, Takuma, I've never used it to heal.'

'Nuru, you are the most powerful mage I've ever known. You can heal a leg.' For a moment, the two proprietors of The Brass Wyvern looked at one another and were as in love as they'd been the first time Hotaru had seen them. Two great, burning celestial bodies revolving around one another. Nuru swallowed uncertainly, head bobbing as she looked upon Zuri's wounded leg. She pressed her hands over Hotaru's sodden scarf.

'*Curarser*.' Golden light poured out of Nuru, casting them all in a great shaft of sun beneath the earth. This time, Hotaru didn't bother to swallow the sweet taste in her mouth; she was too close to the magic to resist its sway. A wave flooded her body, searching for ailment and finding only an unsettled stomach and a small ache in her arm. Nuru's magic swallowed it and went on, revitalising any muscle she'd tugged or slighted in the last several weeks. Several marks on Takuma that were threatening to blossom into bruises disappeared within his dusky skin, and as Nuru reached out, untying the scarf that Hotaru had bound, the gaping puncture in Zuri's hip was sewing itself back together. It was as though her body had forgotten that it had been wounded at all, skin knitting together as if an invisible needle were winding from one end to the other.

'Holy hells,' Zuri breathed, rubbing at her hip disbelievingly.

'I didn't think that would work.' Nuru, ever the optimist, could have likely changed the world had she simply believed in herself as much as Takuma did. 'I truly didn't think that would work.'

'That's some magic.' Hotaru was still gulping down huge breaths, battling the throes of panic that her body did not know how to comprehend. Zuri pulled away from them all, stiffly trotting back down the hallway to where the mass of plants had fallen. Hotaru, yet to trust that she was entirely recovered, followed tight at her side.

'Maybe give it a second to seal properly before you tear yourself open again—'

'Can you save him?' Zuri interjected, looking down at the hound. She kept one hand on her hip to try and stifle bleeding that was no longer occurring. 'There's a real dog in there that did not deserve the abuse it was given.'

Hotaru took one look at the determined set of her jaw and the intensity with which she was staring down at the creature. Any argument was likely to be a nonstarter. She closed her eyes to reach out in the back of her mind to Virnoi, who was peculiarly preoccupied for someone who'd been entirely alone when Hotaru had left him. *She wants to save the hound.*

On the other end of that mental chamber, there was a popping sound, like a distant shower of fireworks. Then Virnoi's attention manifested like a storm cloud. *Show it to me. I saw the thing briefly, but I can't help if I can't see what I'm handling up close.*

As someone who was not a true magus, this was harder for Hotaru to do. It was not just sending a word or shouting into a chamber that she and Virnoi were both in, it was internalising the image of this hound and sending it in its entirety up to her necromancer. She did not know how this creature worked, but in her mind, she placed each component she saw in the beast and sent it forward, brows knitting together as she tried to not miss anything. Hotaru had no idea what was one plant and what another, it all looked the same to her.

Between the ribs will be easy. The dog's a construct bound to a dead soul, no different than raising a skeleton from the earth. Hotaru blew out a long breath and wiped off his hunting knife on her trousers, not wanting the fallen elf's blood to ruin what she was attempting.

'Hush, sweet thing,' Zuri whispered. She was better at kindnesses than Hotaru, who took the moment after she'd spoken to slip the blade within the dog's ribs. The vines shifted out of the way to make space, but Hotaru was unsure what to nick. She had to cut something to give Virnoi access, but this was all dense greenery, with great fans of flowers clustered together to make up the hound's body. Those blooms did not seem so substantial as to equate them with a vital organ.

She picked a particularly large pink blossom and sliced it, barely a nick out of fear that it would fall apart if she tore too deep. Hotaru did not know if it would work at all until the dark shadow left the cuffs of her jackets and sunk within the beast. Hotaru watched it creep through the body, flooding each twisted stalk and fluttering petal with its essence.

The beast's system shuddered and then reset. It began to shift back into place as she withdrew the blade, the plants righting themselves as the hound rose to its feet.

'It's bound to Virnoi now, but he's kept the same soul bonded within the plants.' The poor thing wagged its tail, which looked as if it was made up of a giant bean casing. It shook itself, straightening and stretching as if to test the limits of its corrected form. Hotaru suppressed a smile. 'You now have a dog of your own.'

'Did we really need a dog?' Takuma asked, bemused but not objecting in any true way. He was softer for animals than he was for people. Hotaru had never watched him leave an animal to suffer on the street.

A tentative smile split Zuri's face as the hound leapt up to greet her, tail wagging wildly as it realised its new freedom. 'I guess we have a dog.'

'Feliks,' Nuru said, her voice sharp. She looked at the bastard Thurlowe lying in the hall, still frozen by the force of her voice. With the panic of Zuri's open wound passed, their minds all turned back to the task at hand. Hotaru did *not* want to know what was so exciting above ground that she was hearing shouts echoing through the tunnel, the sudden rise of panic. 'Go get our friend.'

The creature they called Feliks strolled towards the frozen High Elf, took a deep breath, and unfolded. With a wild crack, his rib cage stretched and opened, flesh changing to bark and patterned wood as he pounced upon Llewelyn. He was impossibly huge, his form bending at the roof as he reached down and scooped up the elf. It was difficult to watch; some part of Hotaru wanted to turn her eyes away, but she could only stare. It was the same knee-jerk instinct that stopped humans from looking into the shadows on moonless nights, or possessed them to look into the forest and see shapes among the trees but never cross the invisible boundary that kept them safe. People were deeply, instinctually afraid of their own mortality, and their brains worked to keep them safe, even when it did not comprehend what stood before them.

She'd never quite understood what Feliks was, only that he was particularly useful to have at The Brass Wyvern. Once he was done swallowing Llewelyn into his thorny maw, Feliks' rib cage closed tight again, and he shrunk back into his regular form. He turned towards them and looked to be nothing more than a milky-skinned Nord once more, in his low-hanging trousers and little else. His face lit up as he smiled at them, patting one broad hand on his chest. 'Time to go, eh?'

'Wait!' Another Svarnish voice cut through the noise, and Hotaru whirled to find a stranger standing before them. He was one of theirs, but he lacked horns entirely, tattooed from crown to toe with scattered rings that wrapped his body and dressed exclusively in dark silk. His eyes were not focused on Hotaru but rather Takuma, a wild sense of urgency within his stare. 'Takuma. Let me help you. Things are going strange in the playrooms. If what you're doing will end this night, we need to do it now.'

'What do you mean by strange, Mosi?'

'Thurlow's got ghosts on the premises. There are spectres coming out of the walls. The elves haven't figured it out yet because most of them have got

Svarnish face-blindness, but they will when they walk straight through them.' Hotaru reached out in the back of her mind for Virnoi once more, and was struck by laboured breathing that was not her own. That sense of unfettered victory over another – *he was fighting with someone.* He was winning, which was perhaps what mattered most, but their time was burning down. 'You know what happens when they start turning on Svarnish faces.'

Their own would become quick targets. She did not know what Virnoi had done and, despite her tolerance for his undead shenanigans, even Hotaru understood that this could be disastrous for the dragonfolk who'd been dragged to this night. This had not been in the plan. Takuma's jaw clicked.

'Fine, sure! Another pair of hands on deck,' Takuma said, rolling his eyes. 'Hurrah!'

Chapter Thirty-Five

THE IMPERIUM

Chaos had unfolded below – was Virnoi surprised?

There had been too many variables to control. This heist wasn't ever going to be easy – they were trying to rob a man while he was not only at home but throwing a gala populated by people who'd throw them into a prison without a second thought. They were always going to spend the evening competing with the many eyes in this place, with every magical word that they knew.

The murder was a pleasant surprise. The Wyverns were usually reluctant to resort to bloodshed, Takuma excepted; he hadn't thought they'd committed quite so far into this mess.

He sighed, his mouth tingling. Such excessive use of his magic set his whole body on edge. Acutely aware of every breath and inch of flesh, each seam of fabric grinding on his sensibilities. This evening was proving to involve more overlapping spellwork than Virnoi had done in a long time. His tome would support some of the work – the ghost that held it in his absence had enough spectral focus to support his spells once cast – but the rest he juggled alone. He was the only mage that had any true classical training. Nuru's Blessing was too temperamental to rely upon without an intensive academic course that Virnoi didn't have the patience for.

This would be one more spell to add to the ever-expanding list. At least he would not have to maintain it for long. Like severing a length of rope with a knife, all it took was a flick of his wrist.

Virnoi leapt into the dragon's dome, taking himself not to the floor but into a tree planted on the island. There was a thick fork that he suspected would hold his weight, and it barely creaked as he materialised in a flash of shadowy smoke. Perhaps he had spun a mistruth to Takuma about their entry into the dome. He could not get the Svarnishman into the dome, but that did not mean that he couldn't pry into what lay below.

The beast had stopped its agitating pacing and settled in a nest of crushed saplings. Heat rolled off its hulking form in waves that threatened to overwhelm Virnoi, forcing him to grapple for balance as his head spun. It was expelling blistering waves of gas. Within a few hours, whatever sedative Thurlow had been feeding the dragon would burn out of its system and that gas would be flame once more – Virnoi planned on not being in the beast's direct vicinity when it happened. He just hoped that Nuru was right about their ability to calm it.

She was a secretive creature. In the time he'd spent staying in The Brass Wyvern, she'd often been prone to naming Takuma as the secretive taskmaster of the brothel. But Virnoi had watched Nuru pull at strings for too long not to think that there was something in play he hadn't been made aware of. There was always so much that they were waiting on, just hoping that everything came together in one cohesive bang.

His primary interest at the moment was not the dragon itself. Like he had told Takuma, he was not a healer. He wouldn't be able to do anything with finesse to a living thing, not without a second caster at his disposal and a comprehensive diagram that bisected a draconic body. Yet he had spotted something dead when peering through the glass, and he wanted to get a better feel for it.

The thing – the dragon, he was still rewiring his mind into thinking of it as a sentient being – was staring at him. It was hard to think of something so enormous, so alien, as a being that one might converse with. Nuru spoke of them so fondly, like they'd both sit down and crack open a bottle of wine together with two vastly different glasses. She also claimed that they were highly intelligent polyglots.

Not here for you, Virnoi signed. It was an easy thing, to look in someone's eyes and see that they did not understand when someone was speaking with them. He was faced with no such failed comprehension with the dragon. *I need to see the bones.*

He tugged one of the gloves off and placed his bare hand on a pale rib, the hairs on the back of his neck standing on end as palm met bone. Suffering. That was what came to Virnoi first, the type of suffering that killed all light within a person. A gale force wind that was too strong for a man to fight against. Virnoi almost found his feet slipping out from beneath him at the sheer force of it. He swore and found no air in his lungs, unable to make a noise. He had to drag himself away, pulling his hand from the being that wished to drag him down.

People liked to pretend as if the dead did not much care what happened after they were dead. This was only partially true. For a little while, all people held on to their sense of self as spectres. They lingered over their body while death settled over them, rolling through their life and the most formative moments of their life. Those with Blessings and spellwork proficiency had the propensity to transform into the undead if they managed to hold on to their willpower and sense of vindication. If Virnoi ever died unexpectedly, he planned on making the shift to lich quick enough to kill the man who'd slain him.

Creatures of magic held on to themselves for an eternity. They did not have an afterlife quite the same as humans; as long as their remains were intact, their being lived on. Whomever or whatever this dragon was, lived on in those bones with a vengeance. It had created something that was just about unheard of and impossible to come by if one was against slaughtering magical creatures: a necromantic source. Deathly magic poured from it, as potent as any vein in the earth.

He could work with this. With the evening deteriorating before his eyes, Virnoi needed a contingency plan, and this was better than anything he could have hoped for. He looked at the dragon and found that it was regarding him warily, the look within its eyes entirely too complex for him to be comfortable. Nodding to himself, he drew a mental rope back to the top of the dome, where his tome remained.

A voice broke through his scheming as he flickered back into existence, full of a prim elvish lilt. 'You're not supposed to be here.'

Truls Thurlowe stood on the rim of the Prismarium dome that topped his father's estate. The eldest of the Thurlowe brood looked every bit an elvish king. He wore gilded armour for the festivities, an undershirt embroidered with iridescent thread peeking out from beneath his metallic trappings. On his chest plate, two great winged stallions reared at one another amongst elaborate engravings, a great blooming night-lily at his heart. Glamour magic cloaked him, for he was surrounded in a halo of soft golden light that Virnoi sneered to behold.

Virnoi chuckled, rolling his shoulder thoughtfully. He was not one to mince his words and could not come up with a clever excuse or misdirection, so he found himself falling into an old black humour. 'No shit.'

What a sight this would be, atop one of the grandest states in the empire. The necromancer and this gaudy piece of work fighting in the firmament.

He unfolded slowly from where he had been working, and for once in his life, he allowed himself to come to his full height. He spent so much of his time stooping to ensure that his Svarnish friends did not feel crowded by him, twisting his ivory spine into knots so that they did not have to strain their necks. It was peculiar to allow himself that luxury and to know how tall he truly was, how much space he took up when his posture cracked back into place. What a creature he had become.

Truls' porcelain face scrunched up in a confused knot, eyes raking over Virnoi.

'You're—you come from the Wyvern. You're one of Nuru's friends.'

That was enough to give Virnoi pause. Both men regarded the other in an entirely different light. The two had never had a conversation. Virnoi had given Truls a wide and considerate berth, avoided him in halls and the great gathering chamber. He had been careful. He had been cautious. Yet Truls had seen him all the while. Perhaps he'd been underestimating the man's intelligence just a touch. Perhaps they all had.

'Fucking hell,' Truls swore as all that had happened in the last few weeks fell into place in his mind. 'Fucking, fucking, *fuck.*'

Less of a princely tongue than one would think. Not that it mattered.

'I can't let you leave.' There was almost a reluctance in his tongue as Truls shook his head, clasping his hands before his chest. There was a glimmer of magic that leapt between his gauntlets, and from it sparked electricity. It crackled to life and then solidified as he took it in his hand, extending into an elegant long sword. There was a real blade beneath the charged halo that he'd drawn from the air, but Virnoi found himself less concerned about steel. 'I'm truly sorry, but you can't be here.'

So, I'll strike you down.

'Bold of you to presume you could take me.' Virnoi had the advantage. He'd been brawling with raw magic casters since he was a boy, he had a book of shadows at his beck and call. He had conviction. What did this prince have but some pretty armour and some extra schooling?

Truls did not trade any more words with him. He lunged with lightning in hand. Virnoi leapt out of the way, feet caught by a buoyancy charm he'd lain over the whole dome that would allow him to float around the roof without risk of falling to his death.

The grey ghost that held his book of shadows thrust it across the dome and into his hands, pages fluttering in the wind. He had to withdraw his magic from his many whirring wards to focus it upon this fight, winding them back to him like rope.

Takuma, Virnoi called along their mental thread. *Don't go into the dome yet. We've got trouble up top.*

There were no words from the other end, only a vague sense of affirmation that let Virnoi know that he'd been heard. Truls came for him again, but he would not step off the dome, unwilling to risk embracing Virnoi's spellwork. It would have made this all entirely too easy to drop him down several hundred feet to his potential doom.

'*Taculo,*' Virnoi said as he found the spell he'd been looking for in the parchment. '*Vacia.*'

The ring that sat at the edge of the dome lit up as mist poured from the glass. Tentacles shot out from the dome from where the mist was thickest, as black as obsidian and forty feet tall. They slammed down towards the scion of the Thurlowe empire, grasping at him. Truls turned away from Virnoi with a snap, swinging his blade in a sharp arc to try and cut himself free of the first that had snaked around him. He did not have enough force beneath the swing, and his blade ended up stuck in the flesh.

'This would be a bad place for you to die, up where no one could see you disappear.' It was peculiar how easy it was, to find his animosity uncoiling like a viper when he'd been so mindful for so long about keeping it restrained. 'Your father warded this entire dome so that the city below couldn't see anything that happened atop it. Isn't that funny?'

Truls hooked a foot under one tentacle to give himself leverage and swung backward, wrenching his blade free and gouging a deep slice within the tentacle. It writhed and flipped away momentarily before it slammed down on the glass, swaying wildly from side to side. He turned on his heel and lunged along the narrow, flat portion of glass that surrounded the dome.

The tentacle spell was a nasty variation of a summoning he'd picked up from a sailor in the western reaches. He'd had to finesse it to make it work for him, find something in the ephemeral plain that would answer his call, but it was a mean thing to fight. If all seven tentacles weren't vanquished at the same moment, she remade them, reforming her torn flesh and continuing her service.

Truls was a brilliant swordsman. He fought with the grace of a godly Blessing, never once letting his weapon slip from his fingers. Virnoi vacillated wildly between wanting his immediate death and wanting him restrained so that he could take a moment to figure out what to do, so he traded blows with the prince while he watched imperiously. Rooted in place, the obsidian tentacles had little room to move within the mist, but they were wildly flexible, swinging down hard to try and strike him. It would have been entirely too easy to throw Truls off into the abyss, but it lacked the control Virnoi needed.

In a particularly impressive move, Truls leapt into the air and sliced straight through one of the great tentacles. Sliced in half, the disconnected mass collapsed over the side of the tower and dissolved into ash as the base slunk back within the mist. The High Elf landed on his feet and took a moment to breathe, chest heaving as Virnoi saw an opening in his stance. The remaining tentacles swayed and shifted, swirling towards Truls in an attempt to grasp at him.

Virnoi floated further inwards, swinging past Truls so he could levitate above the top of the dome. His tome flicked between pages on its own, eternally searching for another spell to make use of – but he waited. The keener his eyes were, the keener the perception of the tentacles, so he planted his feet on the apex of the dome and watched as Truls scrambled to get away. The tentacles swirled and looped in on themselves, tangling to try and grab at him.

It was clumsy. He was fumbling. Virnoi dug his fingernails deep into the palm of his hand and found that it sharpened his attention, allowed him to focus in on the finer details. Spellcasting in such mass was violently distracting. It cast a haze over the brain, drew the mind towards a second set of eyes that saw the ethereal instead of the physical. Pain anchored the mind in the body, grounded it to allow him to focus on the task at hand.

Truls plunged his sword into the centre of one of the tentacles, and it sank to the hilt of the blade, the length jolting and jerking in response to the blast of lightning it channelled. The elf went to withdraw it and struggled, a split second which Virnoi capitalised on. Another tentacle emerged from the mist, reached for him and snaked around the dome, wrapping around the Thurlow son in one great swing.

'How are you doing this?' Truls snarled. The look in his eyes was wild, a flash of panic that sent Virnoi's memory flickering back to the white of a beast's eyes against the thick forest. Back then it had been just the same: a boy, a beast, and the knowledge that if Virnoi had ever lost a fight he would have been dead. He hadn't grown up in a castle, he hadn't trained against a sword master or a collection of his father's finest knights. He'd been trained by the dead.

'Prismarium glass is impervious to any magical shattering, but it isn't impervious to having it cast upon it at all. It doesn't just absorb all magic. Otherwise, you wouldn't have been able to ward it so heavily from the rest of the Imperium.' Did he truly not know this? Virnoi cocked his head to the side, studying Truls. Was this something not taught in the Imperium as a standard? 'It holds magic quite well, actually. Like obsidian.'

Materials that were impervious to shattering were truly fantastic bases to cast off. Obsidian conducted magic along its surface, igneous rocks resisted all frost magics by reflecting them off their surface and bouncing them into one another. It amplified it into a blizzard. Prismarium glass, in its original form, had been a creation of Virnoi's people used in temples and hunting grounds to carry spells great distances with minimal effort. It turned the very top of the tower into the easiest summoning circle she'd ever hoped for.

'Just tell me one thing.' Truls hissed at him as the tentacles snaked tight around him. 'Was Nuru a part of this?'

It was such an absurd question that Virnoi stopped, floating down until he was standing atop the apex of the sphere. He sat and stared down at his adversary, twisting his mind around the question.

'Did you think you were friends?' he asked, brows knitting together in confusion. 'Did you think that you put your hand up her skirt, threw some money at her and that made you two *friends?* Truls, she's in love with your brother. You know that. Yet, you continued in your dogged pursuit of the carnal – it's not as if you were ever in love with her. It's not as if you were ever going to marry her. But you had to possess her. Because what are siblings if not children fighting for a shiny toy? You don't pay your friends.'

Virnoi, a voice warned from far below his feet. He stepped upwards and into the air once more, allowing the wind to send his cloak billowing around his form. The voice was Hotaru's, drawing him back gently from his fury. He had already said too much.

'I don't speak for Nuru,' Virnoi admitted finally. 'Maybe you'll get a chance to ask her yourself if you survive this.'

The two tentacles holding Truls threw him off the side of the tower, and a third slammed him downwards. Virnoi floated out to watch him fall, lifting one hand to his mouth. He curled his thumb and index finger into a ring and blew a sharp breath through the hole. As Truls shot down the tower, leaves flew in a flurry from the wind Virnoi had blown and swamped the ground at his back, burying the princely man in a mountain of dry autumn leaves.

It cushioned his fall, but not enough to save the Thurlowe boy from unconsciousness. Once he was buried, he did not rise, though he continued to breathe. The great flame that sustained Truls barely flickered, untouched by the winds of fate.

Out here on top of the world, floating even away from the tower, the wind that filled the skies threatened to carry him away from the world. It would have swept him away had his magic not anchored him in place, binding him to his own spellwork like a spider upon his web.

He had never felt the winds like that before. Taking up along the side of the building like a gale force, threatening to carry Virnoi off into the south. It was the type of wind that would have brought in great, slate-grey clouds back when he'd lived in the woods, the type that promised a downpour. But the heavens were clear and bright, full of boundless infinities and the dead who watched from far above. This must have been what the Svarnish were talking about when they spoke to the sky.

Killing Truls would have been easy. All it would have taken was one well-aimed curse thrown down to the earth, but it would not help their cause. It would not accomplish anything other than killing a Thurlowe before he'd been made to suffer for his dynasty's sins. His Wyverns were still in trouble.

Virnoi stepped away from the darkness and back to where his spectre waited impatiently, staring up at him.

'I know,' he spoke to the ghost, shaking himself free of his fixation. 'I know.'

The tome fluttered in his hands as he passed it back to her, descending back into the spells that he'd cast aside when Truls intruded upon him. They came whirring back to life one by one, the last threads of a rope that he'd been unwinding since his arrival. Thurlow's wards snapped beneath the force of Virnoi's focused fury, the heat of the battle turning his power down to make the final move. Had he been more careful, had he cared more, had the situation not unravelled, Virnoi might have undone those wards in such a way that he'd be able to reactivate them. But they did not have the time.

Takuma. Now. Freed from beneath a lifetime's worth of frightened spells, Thurlow's ghosts came screaming to Virnoi.

CHAPTER THIRTY-SIX

SVARNA

'Men, stand your ground! Show no fear!' The cry came as Thurlow forced his way through Morouqdi's shield. The magic shook, crackling as it tried to seal the breach, but Thurlow Thurlowe would not be barred. He forced his arm through to the shoulder and then reached down, the chain of the necklace still wrapped in his hand, and clawed at the magic. He tore jagged holes in the wards until there was enough space to press his torso within.

Thurlow had murdered their queen and taken her necklace – that was why he'd struck the palace first. He'd known that she'd carried an artefact that would allow him free rein to bypass through anything in Svarna that should have otherwise kept him out. That was why no one before them had been able to stand against his army – they'd been trying to hold fast against the reach of their queen.

Ohba held out a hand and the temple produced a great blade from the earth that flew to his grip.

'You're the true anchor of this place, aren't you?' Thurlow asked idly, as if he was not peeling his way through an ancient power pressing through the door. Adil pulled Eulalia and Bronnuq back from where they'd stood; the holy man was breathing hard and fast, his eyes searching past Thurlow's form as if Fidela would reappear from the dust. 'You, with your fury and despair. You think you're different from the men who've stood before you?'

The holy men who were left, older men with silvered hair and those who could not fight, stepped forward, closing around them. Bronnuq shook like a stiff leaf as he reached out, blindly grasping the air, until he had taken Eulalia's hand in his. She held it fiercely, allowing the sensation of his hand to steady her – his calloused palms and his tender fingers.

'No. I am no different from my kinsmen, but I am no coward.' Thurlow summoned that icy spear back once more with an elvish word, a flurry of snow falling to dance along the stone, and swung. Ohba met it with one quick, sharp flick of his weapon, and the metal sung. He sneered at the High Elf, and in that moment, he was a titan of history. 'And you have lived too long.'

Nequit was waiting on her. His horrified stare flashed in her mind, a distraction from how Fidela's final breath had stuck in the quagmire of her shock. If she did not force herself to think as Ohba fought, they would all be slain and there would be no saving those hidden in the tunnels. Nequit would wait on her until Thurlow skewered their corpses and hung them over the temple, announcing the council's death to all those left in Muqdah. She could not leave him alone in this world.

Ohba and Thurlow clashed, but it was not quite right. She had seen her love spar hundreds of times in the years that they'd known one another, but he'd never fought a High Elf. Thurlow had several feet on Ohba and used them to bear down upon the anchor of Muqdah, his spear showering broken ice onto the stone when it struck against Ohba's weapon. The Svarnishman fell into a defensive stance, allowing Thurlow space while he was forced to swiftly learn what this fight would be.

It was far from fair. As Ohba's blows hit, they glanced off Thurlow's personal shields, while any slip of the elf's blade drew blood. Yet, she had never seen Ohba so rife with fury, barely flinching as thin lacerations bloomed on his body.

'You loved her!' Thurlow crowed. 'That stupid, foolish woman out there – you loved her!'

Ohba snarled, baring his teeth. His resolute nature had started to fracture when he had begun to realise how near the end they were. But within the stone lay a molten passion. All at once, the tide of the fight shifted and Ohba was advancing upon Thurlow. He lunged around the great spear that Thurlow wielded and swung upwards, slashing at his forearms and dancing away as the elf shifted stance to defend himself.

Eulalia loved Ohba, who loved Fidela, who loved Adil, who loved Ohba. They had all loved each other unselfishly, which Thurlow could never have comprehended. They would have never bothered to explain it.

'She was one of the bravest women I'd ever met.' Ohba dropped beneath Thurlow's guard and landed a cruel puncture through his shield, tearing it open just as he had forced through the door. It was common amongst nobility to swathe oneself in magic to protect from errant, glancing blows and injury, but Ohba was not a normal swordsman. His eyes were aglow with Muqdah's blessed magic, overflowing with golden light. He sunk his sword into Thurlow's side, shifted his grip to one-hand, and then cast a spell with the other. An invisible force slammed into Thurlow's wound, tossing the two apart, a sharp pull allowing Ohba to keep his sword in hand. 'She deserved to die wrinkled and old, surrounded by her grandchildren! But you – you who look at this world like a chessboard. You value nothing. You could not comprehend the value of a life.'

'I value our lives quite well. We are High Elves, we are denizens of the Eschalion's Empire. We deserve the lives we are given. We serve the greater purpose.' Thurlow pressed a hand to where he had begun to bleed, Ohba's blade drawing forth a river, and all at once the flow stopped. He tilted his head at Ohba. 'What greater purpose do you serve?'

'Myself,' Ohba hissed. 'I am no dog on a leash. I care for this city as its anchor, but I'm not dragged to heel – not like you.'

'It's funny that you think that,' Thurlow said. He swept his spear in an arc in the air, a controlled motion unlike anything Eulalia had seen before. Thurlow was not posturing, he was not gauging an attack, he was *casting*. Floating shards appeared in the air, each one upon the line of that arc Thurlow had traced. Eulalia opened her mouth to warn Ohba, but before the noise had found its way out of her strangled heart, frost exploded within Morouqdi's heart. It shot towards Ohba in a half-dozen icicles with jagged edges. He was forced to dive out of their way, leaping and lunging in a panic-stricken attempt to dodge the assault. Thurlow stared down his nose at him, expression stony. 'I guess your death will mean little, then.'

'Eulalia, you should go,' Adil begged. She realised then that he had been begging her to leave for some time, and she was entirely frozen in place, determined to see this through to the end. They had made promises to one another. She would not leave Ohba.

Ohba dropped low and broke the icicles with a sweep of his hardened arm, only for the frost to creep onto the leather armour he wore. It crawled up his bracer until it slipped into the sliver of brown skin at the elbow. Ohba cried out hard, frantically trying to rip his armour from his body. Eulalia's mouth went dry, and she wrenched her hands away from Adil and Bronnuq, who were still trying to pull her away. She did not understand why they did not understand. She would *never* leave Ohba.

An icicle struck him in the lower back, straight through his spine. That was all Thurlow wanted, the other pillars of ice collapsing into showers of soft snow.

Her beautiful man fell to his knees as the ice consumed his arm, turning his fingers purple and bruised. He was making a low, pained nose from his belly that rattled. Eulalia's vision swam as she found herself panting, blood thundering in her ears. She reached out frantically within herself for a whisper of magic, of power; she begged with Morouqdi to protect her man and found only darkness in the earth. Thurlow picked his way across the stone, a smile creeping onto his maimed features.

'It truly is pitiful, how you all fight against your fate in some futile struggle to escape what you were meant for.' The elf levelled his spear at Ohba's chest, tutting as he did. 'You were meant to die. How easy this would have been if you'd just lain down and recognised your inferiority.'

Ohba could not fight. Instead of entertaining this raving lunatic, he turned his eyes upon Eulalia. His eyelashes were dusted with white snow, and there was a creeping darkness at his neck, a black, watercolour ink thrown by the gods themselves beneath his brown skin. His mouth opened in a soundless prayer, one final breath – *I love you*. The dragons screamed, all at once, a cacophony of grief.

Thurlow's arm jerked as he thrust his blade forward, taking from Ohba what he had no right to. The air rushed out of Eulalia as the body of the only husband she'd ever known collapsed, lost to the wind. His eyes stayed frozen in that final moment, fixed on Eulalia, and she could not tear herself away from him. The rest of Morouqdi was thrust back within the mud as she began to weep, a river torn open within her mind. Fate reached within her and ripped out what beat within her chest, peeled her apart like her insides and rendering her a shell. It was making space for the sudden despair that burst to life within her.

'He loved you, too,' Thurlow was saying, his shockingly blue eyes now fixed upon her. There was a childish fascination in his swollen face. 'You Svarnishmen are interesting.'

Thurlow flicked his hand at her and bright flame flew from his palm, an inferno manifesting in an instant. Eulalia's heart stopped as a flutter of relief flew through her – it was so quick, and she would be carried to the other side, to join Ohba.

As the fire filled her vision, Bronnuq stepped in the way and was swarmed. Thurlow's flame did not act anything at all like true fire – it should have blown through Bronnuq's frail form and marred her as well, but it had been cast with the intent to incinerate. It coursed through her grandsire's flesh, burning away skin and muscle and any feature that made him Svarnish. His elaborate horns fell to ash first before the flame worked its way down his body, though his eyes had closed far before Thurlow's magic took his body from him.

Adil pulled her back sharply and did not let her go as the violence of Bronnuq's death progressed into a wave of chaos. The duel had somehow frozen the world in stasis, broken as everything spun forward to catch up with the minutes they had lost. He dragged her away as spells were cast and Thurlow shouted for his men, the stench of death thick in the air. 'We have to go!'

Pain thrummed in her hips and with a lurching step, Eulalia realised what was happening within her. Bronnuq's spell upon her had been undone the moment that he'd died. Her body was whirring back to life, which meant that her babe would soon be here. She opened her mouth to tell Adil and instead cried out. Adil, set upon his path, did not stop to look back at her. He dragged her out of the main chamber and into a narrow weaving room, devoid of its looms but still decorated with the tiny tapestries and shawls of those who'd been last working here. Adil pulled her on.

If Morouqdi had answered her in the dark, why had it changed nothing? Why had it allowed Fidela and Ohba and Bronnuq to fall, the best of them all? She had been clutching within herself for that infinite power she'd felt when she'd spun out into the greater reaches of Svarna, but it had slipped away from her, like trying to grasp at smoke.

'We have to close the tunnels,' Adil was saying. His voice emerged from within the torrent of shock that threatened to drown her, with the clarity of a bell. 'If we do not close the tunnels, everyone will die.'

Nequit. Fidela. Ohba. Bronnuq. Ohba. Fidela—Nequit.

'You can't close the tunnels on your own.' She sounded entirely unlike herself; Eulalia's words came shakily from her useless tongue, but she needed to speak with Adil. At their backs, the dragons roared as there was an almighty clash within the First Temple. 'All of those men fighting will die if we close the tunnels, we'd be cutting ourselves off from the dragons – and you can't do it on your own.'

'I'm not doing it on my own, Eulalia. Ohba named you to inherit the role of anchor to Muqdah. You are going to help me. The men will be able to flee the fight or surrender once we've ensured the safety of our people. The remaining dragons will take to the skies. It's our last chance to save what we can.' Eulalia had never understood why Fidela had loved Adil, why Ohba had found peace in his companionship, yet as she looked upon Adil, she saw how his fear had forged the wrought steel from which his expression was made from. 'We have to close the tunnels.'

Nequit was in the tunnels. If Adil was right, which he had to be, perhaps together they could save the remnants of Muqdah. When that was done, she would tell him that the babe was coming because the thought of the labour changed nothing.

She had become an anchor of Muqdah at the most inopportune time, a woman of no magic or grandeur. It took years for the mages who'd inhabited the role – Bronnuq and Ohba and those before them – to learn to express their control over the city with any finesse. She did not know if Ohba had the power to thrust that upon someone without a single Blessed marking on her skin, but Morouqdi, this temple that needed its people, might. Adil was chanting in Svarnish, his chest radiant as the magic that lived within his heart grew so potent that it could shine through linen. The longer he chanted, the quieter their tread grew on the stone. Eulalia could no longer hear her own laboured breathing.

Ohba. Ohba, Fidela, Bronnuq – Nequit. Fidela's trembling hands and Ohba's breath atop the crown of her head. The hours that she had spent with Bronnuq in the quiet, struggling to teach herself to weave at a tiny loom. Nuru. The way that her daughter had stared at her from the caravan, the weight of Rasyl upon her hip as his tiny hands clasped in her hair. There were still people who needed her. There was no one else who would be this babe's mother. She could not leave him an orphan.

As they walked together through the remnants of a shattered peace, Eulalia found that she was holding Adil's hand. He was no longer dragging her through the temple, they were walking in step. When they finally reached the descent, a steep set of stairs into the earth, Adil turned and picked Eulalia up so that she would not have to struggle down while she could not see her own feet. Eulalia closed her arms around his shoulders and choked on another contraction.

Whatever magic Adil had cast engulfed them in quiet, swallowing her words as she tried to speak with him. The contractions were entirely too close together for her liking, and though there had been some small seed of hope in her that this was a false labour, Bronnuq would have not made this mistake. Leaning heavily on the wall to ensure that he did not slip, Adil carried her down the steps.

She closed her eyes and took several long breaths as they went, trying to imagine herself somewhere far from here. In a hot bath. Sitting somewhere quiet, basking in a cool breeze. She'd learned from her last two labours that the brain was the most powerful weapon in mitigating pain, but it was so fucking hard not to pay attention to the babe about to burst out of her, Eulalia could have screamed. She wanted to scream anyway – the pain was threatening to cleave her in two.

Her sandalled feet touched stone once more, and she realised, not from sound but by gut instinct, his chanting had stopped. Adil was staring at her, concern on his features as he held her shoulders. She began to hear the rustling of their clothes and her own laboured breathing once more, which meant that their bubble of silence had passed. She was grateful for the lift, but the return of sound took her attempts at disassociating from the pain away from her. 'Eulalia – Eulalia, what's wrong?'

'What do you think?' she snapped, before she groaned, low and long. The labour had begun while she was unconscious and Bronnuq had swallowed that pain with his spell, but that meant Eulalia had no clue how far along her body had come. Nuru had been a long labour, and Rasyl had barely taken an afternoon. Neither birth had felt similar. 'The babe is coming. I do not know what you think I'm capable of, but I don't have magic. I can't close the gates. Muqdah has only ever answered to me when the whole council has been behind me.'

'You have to try.' Why had Fidela loved this strange man? This cowardly beast, who'd been scared of destroying a legacy that they wouldn't even live to see, who had suddenly hardened beneath the pressure to become something else entirely. 'We have to save what we can, you can't just give up on me now. There's only two of us left in the council,'

'You don't tell me what to do,' she snarled. 'If Ohba and Bronnuq had thought they'd save the city by closing the gates, they would have. I have no magic. I couldn't light a candle with all the power in my body. Even if I wanted to help you, I couldn't. You should have saved Bronnuq.'

'Why don't you think Ohba wanted to close the gates?' Adil muttered. 'All the other holy mothers, they went below before the army's arrival – you and Fidela stayed out here. You'd never leave him. Ohba was a fool for not doing it earlier.'

She swung hard and struck him across the face. It did not deter Adil from his convictions, his head snapping back into place.

'You know that I'm right, Eulalia. Of all people, you know that Ohba would have risked the world to save you.' Regrettably, she came to the burning realisation that Adil was not wrong. It would have been far safer for the city to close the tunnels, seal off the world, and save anyone who'd taken below. The strategy spelled death for everyone above the earth, a closure that could only happen once a season, but it would save thousands. Everyone she had sent down into the ground, who'd been wise enough to stay in the only place dense enough to provide some semblance of safety.

The men were still fighting above the earth, though the distant explosions and singing metal had devolved into shouting. There was strange, distant mechanical whirring – sharp sounds, followed by a thunderous crack. She took several quick, sharp breaths as she tried to get a proper lungful of air within her. She knew that she had to steady her breathing, that hyperventilation was the last thing one should do in the early stages of labour, so Eulalia placed her hand upon Adil's shoulders and braced forward.

The thing of epics. A final duel. Had that been what Ohba hedged his bets upon? They had spent so much time tangled in one another's arms, trying so intently to ignore the horror encroaching upon Muqdah, that they had not discussed what his plans had been or what he had thought of it all.

A breathy sob escaped her. Adil's iron features softened, and as Eulalia tried to pull herself away from him, he dragged her into a hard embrace.

'Morouqdi, mother of Muqdah, the haven of all those in Svarna who'd dared to look,' Adil began, his tone frantic. They stood together, their hands planted upon one another's shoulders, horns touching as they reached, finally, for their last resort. 'We ask you this, as the vestiges of the council that once protected you – we need you to close the gates. Close the tunnels from Morouqdi to Hinamour, to save all those who've gone to ground in this great war. Close the gates of Muqdah and save those that we can.'

Eulalia closed her eyes and turned inwards, reaching within herself. What fire had once burned within her was now entirely out of control, scorching the clay and earth that she'd been crafted from, turning her brittle. There was no steel where her spine should have been, only grey driftwood. Her grief flailed in the cavity that her compassion had once lived. She pushed deeper, sobbing as her legs threatened to give out beneath her, and she found a whisper of what she'd once been.

Mother of wolves, that distant voice called. *You have done all that you could.*

'Close the gates,' she whispered.

Chapter Thirty-Seven

SVARNA

'I should not be here.' That was the Child's decree after a good bout of thought, as she processed that she had been abandoned. The Child followed Bronnuq's great ox of a grandson; brows knitted hard as she stared up at his shoulders. She was panicked and her voice wavered with frightened conviction. 'I should not be here, I should be with them.'

'Your mother left you in my charge,' Imamu explained. His voice was even, but his tone was clipped and quiet. 'Your mother decided you should be left here. I am not going to allow you to run off and risk her life.'

'I could fly out of here. Kine is a good dragon, she's quick. All it would take was enough time for me to mount her, and I could lead the dragons out. I could get Eulalia.' A distant din of panic had filled the space in which the birds had once sung, screaming and clashing blades now a quiet operatic. Her heart thrummed high in her chest, demanding that she take flight. That she flee the violence. The Child steeled herself instead, planted her feet. 'Why are we running when we could be saving people?'

'Eulalia is heavily pregnant and won't be able to ride a dragon. That is why I offered her a place with us, which she refused. I cannot force her onto this caravan, girl.' Imamu's step paused, and he turned, lowering his great height down to look her in the eye. 'She has picked safety for you, respect that. She's done what some mothers could not and would have killed to do.'

Her chin dimpled, and she fought back furious, frustrated tears that sprung to her eyes. It was a curse, to grow angry and to cry – it immediately rendered one a subject of distress upon the other. Imamu paused, regarded her, and sighed. His features held a profound amount of sadness, but the relative stranger was also tired. He had a grim set to his jaw.

'I know how hard it is to leave your loved ones behind, Nuru. I do not know if it gets any easier, but I do know what your mother wants for you.

Safety.' Eyes of deep brown and slate grey bore into one another, and Nuru, the bravest and greatest dragon rider of the First Temple, sobbed. Her shuddering broke through the panicked façade, and this young man took her carefully in his arms, crushed her against his chest. She shifted and shattered, strong no more.

They had fought. They had all fought so hard, and Eulalia had come all this way, only for her new home to fall to pieces. Nuru had burned hundreds, but it had not mattered amongst the thousands at Muqdah's doorstep. None of it *mattered*. Hopelessness fell upon her in a tidal wave that made her want to claw at her own throat, rip her golden Blessing from her skin and denounce the gods that had given it to her. What was the point in making her what she was if it changed nothing?

'I am sorry,' Imamu said. This was, perhaps, the first time in her short life that Nuru had felt a stranger understand her. 'Your life was not meant to be this hard. You should never have known such pain.'

Nuru took a long, trembling breath. Eulalia wanted her to be safe. Eulalia wanted her to abandon them, the only family she knew, because she believed that Nuru would be safer on her own. If Morouqdi was not safe, where in the world could they hope for protection? These caravans would do little to shield them if the monolith of temples was not armour enough. But she looked in the eyes of a relative stranger and understood that Imamu would not have this argument.

He believed that he'd been left in charge of all these wards, children forcefully split from their homes, and Imamu would do everything within his power to do right by those who'd brought them here. He would try to enact Eulalia's will upon her, which meant that he could not be trusted. So she nodded, bobbed her head and tried to feign some quiet submission. Bronnuq's grandson inspected her, eyes narrowing only slightly, before he stood once more.

'Please – please, Nuru, stay here.'

She was left on her own amongst a sea of familiar faces. What a dangerous thing to be. To float for a moment completely untethered from the girl she'd thought herself to be only hours ago, to know that Eulalia was out of reach. The only person in the world that was really hers was Rasyl. Imamu had yet to put her little brother down, talking to a stranger while he bounced the infant against his hip. She could not totally blame her brother for settling into the giant's arms; he was too small to understand the gravity of their change in scenery.

With empty hands and a reeling mind, Nuru shifted her focus away from feeling sorry for herself. She could fly Kine from here, she thought, she could take most of the dragons into the sky if they'd not yet fled the temple. She could have never convinced Eulalia to do a thing like leave if she was set upon staying, but Nuru couldn't bear the thought of Kine wondering where she had gone.

The temple called. She felt it like a drumming in her soul, pounding within her skull. Somewhere within Nuru, there was not a flicker of doubt about what she had to do. *Who could stop her?*

Before Nuru had even grasped what she was doing, her feet were flying along the brickwork. She threw herself up onto the temple dock and searched the walls in a panic, knowing that it would not be wise to take a passageway anyone could enter. She needed to go straight to the nursery. Her heart shot her like an arrow towards the second half of herself, and somewhere within the temple, Kine called into the open air. Nuru could leave Eulalia at her request, but Kine had no say. Kine would not be left behind.

'Nuru!' Imamu shouted after her. 'Nuru, stop!'

She tapped once on the wall, but the energy was high, thrumming in the air. The temple was answering her call before she'd even spoken the words. The bricks peeled away to reveal one of the temple tunnels meant for the children, and she leapt impatiently from one foot to the next, ignoring Imamu's shouting.

The holy council had called her the voice of Svarna, the true child. Nuru took commands from no one. She had slain a thousand elves. She would save her dragon.

'Mosi, get the caravans moving, I'll teleport us back to you once I've got the girl!' He was far too close, and as she slipped into the passageway, his fingertips brushed against the back of her dress, grasping to pull her back. She burst into the temple, quicker on her feet than the acolyte, her hair streaming behind her as the magic of the stone pulled her forth. 'You're going to get yourself killed!'

She would have thought him too large to fit within the walls, but when Nuru glanced back, he was clutching Bronnuq's staff in one hand and the walls were opening to allow him space. She shook her head – she could have met him outside Muqdah if he'd only worked with her, allowed her to retrieve her dragon. 'If you had a dragon, you would not have left him! I saw the eggs that they carried, I can bring Kine!'

They charged together into Morouqdi's heart. Several younglings were swarming a screaming elf in Nuru's path, shredding him down to a mound of flesh, barely recognisable as anything mortal. Nuru whistled sharply, and they split apart from their feast to allow her to leap over them, stopping on the rim of the pit in which the dragons often slept. They were in one of the nests mounted on the lowest floor of the nursery, tucked into the wall, and what surrounded them was a war zone.

A net of crackling light sat across the hatchery pit, where the youngest babies would have been sequestered as their wings developed, guarded by an elvish spellcaster. He held a great tome aloft in his hands as he threw up a frantic cocoon of shields around himself. They would not protect him for long, not when the dragons were coming for their young. The mage was protected by a semicircle of warriors with locked shields and great spears pointed outwards. They were surrounded by scaled beasts who were yet to grow past the size of horses, baring their fangs and screaming their warning – one wrong move, and they'd be devoured.

The only thing that was saving this army from their wrath was the fact that they did not want to hurt one another, both creatures of community. In other corners of the nursery, the elves were not so lucky, trying to take their chances with the greater beasts and being indiscriminately devoured.

Idunn keened, a mourning song. Idunn had never hurt a person in all the time that she'd lived, not with her flame nor her claw – she was the gentlest creature that lived in this nursery. Nuru did not know, at first, why she was calling into the abyss until she looked closer at the eggs that surrounded her nest, how each had been meticulously shattered. Idunn was surrounded by fallen bodies of those who'd dared assault this sacred place.

Her heart spiralled downwards as she launched herself down the wall, climbing along the narrow handholds that helped the dragon handlers scale this place. She ignored Imamu's call at her back as she took a spear from a fallen soldier, found that it weighed nothing within her hands, and plunged it through the breastplate of another. Idunn had not defended herself from this assault, had never wanted to hurt a living being, but her children had come. They had poured out from the alcoves and onto the stone, gleaming scales shining. She ducked hard beneath a tail and pushed off another's limb, intent upon her path.

'Idunn!' she called, standing on the balls of her feet in the one patch of free stone. 'Idunn, I am with you!'

She did not think the dragon could hear her beneath that deafening sound, but Nuru's great mother stopped. Idunn looked down at her with kind eyes, lowering her head to greet her. Nuru cast her arms into the air to wrap them around what she could, her vision awash with tears as she found herself wracked by sobs once more. There was a rage that only tears could bring, flourishing within Nuru's body, within her skull and her throat, in the trembling tone of her voice. 'I am sorry, Idunn. I am *sorry*.'

Go, Idunn's voice came from the ether. The she-dragon closed her eyes and nudged Nuru with her titanic head, lifting her off her feet. *One of my children must live. Go.*

Nuru would make it two. If Morouqdi fell today, she would take herself and Kine and live. There was a flurry of dragons taking to the sky, but the invisible thread that ran between them was still tight and close, which meant that her heart was still here.

'Your children will remember you,' Nuru promised as she stepped away from the dragon that had loved her, who had cared for even as before she'd found her feet. As Idunn rose her head, there was a great mechanical *snap*. Above Nuru's head there was a jerk of motion as a great metal bolt, longer than she was from tip to toe, was shot into Idunn's neck. Horror rolled through her as Nuru stumbled away, eyes fixed on the spear, but even then, Idunn did not rise. She would die here, Nuru knew. 'I will avenge you.'

Live, came the call – and so Nuru ran. She whistled into the air, unsheathing the sword kept at her side, listening intently into the chaos. It would be impossible to hear if she did not know Kine's call amongst the many, that clicking tongue.

'Nuru!' Imamu shouted, grabbing at her arm. She had not realised he'd been so close at her back, and she turned on him, her dark eyes tear-bright and alight with a holy fury. 'Where is your dragon? We'll be killed here.'

He was not dragging her away. There were soldiers who had pressed forward into the nursery, on the opposite end of the chamber. The dragons could have been okay had the group of army men not pressed any further. The only threat to their continued existence was the machine that was throwing bolts, a beast of glowing silver and crystal that sat behind the door with several men mounted upon it. She could have stopped them in place if only they'd been able to hear her, but Nuru could not think of that. They had not returned to fight this battle. They'd returned to save Kine.

Live, Idunn insisted. Nuru cupped her fingers around her mouth and whistled again, a call to the air. She repeated the sound thrice before she could hear through the shouting. Kine stood amongst the tides of chaos, tucked low to the ground with her wings outstretched. She was calling for Nuru in a low, frightened sound, which meant that she could not see her rider in the chaos. She wrenched her arm free from Imamu and pointed at the sapphire dragon, waiting for him to locate her as well so that he would not get lost in the fray. Together, hand in hand, they went to save Kine.

'Get the mage!' came a distant shout, from someone Nuru could not lay eyes upon with the rush of dragons around them. At their sides, a garnet-coloured dragon took flight and spiralled upwards, and there was another mechanical *snap* as another great bolt was thrown into the pit. It miraculously struck no living thing, but the pillar that stood at the centre of the grand nursery cracked. Thin, dark lines spiralled around the stone, and any dragon left in those ascending nests broke free now, taking to the sky. Plenty of them would escape, but it was the mothers, the parents, and their children who'd be stuck.

The pillar tipped and Imamu roared, thrusting Bronnuq's staff into the air. Golden light exploded from where the bolt had landed. The magic sealed the stone shut at an angle, creating a bridge of rippling rock between the two halves. He shouted a curse again and cast a spell *around* the pillar, sending several balls of flame into the knot of soldiers that exploded against shields. He barely had to speak. Just like Bronnuq, Imamu cast magic as easily as he breathed.

The sea of flesh and scale broke apart, parting before Nuru. Kine looked up and found her in the gap, calling excitedly to Nuru in a high whistle. The she-dragon rose from where she'd been huddled and closed the gap between them, crying out for her rider. She had two of the hatchlings clutching at her underside, so young that they should have been in the pit, and she was holding *an egg.* Kine had it clutched in one of her claws.

'Kine!' Nuru cried just as there was another mechanical *snap.*

'No!' Imamu shouted. He was aglow, the staff a shining star as it poured magic into the world and stopped the bolt in place above their heads. It would have caught Kine in the skull had he not reached out and grasped it with those invisible hands, tossing it to the side. Nuru's stomach seized tight. 'Get on the dragon, Nuru!'

She threw herself up onto Kine's neck, grasping at her horned frill, but Nuru couldn't leap quite so high on her own. She hit the ground hard, swearing, and then remembered herself. She whistled a two-note tone as she got back to her feet, and Kine lowered herself, leaning down to allow Nuru onto her back. It would have been a death sentence for most to ride a dragon with no saddle or strap, but left with no choice, Nuru would have flown Kine through the void to save her. She climbed onto Kine's leg and leapt up once more, trying to find a hold on her side.

Snap. Kine's body jolted backwards and the thread that tethered them frayed wildly. Nuru looked to her side and found the jagged head of the bolt sticking out from between Kine's ribs. She dropped back to the stone as Kine fell on her side, wheezing and whistling unsteadily. The winds who had given them both so much, taken them to the firmament, left them in one great unceremonious gust. Nuru foolishly tried to grasp at the dragon-killer barb, to push it back out from within the other half of her heart. The weapon was slick with blood and immovable, but she fumbled at it anyway, her tiny hands slipping against the metal.

A frustrated scream tore through Nuru's body as she sat with a dying dragon at her front and the hard stone at her back, trying to find a way out of this. *What use was being the chosen one if she couldn't save anyone?*

'Kine—' Sheltered by the great mass that was her dragon, Nuru pressed her hand beside the eye that she could reach and looked down upon her. She did not have the time to despair, but she would at least say a proper goodbye. She would not let Kine off into the dark without knowing that she was there. 'The winds welcome you.'

The she-dragon crooned, an apology that only Nuru would understand, and collapsed. It was the mewling of Kine's hatchlings that forced Nuru to leave her side, knowing that her dragon was lost. Imamu was already pulling them out from beneath her round chest, two babies less than a year old whose scales had yet to take colour. A rumbling filled the air as Nuru wedged herself beneath Kine, listening to the dreadful withering within her body. One could never truly kill a magical being, the power within the dragons would live on, but one could strike them down.

Idunn roared as she rose from her nest, untethered by the loss of her children. The bolt that had hit here was too small to fell the mother of all, and the alcoves cracked as she spread her wings, bellowing into the air. It was the sound of the heavens cracking open, the celestial downpour that Morouqdi needed. Light bloomed at the back of her mouth, balling until the flame brimmed between her sharpened teeth.

'Time to go, Nuru!' The two babies were clinging to Imamu's shoulders, tails curled around his arms. She snarled as she pulled Kine's egg free from within her claws, only saved by Imamu's swiftness as he placed his hand upon her shoulder, hauling her backwards against his side. Nuru blinked. Imamu had transported them back up to the alcove from whence they'd come. She clutched the egg against her chest, her hands trembling.

Dragonflame poured into the nursery and Nuru stood, watching the sea of flame rise.

Chapter Thirty-Eight

THE IMPERIUM

'This looks like a normal window,' Takuma remarked blandly as he regarded the stretch of glass before them. He looked at Nuru, who had one hand propped on her hip. 'This is a normal window, no? A large window, but a window. I expected something grander.'

His eternal companion made an uncertain noise, but her eyes shared all of his disbelief. It was huge, stretching a hundred metres down the hall, but it looked like perfectly respectable glass. Despite the fact that Takuma was surrounded by magic, he had never found himself lost in the spectacle of it, he just continued to be uncertain.

'It looked like a normal window until Thurlow touched it.' Hotaru pushed through the group until she also stood facing the glass. She pressed her hand against the glass, her gilded fingers aglow, but it changed nothing. The window sat immovable, exactly as glass was meant to. She slipped out a blade from within the cloak that Nuru had gifted her and flipped it around, swinging the pommel in a short arc against the window. It bounced away as if it had struck solid stone. 'Not normal glass, see? Feliks, come here.'

She was joined at the shoulder by the great auburn-haired man.

'Stick your hand through the glass,' she commanded, with entirely too much haute for someone of her size and stature. Feliks appeared briefly bemused, but honoured her wishes by promptly sticking his hand through the window. His hand passed directly through the glass without a whisper of resistance, and that thin, see-through wall of glass rippled like a lake. 'See? No window.'

That was certainly a trick. Hotaru reached out, grasped his wrist and thrust both their hands through the window in one push.

'Feliks holding the bastard qualifies as touching him, which means that we're getting a personal escort to our dragon from our captive Thurlowe.' That made things easier. He hadn't been sure that Feliks' wondrous rib cage would work that well.

'It's just like a big hug,' Feliks chirped before he wrinkled his nose. 'With a very unpleasant man. He's an elvish miasma.'

'Where is this Thurlowe?' Mosi asked distantly, bewildered.

'In Feliks' ribs,' Takuma responded. It was fun taking Mosi off guard, though really the man should have wondered why they weren't toting around a corpse of some poor elvish lout. He looked at his mentor, the confusion in his stare, and shrugged. Mosi leaned back on his heels and inspected Feliks. His sharp eyes narrowed. Takuma couldn't stop the chuckle that burbled up in him. 'He ate him. Like a gator.'

He'd let Mosi chew over that one for now.

'Well, it's now or never – everyone hold hands.' He couldn't pretend that he didn't feel nervous. Every step of the way, Takuma had found himself painfully wired with anxiety. Yet here he stood, disbelieving that they'd even come this far. The upper echelons of the world, these machinations, they were locked tight with a golden key. Anyone who'd dared poke their head within them had them promptly decapitated. There was some part of Takuma that had never ascended past boyhood, still stealing handfuls of grain from the caravan stock.

Takuma reached out and clasped Nuru's hand on one side, and Mosi grasped his opposing wrist, trying to ignore the thunder rolling around within his chest.

Something was wrong. His gut knew it, and that was something he'd once trusted. Takuma took a long breath and felt the world askew, time snapping at their heels. In the back of his mind, he inspected the game of the night, the many revolving pieces that were in motion, and wondered what had shifted. Yet there wasn't nearly enough time to contemplate that.

'Jump once and jump big. Keep a good hold on one another. The last thing we need is someone getting their arm cut off because the glass reconstituted itself.' If the strangeness of the game reared itself this late in the heist, they would simply have to handle it. Nuru counted down from three, their hands tightening on one another's wrists, before they leapt together.

And the denizens of The Brass Wyvern entered the dragon's den.

'A child comes, a child with a voice of gold. A child of whispers and winds who will be bestowed the glory of Svarna. She who will tear the great empires to the ground and weave a home for us with branches pulled from the fey's own forests. Most importantly, a child comes, a child like no other — a child who heralds a new age for us dragonfolk. May the gods help us when she does.'

— Florentina, a prophet of olde.

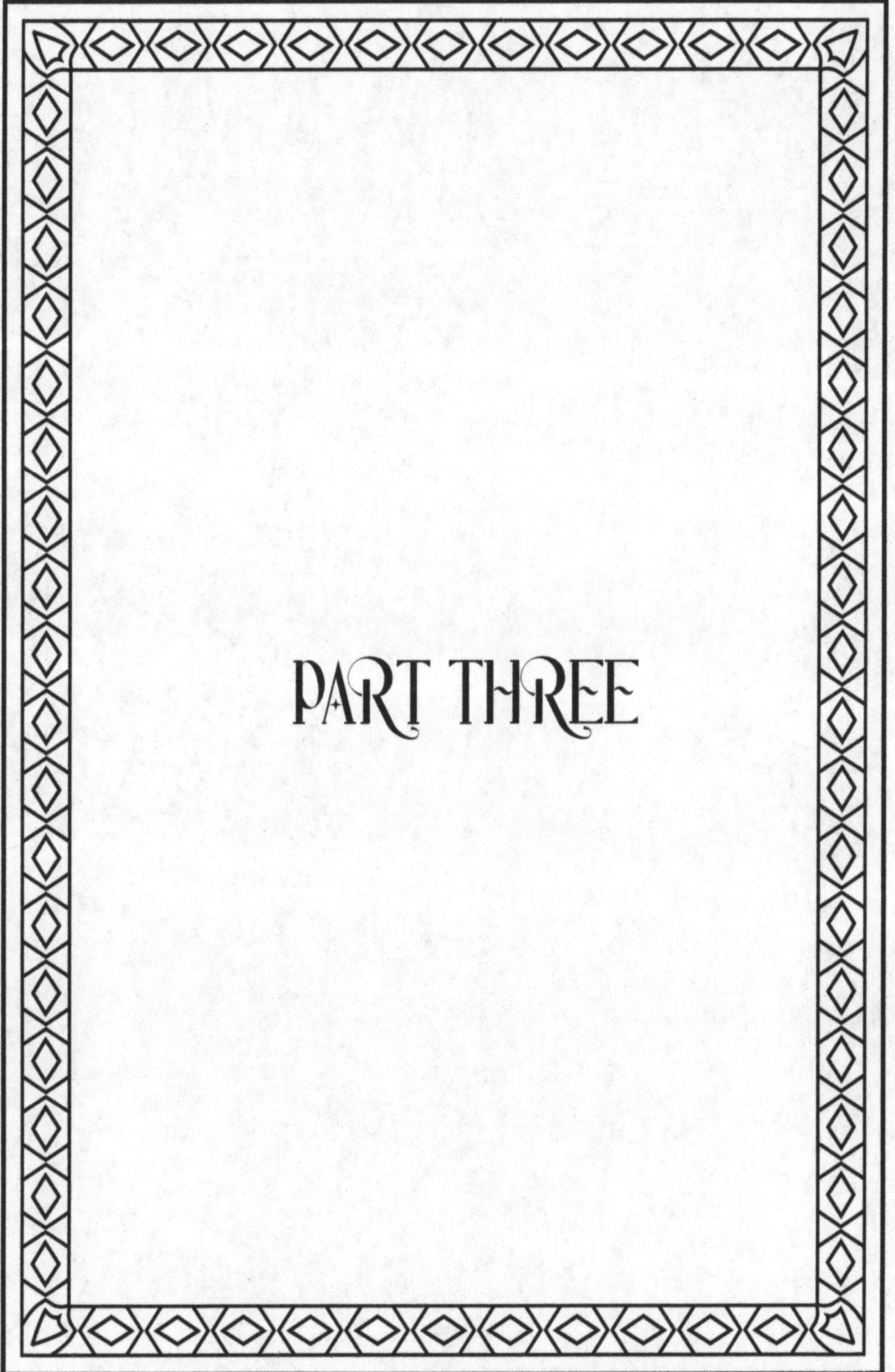# PART THREE

Chapter Thirty-Nine

THE IMPERIUM

Frosty water was not a friend of the mortal body, and as Nuru hit the moat, her whole body seized and bucked.

She had thought herself appropriately braced, but it flooded her, rushing into her nose and ears. Her mind went bright and white, unable to articulate anything but that sudden icy thorn that was tearing her skull apart. Only when her feet hit the floor did her body begin to move without her input, her magic swelling to pull her upwards. Nuru kicked off the ground, bursting out into the dragonpit and onto the steep shore.

Swimming was something she had learnt only because Takuma had thought it vital for their continued survival. Evidently, all of his ideas weren't disastrous.

'Fuck!' Takuma swore as he came to surface several meters to her left.

Nuru was the first upon the ground, pulling herself out of the water and scrambling to her feet, her corset and her dense skirts soaked. There were several huge splashes at her back as her compatriots followed, great impacts in the water. She stuck out an arm to help haul Takuma onto the island, and together, they pulled Feliks' bulk from the surface. He did not have to struggle at all in the water, his strange physique keeping him afloat when it made no sense at all. He drew Zuri to him without a breath of exertion, clearly pleased with himself. Each of the Wyverns shivered; they were dragonfolk. They were not meant for such cold, to feel the ice try to crawl its way inside their skin. It was unnatural.

Mosi seemed entirely unfazed by the frost. Nuru shed her underskirts while she waited for them to surface but kept that heavy layer, clinging to it like a life ring, the only thing that had emerged unsodden. The air stank of incendiary gas. All the way along their descent Nuru had been smelling it, a sharp note that burned the nostrils, but here it was thick. A side effect of

the idiocy of sedating a dragon in an attempt to stop it from expelling flame
without treating the source of it, instead allowing the gas to gather and pour
out from the thing. The island radiated warmth – not a deadly heat, but it
would burn away the water they'd been submerged in quickly.

'If the dragon turns on us, you dive back into the water.' Nuru kept her
voice even, but there was a severity creeping up on her that harkened back
to a much taller woman. A woman who would have truly known what she
was doing instead of playing at the game of power, praying that she was not
fumbling her piece. She had once been hailed as the golden child of the holy
land. Yet, now, that child felt like a distant echo of a dark sky. 'It's cold enough
to buffer dragonflame. If we're lucky, they've charmed it so that it would not
boil.'

It was a common trick in Svarna when a dragon had to be kept away, to
heal or to be checked or to hatch an egg, that there had also been chill water
within reach. Thurlow, who was supposed to be the second-best caster in this
place, should have managed to scrape together that much information from
Svarna's butchering. If he'd been a total idiot, he would have been killed when
he'd crossed the northern border.

The den they had built this dragon felt even more vast when one stood
within it than it had looking at the dome from afar. The Imperium was all built
at a beautifully grand scale, more fit for giants and gods than elves, but this was
absurd. Imperialist grandeur scaled upwards into infinity, but it was so hollow.
It would suffocate anyone within, over time, as the mind slowly emptied it of
anything in search of deeper meaning.

The dragon was on the other side of the narrow island, blending into the
thick mess of vegetation upon the island. The dragon should not have turned
on them, but Nuru would not bet on the stability of a magical being that had
been demeaned and abused and treated as a pet. She could barely count on her
own stability most days. After standing on a caravan and watching as Muqdah
fell, she'd then watched an entire empire rise to celebrate the collapse of her
people. Nuru knew that if the holy men and their prophecy had been right,
it was something she'd been meant to avert. Somehow. Whatever her fate had
been meant to be, it had wildly rattled off-course.

Chosen ones did not exist in the new regime. No holy word was enough
to challenge the might of the Eschalion. If there had been some fated glory for

her, Nuru had never felt it. She had not been able to close her hands around it.

This poor dragon had also likely felt the world unspooling. It was large enough that it would have been alive to see the glory of Svarna, to know how far it had come.

Zuri whistled between her teeth and slowly, the dragon emerged from within the thick forestry. Nuru froze as the world shifted around the creature, some distinct subset of its worldly power unlacing the foliage from its scaled back.

This was not a dragon or hatchling of Muqdah. This dragon was older than Kine would have been, but far younger than Idunn. It also filled a space which it had not a moment ago, a trick of magic. Nuru had only ever heard whispers of vanishing dragons. The nursery dragons had been those that were most accustomed to the human touch; they had not used this sort of magic to shield themselves because they had never been threatened.

Zuri planted both her feet firmly on the earth, kicking up dust with her boots, and Nuru watched in wonder as the captured dragon breathed in Zuri's scent, nudging her with the tip of its nose in a distinctly playful manner. It felt absurd to stand before such a beast in the clothes of a bedworker, scraps of linen and cloth. Nuru longed for a sword or some whisper of armour, especially as Zuri reached up to hesitantly run a hand along its scaled head.

She watched from afar and in the same way that one recognised a glimpse of their former self. Nuru realised that Zuri would have made a brilliant dragon rider. It was the lack of fear in her stance, the way she never drew away from a creature that could have turned her to ash.

'We're here to free you,' Nuru spoke, when she had found her voice once more. She sounded entirely her age for a moment, not a mother but a girl of Morouqdi once more. 'I—she came back to free you.'

She couldn't take that much credit for it. The dragon turned, studying her as it chittered into the open air. The hues of its scales flashed and shifted from that verdant green to bright opalite and back.

Our people, the voice came. It was sonorous and easy to listen to. She was reminded of the clarity of a cello that she'd once heard on a quiet night in the red-light district, when she'd been listening to the world from her window. *Good people.*

'I'd like to think so. We're definitely Svarnish, at the very least.' She was not sure that anyone amongst them was what strangers would call *good*, but no dragon was a stranger to the Svarnish.

Nuru waved at Zuri as she approached, reaching out tentatively to allow her fingers to dance along the dragon's scales. The dancer had already drawn her hands away, likely having been scorched by its warmth – the dragon was leaning back into its magic. As its body figured out heat regulation, how to carry the flammable gas it would use to create its flame, it would grow truly scorching. 'She's the best of us, this one. You did a good thing, freeing her.'

She fought. An image slipped into Nuru's mind, sent by the creature. It was the view of the windows from the island, in the black curtain of darkness that came with a nocturnal storm. The bastard Thurlowes in their triad, passing through the glass with a screaming Zuri in tow. Though the High Elves were wrapped in a tepid, uneven light in the dragon's eyes, it had been Zuri who'd glowed like the sun. In the midnight hour, as she was dragged through the air and onto the island, her feet appeared to be enclosed in the sunlit glow of a Blessing. Zuri had been howling and clawing at Llewelyn's hand, that had been tightly enclosed around her twisted horns. *She is a fighter.*

'Most of us are,' Nuru mused. She allowed herself to lean forward, resting her forehead upon the side of the dragon's head, her whole body swallowed in a heartache that she could only allow herself to indulge for a moment. 'I know you are, having survived this long.'

'My gods,' Takuma muttered from behind them. 'She *can* talk to dragons.'

With the pleasant greetings passed, Nuru turned towards their slimmest companion. Hotaru stood several meters away from them, her wet curls springing to life but her cloak miraculously dry. A twinge of guilt thrummed somewhere in Nuru. Truls had largely been a good client, if a little greedy, and he'd treated her well. They'd only come this far because she'd managed to steal the plans to his family estate amidst his usual foolishness. 'Hotaru – is the dragon's throat as swollen as it was when you saw it earlier?'

Hotaru shook her head, sending a tiny rainfall of droplets onto her slim shoulders.

'That's good. That means he'll likely be flight-ready by the time we're out of this place.' They could have attempted it now, if they'd truly needed to, but she wouldn't have trusted how steady it would have been. Perhaps he would have taken to the air, but he'd likely destroy several buildings if he could not trust that flight bladder.

You will take eggs, too. Nuru stopped, mid-sentence. She looked back at the dragon, mouth quivering. *I would like to be free. But I would like her children to be free more.*

'Nuru?' Takuma reached out to rest his hand upon her shoulder, squeezing gently. Dragons did not mix words. They spoke to the mind, not the ears. They spoke in concepts that the mind translated into whatever language the beholder was most comfortable in. 'What is it saying?'

'Show me,' she told the dragon. The dragon turned and strode away, slipping back within the dense knot-work of forest. The Wyvern workers stumbled after her, Zuri first and the rest at her tail.

Nuru looked frantically back to Takuma, struggled to find her voice, and then all the words fell from her at once. 'He has eggs. He wants us to take her eggs.'

She had her contingency plan, but last resorts were meant for when the world was falling to pieces. She looked to Takuma for answers as he helped her through the underbrush, the branches trying to catch on the slips of linen that she was left in.

'How do we take two?' Nuru asked.

'We *do* still have Feliks as a walking pocket.'

Despite Feliks' size, he had no issues amongst the mess of greenery. Arcing through the forest, he was a red-headed ghost in her peripherals. As he walked, he shifted between human and winding tree – an effect that one could have easily dismissed if they weren't paying him too much mind.

Takuma continued, 'We'd just have to deposit the Thurlowe bastard, pop the egg in, maybe pack it with something to soften the grip. There's plenty of leaves here.'

That was true, though they could never really comprehend how delicate being held within Feliks was. There were several long-standing bets that ran between the pair about who'd be the first to trust their resident bouncer with an eldritch bear hug – neither was yet to bend. They could play at bravado all they wanted, but they weren't taking chances with Feliks.

From within the island emerged a pattern, a path that the dragon had carved between the split trees. The first glimpse of death that Nuru caught was an ivory rib on the opposite side of the island, curving upwards through the trees. Then another. Then slowly, through the web of branches, Nuru began to make out the entirety of a skeleton set upon the gentle rise – the remains of a dragon that was as large as the one that trod ahead of them. With her hand firmly braced on Takuma's shoulder, she gave it a quick squeeze and watched his attention snap to where her eyes lay.

They would get no answers as to how Thurlow Thurlowe had brought two dragons of such size from Svarna's wilds, taken them through tunnels without more than rumours emerging from the shadows. Whispers of awful stenches, great beasts, and a secret worse than anything the Nords could have concocted. It was not Nuru's place to know but, she longed to, her mind churning. Their living dragon passed by the skeleton entwined with wild greenery and retreated to a crushed nest of young trees, all of which had been methodically flattened. He circled around to allow them to clearly see the pair of eggs sitting in a bed of haphazardly gathered moss.

Nuru rushed to the nest, kneeling beside the two greenish eggs. She pressed the back of her hand to both and found the warmth within them painfully absent. There was a faded, flickering furnace within their shells, but there was nothing on this island to insulate the eggs. The nursery nests were packed with sand because of how well it retained heat; without a father who could breathe fire and a severely malformed idea of a nursery, Nuru did not know if these hatchlings would make it. She made an uncertain noise, to which Takuma hummed warily.

'We were prepared to save you, but protecting eggs is much trickier. They're weak. They'll need caring for. You need to leave this place as fast as you can, you'll be slowed down by these.'

Three marks. One shrunken and rushed through a hidden tunnel, the other clutched in Feliks' peculiar rib cage, the third carried. Even if it was by hand. She had carried other dragon eggs before; Nuru knew the weight of a child and how one had to be mindful to protect it. Her dark gaze looked up from these Svarnish jewels and met the dragon's stare, full of an unbidden intensity.

You can bring them to me. When they are healthy. I will build a den. The verdant dragon was picturing a hole carved out of a mountainside, somewhere far warmer than the Imperium. Nuru nodded. That they could manage – even if she could not stray far from Nema, they could use the caravan network to carry the eggs to wherever he made his home. If the hatchlings survived at all; they needed to be warmed.

'He wants us to bring him his eggs once he's fled,' Nuru explained. When she sought the council in the faces of her friends, she found no resistance.

'When we get him out of here, I'll bring him a golden goose. Who am I to refuse a dragon?' It was only the amazement in Takuma's tone that reminded Nuru this was the first time he'd ever met a dragon. That explained why there was an unguarded wonder in his face, something which betrayed his true youth. He stayed with his feet planted outside the nest, keeping his distance from the structure. She flicked her gaze from Takuma to Feliks.

'Zuri—' the dancer was the closest to the nest, but even she seemed reluctant to cross that boundary. 'Zuri, do you want your vengeance?'

There was no justice for someone who'd undergone what Zuri had. Justice implied a righting of the equilibrium, that Llewelyn would be made to suffer all the pain that she had. But Zuri bore her fury in the deadly way only a woman could, marked by the tightness of her jaw. Her suffering was unique to her, it could not be replicated or remade in another. Zuri looked at her and then to Feliks.

'They were going to feed you to a dragon,' Nuru said. 'This dragon, this one we're trying to free, he needs food. He's already burnt through whatever they fed him because they've got no clue how to feed a dragon, so he'll need something more for this escape. I'm not saying that elves are good eating, but—'

'But they were going to feed me to a dragon.' Which had been stupid because though dragons would eat a Svarnishmen if provoked, most wouldn't resort to it for an afternoon snack. Zuri's jaw ticked. 'Will the dragon understand me?'

Nuru nodded. 'They understand most every language, they just can't speak back.'

Feliks unpeeled, ribs unwinding as they became a shifting latticework of wood before their eyes. The primal part of Nuru demanded that she look away from the show as Feliks' eyes glazed over, turning glassy and inhuman, so she stared instead at the eggs. These two little children, with their wavering spirits, who'd come from a fallen mother and would have likely been sold to the highest bidder if she knew anything at all about Thurlow Thurlowe. Had their jailor paid any attention whatsoever to the country he'd destroyed, he would have known what he was doing would kill what he'd worked so hard to steal.

There was a choking sound and then a burp, followed by a thump as Feliks deposited Llewelyn Thurlowe on the earth. He was gasping for breath, scrambling to get to his feet, which Feliks promptly knocked out from beneath him. The bruiser was putting himself back together, seams vanishing within the smooth cover of his freckled flesh.

'You remember this man,' Zuri said. She barely looked at the silver-haired High Elf, her bearing stiff and tall. 'He does not deserve the life his gods gave him.'

As much as a dragon could, the father of two dying children sneered at Llewelyn. A sound came from within his chest, a slow gravelly thing that snaked through the air. That was the hum of death, a sound that Nuru knew. Llewelyn was finding his voice, begging in High Elvish for his life. She knew that from the desperation within his tone alone, the repetition of *vitali*, a word she'd heard Taliesin speak before. When her priest spoke the words, it sounded like a prayer with the reverence beneath it. Llewelyn just sounded pitiful.

'He raped me, he abused me, he kept me in chains – he flouted his power all his life because he thought himself better.' Zuri spoke over his begging, her voice clear and bright. When Llewelyn grew louder, she simply met his volume. Whatever strength Llewelyn had once held was entirely stolen from him during his ordeal. The elf attempted to get to his feet once more, and Feliks lazily hooked his foot around his ankle, leaving him to fall hard back on the earth. 'I hope you know this, Llewelyn, that I hear you. Just as you heard me. I do *not* care. You had a thousand chances to prove yourself worthy of the heart that beats within your chest, worthy of your eyes and your tongue. Instead, you ruined my *life*. You took a little girl who believed in magic and you made a point of slaying her. Now, you're left with the thing you made. A life for a life, I'd say.'

Hairs prickled at the nape of Nuru's neck.

A life for a life.

Zuri hissed, a visceral sound, and the dragon snapped. Its jagged teeth closed around Llewelyn and in one sharp movement, his soft tissue was torn apart. Cleaved messily in half, his voice cut away before he'd even had the chance to scream.

The dragon tossed back the top half of Llewelyn's body and then picked at his legs, bone snapping as he chewed through what was left of the bastard. Takuma looked like he'd gone slightly green around his beautiful features; whereas Nuru, having entirely tired of gore in her life, found a point in the trees to focus upon.

Llewelyn is dead. Nuru sent the thought spinning out along the tenuous, delicate bond she shared with her priest.

Taliesin's response came swiftly and still, Nuru found herself nervously believing she'd be overheard despite the voice existing only in her mind. *Yes, well, such a pity. You've got Father heading in your direction.*

'Do they just ... digest the clothes as well?' Takuma asked.

'They throw it back up eventually, like owls. Anything that couldn't go down.' She swallowed. She'd been grateful that she'd never had to clean up that specific by-product during her dragon-keeping training. The green dragon gurgled happily, turned from a destroyer into a pleased creature once more. Zuri's chest heaved as she was flooded with a torrent of relief, cheeks marked by a glistening tear.

Feliks was first to close the gap between them, putting a strong arm around her shoulders – perhaps it should have been Nuru. Yet, she found herself strangely mercantile, settled on the thought that they could process all that had happened this evening when they were safely free of the Thurlowe walls. 'We have to move. Takuma, we're running out of time. Where's your husband?'

Virnoi appeared in a flourish of black smoke, as if summoned by the mere mention of him. He floated far above them, cloaked in the shadow of his magic. Her hands still pressed upon the eggs, Nuru studied him from afar. Though he was largely tucked away beneath his hood, his eyes cast sharp shadows over his features with an arcane glow. She glanced at Takuma and found him fiddling with his rings on one hand, thumb turning them over on his fingers. Nuru could see that he saw what she did in Virnoi's face.

'Time to shrink the dragon, eh?' Takuma called.

Virnoi sighed. She could not hear it at a distance, but she felt it, a resignation that eked from him. 'I'm afraid not. There's been a change in the wind.'

Chapter Forty

THE IMPERIUM

Virnoi had not always thought himself a calamity.

There had been a time when he'd been just a boy, growing in the mud, his limbs entangled in the roots of the black willow trees. But boys did not survive the grand architecture of the Eschalion's illustrious empire, so he had been forced to decide. One became monstrous or broken, crushed beneath the weight of the world.

He hadn't minded being monstrous. For a hundred years, that was how he'd gone on.

'I'm not going to shrink the dragon,' he sighed. 'I can't maintain a shrinkage spell on one live dragon and resurrect another, considering how huge they are, so I am changing our course.'

Virnoi could see their trust in him burning away like paper set atop an open flame. The bond between them had always been brittle, had never been meant to last. When relationships were founded upon pretence and secrecy, what hope did they have? He considered himself friends with all the Wyvern workers, but they knew nothing of one another. They didn't even know his mother's name, or the forest that had birthed them both. He did not know the ghosts that haunted them.

The understanding that had been forged beneath Virnoi and The Brass Wyvern was always going to be their downfall.

'Virnoi, you don't get to decide this.' Takuma spoke first, his handsome face full of incredulity. He would be the hardest to shake, even when he played at his aloof persona. Whereas Nuru's eyes had gone steely.

'But I *do*,' Virnoi said. 'Where would you have been this evening without my help? Without my magic? Takuma, you're good, but you're not Blessed. I've enabled you all, every step of the way, and didn't ask anything in return. But despite how grand this whole evening has been, you've only been thinking of the small picture. Steal a dragon, free a dragon, vanish into the Imperium and leave no greater mark than a loss upon the nobility. We could do so much more – *be* so much greater.'

'You elves and your monologues,' Nuru hissed. The dragon was watching him in its peripherals, but it had yet to bristle or reel.

Virnoi's eyes narrowed. 'Don't you want this?' He was painfully aware of the edge of desperation that crept into his voice, how he was cracking beneath the pressure of this great hope that had landed on him. He was staring at the beginning of all he had hoped for, had been marching towards since he'd gained any real concept of the crimes that had been committed against his familial line. 'I have listened to all of you snipe about the Eschalion for *years*. I have listened to the hymns and the lamentations of Svarna. I know what you've lost, and you can't pretend as if you don't want to strike at the heart of the empire. Allow me to take the skeleton, and I'll wreak true terror upon this city.'

'Dragonbone retains the memory of the beast that lived long past its death.' Where Takuma faltered, fell silent and uncertain, Nuru rose to the challenge like a mother bear before her cubs. 'You're not talking of just putting together some shambling thrall, you'd be manipulating one of our guardians to your whims. Shrink the dragon, Virnoi.'

Virnoi laughed, a sound that he kept surprising himself with. '*No*. Your magic tongue may work on most, Nuru, but I am not some hapless lecher you can sway. I've been listening to the undercurrents of your voice every single day I've lived beneath your roof. I've felt your Blessing wash over me with every passing moon. You will not take my free will from me like you wrench it from others.'

'Bones are just bones, Virnoi.' Takuma had finally found his voice, buried beneath his disbelief. 'We don't live for the dead. We live for us. We have a plan – that plan can still work.'

Virnoi sucked in a breath between his teeth, the words striking at a soft spot in his side that Takuma had not been aiming for. But bones were never *just bones,* they were the map of how a creature had lived. Every nick and aberration and break bore a memory that they simply couldn't see. This was why Virnoi had never understood the living, had struggled to comprehend their treatment of their past. The dead *cared*. The dead spoke to him more than any living individual had ever dared to.

He looked away from Takuma for a moment and found his eyes resting upon the spectre that never lingered far from him, who now stood tucked amidst a tangled shrub. Her ghostly eyes watched him, mouth twisted in an uncertain line, her soft-fawn ears turned down.

Takuma did not live for his dead. He shed the shadows of his past like an old skin, thinking they'd weigh him down. Some did not have that choice.

Virnoi's eyes snapped back to Takuma's, forest green on emerald.

'It could still work, if I had any interest in making it do so.'

The two men stared at one another, Virnoi's cloak swirling around his shoulders. He had been willing to try and be something different than what he was, for Takuma. He had been willing to play at domesticity and ease into quiet, constant days with his cutthroat lover at his side. The proprietor of The Brass Wyvern had brought out a sensuality in him, a compassion. Yet Takuma would have never compromised a core tenet of his being for Virnoi – and he wouldn't have expected it.

'I am not asking for permission, Takuma. I'm going to bring this dragon back. I'm no miracle worker, but I can resurrect bones, give them some semblance of life once more. I can give this dragon the vengeance that its bones long for.'

'That vengeance is *not* yours to have,' Nuru spat. She turned and strode away from him, her hands working frantically at her waist. A whistle came between her teeth, and the stranger, the one they called Mosi, followed at her heels. 'I won't allow it, no matter what you all have to say. That dragon is dead, not an item for you to add to your collection of curiosities.'

She tossed that thick underskirt layer into the air and it unspooled from her hip, expanding, becoming a great, woven crescent-moon in the air. It was a masterfully crafted image of a city tucked away beneath a sphere of shimmering thread, a sea of temples that clambered to meet the sky. Half-folded on the ground, Nuru tossed it again like she was straightening a blanket and held it out upon the dusty ground. In all the time that Virnoi had known Nuru, she'd worn that skirt – it stayed as a ready fixture wrapped around her narrow waist. But for the first time, he was truly seeing it.

He'd seen it a thousand times. Wrapped around Nema, thrown haphazardly across Nuru's bed, a tapestry sealed by magic that would make it last for an eternity. A mashjor.

'A notice-me-not,' he remarked, eyes fixed upon it. It was something one learned when they began the study of illusionary magic, a spell of moderate complexity meant to draw a person's attention away from an item. It didn't render the item invisible but merely uninteresting, just something that the mind did not need to take note of. As he raked back through his memory, he realised that it had always looked like that – a constellation of meticulous threadwork, richer than anything the other Wyvern workers wore.

'You are not a monster, Virnoi,' Takuma said, with such finality that it drew Virnoi back from the curious magic. His eyes were alight with the fires of one of his many intense convictions – yet he may have met his match. 'We won't let you become one.'

'What is the difference between man and monster?' Virnoi shot back. 'Can one person prevent a comet from becoming a meteor? You cannot stop a change in the wind, Takuma. I'm sorry.'

'He never had any intention of helping us! Can't you feel it? This whole tower is unprotected. The rest of the estate feels enclosed, unshakeable, but here you can almost feel the wind! He's taken off *all* the protective warding because he intends on taking off the top of the tower. He was never following our plan.' Nuru suited rage far more than she should have, her voice took to it like a drum took to thunder. Virnoi levelled her with a stare, but she barely looked up at him. 'We can do this on our own. *Toro.*'

And then Mosi said, in a voice that was not his own, 'I knew you'd never sell the tapestry. You best keep your promises, Nuru. *Abrorse.*'

Pure magic poured out of the tapestry, a deluge of light and power. It tangled around her feet, swimming to her ankles and setting the sun upon the island. Virnoi threw a hand up in front of his eyes, floating backwards until he was resting both his feet upon the dragonbone. The power of a great, dead thing flowed within him, and with all his other spells having fallen away, he could focus entirely on drawing from that torturous rush. Something would be born from the suffering, whether Nuru liked it or not.

A hand thrust out of the tapestry, ephemeral and see-through. The image of a woman ascended from it, a severe Svarnish woman whose hair was silvery moonlight wrapped around her skull in an elaborate braid. She was a grandam, donning armour marked with an array of dragon scale as she rose from the abyss. An almighty laugh rung around the tower, humming in Virnoi's marrow.

'Vioqtria, Goddess of Wisdom and Victory, I free you!'

Daughter of dragons and the son of the dead, right the equilibrium of fate. With the declaration spoken, enunciated by an otherworldly power, the apparition vanished. It vanished into the shadows, leaving the air alight with electricity.

He did not have the time to enter a trance to cast a full ritual, but he didn't think he'd need it. Virnoi threw out a hand and his power snared around the boning in Nuru's corset, which he'd meticulously replaced. He froze her in place before he promptly threw her as far from the tapestry as he could manage, depositing her precisely in the water. It was the softest landing he could find.

Takuma, who had never had any palpable patience, turned sharply on his heels and fled – taking the tapestry with him.

'This is my decision, Takuma!' he cried, railing against their stubbornness in his quiet way. 'You will hear me. This will be great.'

Chapter Forty-One

THE IMPERIUM

If Takuma gave himself the chance to grieve Virnoi, it would incapacitate him.

The man that he had known, whom he had bedded and loved, was not just a blood mage. He did not simply participate in the rite of sacrifice that the Svarnish magi once had. Virnoi was a necromancer – the emperor's ancestrally bound practice. The only necromancers in the Imperium had the blood of the crown running through their veins.

Takuma could not reconcile that thought with his Virnoi. He could not grapple with that right now.

Instead, he took the tapestry and plunged into the island forestry. He was at a severe disadvantage against the necromancer, with not an ounce of magic, but he was resourceful. He could make himself a distraction while he figured out how in the hell they would blow open the tunnel. There had never been the faintest whisper of doubt in him that Virnoi was always going to be their failing factor. Perhaps Takuma would have forgiven the diversion – it wasn't as if he were particularly attached to his draconic ancestors – but no one was allowed to lay hands, magical or otherwise, on Nuru.

Virnoi knew that quite well.

There was no time to linger on Virnoi, not even as his presence hovered over the trees. Takuma stumbled, hooked his nail beneath the threads of dark hair that were tied around his index finger, and snapped the mental bond that bound he and Virnoi. It would also disconnect him from Hotaru, but he had to trust his little crow. He couldn't leave Virnoi with an open channel into his mind.

Mosi was the only one quick on his heels, an arm's length behind him.

'What's the plan here?' Mosi asked.

'He wants to cleave the tower in two and take to the sky,' Takuma muttered. 'If we do that, we're marked for death – we can't go home. I won't do that to them. Nuru needs to be able to go home to Nema. Which means that we need to open our exit on our own.'

'Where's the exit?' Mosi asked, his eyes glancing briefly towards the window from whence they'd come.

'Sealed tunnel on the south wall, set into the ground. Half-submerged under the moat. One good spell would do it, but I suppose you can't quite cook that up, can you?' This was one of the litany of reasons why Takuma hadn't wanted Mosi along – he knew none of their plans. Imamu's eyes flashed in Mosi's skull, changing with a blink.

'I can only channel temple spells through Mosi,' Mosi said, in Imamu's voice. 'No explosions. I've got no sway over these bricks.'

'I knew you'd be useful.' Takuma rolled his eyes. Had there been no consequences for their actions, Takuma wouldn't have thought twice about handing the night over to Virnoi, but they were mere mortals. Virnoi would live a thousand years. He'd have the freedom to fuck up frequently, only for the consequences that hurt him to eventually pass. The Svarnish lived small, shining lives like shooting stars in the night, and if they'd found some pocket of peace, they had to preserve it while they could.

'Takuma.' The call came. It was peculiar, how he did not have to yell to raise his voice. 'I don't *need* the tapestry, but you can't handle that sort of magical artefact.'

When faced with a super villain of any variety, Takuma found it generally unwise to hand over whatever they'd set their eyes upon. He shook his head and broke out onto the edge of the moat, where Nuru had been thrown in. He dumped the tapestry and dove into the water. It was a wonder that Nuru hadn't drowned trying to swim with it attached to her in the first place, given how hefty it was. She was struggling now, slowly sinking, kicking and clawing at the rising bubbles, but being dragged down all the same. Takuma closed an arm around her and pulled toward the surface, heaving hard.

He pushed her onto the shore before he pulled himself up, entirely unnerved by the silence that echoed within his skull. It was strange to suddenly feel a yawning abyss where Virnoi and Hotaru had lingered.

'I can't move,' Nuru sputtered. She sat on her hands and knees, spitting up water onto the sand between words. 'Mother*fucker*.'

Takuma looked her up and down before he placed both hands upon her corset. He apologised, knowing that she was quite attached to the garment, and tore it open. It resisted more than it should have. Virnoi was clever, but he wasn't getting this one over on Takuma – a necromancer was more of a bone-witch than a purveyor of flesh. There was boning in the corset, bones put in the hilt of his knives to allow him a better accuracy, chips in Virnoi's cuffs and decorating his ears. He was frantically trying to catalogue anything manipulable that Virnoi put on them, and was suddenly grateful he was barely dressed.

That was why Hotaru's leg had taken Taliesin's intervention to make whole. Virnoi could manipulate and reconstitute flesh, he could make a skeleton dance, but he could not bring it back to life.

Nuru stumbled to her feet, snatching the tapestry up once more. They looked at each other once, then fled back within the forest line, knowing that cover was always safer.

'Virnoi wants us to be on his side,' Takuma muttered as they crouched together within a thick knot of underbrush, ignoring how the plants and twigs scratched at their exposed arms. 'If we can get the dragon out on our own, we won't need him. So we keep the tapestry out of his hands. This is what you're going to use to get the dragon out, right?'

Nuru nodded. 'Now that it's empty, we've just got to be able to touch it to the dragon, and it should hold him. Then it's just the tunnel.'

Yes, the great sealed tunnel that Takuma had been relying upon Virnoi to open. They sat together in the underbrush for several long breaths. Virnoi did not want to harm them in any meaningful way, but they had slain two Thurlowes tonight – there were plenty of people on their trail who would.

That stench filled the chamber, the gas cloying and thick, not allowing Takuma a singular breath of fresh air. It was oppressive.

'I see you, interlopers!' a shrill voice screeched. 'I see you!'

'Thurlow Thurlowe.' Virnoi's voice reverberated on the stone, amplified by some magic that projected his usually muted tones. 'Eschalier's mad dog. You and I have yet to be acquainted.'

'Mosi, Virnoi has a spellbook – that's his arcane focus. He's going to need it to summon that dragon. When he summons it, you grab it.' Mosi nodded and trotted off into the island, seemingly unconcerned with the looming threat of a necromancer; being a construct had its perks. He may have been on the outs with The Brass Wyvern, but Mosi was accustomed to working in a team, at least, and taking orders. Takuma never thought he'd see the day his order would be the one Mosi responded to.

Carefully, Takuma unwound himself from the plants that wound around his legs and stepped out into the more spacious reaches of the forest. He waved Nuru along carefully, recognising a malevolence in Virnoi's voice that he'd only heard whispers of in the past. Feliks materialised from the liminal space between the foliage and the red bark, mouth set in a thoughtful line.

'We'll get the dragon,' Takuma whispered in Svarnish. 'You get positioned near the tunnel. On the shoreline. Find something to start a fire.'

He was rearranging the game in the back of his mind, shuffling through the papers he'd piled on top of one another back within The Brass Wyvern, and a plan was slowly forming.

Feliks nodded and touched his chest before he melted back within the trees.

'*Who are you?*' A hiss rose, echoing within the forest. The world fell silent as each of the Wyverns drew to a stop, frightened that a snap or errant murmuring of a branch would give them away. They stared at one another, ears turned into the open air. There was no wind in the dome. There was only them, the six Wyverns and the dragon they were about to steal. 'You aren't meant to be here. You've assaulted my home. You are an *intruder* upon my land.'

'This isn't your land,' Virnoi remarked. 'That's absurd. Have you forgotten that before the Imperium was built, this was the Nordlund? Have you forgotten that the Wood Elves and the frost lived here, long before you came down from your isles and planted flags upon the earth? It was the Nords that gave you your gods and the Wood Folk that gave you your precious glass. I'm no more intruding upon this land than you have superimposed yourself upon the world. Do not let my height fool you, we are far from alike. Our people are entirely different breeds.'

'Nuru, stay undercover until I signal for you. Stay close.' Takuma glanced at the tapestry and wondered if he should take it from her, but Nuru was clutching it, white-knuckled and tense. She was the magical one – the tapestry was hers. That was why she'd lied between her teeth when confronted with Imamu's claim upon it. Nuru was the only person who was going to be able to use the tapestry to its full potential. She looked at him with those big, black eyes filled with trepidation and flame, awaiting more from Takuma. He reached out and embraced her in tight arms, her soft shoulders chilly and trembling. 'We get out of here tonight, Nuru. We get that dragon out of here tonight.'

Even if Virnoi had tried to strong-arm them, he was a Wyvern. He walked slowly along the tree line towards the mage, treading carefully until Virnoi drew back into his line of sight.

Gentle, soft Virnoi had evaporated and left a dark reaper in his place. A ghostly glow overwhelmed his eyes, cutting through the stark darkness that had engulfed him.

'Perhaps you should educate yourself about our culture before you go running around in our homes, like the riffraff that wander in from the gutter.' Takuma snorted.

'Are you embarrassed by your audience?' Virnoi asked. He was using his dramatics to let them know that there were others laying witness. The shadows rose like ghosts from the walls, melting into one great echo of Virnoi cast upon the great tower. 'Are you embarrassed by the thought that they see you for what you are?'

He caught a glimpse of the great viewing windows through a stretch of trees, in a spot where the canopy parted momentarily on the island and allowed Takuma a view of the far wall. In truth, Takuma didn't understand how anyone took Thurlow seriously. He was ridiculous looking, in the way that all High Elves were, but all their worst features were amplified in this fool of a man. From his gangly limbs to his knife ears that sat entirely out of proportion to his pointy, weaselly little face. At least the leaders of the Svarnish looked impressive – as much as Takuma disdained Imamu, he could understand why he drew a crowd.

Thurlow Thurlowe was not alone. He was flanked by Taliesin and another High Elf, a stranger who was dressed in robes that outdid Thurlow's in every way. Instead of the jarring, mismatched blues that Thurlow wore, the ebony-haired stranger wore the deep, jewel tones of the forest floor. A blackened green shot through with a sapphire sheen, a thick band of jewels set upon his neck. Takuma took in a short, sharp breath and turned away – almost afraid that those all-knowing eyes would find him in the forest.

Shit. There were far too many important people in one place for his liking. Takuma did not want to make his debut into elvish society in front of Eschalier, the sixth Eschalion.

Hotaru had not gone far. She stood where Takuma had left her, watching Virnoi, having neither fled into the woods nor joined Zuri by the dragon. Her lips were pressed together in a hard line that Takuma understood. He knew he would never comprehend the debt owed between the two of them, but if he could draw Hotaru's mind from the trade-off at hand, perhaps he'd be able to retain some of her usefulness before she picked sides. Their first conversation had begun with Takuma slipping a mild sedative into her food; he wasn't about to put his faith in that versus the man who'd given her back her feet.

'I am embarrassed by nothing. Certainly not some run-of-the-mill burglars. It will be a simple thing to handle you.'

'Little crow,' Takuma called, keeping his voice low. Her eyes snapped towards him, hesitating momentarily before she crept backwards. Virnoi's attention was elsewhere. 'Have you still got blood on your knives?'

She shook her head. *Right.* Leaping feet-first into a body of water would wash away their more murderous sins, but they had more blood. The dragon had not killed Llewelyn cleanly, which meant that a small collection of his entrails was left on the earth. He pointed to them and made a quick wiping motion against the leaves at his feet. Quick-witted Hotaru didn't need it spelled out for her and circled back towards the entrails on light feet, avoiding stepping directly into the mess as she took two throwing knives to the muck.

'We are *anything* but run-of-the-mill.' Virnoi snapped his fingers and his tome appeared in a flash of smoke, thrown from some unknown reach. 'I'd like to see you try.'

'Thurlow,' a stranger's voice rose, accusatory. 'What have you done?'

Zuri was watching, still taking shelter by the dragon. He made eye contact with her briefly and nodded, not knowing what he could say from afar. He was almost certain that she'd be fine on her feet.

Hotaru trotted back to him, staying an arm's length from him, silent.

'I do not care if you pick Virnoi, little crow, but if we don't act quick, Thurlow will spell the end of us all. We need Thurlowe blood.' He did care. He cared ardently. He had gone out of his way to save Hotaru because he hadn't been able to watch her die, starving and alone on their doorstep. But he could not place the burden of his care on this woman, who needed to be where her heart demanded. Perhaps he was still hoping that Hotaru could pick them both. 'Go to the trees and look for the window. We want eyes on Thurlow Thurlowe – wait until the glass turns to water.'

She went to turn away but stopped, fixing him with a pensive look.

'Don't you want to see the Eschalion fall?' Hotaru asked softly, the words barely more than a murmur. 'Don't you want to see them be held accountable for all they've done?'

'I've lived through the fall of one country,' Takuma sighed. 'I'd rather not see another burn in my lifetime.' On that, perhaps, they disagreed. They'd never discussed it. Takuma hadn't thought her political. His little crow vanished, and he caught a glimpse of her scaling a thick tree mere moments later, just another shifting shadow.

He approached Virnoi slowly, the way in which one might approach a bull roaming within an open field. He may have imagined Virnoi's glance downwards, but at the risk of giving away his position, Takuma did not call out to him. He kept an eye on Nuru in his peripherals, her familiar silhouette slipping through the narrow gaps between the trees.

Mosi had done a swift, full circle around the island and was approaching Virnoi from behind. He climbed onto the dragon's back and did not stay long, taking a running leap at Virnoi. He flew through the sky and stole the floating book from Virnoi's loose grip, both of his patterned arms clutching the tome to his chest as he hit the earth once more. Virnoi whirled on him, snarling, but Mosi had taken off once more. It wasn't as if Takuma had told him where to take it; they just wanted it out of Virnoi's hands.

Takuma whistled, something that vaguely resembled a bird call. Nuru broke through the trees and threw her arms out, brandishing the tapestry in front of her. Zuri tapped on the dragon twice, and he charged towards Nuru in a frightening display that would have shaken anyone, had it not been their holy mother. The instant that the dragon's nose should have torn the tapestry in twain and thrown Nuru aside, its body was instead rendered light. A thousand starlit threads poured down into the tapestry, from the crest upon its head to the very tip of its tail.

The shadows unleashed upon Mosi, let loose as Virnoi's control upon them broke. A flurry of crows fell upon the man's tattooed shoulders, slashing at him while he dove out of the way. He would need to take care of himself.

Takuma went to Nuru first and used his steady hands to tie the tapestry back in place around her waist. They would need it secure for what was to come, as long as Feliks had found his mark.

There was a distant shout and a clatter from the viewing windows. Hotaru climbed down in a swift blur, dropping from a branch several metres above the ground. She emerged from the tree line and her blue eyes flashed between them. With his tome stolen from him, Virnoi slowly floated down towards them. He kept his distance – dared not lay his feet upon the earth again – but he'd turned his focus onto them now.

'You have no right to touch that tome.' That sound was something else as it rose from Virnoi's throat, a venomous hiss. 'Don't make total fools of yourselves. Give it back before it kills you.'

The threat was likely genuine. Takuma had never known him to throw around words needlessly, though his lover was a little more frantic than he'd ever been in the years they'd spent together.

Zuri ran to where Mosi had stopped, bent over defensively. The shadowy birds were doing what crows would, swooping for his eyes, and he'd doubled over to try and shield himself from their attack. The dancer snatched a broken branch as she went and waved it in the air, swatting at the shadows.

Takuma tied the knot at Nuru's waist twice. 'Open the tunnel, Virnoi.'

'No. Someone has to strike at the Imperium, and we are the best people. If the world sees the Eschalion take a hit from people like us, it will mean something. It *should* mean something.'

Someone would have to strike out at the nobility eventually, but it would not be them. It would be some princely, straight-edged avenger of Svarna who was more figurehead than mortal. Someone who had a shell of a community closed around them to weather the flame that would come after the spark.

'It will mean something, Virnoi.' Takuma said, finding his charm distinctly lacking. 'When it happens. But we're not those people. I think you know that. We can't be those people, and we – you and me – we should leave here together.'

Virnoi's face softened for a moment as he studied Takuma. Then he sighed. '*Fermare.*'

Takuma hadn't been paying nearly enough attention to where his little crow had flown. There was a flash on the other side of Mosi as Hotaru leapt out of the trees. She threw her intact horn into Mosi's back, and when he twisted sharply to get out of her way, his grip on the book grew loose enough for Hotaru to lunge around his waist and knock the tome loose.

She had picked her side. The moment the book fell free, it took a snap of Virnoi's fingers for it to return to him. Hotaru pivoted hard on her feet and dove past them, stumbling to close the distance and join Virnoi.

Takuma looked at the three companions that stood by him. With the spell book returned to Virnoi, there was no more arguing their point. It was time for them to make a break for it. He disdained the resignation in his voice when he spoke. 'Get the eggs, meet me at the south wall.'

'Come with us, Hotaru,' Nuru demanded, her face flushed crimson. 'Don't stay here, he's made his bed.'

'Go,' Takuma insisted. They would make their own way out, but Takuma still needed to know that Virnoi would break free. The three fled, charging past Virnoi to the nest. Mosi cast a brief look back at him, but he understood the sense of urgency required for what faced them. Their time was burning down.

Hotaru was still standing with Virnoi as the elf flipped through his book, searching for something within the pages that Takuma didn't feel like standing by to wait for.

'Hotaru,' Takuma called. 'The path he's going down is a dark one. Darker than ones even you have seen. I wanted you to live so that you could see a long life, little crow, not this violence. You deserve that.'

'I deserve the fate that I make. The one I forge.' Hotaru looked up, and she was a different creature entirely than the one Takuma had plucked off the broken streets, that feral stray cat who'd hissed and spat at any hint of kindness. Perhaps there was something in that delicate face that was marked for a fate that Takuma had no part of. She swallowed, her hand flexing. 'I want to see a world where we don't have to fear the Imperium. But I'll come back – I won't leave you all, I swear that.'

A whoop went up from the far side of the island, a warning call from Feliks. Takuma withdrew as Hotaru retreated into the dragon skeleton, Virnoi stopping only for a moment to look at him properly.

There had been no time in all their courtship that the two had minced words or needlessly spoken, silent lovers at their most severe. So, he started to walk backwards, keeping his eyes forward to watch as he prepared to flee. Virnoi rose slowly, anchoring himself inside the fate he'd forged for himself, only tearing his eyes from Takuma when he turned his back.

'Thurlow Thurlowe, I know that you remember me. You'll say my name before this evening is done.' The air hummed, vibrating with a thousand voices that Takuma could not place. The tome opened to a set page and glowed, greyish and ghastly. '*Alzar—*'

Virnoi was cut off by a hiss of elvish. A crimson line bloomed across his throat, grazed by a dark curse that Takuma saw fly like a glistening barb through the night. The skin opened and Virnoi pressed a hand over it, snarling silently. This was going to be a brawl.

Instead of watching any longer, Takuma ran. He plunged through the trees and hit the shoreline, where his Wyverns were lingering. Nuru was hopping from one foot to the other, swearing beneath her breath.

'Feliks, take Zuri's egg! Quick now!' His mind was thrumming with adrenaline. There was a sound like the shell of the earth splitting apart and a roar unlike anything that Takuma had ever heard, shaking him to the bone. There was no great unwinding from Feliks, no slow change; this was a snatch. His flesh made a half-shift into a whorled mix of wood, and he reached out with his ribs and grabbed the egg, tucking it away in a blink.

'It won't survive long in there,' Nuru said.

'Then we best move quick. Get in the water. Feliks, hands up!' Together, they thrust themselves back into the icy water, with Feliks keeping one hand high. 'We go under, you light it up.'

The dome had been sealed months ago, and ever since the dragon had been trapped in a tower with poor ventilation – if there had been proper vents built into the wall the smell would not have been nearly as oppressive. All it took was one dry snap from Feliks' wooden hand to start a flame, which burst into the air above the river in an entirely unnatural way as he waved his hand around. It swam above them as if the world had slowed, surreal to watch from where they hid. Takuma was reminded of a fish as he watched from below the water, swimming deeper within the moat to try and put space between him and what was to come.

The world above water turned into a living inferno as the sky exploded. There was a muffled, thunderous *boom* as a godly hammer swung through Thurlowe tower.

If Virnoi wanted to strike at the Imperium, he could take the blame for this blow. The Brass Wyvern would not be marred by flame; they would escape by the skin of their teeth and by Feliks' singed, blackened hand. All Takuma had done was find their way out. The tunnel burst open – the only channel to the outside world that had not been reinforced when Zuri escaped. Water poured out of the moat, rushing into the quickly widening gap.

Takuma grabbed the back of Nuru's dress and pulled her towards him, her arms laden with a dragon egg. The water dragged them with it, and for several seconds they were both pressed against the remains of the wall. A huge pressure weighed down upon their chests, but it was pulling them in the right direction.

It poured down into the abandoned tunnel and drew them along, dumping the Wyverns together on the slick stone. It was only Takuma's white-knuckled grip that kept Nuru from being pulled away. He twisted as they went through the swiftly widening hole and was thrown straight onto his back, sputtering and swearing and grateful for the air in his lungs.

That was until Nuru landed hard on top of him, ridding him of any breath he may have taken. They stumbled to their feet, Takuma pulling Nuru up to take quick stock of their people. He counted himself lucky that they'd all made it through as Feliks unwound his branching arms from around Zuri, and Mosi spat up more than a mouthful of water, each of them soaked and bruised – but alive.

'Time to go, and go quick – we've got a distraction, let's get out of here!'

Chapter Forty-Two

THE IMPERIUM

Hotaru had almost slipped.

She had shuffled forward on the branch to get a better vantage point, hilt of her knife gripped between her teeth and her hands sidling along a branch above her head. She was a child of the city, of cobblestones and alleyways – she was not nearly as adept in the organic reaches of the trees. Perhaps she had been more frightened than she had thought. When she'd tried to place her foot, it had slipped out from beneath her. Her hands had shot out to catch her as she fell, throwing her weight onto the opposite leg to counter the fumble. She fell hard and thumped into the wood.

Getting punched in the crotch *hurt*, especially when what was catching her was a hunk of tree. The only reason she did not swear was the knife between her teeth, which would have slipped and sliced her face in two should she have indulged the urge.

Virnoi's whispering was the magic that nudged her balance into place. *Upright, little crow.*

She was frightened of heights when the only thing that protected her from the earth was a series of branches and underbrush. She was scared of death, and falling, and the imminent rage about to fall upon them from the highest reaches of the Imperium echelons. Takuma had not known how frightened she was. She'd thought that it was quite reasonable that she be afraid, after all the stories she'd heard of the arch mage of the Imperium, how as a girl she'd been able to follow the river of blood left in his wake. The tearful women who'd been left on street corners, indigo and navy in the shadow of the Imperium.

She clenched her legs around the branch, taking the bloodied knife between her gilded fingers. Her whole body shook with the force she was using to keep herself anchored upon the tree. Hotaru did not trust her own body, but one of those legs was not entirely her own. It had not been for years. After

Virnoi and Taliesin had worked as life and death would to remake it from scratch, it had always been a little stronger than the right. Less prone to losing its footing. It played no small part in saving her upon that tree.

Hotaru was not special. She was what the world had made of her, the magic that bound her flesh to its bone and her fingers in place. She could not remake the world with a whisper, would never commune with empresses or the dead. There was no one on this earth who looked at her like the rising sun. For the minutes Hotaru sat in the tree, she was struck by how entirely out of her depth she was – left on her own to watch and to strike at a man who had struck down a country. She was not sure what collusion of fate had brought her this far, but fleeing, suddenly, was not an option. She wanted to strike at the heart of the Imperium just as badly as she wanted to be free of this place.

She had never been special. Yet, she kissed the pommel of her blade, as if the steel would make her brave.

Hotaru wished that someone had been there to see how well the knife had flown, hurled by her tired fingers. How, when Thurlow Thurlowe had pushed his arm through the window, she had been holding her breath to make sure that her balance was as steady as it could be. No one but Hotaru had seen how the elf's eyes had found her, burning with an incensed rage, as she let the knife free. She had never thrown a knife so well, felt her magic work like the gods itself had intervened in her aim.

A chest was an almost impossible thing to hit at such a distance, with so much resistance beneath their sternum. A knife should have lost speed, should have bounced off – but there was something in the air.

Her knife buried itself in Thurlow's chest and he reeled, eyes wide.

Nobody had seen how Thurlow Thurlowe stumbled back, wounded by a blade thrown by a woman forged by a city that had almost spelled her death.

Hotaru scrambled away, terrified that if she threw another, she would ruin her luck entirely. She held only one person in mind as she'd dropped to the island, knowing that her choice was already made.

After the lords of the Imperium had tried to slit Virnoi's throat, he had taken the wash of blood and wiped it across his pale neck. It left a red mark beneath his jaw, giving the impression that he was marked by gore. When he opened his mouth to speak, his voice didn't come, so instead he made a symbol with his spare hand. One need not know the intricacies of the language to know that, despite the fact someone had stolen his voice, Virnoi continued to cast.

Rise. The word formed between fingertip and palm, and beneath Hotaru's feet, the dragonbone spread to create a platform several inches thick, wide enough for her to balance upon. The skeleton rose, and when a shout in Svarnish came from the far wall, Virnoi sheltered with her within its ribs. The explosion threw them both, but the dragonbone was more protection from the heat than any armour could have been. It closed around them, a cocoon of magic, cool and smooth to the touch.

Prismarium glass was impervious to magical shattering, but dragonflame was something else. When Hotaru stared back out through the ribs, Virnoi having put the bone back in its place, they were overwhelmed by a crystal shower that fell from above.

The dome had not simply broken, but shattered into several thousand pieces. Takuma had lit up every ounce of gas that accumulated within those ivory walls.

There was nothing more gratifying than seeing the Thurlowe sanctuary cleaved in two, or the horror in their eyes as wings of bone took flight.

It was worth it, truly. No one ever wanted to talk about how violence could make a mark for the better.

Chapter Forty-Three

THE IMPERIUM

The Wyverns took flight. They flew through the broad tunnel, unmarked by guards or obstacle, which led out to a low, subterranean door. Feliks forced it open with a sharp shove of his brawny shoulder. The Thurlowe tower was falling to pieces, and they needed to put plenty of distance between them. Nuru did not care how tired her legs were or how battered she felt, she made them work. The water chased them, icy throes nipping at their heels as they ran.

She was not sure when she lost Mosi – one second, he was at her side, and the next he'd turned and disappeared into a branching path, not speaking a word as he went. The tunnel came to another low, broad door set into the earth, and Feliks did not wait for them to speak before he burst through it, and they fled out into the Thurlowe gardens. The four Svarnishmen poured out onto the lush grass, amongst the revelry and the wine-drunk, and found that all those celebrating had turned their eyes upwards.

Against the dark velvet sky, Virnoi rose, mounted upon a skeletal dragon. The light of his magic flowed through him, lighting the night like the northern star, rising from the ruined peak of the Thurlow estate. Nuru stared only for a moment before Takuma pulled her along, his strong hand at her elbow. They were not the only ones fleeing the wreckage. They had promised Imamu a distraction and, after the explosion, those who did not wish to be dragged into the arrests that would follow burst from the main chambers.

The Svarnishmen, directed by a roaring patriarch, took to the crowds with bright-eyed Nuru, quick-fingered Takuma, angular Zuri, and hulking Feliks amongst them. Nuru kept the egg clutched tightly to her stomach, so much smaller than it should have been, thrumming with panic at the mere thought that at any moment she could be thrown to the ground and the child could be lost. Zuri kept at her back as they pushed through the throng of bodies that poured out into the city.

'Find the thieves!' Thurlowe's shrill voice screeched distantly over the din, so far away that Nuru may have been imagining it. She glanced in the direction of the voice and only saw Takuma pressing in behind them, blocking both the women from easy view.

Even as they pushed forward, the people behind them threatened to bowl them over. Nuru could barely manage to find her feet, so focused on protecting the egg that she was half a second from being swept away in the rush. He reached out and grasped the back of her dress with one hand and grasped Zuri's hand with the other and pulled.

Any Svarnish child who'd been to the coast was taught about how quickly a riptide could kill you. They were taught that if they felt the draw of the ocean pulling them out to their doom, they should work against it, cutting horizontally across the current rather than along it. Takuma was trying to help them cut the current, but the moment they pressed back, the wash of people pushed against them. A hard shoulder shoved into the back of Nuru's head, threatening to upset her balance.

'Watch yourself!' Takuma swore and spat back at the people pressing them and heaved twice, pulling Nuru out from beneath that oppressive weight.

Her blood thundered in her head and she began to wonder, for a breath, if she would die there. Trampled by her own people with the last hope of Svarna clutched to her chest. They had slain the dragons and captured the young, but a wild dragon egg could birth a lineage.

A strong force seized the three Wyverns and pulled them out of the human river. Nuru, the smallest and softest of them all, clutched the egg as she was lifted along. The fire within it licked at her palms, demanding she pay them heed. 'God damn it, Nuru!'

The great bull Imamu stood, one hand gripping Takuma's shoulder and the other anchoring him and his staff between two bricks. Mosi stood at his side, pulling people roughly out of the riptide, loosening the crush of people below them.

Once they had a moment to breathe, Imamu placed his staff upon the stone and a platform appeared beneath the crowd – lifting them up and out of the narrow channel. Nords and Svarnishmen both fled, the snowy-haired mixing with the dragonfolk. The crowd split apart, no longer trapped into the paths between the gardens, and fled like a hundred deer from an oncoming bear.

Nuru looked up at Imamu. He'd been a travesty of a husband, but still stood so stubbornly for what was right. He wielded the staff of Muqdah, tucked away beneath a dozen glamours to hide its appearance from those who did not know what to look for. He was the one who'd taught her the notice-me-nots existed, but it had been Taliesin who'd cast the one on her tapestry, *hers*, a bridal gift from Imamu. A gift did not stop being a gift when the relationship fell apart.

Her dear husband looked as if he wanted to say something, opening his mouth in some contemptuous way, as if something snide couldn't resist escaping him. But it never came. Instead, his bronze eyes flicked away from her. 'Mosi, take them and go. Wait with them until the heat dies down.'

Mosi shared a look with Takuma and they both nodded. Zuri looped her arm through the crook in Nuru's elbow, careful not to dislodge the grip she had on the egg. The job was through, but their night certainly was not. There was a chorus of authoritative elvish shouting breaking across the estate, that tone of voice with which only guards spoke – people who thought that they were the law.

'Back to The Brass Wyvern,' Takuma said, 'but through the city, first. We need to lose those guards – and they're coming.'

The Imperium was ablaze with colour. The swathes of people they'd seen gathering earlier in the day had proliferated into an ocean of faces, an immovable wall of flesh in the street. A parade had filled the sprawling promenade, towering floats and grand carts marching from the heart of the Imperium to its grand entrance – all to the sound of an almighty music. A marching band that must have been a thousand wide was scattered through the procession, hands full of instruments that Takuma couldn't even name.

He knew the drums, though – he'd been born with those banging in his chest.

Takuma's mind churned as they pushed along the side of the street. It would have been easy to disappear into this sort of crowd on his own, but there were twice as many guards stationed on the street to compensate for the swell of people. All it would take was one wrong shoulder, and they'd be had. If they'd had Virnoi's magic, it would have made this a very simple escape – some traitorous bastard he was, leaving them all in the dust. The least he could have done was teleport them to safety before he decided to be a complete ass.

They could not flee to the Wyvern without shaking the Thurlow guard. The Brass Wyvern was a ghost in the red-light district; it had to continue to not exist within the greater scheme of the Imperium. If they did not shake them off properly and stupidly led them home, there would not be a safe spot in the world for them that was not on a caravan. He would not resign he and his to that life, one that they did not deserve, because of Thurlow Thurlowe.

'Onto the parade!' he shouted and, with little delay, dove into the throng. He broke through a line of dancers in rivers of silk and onto the grand stretch of road that announce the Imperium. If Vioqtria was truly on their side, then he was going to put her influence to work. He let Nuru go, knowing that they'd have no luck if he was dragging them along in this sort of chaos. 'Go, to the other side!'

Chances were that they could not hear him at all, one singular voice in the many. He waved them forward across the parade and together the Wyverns went, Mosi bringing up the rear. The watchdog of the caravan glanced back frequently, a sharp-eyed presence at Takuma's back. They forged a path through the dancers and tried to cross through the first gap they met, but in their rush, Takuma almost led them headfirst into one of the many bands that was carrying that grand tune. The absurdity of having a marching band of harpists was not lost on Takuma, who was desperately trying to swallow the hysterical laugh rising in his chest.

It was funny. There was so much about this that was funny, most of which would be even funnier when several weeks had passed.

The Wyvern workers danced down the parade, shouting to one another in Svarnish as they struggled. They were dragonfolk, not fish, and weren't much suited to swimming upstream.

There were other Svarnishmen flooding into the parade, stopping the great floats in their tracks and drawing alarmed stares from the entertainers; threads of darkness and plain linens crept into the frivolous display of luxury, the Svarnish moving like river-water finding its way along the mountain's barren side. Takuma stared, struck by the sudden spectacle. Thurlow's guard in the familial blue were trying to push along the walkways, and the dragonfolk were doing what anyone with half a brain would to escape arrest – fleeing in the only direction they could go. Scattered clusters of people flowed ahead of them, having evidently had the same thought.

Others would have gone to the scattered alleyways and under crofts that lead off from the Golden Quarter, but the panic would have left plenty without any control of where they went. The parade was moving forward, though, which meant that eventually it should pour out into the front of the city. They simply had to follow it. The Golden Quarter was the core of the Imperium, where the nobility was at its strongest, but the further they went, the more the streets would fill with Nords and half-elves. They would be safer there. They could do something with that. It was just a matter of outlasting those who followed them.

A shrieking cry rose in the distance. He could not make out the words, but there was no doubt that Thurlow Thurlowe had followed his guard, thinking they would swoop down upon the thieves and reclaim his lost eggs. He swore beneath his breath, and stepped almost directly into Zuri, who had stopped. She looked at him with those inky eyes and they both swallowed.

He was not sure what he was saying until the words tumbled out of him. Takuma didn't even know if she could hear him. 'If we get out of this, you should let me take you to dinner. I mean, I would like to take you to dinner. To court you. If I'm not imprisoned.'

Fearing for one's life tended to put things that were important and otherwise needless in precise focus. He'd been plagued by doubts, having been deemed mildly obnoxious his whole life, and often judged for wearing his bedwork career proudly. But worrying that his attempts at courtship would be written off suddenly seemed useless when, in truth, Takuma suspected they'd be brilliant together. Zuri was beautiful and brave and more ruthless than he'd ever been in his life. He wanted to know the ins and outs of her, the way all of her pieces slotted together to create the woman that could brave the depths of hell.

Zuri looked at him, bemused, and then burst into pealing laughter. Slowly, her head bobbed into a tentative nod. 'If we're both imprisoned at the end of this, you can still court me. Maybe we'll start with a date.'

That was good enough for him. His survival instinct distracted from her radiant features, drawn towards the waves of shouts that rolled through the crowd. Great, dramatic gasps that the High Elves had such a talent for. The four Wyvern workers pressed themselves up against the back of a parade float and turned their eyes to the sky, where Virnoi appeared. The necromancer had swooped low, crouched upon the spine of the undead beast, and within the cage of its ribs sat Hotaru.

Takuma did not know what Virnoi would have done, had he not looked down in that moment. Perhaps Takuma imagined the shift in his gaze towards the muddled parade – how the arcane light that sat within his marble features found him for a breath. Takuma did not know what type of death a bone dragon could rain down upon a city, and he did not find out.

Instead of bringing destruction, Virnoi tipped his chin upwards. The dragon beat its fleshless wings twice and soared back up to the sky, soaring past the parade and away from the city.

Relief formed a hard lump in Takuma's throat that he did not have time to savour. He swallowed and turned away, hip-bumping Zuri along. It nudged them all in a great chain, and they broke into a run once more, with Nuru leading the way. The chaos breaking out behind them at the sight of the undead dragon was enough that, when Takuma looked, the guards had largely stopped in a horrified stupor. There were supposed to only be two necromancers who lived in the whole city, the Eschalion and his daughter, neither of which Virnoi was. This would certainly make the papers in the morning: *Necromancers invade the Imperium to rain on parade! The Eschalier's bastard child running amok in our grand city?*

Better Virnoi in the papers than Takuma's precious brothel.

Somewhere, the great lord Thurlow Thurlowe screamed with an incensed rage – or perhaps that was raucous laughter that rung in his ears, it was impossible to tell.

They were almost free. If they could reach the outer wall of the Imperium, they could release the dragon into the open air. It would be a short trip to the mountains or to the Black Forest. There were plenty of places within the Nordlund that a dragon could disappear, great reaches of the wild where the High Elves held minimal sway. With all the magic in Thurlow's little finger, Takuma did not trust that he would not track the dragon on Nuru's hip if they tried to sneak it away into the city. No, tonight was the night. Under the cover of all this festivity, the patriotism that dripped from every banner, they would see that dragon take to the sky.

Takuma's eyes sought a way out, something less suspicious than several Svarnishmen fleeing into the outlands of the city.

The Roasted Apple inn, packed to the brim. The frost-bitten tavern that stood to welcome all who wandered in through the Imperium gates was overflowing with snowy-haired Nords, who had taken to the celebrations as thoroughly as anyone else along the parade road. The city had been so heavily adorned that Takuma had not even realised how far they'd fled, the parade finally coming to a lurching stop in the confusion.

Nuru was tucked against the back of a huge carriage, waving frantically to them. Their kinfolk were shouting and trying to force their way out of the parade, but the bewildered guards were beginning to close off the street as they tried to figure out what they were supposed to do with this chaos. When pressed hard enough, they would defer to the nearest show of Imperium strength, and they couldn't have that.

Nuru handed the egg to Zuri, then looked at the three men who stood before her. 'Give me a lift!' she demanded, and it was Mosi who knelt, lacing his fingers together to boost her up onto the elaborately decorated body of the carriage. 'We can't do this on our own!'

Nuru was a soft woman, not a warrior of the world. She stood atop the carriage, mostly skin and diaphanous silk, her braids fallen loose. The wind pulled at her wet hair, a river of curls that billowed around her. She took a long breath, summoning something from within her, and the gilded cage that wrapped around her neck began to glow once more. He did not know what she would do, but in that moment, Takuma would have trusted her with all of Svarna.

'I am a daughter of Morouqdi!' Nuru bellowed, and her voice was tenfold greater than it should have been. Her cheeks were crimson, chest marked with the warmth of her fury. Goose flesh rose on Takuma's arms as he saw her face twist. 'And I kneel to no man, no elf! This is our final call before our eternal silence. If you can bear fire or a blade, come and fight for all that is good!'

An unnatural silence fell over their section of the parade, the dancers and instruments falling still as they turned their eyes upon this small woman who stood astride a noble carriage. That quiet unsettled Takuma's stomach, his eyes searching the masses of people for an ally amongst them that did not bear their horns.

Then there was the sound of a horn, a singular sonorous hum that came from the west. From The Roasted Apple. A second joined the first, and then a roar from within the inn's overcrowded walls.

The Nords, those who had not had the chance to save Muqdah in its day, who had been too far away to ever save the Svarnish – they were the ones who came. An army of brawny warriors, flushed red with drink but still bearing their battleaxes, poured out from The Roasted Apple, roaring and shouting to one another. The High Elves were forced to part as the broad-shouldered warriors dislodged shields from their backs and spears, flipped swords into their hands. The last person to fill the inn's door was Grenh, leaning heavily on her walking stick, a toothy grin splitting her wizened features.

'You called for a warrior?!' The call came from that little old lady that had always given Takuma a hard time, brusque and full of good humour. 'The Nordlund hears you, Svarna!'

Her words carried across the sea of ice that had flooded into the parade. *The Nordlund hears you.* The Nordlund would not be pushed around. They cut the Imperium's grand parade in half, a line of muscle and steel, and Takuma saw his kinfolk fleeing for safe harbour. He saw Nords pull women behind their line, saw the natives of this land joke with dragonfolk as if they were not saving them from a fate worse than death.

Takuma looked up and saw Nuru, her lips fallen open in disbelief, having seemingly forgotten that she had made this call at all. She snapped back to herself, eyes setting upon some distant spot, and the grin of the victorious filled her features like an unending joy.

'The Nordlund hears us!'

And then, well, the Nords did what they did best. They fought.

Chapter Forty-Four

THE NORDLUND

Nuru launched herself back off the carriage and into Mosi's hands, her heart drumming like a herd of wild horses had been let loose in her chest.

The guards took the bait, and steel met steel as they fought with the Nords, who took this whole thing with the grand humour she'd come to expect of them. That had been her last-ditch effort to find them a path out of this mess, driven by desperation and the panicked thought that she would not make it back to Nema by morn. It was bizarre to know that the world had listened, that reality swam before her eyes as she tried to right the wrongs of the world.

'Go to the tavern!' one of the warriors shouted, a man with a hefty beard and a great hammer clutched in his hands. Nuru nodded, the tears of the thankful bursting to life in her eyes, and together the Wyverns had their way out. They wove around a tangle of violence that was spreading through the Imperium and dove into The Roasted Apple, where Grenh awaited. She stepped aside, greeting them as one would a family member arriving at the crack of dawn.

'Back door,' she said simply. 'Through my rooms. It will lead you straight out to safety.'

'Thanks, Granny!' Feliks cried as they went, muscles crying for all the work they had done today.

They piled through the inn and through the cluttered rooms. Nuru had never seen it so entirely devoid of people, and through the cluttered rooms of an elderly woman until they came to a narrow, tiny door that looked as if it had been made for The Roasted Apple's proprietor. They squeezed through it one by one, Feliks bending and shifting to pull himself through the frame, and fell into the Nord's corner of the Imperium. A safe space that only those who'd been here the longest could have carved out of an otherwise cruel city. Those who were not warriors crowded the streets, with their luminous eyes peering at the Svarnish interlopers.

'This way!' a woman called who stood outside a bakery, a baby wrapped on her hip and a younger girl lingering at her back. Nuru did not doubt her feet as they rushed down the stricken street, ushered down and around the building. 'You need a way out, no?'

Nuru nodded, and the mother pointed them along. Zuri spoke her thanks as they went, tripping over themselves to flee the symphony of steel at their backs. At each corner, there was another Nord to lead them on, whispering conspiratorially and guiding them through a corner of the Imperium marked by garlands of candied oranges and pine branches. The labyrinthine city shifted, an entirely different creature when led by another, until they were deposited at a square in the outer wall of the city.

She had never seen a place where the Imperium opened to the broader world, but here there was a great set of gates that were left open. It was a community square with a great tree at its centre, whose broad canopy was adorned with clusters of pale blue fruit. As Nuru stepped down into this grassy sanctuary, there were a hundred eyes that peered out from the homes lining the Frost Quarter, waiting to see what these Svarnishmen would do next. The only person guarding them was a white-haired Nord wearing the uniform of the royal guard, who was buried in his book. He gave them nothing more than a cursory glance as they approached.

'The Nordlund hears you,' was all he said, speaking under his breath.

The denizens of The Brass Wyvern stepped past him, stopping short of exiting the Imperium entirely. The celebrations had filtered out from the city to the pilgrims who lingered outside the wall, but few dared to linger so close to the forest, which stood watch. The world here was quiet, in the way that the world in Morouqdi's many chambers had once been. With shaking hands, Nuru tried to unlace the tapestry from her waist.

As she struggled with the knots, Takuma found his way to her, breathing hard as he pulled the thing off of her. It was fucking heavy, carrying around the weight of a broken marriage on your hip. She took the thing in both hands and looked to Mosi, who stood with nary a bead of sweat on him. '*Toro*—'

His eyes flashed and Imamu's voice spoke from within Mosi. '*Abrorse.*'

The tapestry rippled as Nuru spread it away from her, the holy magic unfurling all sealed within. Zuri's dragon, verdant and shifting in colour, burst to life. The thousands of magic threads that had carried him now wove themselves back together, recreating the planes of his scaled body and his vast wings. Glowing with the magic of Muqdah, he flapped his wings and rose into the air as his very being reformed from within the reaches of Imamu's weaving.

'You're free!' Zuri shouted, her call breaking the quiet of this place almost more than the sound of the dragon unleashed. She had not let go of the dragon's egg since Nuru had thrust it upon her, and was arguably far better suited to holding such a thing, long-limbed as she was. 'Go! You have your freedom!'

Were there any words in all the languages in the world to articulate the gratitude that poured down from the dragon into Nuru? What use did a dragon have for thank-yous? The theft of one's freedom was an unthinkable evil and, somehow, The Brass Wyvern had righted this.

As she stood, staring up at the creature she'd fought for, she could not believe what they had managed. The wind buffeted them as they stood beneath the beating wings of a wild dragon. Nuru's hand found Takuma's as her feet slipped against the grass, clutching at a man who had always been her closest companion. Who would likely always be her closest friend.

Nuru knew that the dragon was thankful, and they had promised to bring him its eggs, so instead he rose into the firmament. It took to the winds with a torrent of bright flame released from within its thick throat. It did not make any sound, instead rising further into the night until it was nothing more than another patch of darkness in the sky. A round of quiet applause rose from their backs, and the Wyverns turned to find their curious crowd had emerged to cheer on their evening's great finale.

Laughing weakly, Takuma blew kisses into the crowd. They stood together until Nuru's feet felt as if they were no longer made of jelly. Zuri nudged her with a sly smile as the first true glimpse of relief rolled over the willowy women's features.

With their job done and a parade pouring into the quiet land that stood with its eyes turned towards the sky, the Wyverns went home to their crimson streets. They went home to find a furnace, a drink, and several days of sleep.

THE END

ACKNOWLEDGEMENTS

There are entirely too many people for me to thank where this book is concerned, so I'll aspire to hit the major notes of the melody and hope that the symphony understands if I miss a beat here or there.

Firstly, my thanks to my wife, who forged this world with me. We've spent years carefully building The Brass Wyvern from scratch, and your essence is so entangled in the dragonfolk that I could not have written this epic without you. How shocked everyone shall be to discover that *you* are Takuma's mother and I simply adopted him.

To my mother, who read this book and told me she loved it despite her intolerance for sprawling fantasy casts. I love you. I couldn't ask for a better Mama.

My thanks to Isa, Saint, and Ophelia – my writing buddies who listened to all of my rambling. To Danikka, my editor, who dared to write* my grammatical wrongs. We are nothing without our friends, and you have all saved this book a dozen times over, without ever knowing it.

What a horrifying joy this process has been. I am truly shocked I survived. Here's to doing it again.

*I'd also like to acknowledge that Danikka caught this, and we decided to keep it for the irony.

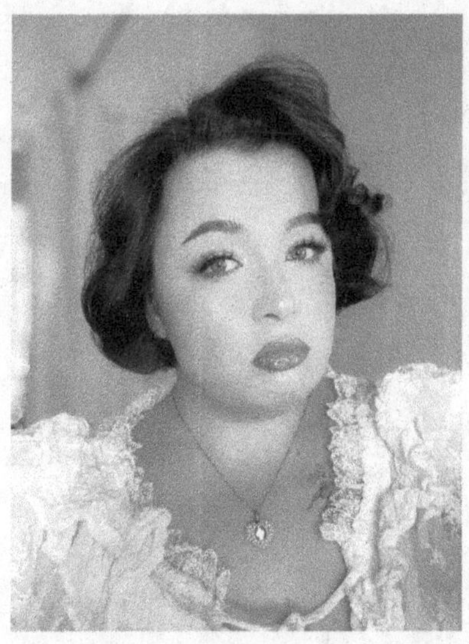

Bronte-Marie is a fantasy author from Sydney, Australia.

A bookseller by trade and content creator for a giggle, she's a never-ending storyteller with a highly visual brain ... so she writes.

From love letters to fun fantasy epics, Bronte credits her wife with giving her the push she needed to improve her craft and start writing fully formed books. Now, wrangling the incessant voices in her head onto the page to tell the stories she's dreamed of since childhood is her passion.

When she's not lost in her imagination, Bronte escapes into her latest gaming obsession and exercises her creativity through dabbling in illustration.

Find her on:
Instagram: https://www.thebrontemarie.com
Patreon: https://www.patreon.com/bmsbeautyhaven
Her website: https://www.thebrontemarie.com